POWER
IN THE
BLOOD

A John Jordan Mystery

MICHAEL LISTER

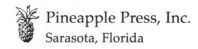 Pineapple Press, Inc.
Sarasota, Florida

Copyright © 1997 by Michael Lister

Inquiries should be addressed to:
Pineapple Press, Inc.
P.O. Box 3899
Sarasota, Florida 34230

"Small Town" by John Mellencamp © 1985 Windswept Pacific Entertainment Co. d/b/a Full Keel Music Co. All rights reserved. Used by permission. Warner Bros. Publications U.S. Inc., Miami, FL 33014

LIBRARY OF CONGRESS CATALOGING-IN-PUBLICATION

Lister, Michael.
    Power in the blood : a John Jordan mystery / Michael Lister.
— 1st ed.
        p.   cm.
    ISBN 1-56164-137-5 (hb. : alk. paper)
    I. Title.
PS3562.I78213P69   1997
813' .54—dc21   97-26866
                                                                    CIP

First Edition
10 9 8 7 6 5 4 3 2 1

Design by Carol Tornatore
Printed and bound by Royal Book Manufacturing Company, Norwich, Connecticut

For the love of my life

ACKNOWLEDGMENTS

On the publication of my first novel, I would like to acknowledge my firsts:

Lori, my first reader. Thanks for the support and encouragement. And your notes to "keep it coming."

Jesus, my first love. Thanks for the passion, compassion, mystery, and romance.

Pam, my first lover. You have, like Jacob of old, wrestled with God and with man and have prevailed. Thanks for teaching me the fine art of wrestling.

Meleah, my firstborn. You are my inspiration as surely as your brother, Micah, is my expression. And you both are the essence of all I hope and dream.

June, my first editor. Thanks for seeing what was . . . and what could be. And then putting your refined skills and love for language to work, shaping what was into what could be.

David, my first publisher, a true gentleman in an industry and indeed a world where sadly there are few. And to everybody at Pineapple Press for their dedication to excellence, especially Amanda.

The first novelists and writers I fell in love with who showed me the power in the blood of opening up a vein and pouring it out on the page: Frederick Buechner, Andrew M. Greeley, M. Scott Peck, Robert B. Parker, Pat Conroy, Patricia Cornwell, and Stephen King.

The first teachers who taught me to truly love words other than the Word and how all words relate to the Word: Tricia Weeks and Lynn Wallace.

My first . . . everything: Mike and Judi Lister. You were the first image of God and of the world and of myself I ever had. No wonder I adore God, think it's a half-full world, making possible a wonderful life, and truly love and accept myself.

Aimee, my first friend.

Herman and Bobbie, the first family members I ever got to choose. You are not in-laws, but family, having everything to do with love and nothing to do with law.

Jenny and Helen, my first fans.

My first superintendents, Ron McAndrew, Al Solomon, Dinah Poore. You are the reasons I believe in the Florida DOC. And my first prison, Gulf Correctional Institution; my parish; my friends; the staff of Gulf Correctional Institution; and the inmates, my firsthand exposure to prison ministry.

AUTHOR'S NOTE

This is a book of fiction. I write fiction because it is the best way I can think of to tell the truth. However, the truth I am telling here is not a factual truth, but a philosophical one. The characters and events in this book are entirely my creations, not God's. Though much of this book is based on the reality of life in prison, it should not be viewed as a factual account of life inside the Florida Department of Corrections. I do hope to write a nonfiction book one day on life inside, but this is not that book. Thus, this is a true story, though none of it really happened.

*T*he blood will be a sign for you on the houses where you are; and when I see the blood, I will pass over you. No destructive plague will touch you when I strike Egypt.

Exodus 12:13

Then he took the cup, gave thanks and offered it to them, saying, "Drink from it, all you. This is my blood the covenant, which is poured out for many for the forgiveness of sins."

Matthew 26:27-28

When Christ came as high priest . . . He did not enter by means of the blood of goats and calves; but he entered the Most Holy Place once for all by his own blood, having obtained eternal redemption. If the blood of goats and bulls sprinkled on those who were ceremonially unclean sanctified them so that they were outwardly clean, how much more will the blood of Christ cleanse our consciences from acts that lead to death?

Hebrews 9:11-14

ONE

I WAS STANDING AT THE GATE of Potter Correctional
Institution staring at him when he was killed. Actually,
I was looking into the back of a garbage truck. As I waited to
be buzzed into the pedestrian sally port, my view was slightly impaired by the chain-link fence and razor wire that surrounded the vehicle sally port. The hot July sun reflected off
the razors as it would from the mirrored shades of a redneck
police chief, waves of heat dancing through the circles of
steel. The air was thick and hard to breathe. The clear, blue,
cloudless sky offered me no shelter from the sun's assault,
nor any promise of rain for the parched planet beneath my
feet.

I didn't know I was witnessing a murder at the time. All
I saw was a rather young corrections officer, with a bad com-
plexion and wide hips, standing on the back of a white, one-
ton Ford flatbed truck loaded with trash bags. He was
thrusting a long metal rod through each bag. His hips made
him look like he was wearing football pants with full pads.
Sweat poured off his face, and his light brown uniform was
soaked through. What caught my attention in the first place
was the enthusiasm with which he executed his task.

I understood the need for a security officer to check

1

every vehicle and everything those vehicles carried before they left the institution. Recalling just one of the many real-life horror stories recited during my recent new-employee orientation about the brutal and bloody trail an escaped inmate leaves behind was more than enough to convince me of that. But as I stood at the gate waiting for it to open, I was awestruck by the violent blows each bag received. It seemed to me that there must be more effective and efficient ways to search the trash. Of course, the manner in which he was searching was a warning to all the inmates looking on as much as it was a search for an inmate trying to escape. Like a prehistoric sign language or an antiquated form of Morse code, every violent stab by the officer was a character of communication. Taken together, they sent out a concise message for all who had the eyes to see: Attempting to escape PCI in the back of a trash truck was a bad idea. And, although inmates were sometimes treated like trash and, at times, acted like trash, they were not going to escape by pretending to be trash.

Preparing to stab the final bag in the center of the truck, the officer stumbled over the outer ones and stood above it. Raising the weapon above his head, he brought it down with incredible force. When the rod entered the bag there was a deep thump followed by the sound of twigs caught in a lawn mower. This time the metal implement did not return when the officer attempted to retract it. He then took another stance and yanked even harder. On his third attempt in that position he pulled it free, ripping open the bag as he did. It was dripping with blood.

At first, I thought he had stabbed a can of chocolate syrup from food services or an old oil can from maintenance, but his reaction quickly convinced me otherwise. The officer lost all his color and stumbled backwards. He dropped his spear and reached for his radio only to discover that it wasn't there. This only made him more frantic. I waved to the officer in the control room, who immediately buzzed me in. As I ran in, the officer on the flatbed began yelling.

"Chaplain, get out here now. Call for help!" His voice was weak and tight. Then his voice changed to the high-pitched cry of hysteria. "Oh God . . . What the . . . Oh shit . . . There's a body in . . . " With that, he passed out.

I rushed over to the second gate that led into the vehicle sally port, and before I reached it, the control room had already buzzed it open. I ran straight through the gate, pausing on the other side only long enough to close the gate behind me. My heart was thumping like a boom box playing rap music in my chest, and my thoughts were a blur of indistinguishable lyrics. Climbing onto the back of the truck, I saw that the officer had landed on a bag of papers that had cushioned his fall. I crouched beside him, the sweat from my face dropping onto his. I could tell he was beginning to come around. My eyes moved down his body. The name tag on his shirt bore the name Shutt. His feet were still touching the last bag he had stabbed; they were covered with blood. It looked like the entire bed of the truck, once white, was now crimson.

"Look at me, Officer Shutt," I said when he first opened his eyes. "Don't look down. Look right at me." He immediately looked down and began backpedaling away from the blood, looking like a sand crab avoiding the approaching tide. Blood splattered everywhere—on the bags, on him, and on me. As the blood splattered on me, I wondered if the red rain might contain HIV or hepatitis B.

In his clumsy attempt to escape, the officer knocked me back into the bag with the body. As I fell, it enclosed on me like a beanbag chair, and I felt warm, sticky liquid on the back of my neck and soaking through my clothes. I lurched forward, pivoting slightly as I did, a morbid part of me wanting to see. Lifeless black eyes stared at me blankly from a lifeless black head, which hung unnaturally. I slid forward trying to get away. When I sat up, I noticed that one of the nurses, a rather tall young woman with blond hair, had entered the sally port with us. Shutt was already off the truck moving frantically towards the gate where I had entered. The officer in the control room had the wits about her not to let him through. I quickly jumped off the truck and had to hold onto its side as all the blood seemed to drain from my head.

Within seconds, officers began pouring into the sally port from other gates like ants through small holes in the earth. Two of them immediately went over to check on Shutt. Another came to check on me as all of them strained to look at the back of the truck, which had taken on the surreal quality of a scene from a B slasher film.

"Chaplain, you okay?" Captain Skipper asked.

"I'm fine," I lied. "But let's get Shutt to medical. He's really shaken up. And he's got blood all over him."

"They're on the way," he said and looked back at the truck. "Damnation. How can there be so much blood?"

"His heart must still be pumping," I said. "How did everyone respond so fast?"

"Tower," he said as if it were obvious.

I looked fifty feet up at the tower to see the officer leaning out of the window observing everything with the radio still in her hand. When I looked back down, I saw that the nurse had her arm around the distraught officer, talking to him reassuringly.

"Chaplain, can you help me for a minute?" the nurse asked.

"Sure," I said as I hurried over to where they were. "What can I do?"

"I'm Nurse Strickland," she said, trying but unable to remove the distressed look from her face. She appeared to be in her late twenties, an attractive and delicate blue-eyed beauty with more makeup than she needed. She looked like the kind of woman who, despite her attractiveness, never actually believed it. Her white nurse's uniform was as wrinkled as her distressed face. She smelled of smoke and cheap perfume, and her inexpensive gold jewelry made hollow tinkling sounds as she moved.

"I need to check on the inmate on the truck. Can you stay with him?" She glanced at Shutt. "He's still very shaken up."

"Sure," I said. "You go ahead and do what you have to. We'll be okay over here."

She turned to leave, but then turned back to Shutt and said, "I am so sorry." She then ran over to the truck and bravely climbed onto the back. Standing on the truck, she snapped on rubber gloves and carefully, but quickly, made her way to the center bag—the bag with the body in it. She crouched down to check the inmate, nearly disappearing behind the bags as she did. She moved with the surety and confidence of a seasoned ER nurse.

Moments later, the colonel and other medical personnel began to arrive. Shutt and I were escorted out of the sally port and into the security building on the rear side of the control room. It was hard to see from that position, but I could tell that Captain Skipper had finished ripping open the bag to discover there was nothing left to do except call the coroner.

"I don't know if post-mortem prayers work, but if you have one, you might want to launch it up," Colonel Patterson said when he was buzzed into the hallway of the security building where we were standing.

He was a short, fat man with thick hands, bushy eyebrows, and messy hair—Lieutenant Colombo gone to pot. His uniform, which always looked sloppy, had large rings around the neck and armpits. His skin was leathery, and his neck was red—literally and figuratively.

In my short time as a prison chaplain, I had met many decent and hardworking correctional officers who performed a difficult job with discipline and integrity. Colonel Patterson was not one of them.

"I don't know either," I said, "but that's never stopped me from making them before."

"Why don't y'all come back to my office. We need to get your statements and have each of you fill out an incident report," Patterson said as he continued to walk down the hallway towards his office.

The hallway, like all the hallways at PCI, was spotless and gleamed with the shine of a fresh coat of wax. Inmates had to have something to do.

In the colonel's office, we waited while he used the phone. His office was decorated with photographs, paintings, and trophies, all related to hunting. His desk was cluttered; a thin, but visible, layer of dust covered it completely. It looked as if it had been quite some time since the carpet had been vacuumed, and a distinct musty smell lingered in the air. Unlike the hallway, Colonel Patterson's office was not cleaned by inmates. Like the hallway, his office was included in their job assignment; however, Colonel Patterson hated inmates and made no attempt to hide it. Rumor was that there had never been an inmate in his office. I believed it. There were other rumors about why the colonel hated inmates, many of which sounded like war stories, involving things like riots, gang attacks, and escape attempts, all starring the colonel himself. My theory was that the colonel just needed someone to hate, and since sixty-five percent of the inmate population was black, it came naturally to him. The only thing missing in Colonel Patterson's office was a large Rebel flag that said FORGET? LIKE HELL. Patterson was a true son of the South, although he was most often referred to as a true son of a bitch.

"I want the yard closed, the work crews recalled, and a count taken immediately. Call the superintendent, and ring him straight through to my office when you get him. Find Inspector Fortner, and get him back to my office with some incident reports."

If the colonel was upset by what had taken place, I couldn't tell it. He always operated at a fevered pitch, always barking out orders, always coming on way too strong, imitating a hockey player attempting figure skating. I glanced over at Shutt. He looked as if he had just killed a man. His whole body, which appeared to be trapped in adolescence, trembled.

"Are you okay?" I asked him while the colonel reported to the superintendent what had happened.

He didn't look up, so I repeated the question. When he finally looked at me, he appeared to be in a trance, not knowing where he was.

"What?" he mumbled.

"Are you okay?" I repeated a third time, this time slowly.

He looked shocked at the question and shook his head forcefully. His pubescent face was pure fear; he was obviously in shock. He dropped his head again. I slid my chair over next to him and put my hand on his back. My hand actually moved from the force of the tremors running the length of his body. Though it was in character, I still found myself amazed at the colonel's insensitivity.

"Colonel Patterson, Officer Shutt needs to see a doctor immediately," I said when he had finished briefing the superintendent.

"What? No, he doesn't. Do you, son?"

Son didn't respond. He just continued to stare at the floor.

"Call medical, now," I said, employing the colonel's method of communication by raising the volume and lowering the tone of my voice.

"Ah, hellfire, Chaplain. He's been trained. He'll be all right."

"Call medical now, or I will. And if I do, I'm going to request the trauma support team. Then you can explain to them why you didn't."

The colonel snatched up the phone, pushed three buttons, and yelled into the receiver, "Get medical to my office now." Then he looked at me. "Chaplain, you need to get a few things straight about the way things work around here. If I wasn't leaving this afternoon for three weeks of special training, I'd take you under my wing and make things real plain for you. But the short version is this. I—"

A quick knock on the door was followed by the entrance of the superintendent, Edward Stone, a deliberate-moving black man in an expensive suit.

"Colonel, Chaplain, Officer Shutt," he said by way of greeting. His eyes stopped on Shutt. "Have you called medical, Colonel?"

"Yeah, they should be here any minute," he said curtly, as if he were talking to a new officer and not the superintendent of the institution.

"He's obviously in shock. How are you holding up, Chaplain?" Stone asked.

"I'm okay, I think," I said, and my voice still quivered slightly with the anger I felt for Patterson and the memory of those lifeless black eyes.

"I heard how you responded to the, ah . . . situation. Control said you reacted with no hesitation. You never know until it comes down to it what a man will do in those kinds of situations. You're still new around here, but everybody's trust level for you just jumped up several notches. Isn't that right, Colonel?"

"Yeah, you never know what a man will do in a crunch," he said, careful to respond to Stone's first comment and not his second.

"Let's have medical check out Officer Shutt and let the chaplain go home. We can take their statements tomorrow."

"Yeah, I think that's a good idea," Patterson said as if Stone had asked him.

"Sir, I'd really like to stay and help out if I can," I said to Stone.

"No," he said, and I could tell that there would be no further discussion about it. "We'll take care of everything here. In fact, the first thing you need to do is get over to the training building and get out of those clothes and get that blood washed off of you. Blood's not something you mess around with these days—especially the bad blood in this place. I'll drop by and see you at your office in the morning."

Before I could respond, the colonel's phone rang and the medical personnel arrived to collect Shutt. As I helped him to his feet, I assured him that everything was going to be okay. The nurses quickly helped Shutt to the door. I followed them out. Just before I closed the colonel's door, he hung up the phone, and I heard him tell Stone that the deceased inmate in the trash bag was Ike Johnson.

After a long, hot shower in the training building, during which I scrubbed Ike Johnson's blood off my body, I drove up to the state park and tried to clear my head.

For as long as I had been a praying man, I had never found a better place to get in touch with God than Potter State Park. The park was roughly sixty acres of palmettos, pine trees, and wildlife, with long, winding trails cut through the dense woods. At its center were two small ponds with a small pathway running between them. That pathway, for me at least, was the path of peace and the way of wisdom. I spent most of the afternoon up there and felt better for it. Had I stayed until nightfall, which during the summer was still several hours away, I might have been completely distracted from thoughts of Johnson's vacant black eyes. I opted instead to drive home and order pizza.

An event, as it turned out, which proved to be distracting in other, less spiritual ways.

TWO

I WAS HALF-UNDRESSED when my doorbell rang. I guess if I were more optimistic, I would say that I was half-dressed—and that the glass of seltzer water without a coaster on my dresser was half-full. My dresser, like every other piece of furniture that I scrambled to get after the divorce, was not worth the trouble of a coaster. It had been a gift—actually its previous owners did not know that it was a gift; all they knew was that they threw it out. The dresser, like the house trailer and the rest of the furniture, did not bother me too much, that is, until I had company, which thankfully was not very often.

I was surprised when I heard the doorbell, not only because I was half-undressed, but also because I had placed my order for pizza less than fifteen minutes before. It had always taken Sal's at least twenty-five minutes to deliver out here in the sticks. Since returning to Florida's panhandle after my world fell apart, I had made my home in a dilapidated, butt-ugly trailer in a small trailer park on the edge of Leon County. I quickly pulled my pants back up and whisked by my gem of a dresser on the way out of my room, pausing only long enough to secure the two folded bills on its corner.

The trailer had been repossessed, and its previous owners were obviously not a gentle breed. It was situated on a
thatch grass prairie on what was supposed to be Phase II of
an expanding mobile home community called the Prairie
Palm. Presently, Phase II was a community of one, due in
large part to Phase I, which resembled a trailer junkyard
more than a place where people actually lived. The trailer
park got its name from the lone sabal palm, Florida's state
tree, that stood in the center of the sixty-acre plot. The lonely
tree seemed to me to be an appropriate metaphor for my isolated existence here and for the state I so loved. For Florida is
a lonely appendage on a continent it resembles little.

As I walked down the extremely narrow hall of my not-
so-mobile home, passing over the pale yellow linoleum that
curled up so that it no longer reached the thin blond paneling of either wall, I remembered the two-story brick home
that Susan and I had shared on Atlanta's north side.
Amazingly enough, this felt more like home, except for the
filth of course. I opened the door and extended my hand and
the money that it held in one flowing motion, more from
practice than a God-given talent. Expecting to see Ernie, Sal's
nephew, who resembled the Sesame Street puppet of the
same name, I made an audible expression and suddenly felt
naked without my shirt when I saw the pert young delivery
person with big brown eyes staring up at me. She was actually more than pert; she was beautiful—but her orange,
white, and blue uniform, which included wonderfully fitting
navy blue shorts and a baseball cap, made her look quite
pert. She had shoulder-length brown hair pulled through the
hole in the back of her cap to form a ponytail that swung
from side to side as she moved her head. Her dark skin,
which I first noticed on her muscular legs, seemed to be her
natural skin tone rather than tanned. Her face was kind and
soft, with features that reminded me of Bambi. Though
Bambi was a boy, and apart from the muscular build of her

body and the uniform that covered it, or at least part of it, there was nothing boyish about her at all—at all. Her face was flawless, with the one exception of her slightly crooked nose, which apparently had been broken. However, it made her all the more attractive.

She looked confused as I handed her the money and seemed to take it more out of reflex than anything else. I took the box from her and realized why she looked confused. It was a parcel and not a pizza. The oversized blue block letters on its side read QVC, and then I remembered.

Sometimes late at night, when I couldn't sleep, I would lie on my old green vinyl couch and flip through all the channels for hours—the exciting life of a bachelor. Last Friday, as I flipped past the QVC home shopping channel, I saw the IBM Thinkpad sub-notebook computer at an unbelievably low price—on their easy-pay plan. The easy-pay plan was a wonderful plan whereby one—me, in this case—can buy things that one cannot otherwise afford.

"Actually, this job pays very well. All I need is your signature," she said with a notable measure of amusement.

"I'm sorry. I was expecting a pizza," I said, a little unnerved by such a stupid mistake in front of such a beautiful woman.

She handed me the pen and electronic clipboard that required my signature as she cut her eyes toward me and flashed me a quick smile. As I signed the pad, I sensed her staring at the round pink scar on my chest and long, thin white scar across my left oblique. I looked up at her.

She looked away. "Pizza, huh? You one of those health-food freaks? I bet you have a Sony Walkman and one of those nifty little exercise bikes, don't you?"

After I signed the pad, she attempted to decipher what I had written on it. In the distance, I could hear the sounds of poverty coming from Phase I of Prairie Palm. The sounds of poverty were those of people—people with time on their hands and not much else. Children yelling and laughing, the revving of automobile engines, and the loud distorted music of cheap car stereos and boom boxes swirled together into the sad and badly mixed sound track of life in the rural South. The only artist my ears could discern was John Mellencamp, which justified the volume. Appropriately enough, it was an acoustic version of his tribute to life in a small town.

I was born in a small town and I live in a small town. Prob'ly die in a small town. Oh, those small communities.

"I'm sorry," I said. "I should have introduced myself. My name is John Jordan."

"Why?" she asked. Her severe expression made me feel as if I had said something wrong.

Educated in a small town. Taught to fear Jesus in a small town.

Used to daydream in that small town. Another boring romantic that's me.

"Why, what?" I asked.

"Why should you have introduced yourself? I'm just delivering a package. This isn't a social call or anything," she said. She seemed annoyed. "You're not making a play for me, are you?"

"Well, I'm just saying it's polite, and you know . . ."

"Relax. It's perfectly all right. I'm sure a man in your profession introduces himself to nearly everyone he meets, whether they want him to or not. What are you, a priest? Wait until I tell my friends I was hit on by a priest."

For about a second I couldn't figure out how she knew, and then it dawned on me that my clerical collar still hung around my neck.

But I've seen it all in a small town. Had myself a ball in a small town. Married an LA doll and brought her to this small town. Now she's small town just like me.

"I'm the chaplain at Potter Correctional Institution," I said touching my collar.

"Oh, I see," she said with a tinge of what seemed to be embarrassment for me. "I make deliveries over there sometimes. Big place."

I made a mental note of that.

No I cannot forget where it is that I come from. I cannot forget the people who love me. Yeah, I can be myself here in this small town. And people let me be just what I want to be.

"My brother, Stan, is a Methodist preacher. He says that chaplains aren't real ministers. He says if he ever can't make it as a pastor, he knows that he could always become a chaplain."

"I'm a real minister," I said, the wounded child inside showing through my voice slightly.

"Relax. I'm just kidding." She turned to head back down the rocks and pebbles that served as my driveway toward her big colorful Federal Express truck that matched her uniform. The rhythmical blinking of its flashers—slightly slower than my heart—had a hypnotic effect on me.

I was just about to ask for her name and maybe even her number when Ernie sped into the driveway, jumped out of his car, and ran to my doorstep, where I was still watching her in amazement.

Got nothing against a big town. Still hayseed enough to say look who's in the big town. But my bed is in a small town. Oh, and that's good enough for me.

"Sorry I'm late, JJ. Uncle Sal's getting slower and slower," Ernie said.

"It's okay," I said. "Sal's pizza is still worth the wait." I looked at him only momentarily and then back with the eyes of a hunter towards Bambi. She had disappeared inside the truck. Ernie had seen her too. He was trying to hand me the white pizza box in his left hand with little success. I wanted to look at my future just a little longer first.

"Do you want the pizza or the pussy?" he half-whispered.

"What did you say?" I asked as I dug into my pocket for the pizza money with one hand and slapped him on top of the head with the other, knocking his cap off in the process and revealing a shock of black tangled curls roughly the texture of Ernie the puppet's hair.

"I said, that will be eight dollars and eighty-nine cents," he said as he handed me the box.

I was still feeling around in my pockets for the money when I decided to take one more glance at the truck. She was standing in the opening on the passenger's side waving Ernie's money in the air.

"This one's on me, Preacher. I need the tax deduction," she said.

"Thanks" was all I could say. There was a time, not so long ago, when I would have had a very nice buzz going by this time of the day and I could have come up with a better response than "thanks." I always found that I had plenty to say once liquor had removed my inhibitions. I used to be able to charm the pants right off of them, although not this one I suspect. Recovery has its disadvantages too.

Ernie ran down the driveway and across the road to her truck and got the money faster than I thought possible. They exchanged a few words, laughed, and then she drove off. I was instantly jealous. As Ernie crossed over the road again, I walked down the driveway to meet him at his car.

Well I was born in a small town. And I can breathe in a small town.

Gonna die in this small town. And that's prob'ly where they'll bury me.

"Please tell me you know who that was," I said, sounding a little more desperate than I would have liked.

"Sure, that's Laura Matthers. Her sister Kim and me are on the homecoming court together Friday night."

"This Friday night, as in day after tomorrow?"

"Uh huh."

"Thanks, Ernie."

"She's got a boyfriend," he said unaware of the damage that those words would do to me.

"They almost always do, Ernie."

"Uh huh," he said, and then added, "Nah, man, I'm just joking," and began to snort and laugh obnoxiously.

I stood for a while in the middle of my driveway after Ernie drove away. The sun was setting, its fiery bite replaced by a glorious orange and pink beauty. To the east, toward Tallahassee, the Apalachicola River snaked around the corner of the Prairie Palm property. Its banks were lined with pines, cypresses, and a seemingly infinite number of other trees and plants so unique and beautiful that one Elvy E. Callaway, a local lawyer and minister who ran for governor in 1936, had written eloquently that this was the very site of the original Garden of Eden.

As I walked back up the driveway toward my little tin home, I thought how appropriate that the little tin man lived here, but I also thought that a woman that beautiful who drives a one-ton FedEx truck had to have had a tragic life. We were perfect for each other. And though I still couldn't shake the image of those lifeless black eyes from my mind, I also had the feeling that things were heating up in the small town.

THREE

THE FOLLOWING MORNING, I stood in the chapel office of Potter Correctional Institution. A stack of mail and the package that housed my new computer lay on the desk before me. I moved the unopened mail to one side of my desk and set the box in the center. The box took up so little space on my small desk that I felt justified in having mistaken it for a pizza. Opening the package and extracting the computer inside released a flurry of small packing peanuts into my office, many of which were scattered abroad by the small fan oscillating on my file cabinet.

The dull gray walls surrounding me added to the illusion of a snowstorm. Watching the flying peanuts sail through the vacant room inspired a troubling thought. If as a pastor of a prestigious church in north Atlanta my ornate office had been an expression of who I was trying to be, maybe my current empty and sterile surroundings were an expression of who I really was. My office had nothing personal save three pictures that inspire me hanging on one wall: Martin Luther King Jr. and Billy Graham, for obvious reasons, and Jimmy Carter, to remind me that the best man was not always the best man for the job. A portrait of Jesus weeping sat on the right corner of my desk, his dark eyes drinking in the sorrow and suffering of the world. Daily I read his words, "I was in prison and you visited me."

At the height of the peanuts' performance, Superintendent Stone walked in without knocking. I felt every muscle in my body grow tense: an instinctive reaction—like braking at the sight of a Highway Patrol car.

"Chaplain Jordan, may I speak with you for a moment?" Stone said as he closed my office door. He made no attempt to hide his annoyance at the floating Styrofoam swirling around him.

"Of course. Please have a seat." I motioned him to the blue vinyl chair opposite my desk that inmates used when they had spiritual and some not-so-spiritual problems. He paused before sitting and removed two handfuls of packing peanuts from it, ever diligent to care for his expensive suit. Had he been aware of the sweaty, soiled inmate uniforms that normally occupied the seat, he probably would have left the peanuts in place.

As I sat down, the envelope on top of my lopsided stack of mail slid off, revealing an inmate request form from Ike Johnson. I was stunned. Quickly, I opened my center drawer and placed it inside.

Before he started talking, Edward (not Ed) Stone paused to clean his charcoal, wire-rimmed glasses. Like everything he owned, they looked expensive. As he removed them carefully from his face and wiped them with the spotless white silk handkerchief bearing his initials in bold black block letters, he treated them like they were costly jewels. I suddenly realized that the glasses, like everything he owned, seemed so expensive because he treated them that way. As he made these exact, intentional motions, I had a chance to really look at him for the first time. He was much leaner than I had thought. I had seen skin that was darker than his, but not by much. He had all the African features of a man from Nigeria. His nearly hairless skin was smooth and had a slight sheen about it. His movements were slow—not hesitant, but deliberate and economic. He knew exactly what he was doing and the precise amount of energy required to do it. He did everything as if it were the most important thing he would do that day.

Edward Stone's minimalist actions and conservative policies reminded me of the effects poverty has on people. No matter how successful they become, they always keep plenty in reserve for fear they will have to do without again. My grandmother, a child during the Great Depression, was the same way. It was apparent that Edward Stone and I came from different eras, mine a result of his.

"How are you doing," he asked, paused, then added, "you know . . . with what happened yesterday?"

"I'm okay. I appreciate the time yesterday afternoon to pull everything together."

"That was a bad thing you had to see. You'd have to be an idiot to try to escape, but to try it in that manner, you'd have to be suicidal."

"Perhaps he was," I said with a slight shrug.

"Maybe. I don't know. But that's what I want to find out. The thing is, his name came up in another matter that we were considering investigating."

"Really?"

"Yes. I had not put much stock in the earlier reports, but now . . . I am not so sure."

"I can see how this would give the investigation a new priority," I said sarcastically, but only slightly, and he didn't seem to catch it.

"You can? Then you'll probably understand what I am about to ask."

"What's that?"

"Chaplain, we have a situation that I need your help with." A little alarm began to ring inside my head.

"I'll be happy to help if I can," I said, pushing my mental SNOOZE button.

"Well, I appreciate that, but your help in this matter will

not be easy. In fact, it will be extremely difficult, not to mention that it is totally out of the purview of your job. But I honestly do not have anyone else I can turn to."

I raised an eyebrow and nodded encouragingly. When he didn't say anything, I said, "You've certainly piqued my interest."

"I need your help with the investigation being conducted on our compound by the inspector general of DOC into the death of Ike Johnson."

I started to object. He stopped me with a single authoritative wave of his hand.

"I conducted a thorough background check on you long before I ever decided to approach you with this, and I know that you and the IG don't care for each other very much, but there's no other way."

"Even if you could convince me to work with him, and I'm not saying that you can, you'll never be able to get him to work with me. Never."

"I've already taken care of that through the secretary."

"His *secretary*?" I asked.

"Of course not. The secretary of the department," he said with an amused smile. "So, like you, he really doesn't have a choice in this matter."

"I still don't understand why you are asking me and not someone more qualified."

"You are more than qualified. Your father has been in law enforcement all your life and is currently the county sheriff, and you nearly completed a degree in criminology before dropping out to attend seminary. I know you served as a police officer in Stone Mountain while you were in school there. It's even rumored that you were the one who stopped the Stone Cold Killer."

"As impressive as that is," I said sarcastically, and this time he caught it, "wouldn't our own prison inspector be the more logical choice? I don't get it. Why me?"

"To be completely honest, I don't trust Pete Fortner. Ordinarily, I would have the colonel assist in this kind of investigation, but he'll be gone for over three weeks."

"Why don't you trust Fortner?" I asked.

"First of all, I need to know if you'll do it," he said, his voice reminding me I really didn't have a choice.

I thought about it. I had, after leading a violent life, dedicated my life to a nonviolent struggle against violence. Fighting fire with fire had only gotten me burned. Conducting an investigation was a part of the violence I had walked away from, but . . .

I could feel the strong pull of what was being offered to me. It was seductive. Like an inmate continuing to do the same things and expecting different results, I was going to play with fire again, hoping not to get burned.

"I'm a chaplain," I said. "That comes first. But if I can do both, I am willing. I will. But I will not work closely with the IG. I don't trust him."

"Okay, the reason I'm asking you is because Daniels is Fortner's boss. Fortner's looking for a promotion, and he'd sacrifice my institution to get it. I don't trust the two men together. You, on the other hand, Daniels hates. You're the man for the job."

"God help us," I said.

"That's what I'm counting on," he said.

At that moment, my phone rang. As I lifted the receiver, I half-expected it to be God saying that he was too busy just now to help me conduct an investigation at PCI.

"Good morning. Chaplain Jordan," I said into the receiver.

"Chaplain, this is Officer Jones in the control room. Is the superintendent in your office by chance?"

"Yes," I said, but I thought, *No, not by chance. He leaves nothing to chance.* "Hold on just a moment." I handed the phone to the superintendent. He took it without comment or expression. Like I said, he's into conservation.

"Superintendent Stone . . . Yes . . . okay, send him over to the chapel right away," he said into the phone and then turned to me. "It would seem that your new partner has arrived. Before he gets here, I just want to make clear your responsibilities. You are to assist him in the investigation in any way that you can."

"Got it," I said. I could tell that arguing was futile.

"But, that's not all. I also want you to look out for the interests of this institution and its administration—and report to me every step of the way."

"Yes, sir," I said and immediately wondered if he had something to hide.

As I heard the front door to the chapel opening, I whispered to myself, "This will not go well."

"Make it go well, Chaplain," he said, confirming that I had not said it softly enough.

"Or?" I said.

"There is no 'or'—just make it go well."

The superintendent stood to open my office door for the inspector. I remained seated, preparing for the worst. This was definitely shaping up to be one of those half-empty days.

"Good morning, Inspector. I'm Edward Stone." He rose as the IG entered.

"Good morning. I'm Inspector Tom Daniels." The inspector was fifty-five, but looked sixty-five. His battleship-gray eyes matched his hair, which still showed no sign of receding.

When they had finished shaking hands, Stone sat down again, pulling his pants legs up slightly and crossing his legs—the way sophisticated men in expensive suits do. He then steepled his hands together in front of his face as if praying, the tips of his fingers at his lips. Daniels just sort of collapsed into his chair.

Tom Daniels had the look of an alcoholic; I knew, being an alumnus myself. His face was red and swollen; his step was hesitant, matching his slow-moving gray eyes. He was, however, a socially acceptable drunk. He never missed work; in fact, he was an overachiever. Yet he was often late , and, though he worked hard, he didn't produce the results he once had. Most people attributed that to age, but I knew better. Also, he made a great salary, lived modestly, and yet had financial problems. His nose was pink and puffy, offering contrast to its blue broken veins. He dressed in gray slacks, which matched his hair and eyes; white shirt, which matched his pale skin; and a red tie, which matched his bloodshot eyes. No doubt his enabler, in this case his wife, made sure his clothes were cleaned and pressed to aid in the deception. All that effort, and still so obvious.

The effect of alcoholism on Tom Daniels was severe; however, its effect on his family could scarcely be overexaggerated—not because they were beaten or abused, but because they were neglected. Not only did his children have no father who was emotionally available for them, but their inheritance was turmoil and pain. This caused his son to begin drinking at the ripe old age of fourteen. Nine treatment centers and ninety-four thousand dollars later, he was still a religiously devoted addict. His daughter, though a teetotaler, lacked confidence and any idea how to relate to men in general and a husband in particular. She attracted, and was only attracted to, alcoholics. I knew. I had been married to her.

"I believe you know our chaplain, John Jordan," Stone said.

"Yes," Daniels said without so much as a glance in my direction.

"As I am sure you are already aware, he will be the official from this institution who will be assisting you in this investigation. He grew up here and knows many of the employees of the institution," Stone continued.

Actually, I had been away for so long that I didn't know many of the people anymore, but the point was moot.

"I have been told that I don't have a choice in the matter," he said irritably.

"So has he," Stone said nodding toward me.

Daniels cut his eyes in my direction. They were cold, dull steel. He smirked. "What about the inspector of this institution?" he asked. "He's all the help I need at this time."

"He'll be working with you as well, but you are to limit his knowledge of the investigation and its revelations."

"You better have a damn good reason for that," Daniels shot back at Stone.

"I do."

When he didn't explain, Daniels said, "And what's that?"

"A good reason."

"No. I mean what is your good reason?"

Stone smiled. That was all Daniels was going to get.

"I understand what you're saying, Ed," Daniels said patronizingly, trying to be patient with the dumb colored, "but if you're keeping something from me or if I want to change our little agreement for any reason, I will. You know I have the authority. Now, why don't you brief your little chaplain here, and let's begin."

"You have copies of all the files and reports that I have. You know as much about it as I do. So, I'm going to let you brief Chaplain Jordan. At the end of the day, report back to me. Both of you."

With that, Edward Stone stood to leave me alone with Tom Daniels, which resembled an old nightmare of mine. I stood as the superintendent left. His steps were slow, deliberate, dignified; however, an unmistakable rhythmic step was present as well. Edward Stone, God bless him, was a large chunk that refused to melt in the American pot. The inspector remained seated.

I sat back down, every muscle in my body tightening again. I felt like a guitar string being wound too tightly, ready to snap at any moment.

"Before we even begin this little exercise in futility," he began, "I want to get a few things straight."

I merely nodded, trying not to break and run. It wasn't that I was scared of him, although I wondered what he was capable of doing to me when I wasn't looking, but it was the enormous guilt I felt about his daughter. I could almost taste the bile that burned in his throat for all the things he wanted to say to me.

"One," he said, raising his fingers to count his items off as he came to them, "I don't like you. Two, I've never seen a more hypocritical sight in all my life than you in a clerical collar, except for the fact that it makes you look like the little candy-ass faggot you really are."

Amazingly enough, I began to relax. The anticipation proved far worse than the actual confrontation, and, like a child who had disobeyed Dad, I found punishment brought with it release.

"Three," he continued, "this is my investigation, and you better stay the hell out of my way. Four, I'll be watching you—hoping, even praying, that you screw up. Five, when you do, and I know you will, I will personally bury your ass."

"Six," he hesitated. He looked desperate to find a sixth point. "Six," he said again, "don't forget one through five."

He stood up and walked out. As he reached my door, he began to whistle. I recognized the tune. It was "Amazing Grace," the song he knew to be my favorite hymn. He had threatened me in my own office, and now he taunted me with a song that was sacred to me. I'm not often right, but when I am, I usually am in a big way. I had been right in a big way: this was not going to go well.

FOUR

IN AN INSTITUTION LIKE PCI, there are all kinds
of inmates. There are those who received a DUI and
resisted arrest, those who sexually abused children, those
who committed murder, rape, or theft—the last usually in
the pursuit of drugs. There are inmates who are very dangerous and others who are themselves in danger in open
population. Putting all these various individuals in one institution is a very precarious endeavor. Some of them are
violent; some are not. Some of them are escape risks; some
you couldn't make leave. Others need close medical or psy-
chological supervision. And, all inmates must be assigned a
job that they are qualified to do, even if it's picking up trash.

The department that is responsible for giving inmates a
security evaluation and a job assignment, as well as deter-
mining whether or not they are a risk or are themselves at
risk in open population, is the classification department.
Since Inspector Daniels made it clear that he did not want me
working with him, and because the feeling was mutual, I
decided to conduct a little inquiry of my own, beginning
with a classification officer named Anna Rodden.

Anna Rodden, God bless her, was Potter County's only
true feminist. She was intelligent, strong, spiritual, and beau-

tiful. The last she tried to conceal behind the first, saying, "I do not wish to be judged by the shape of my ass, but on my true assets."

I once asked, "And once you've been judged on your true assets?"

"Then one may, if one is so inclined, evaluate the shape of my ass, which I must admit, is truly an asset" was her reply.

Anna, who in many ways was like my sister, was in fact my sister Nancy's best friend all through school. She had always been successful at nearly everything she did, with the exception of hiding her beauty. In fact, her attempt at repression made the subtle fire of her sensuality smolder. Her sexuality, buried just beneath the surface, threatened to make men lose their religions and, in the process, find new ones. Judging by her husband's expression of eternal bliss, it was not an idle threat.

"Anna," I said after tapping on her door.

She was seated behind her desk wearing a sleeveless white silk blouse, a fire-engine red skirt, with the matching jacket draped over the back of her chair. Her long brown hair was gathered in a single long ponytail at the nape of her neck held by a red-and-white bow. The white of her shirt made her olive skin look even darker. She was dark in other ways too. She was, like most women, dark and mysterious, only more so. As she looked up from her work, I was again amazed at the depth of her seemingly bottomless brown eyes.

"John," she said, sounding happy to see me. I loved the way she said my name. "Come in. How are you? I heard what happened yesterday."

"I'm okay, really. How are you doing?" I asked.

"I've certainly had better days. Escape attempts produce a shipload of problems and paperwork, but when the inmate gets killed in the process, it produces an oceanload."

"Was he one of yours?" I asked.

"Unfortunately," she said with a quick shake of her head and roll of her eyes. "Which means everyone from central office on down wants to know why I didn't know he was an escape risk. Like I'd be willing to read his sick little mind if I could, which I obviously can't, because I thought he was an institutional man."

"I don't see how you do it all," I said. And then added, "And so well."

"Don't do that," she said shaking her head but smiling at me.

"What?" I asked, shrugging as if unaware I had done anything.

"Don't give me compliments or understanding. I can't afford to be distracted."

"Whatever you say, but a little understanding never hurt anyone."

"Thanks," she said and then put her pen down and stared at me.

"What is it?" I asked, resisting the urge to wipe my face.

"I'm just so proud of you. . . . Serving her the way you do agrees with you." As long as I had known Anna, she had only referred to God in the feminine form. "You're really doing what you were created to do now."

"Thank you," I said.

"*Thank you,*" she said emphatically. "You are a much-needed breath of fresh air around this place. And, I suspect, everywhere you go. You know," she said in a playful manner with a smile on her soft face, "if I weren't married . . ."

"If you weren't married . . ." I said and let it hang there like a dream.

"Are you dating yet? Found anyone special in Potter County?" she asked.

"Yes, to the second question, but she's married. As to the dating, I'm not quite ready yet, but almost."

"Don't rush it. That's the worst thing you could do. Take

care of you for now, and worry about a *her* later."

"I don't feel like I've rushed it. If anything, I've been dragging my heels."

"No, I guess you haven't. Still, you can never be too careful these days. Especially considering what you've been through. Probably best to let me pick someone out for you."

"Could you please? If she won your approval, she would most certainly have mine."

"Well, I'll keep my eyes open."

How could such an extraordinary woman work in a prison in a one-horse county? Living in Pottersville, for Anna, had to do with a promise she made to her grandmother just before she died. Working in prison is the result of a promise she made to herself when her younger sister was murdered. Besides, it was temporary. She was in the final stages of finishing her law degree from Florida State University. I had every suspicion that she was going to be the toughest prosecutor that our state would ever see. She was as strong and as tough as she was beautiful. And, though she acted like she needed her husband or me in her life, the truth was she did that for our benefit. I was grateful nonetheless.

"Listen, I've got this little problem I need some help with," I said.

"Name it," she said, sounding excited at the prospect of helping me.

"Mr. Stone has asked me to look into what happened yesterday. Unofficially, of course."

Before I had finished my sentence, she was shaking her head rapidly. "No, I won't help you. You are already doing what you were meant to do. You are called to be a minister, not Father Brown, Bishop Blackie, or Brother Cadfael," she said, using my favorite fictional ecclesiastical sleuths against me.

"But . . . ."

"But, nothing," she snapped. Her eyes had narrowed and

seemed to glow. "Surely you haven't forgotten what Atlanta was like. Is your sobriety—your serenity—not worth whatever it takes?"

"It is, but I think I'm ready. Besides, this is nothing. Just a simple inquiry, that's all." I said it with so much conviction I almost convinced myself.

"I will not help you with something that will really wind up hurting you."

"I was told not to tell anyone about this. I decided that I had to tell the two people here that I would trust with my own life."

"Well, if Merrill is the man I think he is, he won't help you either."

"What do you suggest I do?" I asked.

"You're going to tell Stone you can't do it," she said without hesitation.

"I can't do that."

She was telling me that not only could I do it, but that I must do it, or she would, . . . when there was a knock at her door. It was Tom Daniels.

"Yes," she said as he stuck his head in the door.

"Hello. My name is Inspector Daniels."

"Really? Your mother named you Inspector? How awful," she said as she sat up in her chair. Her eyes sparkled mischievously. This was going to be good.

"No ma'am. My first name is Tom. I am the chief inspector of DOC. I can't believe you haven't heard of me."

"Oh, I've heard of you," she said and winked at me. "I've heard all about you. What can I do for you?"

Daniels jerked his head toward me like someone suddenly getting a whiff of a foul odor. "It's a private matter. Can I talk to you alone?"

"No, I'm afraid you can't. You see, the chaplain and I are having an affair, and since he's my secret lover, I keep no secrets from him. So, he stays."

My mouth dropped open—for two reasons really. First, I couldn't believe that she would say that we were having an affair, just in case he might possibly think she was serious. Secondly, and more importantly, I knew that as the chief inspector he could give her a world of trouble if he wanted to. She was more than just a little confident. And that was more than just a little appealing.

"Whatever," he said as he came in and took the seat beside me, careful not to look at me. "I'm looking into the death of inmate Ike Johnson. Is he yours?"

"Is he my what?"

"Is he your . . . Are you his classification officer?" he said, obviously frustrated and slightly tongue-tied. Anna's beauty, along with her confident manner and sharp tongue, was too much for any man and most women.

"Yes, I am."

"Can you tell me about him?"

"Oh, yes," she said as if she were going to cooperate, which I knew she was not. "His name is Ike Johnson."

"And?" he asked.

"And, what else would you like to know?"

"I would like to know whatever in the hell there is to know about the bastard so I can find out why he was trying to escape."

"I honestly couldn't tell you. I know of no reason why he would attempt to leave our happy little home here. Perhaps you should ask his pimp."

"His pimp. Who is that, the chaplain?"

"I will speak with you no further if you say another disrespectful thing about the state's finest chaplain."

"Okay. Damn it, lady, all I need is a little information. Who is his pimp?"

"What you need are some manners. His pimp is an inmate named Jacobson."

"What's Jacobson like?"

"An inmate pimp. He pretends to be crazy, but he's not," she said, and then she was silent as she thought about it for a minute. "I say he's not crazy, but what I mean is that he's not crazy the way he pretends to be. He pretends to be loony. What he is, is psychotic. He's dangerous. There are many people who have not lived to regret the fact that they allowed his crazy pretense to make them forget how really dangerous he is."

"So, I should talk to him?"

"I think so, but then I'm not the chief inspector of Florida state prisons."

"Did Johnson have any family on the outside?"

"Grandmother who raised him and an aunt that I know of."

"No girlfriend?"

"He didn't like girls, never has."

"Faggot on the outside too?"

"If you are asking, in your own redneck way, if I am aware of a lover he would have tried to escape for, I am not. He did have four visits from a Don Hall when he first got here, but that's been over a year ago."

"Is there anything else you can think of I should know?"

"Yes, there is. Something very important."

"Well, spit it out."

"My brother, whom I love with all my heart, is gay, and I am offended by your assertion that he or any other gay man should be used for firewood."

"Firewood? What the hell are you talking about now?"

She looked at me.

"The term *faggot*," I said, "came from a period in time when homosexual men were burned at the stake. It means kindling."

He stood without comment, withdrew a card from his pocket, and placed it on the desk in front of Anna. "This is an official investigation of a death within this prison. A death in which you are at least partly to blame. When you get tired of your little grab-ass games and want to help me figure out what the hell is going on here, call me. If you continue to refuse to cooperate or try to play more games, I will become a very big pain in your ass."

"You've already done that. Maybe you could set some new goals for yourself."

He slammed the door, and I felt a wide grin slowly spread across the width of my face.

"Tell me I was correct in assuming that was your ex-father-in-law," she said.

"None other," I said, unable to keep from grinning.

"What an ass," she said in disgust.

"He didn't exactly get to see your best side either," I said.

"I thought my ass was my best side," she said with a smile.

"Not exactly what I meant."

"I guess not, but he's not going to see my best side. He's not going to come within a mile of it. You two are working on the same case?"

"Actually, we are working together on it."

"You don't seem too together."

"We are as together as we are going to get."

"Now," she said with a warm smile, "how can I help you solve this case?"

"What?" I asked. "What happened to it being bad for me?"

"Well, this time you'll have me to help you, and I'm going to help you solve this thing before that obnoxious bastard does. So, how can I help?"

"Tell me all you can about Johnson," I said.

She did.

"Do you know for a fact that Jacobson was Johnson's pimp?"

"As much as you can know such things for facts. They were both assigned to me."

"What was his job assignment?"

"Outside grounds," she said, seeming not to catch how odd that was.

Inmates who worked outside of the institution did so because they were deemed to be a low escape risk. It had to do with their custody, their release date, and past history (had they ever tried to escape before?). It was a gamble, and it was the responsibility of their classification officer.

"Outside the gate?" I asked. "Are you sure? That can't be right."

"What do you mean?" she said. She must have been really distracted.

"I find it interesting that he works outside the gate and he tries to escape in the trash truck on his day off."

The greatest risk and highest percentage of escapes occurred with those who were working outside the gate. Breaking out of the institution was difficult, but once you were outside, well, you had a chance.

"Nobody ever said they were smart," she said. "But I see what you mean."

"What else can you tell me about him?"

"As you can imagine, he spent a lot of time in confinement for physical contact with other inmates and drug use."

"By physical contact, you mean sexual contact, right?"

"It sure wasn't fighting. Did you see how small he was?"

"No. I don't recall ever having seen him. Probably didn't spend a lot of time in the chapel." But I had seen him—his eyes, his lifeless black eyes.

"Well, he was in the beginning stages of AIDS."

Oh, my God, I thought. *I was covered in his blood. Think. Do I have any sores, open cuts, wounds. Think. Focus. Father, please protect me. Don't let me have AIDS. Let me live to serve you longer and to find love again.*

"Do you think that's related to his apparent escape

attempt?" I said finally, realizing that Anna was staring at me.

"Yes, possibly. I don't know," she said. She must have noticed my sudden agitation. "You came in contact with his blood, didn't you? The chances that you could have it are so small you shouldn't even worry about it. Okay?"

"Okay. I'm not really worried," I lied.

"Good. You shouldn't be. Now, why did you say apparent escape attempt?"

"It seems to me that had he really wanted to escape, he could have from his job much more easily than the way he chose. Besides, he sat there in that bag and heard what the officer was doing to all the other bags. He had to know what was coming."

"You're thinking suicide?"

"I'm at least considering the possibility—all the possibilities. But suicide is one of the least likely. There are much better ways to commit suicide."

"What are the other possibilities?" she asked, her voice rising in excitement.

"About a thousand others, but the one I'm thinking about seriously is murder."

"Murder? That's ridiculous," she said.

"Maybe so, but I feel that I must consider it, until I know otherwise."

"Sure, that's good investigating procedure. Keep an open mind . . . but—"

"It's good theology too," I interrupted.

"Yes, I guess it is. But you have a reason for seriously considering it. What is it?"

"Let's just say that everybody at this institution knows how that garbage is checked, and it would be a great way to hide a murder or have one committed."

"Interesting. I never thought of it that way before. So,

you think somebody killed him and then put him in the garbage bag so that he'd be dumped somewhere or get stabbed and it would look like he was killed trying to escape."

"I just think that if it were an escape attempt, he would have lost his nerve there at the end."

"Maybe. Maybe the officer had been paid to miss that bag."

"Maybe. But if he were, that meant he knew the inmate was in there, which meant he knew he was killing him. Which means that he deserves an Oscar for his performance."

"He was shaken?" she asked.

"He was shaken and stirred," I said.

"Sounds like you've given this some thought."

"A little," I said, and then we fell into silence. It was a comfortable silence. After a couple of minutes, I said, "What can you tell me about Jacobson?"

"I was wondering when you would get to that," she said with a smile that said she knew something that I didn't. I saw that smile a lot.

"I can tell you that not only was he Johnson's pimp, but he was also in the infirmary with Johnson on Monday night."

"What?"

"Yeah. And, they had a fight. Tuesday morning Jacobson was taken to confinement and locked up, and Johnson . . . Well, you know what happened to him."

"What time was he placed in the box?"

"Log indicates that it was around six thirty in the morning. Of course, those logs are never exact."

"No, but it's probably close to the actual time, which means he could have killed him and bagged him before he was taken away," I said.

"Maybe, I don't know. Seems to me that whoever did the

deed would have to actually put the bag on the truck or run the risk of whoever did load the bag discovering what was inside it," she said.

"Very good point," I said. "There's something else too."

"What's that?"

"It may not mean anything, but then again, who knows? He was locked up before the shift change. And yet, it was close to the time of the shift change. Too close."

"What do you mean?" she asked, genuinely interested.

To have a woman like Anna Rodden genuinely interested in anything you say is more than most men dream of.

"I mean, from what I've seen, if something occurs that close to the shift change, the officers leaving save it for the officers just coming in."

"That's true," she said. "God, you're good. Do you really think you can handle it better than the Stone Mountain thing?"

"Time will tell, but I think so. I think that I'm a different person. Besides, I have you and Merrill."

"If you need someone to talk to, you know where to find me."

"Thank you."

"I haven't done anything yet."

"Oh, yes, you have. You've listened, you've given me some much-needed female attention and perspective, and, most of all, you've made my day by telling off Tom Daniels."

"You know I love you. Always have. We share something very special. And, you don't have AIDS."

"I know. I love you too. And thanks again. You were amazing."

"Was there ever any doubt I would be?" she said with a small chuckle, pretending to be kidding, which she was not.

*F*IVE

*P*OTTER CORRECTIONAL INSTITUTION was its own little world—a society of captives with their own social order, classes, economy, and laws. In this world, I was a stranger. PCI was my job; it was their home. I spent eight hours a day there; they spent twenty-four. I needed a guide. There were less than three inmates out of fifteen hundred that I felt might actually help me. My first choice was the inmate assigned to the chapel to assist me, Mr. Smith. I was told during orientation not to call any inmate mister or sir, but I made an exception for Mr. Smith.

Mr. Smith was old, exactly how old I wasn't sure—I don't think he was either. His back was slightly bent, causing him to bow forward a little as he walked. Being a black man in America had bent, but not broken this man. As he walked, with his head down, a small bald spot could be seen right at the very crown of his head. He was raised in the old Southern school of repression, in an era when a black man was to be seen and not heard—seen working, that is. We had developed a good relationship since I had been at PCI. After returning from Anna's office, I decided to ask him to explain a few things to me about life on the inside. When I returned to my office, however, there were several inmates waiting to see me.

On an average day, I have contact with over a hundred inmates, twenty of whom usually came to my office with their problems. Issues ranging from family crises to conflicts with one of the other inmates or officers filled the majority of my counseling sessions. Many inmates came to me with things I could do nothing about, especially if they related to security or housing issues; however, since I am one of only a few that will even take the time to listen to them, they come.

Some inmates actually came to my office out of a desire for rehabilitation, recovery, and spiritual growth—that was as refreshing as it was novel. Most came over trivial matters relating to their job or bed assignments or wanting to use my phone.

"Chaplainsuh, I's wandering if you could let me use the phone," Inmate Jones, an elderly, slow-talking and slow-moving black man, said when we were seated in my office. "My aunt is real sick. I need to call my peoples."

"I'm sorry," I said. "As you know, the department will only allow me to place a phone call for you in the event of the death or serious illness of an immediate family member. Even then I have to verify it by an outside official like a doctor or funeral director."

"Just this once. I really need to talk to her. She raise me, you know."

"Is she at home or in the hospital?"

"She at home."

"The only thing I can do is give you a phone pass that will allow you to call collect from your dorm."

I opened my desk drawer to retrieve a phone pass form. When I looked down, there was the request from Ike Johnson. In the events of the morning, I had forgotten it. I shut the drawer.

"She got a block on her phone," he said, failing to see the contradiction in what he was saying.

If she really wanted to hear from him, why would she

have a block on her line? I often wondered how inmates could tell me with a straight face how close they were with their families and yet admit that their families had gone to the trouble of placing a block on their phones that prevented them from calling.

"The only thing I can suggest is for you to have another family member call or write her."

He stood up to leave, obviously angry.

"Would you like to talk about how your aunt's illness is making you feel?" I asked.

"All I want to do is call my peoples," he said, opening my door to leave.

"By the way," I said, "how did you find out that she was sick in the first place?"

"I call my moms," he said before he thought about what he was saying.

"Why don't you call her again and ask her how your aunt is? In fact, if she has a three-way feature on her phone, she can then call your aunt, and you can talk to her that way."

"You don't understand," he said walking through he open door.

"I'm trying to," I said. "If you can think of how I can help you within the rules, I will be happy to do it," I said—more to the back of his head than anything else.

As soon as he left, I opened my center desk drawer and extracted my mail and the request form. Inmate request forms are how inmates make requests of staff members in prison. The top of the request form stated that it was from Ike Johnson and to Chaplain Jordan. The request read: "Dear Chaplin sir, I really need to talk to you very soon. Can I come to your office tomorrow? It's real important. I scared I either going to try to escape or kill myself and don't know who to talk to. Sir, you my only hope. May God bless you, Chaplin sir."

Unlike any other request I had ever received, this one

was typed. Most inmates did not have access to typewriters, and the ones who did were only allowed to use them for official reasons such as law work. I glanced up at the date. It was dated the day he was killed. I should have received the request that day, but, because of the incident in the sally port, I had not picked up my mail. Ironically, his death was the very thing that had delayed my getting his plea for help. I felt sad for him and just a little sick. If he were planning an escape, why would he request to come and see me? Obvious question, I know, but it must be asked. Did he really send it? I wondered what he was going through and if it were the sort of thing that people were killed for.

I reread the request several times. The type had several distinguishing marks, not the least of which was that the letter "t" was missing the right side of the crossbar, the letter "o" was missing the bottom curve, and the letter "a" was much darker than the rest of the type. The typewriter that produced this request would not be difficult to find.

While I was examining the request, Mr. Smith tapped on the door.

"Come in," I said.

"Brother Chaplainsuh, they's two mo' to see you now." Mr. Smith's blue uniform was always neatly pressed and buttoned to the top button.

"Do you know what they want?" I asked.

"One say he didn't get the Father's Day card we sent him. The other one wants you to make copies of his legal papers."

"Sounds like they can wait a minute or two. Would you mind coming in and talking to me for a few minutes?"

"Nosuh, I don't mind," he said as he swaggered in and slowly took his seat. "I done something wrongsuh?" he asked.

"No. Nothing like that at all," I said reassuringly. "Actually, I need your help."

"Okaysuh." He was slumped so far down in his chair as to be nearly horizontal. His head hung down as if it were too much effort to keep it up. His long arms dangled on either side of the chair, nearly touching the floor.

"I'm still trying to understand how things work on the compound and wondered if you could explain it to me."

"'Splain whatsuh?" he asked slowly.

"First of all, how often do you hear inmates talking about trying to escape? I'm talking about serious talks about escape attempts."

He hesitated. "Nosuh, not many ever say anything like that to me. Too hard. Chances are they couldn't make it. Not worth it. This place harder to get out of than it look."

"Has anyone ever tried to escape from here before?" I asked, knowing that he had been here almost the entire three years this institution had been open.

"Nosuh. Not as I know of. Couple from the work camp did, but they caught them lickidy-split."

"What do you think about the escape attempt we had yesterday?

"I think he a fool. Everybody know what they do to the trash. Maybe he wanted to die. Never tell about him."

"But you don't think that it was a serious escape attempt?"

"Nosuh. Either he wanted to die, or somebody wanted him to die."

"I see. What can you tell me about drugs or alcohol on the compound?"

"They's those who have it. They's those that would love to have it but can't afford it. They's those who do anything for it."

"Is there a lot of it on the compound?"

"Nosuh, not a lot. And they's really only two things—buck and hash."

"How do they get it?"

"Most the liquor is homemade. Inmates in food services or the chapel sneak juice or old fruit and sugar back down on the 'pound. Mix it up and let it ferment."

"You mean inmates have stolen our communion juice to make buck?"

"Yesuh. Some go to church on communion night 'cause of it. They hold it in their mouth until they get back down to the dorm and then they all spit it into an old can or a plastic bag they stole. The clerk that worked here before me used to steal some every week and sell it down on the 'pound."

"What about hash?"

"Hash come in during visitation, or some officer bring it."

"What do you mean?"

"Some of the inmate's family members sneak it in and slip it to them while they visit or leave it in the bathroom and the orderly get it when he clean up. And, they is officers that will sell it to you. Not many left, but they always a few."

"Is it expensive? Hard to get?" I asked.

"Cost whatever man's got. Cookies, cards, smokes, or a hit on someone."

"No cash involved?"

"Nosuh. Not enough of it to be able to bribe officers and it don't do no good for inmates."

"Everything's done on trade?"

"Yesuh. Inmate say, 'You do this for me or that for me and I give you my canteen.' They pay—it just ain't with money."

"What can you tell me about homosexuality on the compound?"

"Well, they's the punks, the pimps, the sisters, and then the inmates who use they services. The punks are the real fags. They like it. They was fags before they come in here. They have pimps who look after them, and hire them out. The sisters are faggots who just go with each other. They don't have no one to protect them and they don't hire out. They just in love, I reckon," he said, shaking his head and then growing silent.

We were both silent for a moment. I looked at him. He was looking down, which is what he did most of the time. He was old, with solid gray hair, except for the bald spot. He seemed feeble. His brown lips protruded and his nose seemed to spread across his entire face. His eyelids twitched occasionally—probably wishing they had been closed more often throughout his painful life. His hands were very large and his fingers all came to sharp points at the ends.

"You said that some inmates use the services of a punk, but are they not considered to be punks themselves?"

"Nosuh. They straight on the outside. It's just they can't get none in here. In here they a big difference between pitching and catching."

We were silent again, and I mused about the moral difference between pitching and catching in the social order of Potter Correctional Institution. What a strange world I had entered.

"The punks," he began again, "wear women's stuff."

"Like what?" I asked.

"Panties, pantyhose, perfume. Shit . . . I mean stuff, like that."

"What?" I asked truly amazed. "Where in the world do inmates get women's clothes and perfume?"

"Get it from one of the female officers."

I gave him a look that said, *No way*.

"Yesuh," he said with a world-weary smile. Some of these womans who work out here are lonely. They do lot of stuff for inmates they likes. If they like one, nobody better mess with him."

"Do any of them actually have affairs with inmates?"

"Some do, not many. Not really affairs, but they have sex. Get an inmate to come into the laundry room with 'em late at night when 'most everybody's asleep. Some of the black officers get white inmates. They chance to have a white man. But this don't happen a lot. Too hard in open dorms. But a lot of them let inmates gun them down."

"Gun them down?" I asked as if I had been born yesterday, and in this world I had.

"They jack while they watch the officer in the control room of the dorm. Control room glass, and you can see everything in the bathroom. They got a squad that get together and gun down the female officers, especially the fat ones. Some of the officers encourage it, and some even expose themselves to the inmates. Some don't even know it's goin' on."

"Who all knows about this?"

"'Most everybody on the 'pound."

"Officers too?"

"Some. Not too many. Everything that we do, somebody know about. Everything."

"So if an inmate does something, it's because some officer or staff member allows him to do it."

"Yesuh."

"Most of the inmates trust you, don't they?"

"I got respect. Not the same thing. Inmates don't trust no one. They life say they can't trust no one, not even the chaplain."

"Really? So I have no hope of real acceptance and trust from them?"

"Nosuh. You got mine. You probably get others, not many though."

"I see. What's the overall feeling about the officers and staff?"

"Nobody give 'em much thought 'less they mess with us. The jits are not smart enough to be cool so that the officers don't get in our business. They so stupid."

"The jits?" I asked.

"Jitterbugs. Young inmates. They not convicts like us.

They inmates. A true convict don't get in no trouble. 'Cause if you stay clean or look like you do, officers stay away from you. Convict wants to do his time quiet with no trouble. Jit ain't got the sense God give a dung beetle. 'Sides, most of them don't have a lot of time anyway, so they do it the hard way. But, they be back. Eventually they learn."

"If an inmate—or a convict—wanted to escape, could an officer be bought to help?"

"Nosuh, probably not. They sell you dope, maybe turn they head when you beat up a punk, but they wouldn't help you get out."

"Did you know the inmate who tried to escape yester-day? Johnson."

"Nosuh, not really."

"What about an inmate named Jacobson?"

"Yeah, I know of him. Watch your back around him. Some people say he crazy, but he ain't. He's dangerous. Lot of inmates say they killed before; most of 'em ain't, but Jacobson's a killer for real. I bet he's lost count of the number of people he's offed."

"Is there anybody else I should talk with?"

"Yesuh. They's an old homosexual on the 'pound. He say very little, but he know a lot."

"What's his name?"

He started to speak and then stopped. "I don't know his real namesuh. Everybody on the 'pound call him Grandma."

I couldn't help but laugh a little. "Thank you for all your help. I really appreciate it."

"Yesuh. Thank you for what you do. You the first chap-lain I seen who really care and don't act like he any better than the rest of us."

"Mr. Smith, I'll tell you a little secret: I'm not."

*J*OHN JORDAN'S FIRST RULE of detection: start with
what you have, even when what you have isn't much. I
knew that Johnson spent his last night in the infirmary and
that Jacobson was there too. So I went to the medical building. The medical building, like every other building at PCI,
was gray. At least everybody referred to it as gray; I felt that
it lacked sufficient color to actually be classified as a color,
even a color as colorless as gray. The medical building, which
actually housed dental and classification also, was always
filled with inmates lined up waiting for service. Some of
them were there to see their classification officer, others to
see the dentist, and still others to see a doctor or pick up
medication.

Just inside the building there was a small inmate waiting
room where inmates sat in silence staring at the front wall
until they were called in by the particular official they were
waiting to see. To the left was dental and classification, and to
the right was medical and pharmaceutical, all of which were
behind locked doors. I turned right—the opposite direction
from Anna, whom I would rather have been visiting.

After unlocking the medical department door with my
key, I walked down the long hallway leading to the infir-

mary, wondering how many other staff members had a key to the medical department. It made sense that the chaplain did; I spent a great deal of time in the infirmary.

Along the way, I passed the nurses' station where two nurses—one white, one black, both elderly and overweight—sat. Each had an inmate seated across from her and was laboring to check his vital signs. The inmates' slightly amused slightly fearful looks said they wondered if the nurses had a vital sign between them.

I also passed by two exam rooms. In one, Dr. Mulid Akbar, PCI's senior health officer and my personal advisor to the Muslim religion, was examining the knee of one of the inmates, who seemed to be in a great deal of pain. I couldn't help but wonder if he was just trying to get out of work, and then I felt guilty for being so jaded. It's just that in the few months that I had been at PCI, I had been lied to more than the entire rest of my life. However, I vowed again, right then and there, not to become so callused that I expect to be lied to.

At the end of the hallway and to the left, I entered the officers' station for the infirmary. There I found to both my surprise and delight Nurse Strickland, whom I had briefly met the day before. She was seated on the officer's desk swinging her legs back and forth and chewing bubble gum while warmly conversing with Officer Straub.

"Well, hello, Chaplain. Jordan, isn't it?" Strickland said.

"Yes, John. Hello. How are you two today?"

"Never better," she said in an upbeat voice, but she was looking down. "By the way, my name is Sandra, but everyone calls me Sandy." When our eyes finally met, she glanced at me and then looked away. She was that not-so-rare combination of beautiful and insecure. At that moment, I wished for the chance to help make her more secure. She was beautiful and I wanted to tell her so.

"I've never seen you here during the day before and now I've seen you two days in a row," I said. "Have you been transferred to day shift?"

"Oh, no. I'm too much of a night owl. I wouldn't be much use around here most mornings. Just with everything that happened yesterday and all, I'm trying to lend a hand. We also have an ACA inspection coming up soon, and I'm putting in a lot of overtime to whip things into shape."

"We keep trying to get her to join us here on day shift," Officer Straub said, never taking his eyes off her, "but she just won't do it. I think she's a vampire."

She slapped at him in mock anger and then opened her mouth just enough to expose her vampire teeth and started toward his neck, but then got embarrassed and stopped. She looked down and then back at me to see if she had made a complete fool out of herself.

I tried to think of something to say that would assure her that she had not. "If you want to drain his blood, I can wait in the other room." And then I laughed, but soon discovered that I was laughing alone. She looked upset and a little pale.

"I'm sorry," I said. "I forgot all about yesterday. I know you were the first to check Johnson. It was very insensitive of me. I'm really sorry."

"It was just so horrible. So much blood . . . everywhere. It really got to me. I didn't think it would, but it did. I think I'm going to walk outside for a minute and get some fresh air. Would you like to join me, Chaplain?"

"Sure," I said and then turned to say good-bye to Straub but could feel the intensity of his stare immediately. I had interrupted his play and he made no attempt to hide his anger. I simply nodded and turned and walked away.

Outside, the fresh air was far too hot and humid to be refreshing, but it did restore Nurse Strickland's color. Or perhaps it was the super slim Capri cigarette she was inhaling the way underwater swimmers take in air when they finally reach the surface again. We were standing at the back right of the medical building where the smokers normally congregated, but, for now, we had it all to ourselves.

"I'm really sorry about that. Are you okay?" I said.

"Oh, yeah, don't worry about it. It was no big deal and any other time would have been funny. It's just . . ."

"I know. Did you know him very well?" I asked.

"Who?" she asked as if I had just awakened her.

"Johnson."

"Yeah, I guess. I mean, as well as you can know any of these men, I guess."

"Was he in the infirmary a lot?"

"Not a lot, but still a lot more than most of the other men," she said.

"What can you tell me about him?" I asked.

"Why so many questions? What are you, an undercover cop?"

"No, nothing like that. It's just that I was involved and I'm curious," I lied.

"Well, let's see," she said, looking at me only for a moment and then back down again. "He was kind of small, so he got picked on a lot. He was a little effeminate. I don't think he liked girls very much. Probably hated them."

"Really, what makes you say that?"

"Oh, don't pay any attention to me. I've had a few psych courses, and I like to see if I can read people, but I don't really know."

"You may be right. I've heard that he had a pimp."

"Really, who?"

"An inmate named Jacobson. Do you know him?"

"Not very well, I'm happy to say. He's been in to see us a few times, but I try to avoid him. He's crazy. That really pisses me off," she said bitterly and then looked up at me in shock. "Oh, shit, Chaplain. I did it again. Excuse my French, please. I'm sorry."

"Don't worry about it. What were you saying? I want to know what makes a pretty lady like yourself that angry."

"It's just what this place does to people. People like Jacobson turn sweet little boys like Johnson into monsters, you know. I'm sick of it. If you're not a criminal when you get here, you'll damn sure be one when you leave." A single tear cut a path through the thick makeup on her right cheek.

I was moved with compassion for her. She was right. Oftentimes, the merely misguided became the cunningly criminal inside facilities like these. "It sounds to me like you really care," I said.

"I do."

We were silent for a few minutes. She puffed away, and I waited for the silence to pass while a single drop of sweat trickled down the center of my back, tickling as it did.

"What happened Monday night?" I asked finally. "How did Jacobson get thrown in the hole and Johnson in the back of that truck?"

"I really don't know. It was a relatively quiet night. They were the only two we had in the infirmary. In the early morning hours of Tuesday—five maybe, they started yelling at each other and, before too long, Jacobson was on top of Johnson punching him in the face. The officer on duty, Officer Hardy, wasn't at his desk, so Captain Skipper and I broke them up and separated them. He told them to go back to bed and he would forget about it. I've never seen Skipper do anything like that before. I figured he was up to something. He told them if they did it again, he was going to write them a disciplinary report and send them to confinement."

"Where was Officer Hardy?" I asked.

She shrugged. Her expression said he was often away from his assigned post. "I really don't know. Could've been anywhere. He was not where he was supposed to be."

"Really?" I said. "I've heard he's an excellent officer."

She shrugged. "Don't believe everything you hear around here, Chaplain."

I smiled. "What days does he work?" I asked.

"Hardy? Thursday through Monday, but Monday night was his last night for two weeks. He's on annual leave now. Pretty convenient, huh?"

"Why was Captain Skipper here that night?"

"I think he came to take a statement from one of the inmates involved in an incident earlier that night, but he wasn't here."

"Which inmate?"

"Thomas, I believe."

"Anthony Thomas?"

"Yeah," she said defensively. "Why?"

"I've worked with him and his wife some," I explained. "Where did he find him?"

"I really don't know, but he did find him eventually and locked him up for not being where he was supposed to be."

"How long did he stay?" I asked.

"Not long at all," she said. "He left when he couldn't find Thomas."

"What happened next?"

She gave an elaborate shrug and a took a deep drag on her cigarette. "They must have started fighting again. Obviously, Officer Hardy had Jacobson locked up. I went back up to my desk to finish some paperwork, and that was the last I saw of either one of them. Until the truck," she said, turning pale again.

"Who else was in the building at that time?"

"Well, let's see. There was Nurse Anderson, and our inmate orderly, Allen Jones, was gathering the trash and cleaning the exam rooms."

"What about the trash? When is it picked up?"

"Early in the morning usually. I'm not really sure. Our orderly always gets it ready and puts it out here to be picked up."

"Is that orderly here now?" I asked.

"Yeah, I think so," she said.

"Can I talk with him?" I asked.

"Sure. Let's go back inside," she said, taking a long final draw on the stub of her cigarette and tossing it into the ashtray.

We found her orderly, the same old black man that I had denied a phone call to earlier this morning, in one of the storage closets near the back. She told him that I wanted to talk to him and that we could go into the staff break room, which was just around the corner.

I could tell he didn't want to talk to me, but he swaggered toward the break room nonetheless.

"This won't take long," I said when we were finally seated at the table in the break room. "I'm sorry I couldn't let you use the phone this morning."

He shrugged as if he didn't care, but didn't say anything. I continued.

"I just want to know how you normally gather and take out the trash down here and if you did it any differently on Monday night or Tuesday morning."

Without facial or verbal expression he said, "I gather it all up before I leaves every night and puts it near the back door were you's just standing. Then, in the morning I picks up any new trash and sets them outside the door. The officer and inmate who pick up the trash then come around and pick it up."

"Is that how it happened Tuesday morning?" I asked.

He shook his head slowly. "I already told the inspector. I gathered it all up and put the bag in the back hall, then Miss Anderson come say she need me to clean up a spill in the exam room. When I come back to load it on the truck, the bag was gone. Miss Anderson was with me. She can tell you. The trash wasn't outside the door neither, and the truck was gone."

"Did you see the inmates in the infirmary that morning?" I asked.

"Yes, sir," he said nodding his head. Each time his head went down I wondered if it would come up again. In addition to seeming old, Allen Jones seemed weary, as if every year he had lived was a hard one.

When he didn't elaborate, I added, "Anything unusual about them?"

"No, sir. All three were lying there in they beds sleepin'."

"All three?" I asked, the surprise in my voice obvious. "Who else was there?"

He wondered if he had said something wrong. Then after a long pause, he said, "Johnson, Jacobson, and Thomas."

"You saw Thomas in an infirmary bed that morning?"

"Yes, sir. Well, I thought I did. I could've been . . . maybe I didn't see him. I don't know," he said.

"What time were you in there?"

"Can't say, sir. Don't wear a watch. But I come in at four. It wasn't too long after that," he said.

"Did you see Jacobson and Johnson fighting around five?" I asked.

"No, sir. I's still gathering up the trash and cleaning up. I's all over the building."

I walked back to the nurses' station and called the trash officer, Officer Shutt, whose acquaintance I had briefly made the day before.

"How are you doing?" I asked.

"Better," he said. "Thanks. And thanks for your help yesterday. I just freaked."

"I understand," I said. "It was an awful thing you had to experience. I'm surprised you're back at work so soon."

His voice became slightly defensive as if I had made an accusation. "Whata you mean? I'm just trying to do my job, to stay busy so I don't have to think about it. That's all. It wasn't my fault, just an awful accident I was involved in."

"Of course," I said. "How do you think Johnson got into that trash bag to begin with?"

"Johnson? Who's Johnson?" he asked, but it was unconvincing. He knew who Johnson was.

"The inmate who was killed," I said. "The one in the trash bag."

"Oh," he said. "Well, that's a good question. You see, usually I pick up the trash from every department early in the morning. They set it outside their back door, and me and an inmate pick it up. But yesterday, there was no trash outside of medical."

"So what did you do?" I asked.

"I had already parked the truck between medical and laundry. So I walked over with the inmate, and we picked up the bags from laundry. When we got back to the truck, medical had already put theirs in."

"Have they ever done that before?" I asked.

"Sure," he said. "But not very often. And usually we see that old black inmate 'cause he's so slow, but we didn't see anybody put it in the truck. Why all the questions?"

"I'm just trying to figure out exactly what happened."

"I can tell you what happened. A dumb inmate tried to escape and became a dark meat shish kebab. Everybody's saying what a great job I did. Hell, I'll probably get Officer of the Month. And, if anybody has anything else to say about it, they can say it to my lawyer."

"You have a lawyer?" I asked. It was the most surprising thing I had heard all day.

"Hell, yes," he said. "I been grieved and sued so many damn times by these dumb nigger sons a bitches I had to get one. What kind of world do we live in? A bunch of stinkin' inmates can make me need a lawyer."

"So you think Johnson was trying to escape," I said. "How do you think he got into the bag and into the back of the truck?"

"I don't know," he said. "I really don't. All I know is that I didn't put him back there."

If they were telling the truth, neither Shutt nor Jones had put medical's bags in the truck. But, somebody had, and there was a good reason why that somebody had, and I intended to find out who that somebody was. But, first, there was something more pressing on my mind.

SEVEN

*E*VERY ELEVEN MINUTES, someone in the U.S. died of AIDS.

In Florida state prisons, those with HIV outnumbered those in Florida's free population two to one. In fact, HIV and AIDS was spreading throughout both federal and state prisons at extraordinary rates. Many inmates came to prison already infected with HIV—the result of illicit drug use and unprotected sex. And in prison, it spread. Tattooing, drug use, and especially unprotected sex caused HIV to spread inside prison nearly as quickly as the latest rumor—and only six prison systems in the U.S. distributed condoms. Florida's was not one of them.

"Can I talk to you for a minute?" I asked Nurse Strickland when I had found her again. This time, she was in exam room two looking through some supplies.

"Sure," she said as she turned around to face me, her blue eyes sparkling even under the dull fluorescent lights. She was really beautiful, and so delicate. Laura and Anna were beautiful, but they seemed to be as strong as they were pretty, but this woman was pretty in a fragile, vulnerable way, like a ceramic figurine. "Come in," she continued.

I did. And, when I had closed the door, she looked a little surprised.

"What is it? Are you okay?" she asked, and I sensed her genuine concern. She was a good nurse, I could tell. I had come to the right place.

"I need some help," I said, "and I really don't know where to turn."

"Sure. Anything. What is it?" she asked.

"I don't really quite know how to say this."

"Take your time. It's okay. Whatever it is, we'll figure it out. Okay?"

"Okay, here it goes. I found out today that the inmate who was killed yesterday had AIDS."

She nodded her head slowly. "Yes, I know," she said.

"His blood got all over me. I can't quit thinking about it. I can't concentrate on anything else because I think I might have gotten AIDS through his infected blood."

"Oh, you poor man," she said, sounding like the kind mother I never had. She was a mother—a caretaker, which I was glad of because I needed taking care of just then. "I know how you feel. Blood is such a scary thing these days. I come in contact with bad blood all the time. It scares the hell out of me, too."

"Should I be scared?" I asked.

"Well, he did have AIDS. That's true enough, but unless it penetrated your skin or splashed into your eyes or mouth, you probably have nothing to worry about. And even then you'd have to have an open sore or wound. It's not likely."

"Officer Shutt splashed it everywhere. It could've gotten into my eyes or mouth. I just don't know. I haven't found any cuts or sores, but eyes and mouth I'm just not sure about. What should I do?"

"To be certain, I can give you an AIDS test. That'll clear it up for you and let you know one way or another. But I wouldn't worry. Chances are, you didn't get it, okay?"

I nodded.

She smiled at me reassuringly. "Tell you what," she said. "I'll go ahead and give you the test down here now, and it can be our little secret. Nobody else has to know. How does that sound?"

"That sounds great," I said. "Thank you."

She motioned for me to have a seat on the exam table.

"Stone might ask you to go on leave until you know for certain, and that would just be a hassle. You shouldn't be punished because that little black bastard had bad blood. It's not right. There's no justice in this world when people like you and me have to risk our lives just to do our jobs."

I didn't respond.

She moved around the room quickly and efficiently preparing to take some of my blood out of the place where I most wished it to stay, my body. All the while she spoke of how high the number of inmates with AIDS had become. And how we were all paying the price for their sins.

While she continued to talk about the same things, my mind drifted. I began to think of how ironic it was that I might have AIDS. Not only had I been monogamous and careful even then, but I was extremely careful in daily life as well. My daily routine in prison involved washing my hands so many times as to be almost compulsive. I didn't take chances with AIDS, hepatitis B, and the like. I had visited enough hospital rooms to minister to someone in the last stages of AIDS to know that I wanted to avoid it at all costs. If I had it, I would not let it get the best of me. *I'll kill myself first*, I thought.

When she was finally ready to draw my blood, I watched to make sure that the needle she was about to pierce my vien with had been removed from an unopened sterile package. She put her delicate hands on me: patting, squeezing, caressing, comforting. She even held my hand as she withdrew the blood. And, after she had finished, she gave me a hug. It was, hands down, the best nursing care I'd ever received.

"How long does it take?" I asked. I remained seated on the exam table, not in a hurry to leave. She busied herself labeling the vial of blood and disposing of the needle.

"About a week, give or take a little. I'll have to sneak it in with some other tests. I'll call you the minute I know, okay?"

"Okay. Listen, thanks a lot. You've been wonderful. Truly an angel of mercy."

"You're very welcome. You're a special man. I want to take good care of you."

"Thanks."

"It's funny that you called me an angel of mercy," she said, turning to face me. "I wanted to be a nun when I was a kid. I was raised in a Catholic orphanage."

"Really?" I asked.

"Yeah," she said. "But . . ." She made a sheepish grin.

"What?"

"I like men too much," she said. She walked over to the table and stood between my knees, her face just inches from mine. "Sister said I should become a nurse."

I nodded my agreement. "Forced celibacy is wrong. It's going to do nothing but cause increasingly more problems for the Catholic Church, I'm afraid."

She nodded. "Anyway, I wanted to help people, so I became a nurse."

"You became an excellent nurse," I said.

She smiled warmly as tears filled her eyes. "Thank you," she whispered and leaned in and kissed me on the cheek. I could feel her tears.

"Thank *you*," I said.

She turned, pulled some tissues from the flower-covered box on the counter, and dabbed at her eyes. I hopped off the table.

When she had finished wiping her eyes, I asked, "How did you wind up here?"

"In prison, you mean?" She smiled. "Old sour Sister Mary Margaret said I'd wind up in prison one day. I worked for a doctor in Tallahassee that I needed to get away from, and this came open, so here I am." She backed away from me slightly.

"You needed to get away from the doctor you worked for?" I asked.

"Yes, well, it's a long story," she said. "Bottom line is that we had a relationship. He had a wife . . . and kids. And . . . it was a bad scene."

"I'm sorry," I said. "Tallahassee's loss is our gain."

"Thanks. Anyway, I didn't mean to get into all that, but you are so easy to talk to. And so nonjudgmental. I've heard you went through a divorce and some pretty rough times yourself. I'm sure that gives you a lot of empathy for others."

"I hope so," I said as I walked over to the door and opened it. "Thanks again."

"Thank *you*," she said. "I'd like to talk again sometime, perhaps over coffee."

"Sounds great." I walked out, leaving the door open.

EIGHT

COMPARED TO OTHER INVESTIGATIONS I had conducted, I was finding out information quickly. Prison is such a closed society and so self-contained that rather than having a lack of information about the case, it seemed as though I'd soon be faced with having too much. Having such easy access to everyone at all times, with the exception of the first- and third-shift officers, made this more like *Murder on the Orient Express* than a modern-day investigation.

I was trying to track down an inmate named Jacobson, which on the street would have taken days, if not weeks. In a matter of minutes, I discovered that he was in lockup.

There are four types of lockup in the state prison system. Protective management lockup is for those who are at risk in the general prison population—rapists, child-molesters, ex–law enforcement officers. Close management dorms are for those who, because of their custody, crimes, and behavior on the inside, do their entire sentence inside a cell. Then there is confinement, which has two classifications—administrative and disciplinary. An inmate is placed in administrative confinement when the administration determines that it is best to do so—usually when he is under investigation for a crime. Disciplinary confinement is for those inmates who were accused of a crime and were found guilty. Jacobson was in the latter.

Whereas most inmates in the Florida DOC are housed in open-bay, military barracks–style dormitories, those in lock-up are housed in single six-by-nine cells. Some of the lockup cells house two inmates, some one. All have a sink, toilet, bunk, and a very small window covered with steel mesh. The inmates in lockup are fed through a slot in the metal door about the size of a food tray. Jacobson's was open, and I was talking to him through it.

Squatting down to talk through the tray slot in the door always made my knees ache and my feet fall asleep. I usually chose to talk to an inmate through the tray slot because of the security hassle involved in arranging to meet him in his cell or the conference room. For me to enter an inmate's cell, he must be frisked and cuffed, and an officer must be present at all times. The same is involved if I meet with him in the conference room. Many times what the inmate has to say to me is so short that being frisked and cuffed takes longer than our meeting. Other times the inmates have a lot to say, but are unable or unwilling to because of the security officer standing within hearing distance. I was hoping that without an officer present, Jacobson would sing me a song. He did. Unfortunately, it was one I had heard before.

"Fuck you, motherfucker," he said in response to my first question, which was "How are you doing?"

From the last cell of the corridor to my right, I could hear Inmate Starn yelling, "CHAPLAIN, CHAPLAIN, COME HERE. COME HERE, CHAPLAIN."

He did that every time I came to confinement. It was Wednesday, and I had already seen him twice that week.

It didn't look like Jacobson was going to cooperate. Perhaps I had spoken too soon about the overabundance of information I was going to uncover during this investigation.

Crouching down on the bare cement floor of the confinement hall, I smelled the same smell I always did down there—sleep. The stale air was thick with smells of drool, perspiration, and halitosis. The cell was one of twenty along a long corridor. There was an officer seated at the end of the hall, a round black man with virtually no hair. Another officer, a tall slender man with strawberry blond hair and pink cheeks, was crouched down by a food slot about five cells down from me.

"Is there nothing I can help you with?" I asked. "Nothing you would like to talk about?" Behind me, the gray block wall was lined with empty milk cartons, wads of crumpled napkins, and various other items of trash the inmates had tossed out of their cells.

"Fuck you, motherfucker."

"From what I hear, you would, but I'm not interested," I said, deciding to change my approach. A few cells down, an inmate yelled, "DON'T TALK TO THE CHAPLAIN LIKE THAT, YOU STUPID SON OF A BITCH!"

If Jacobson heard him, he didn't acknowledge it. "I ain't no punk," he said, his eyes seeming to take on a demonic glow in the dark cell.

He may or may not have been a punk, but he certainly did not look like one. His shaved head, pale white skin, sparse beard, and puke-green tattoos made him look like a neo-Nazi serial killer.

"What are you then?" I asked. Somewhere in another corridor a steel door slammed. The noise bounced off the concrete walls and floors and reverberated through confinement. It was, perhaps, the most depressing sound I had ever heard. Another inmate, from a cell to my left this time, said, "We're locked in now, boys." Someone else said, "Yeah, and so is the chaplain."

"I'm Satan, man," Jacobson hissed.

"Don't be so hard on yourself," I said.

"Don't be so hard on Satan," the inmate to my left said and started laughing.

"Did you come to cast me out, Holy Man?" Jacobson asked in such a way as to doubt my ability to do so.

"Actually, I just wanted to see if there was anything I could do for you and maybe ask you a few questions."

"There's nothing you could do for me. I'm well taken care of. What you really mean is, there's something I can do for you. You need something I have."

"CHAPLAIN, CHAPLAIN," Starn continued to call.

"Which is what?"

"Secrets."

The officers' radios sounded at the same time, and because of their distance apart and the cement surroundings, every word was doubled. It sounded like the digital delay that many recording artists overused during the late eighties.

"What makes you think I want to know your secrets?" I asked.

"Believe me, you do. I see evil. I hear evil. I see and hear that which is done in darkness," he said. His eyes were wide and wild, and he hissed his words, placing about fifteen s's on the end of darkness. He was a bad actor doing Manson.

I felt something moist on the back of my hand. It was a small dot of water. I looked up. Above me, hanging from the ceiling, there were two bare galvanized pipes running the length of the hallway. I saw condensation around the joint of one of them directly above me. For a moment, I lost my train of thought, forgetting what he had said. Then I remembered—he knew things that were done in the dark.

"What sort of things?" I asked.

"I see evil. I hear evil. But I speak no evil. I've crossed my heart, hoped to die. Watch it, or I'll stick a needle in your eye. I'll cast *you* out, Holy Man."

"I see," I said. "And hear."

"Don't play games with me. I can have you stuck, just like Johnson. Was it in his eye? Corrections officers are so sloppy, you know. I heard it was very messy. Did all his blood drain out? There's power in the blood, you know. Life and death. Atonement's in the blood. But, I guess you know that. You think he atoned for his sin?"

"CHAPLAIN, CHAPLAIN. CHAPLAIN, I NEED YOU," Starn yelled.

"So you had Johnson stuck? What was his sin?" I asked, trying to keep up.

The officer seated at the end of the hall propped his feet on the corner of the desk and leaned back in his chair. The shortness of his legs caused his feet to fall off the desk when he leaned back in his chair.

"I can have anybody I want to stuck," he continued. As he talked, he widened and narrowed his eyes. I had seen Charles Manson do the same thing on a TV interview. "But I like sticking pigs best."

The officer at the desk stood, pulled the chair closer to the desk, and then repeated his earlier attempt. This time he was successful. However, his new position made him look extremely uncomfortable.

"Was Johnson your punk?" I asked.

"Hickory, dickory, dock—Johnson didn't have a cock, but he got one . . . every night, and now he's taken flight."

"CHAPLAIN, CHAPLAIN." Starn's voice sounded sad and whiny.

"Did you have Johnson stuck?"

"The pig had him stuck because he was tired of getting stuck in the butt."

He jumped up suddenly from his crouched position at the slot and began dancing around the cell, crashing into the sink, bed, and walls as he did. All the while he was singing the old hymn, "There's Power in the Blood." *There is power, power, wonder-working power in the blood of the lamb.*

"Jacobson," I yelled at him, "Jacobson, come here, now."
Power, power, wonder-working power in the blood of the lamb.

Evidently the officer at the other cell heard me yelling because he rushed over and looked through the narrow glass window of the cell door. He yelled for the other officer, who was still seated at the end of the hall, to come quickly and began to fumble for his keys.

"CHAPLAIN, CHAPLAIN."

"Step back, Father, please," he said, his voice an octave higher from the excitement. His strawberry blond hair was very fine and it moved a great deal whenever he did. His face, previously pink, was now a deep red.

I complied. He pulled the handcuffs from the back of his belt and opened them. As soon as the rotund black officer joined him, Strawberry unlocked the door and stepped in, Rotund following closely behind him. As Rotund entered the cell, I could have sworn I saw him smile.

Would you be free from the burden of sin? There's power in the blood, power in the blood.

Strawberry told Jacobson to assume the position, to which he responded with many colorful obscenities, some of which I had never heard before. The next thing I knew, Jacobson was on the floor. It happened so quickly that it took my mind a few seconds to replay it, at a slower pace, so that I could comprehend what had happened. The tall white officer in front told Jacobson to turn around and spread them, and it looked as if he was actually about to when the short black officer stepped up and punched him hard at the base of the neck.

By the time my mind had finished the first scenario, the second one was already over. Jacobson was cuffed, face down on the rough concrete floor. They got him to his feet and spun him around. There was a mild abrasion on his fore-head. He looked as calm as anyone I had ever seen. In fact, he appeared to be in a trance. He seemed to move in slow motion, but his movements lacked both direction and sturdi-ness.

"Let's get him to medical," Rotund said. "See about these cuts." Then he added to Jacobson, "Next time I'm using the gas."

"You better ask your captain first," Jacobson whispered.

"Nobody touch this blood," Rotund said as if he hadn't heard Jacobson. "It's bad blood in more ways than one."

"Let me call the OIC first," Strawberry said, beginning to walk back toward his desk. "Chaplain, can I talk with you for minute?"

"Sure," I said looking back at Jacobson, who stared blankly at the wall in front of him.

As we walked down to the officer's desk at the end of the corridor, I learned that Strawberry's name was Rogers. When we passed by Starn's cell, I stopped and looked in.

"Chaplain," Starn asked, "do you believe that a demon can possess a man?"

"We already talked about this, Starn," I said.

"I'm scared," he said in the small voice of a scared child.

"Nothing spiritual good or bad can happen to you that you don't allow or even invite," I said. "You keep reading your Bible and praying. I'll check in on you later, okay?"

"Okay," he said in an upbeat voice again, easily soothed like a child.

Rogers propped his feet up on the desk without the prob-lems Rotund had had. "What happened to make him go off like that?" he asked. I was seated across the desk from him.

"I really couldn't say. He was okay, and then all of a sud-den he exploded. Does he do that often?"

"He does pretty much whatever he wants to around here," he said, and I could tell he wanted me to ask him for more.

"What do you mean?" I asked.

"I don't know. It's just that certain inmates are looked out for by certain officers, and if the officer happens to be a captain, well, then they do pretty much what they want to. At least on that captain's shift anyway. And, if the captain is popular or powerful enough, the inmate does pretty much whatever he wants anytime."

"Who gives that kind of preferential treatment to an inmate as unstable as he is?"

"He's not unstable. He's a damn thespian."

"You're saying that was a show for my benefit?" I asked.

"I'm saying that everything he does is for show. It has an angle. He is always on the make. Did you say anything about Johnson to him?"

"As a matter of fact, I did. Why?"

"Well, his death really seemed to shake him up. Like maybe he wasn't acting. I don't know, but I think he's scared for real about that."

"Do you think he had anything to do with it?"

"He had everything to do with Johnson. They were both down here constantly. So either he had something to do with it or it scared him shitless, excuse my language, because he had nothing to do with it."

"Like it may have been a message to him?" I asked.

"Yeah, something like that," he said as if that caused a light to come on in his head. "Yeah, that could be it."

Rotund yelled from down the hall, "Come on. What's taking so long?"

"Just a minute," Rogers yelled back.

I glanced at my watch. It was almost time for my meeting with Tom Daniels and Edward Stone.

"I'd better be going now. I've got a meeting up front. What will happen with Jacobson?"

"He'll be taken to medical, checked out, and probably taken to the isolation cell and sedated and watched for twenty-four hours. That is, unless Captain Skipper cuts him out."

"Then what will happen to him?" I asked.

"He'll be sent back down here, I guess," he said with a shrug that said, *I just work here.*

"What's the difference in being confined in one cell as opposed to another?"

"Not much during the day, but I've heard at night all sorts of weird stuff happens in here."

"Thanks for the info," I said.

"Anytime, Father," he said respectfully.

Before leaving, I glanced down the hallway at Jacobson. If he had moved even an inch, I couldn't tell it. He appeared to be catatonic. I walked out of confinement with these words whirling around in my head: *There is power, power, wonder-working power in the blood of the lamb. There is power, power, wonder-working power in the precious blood of the lamb.*

NINE

THEY LOOKED LIKE MEN sitting around a barber shop on Saturday morning or senior citizens on a park bench or mall-wanderers: they had time to kill. Inmates don't have much, but what they have they possess a lot of—time. They sat around the chapel library under the watchful eye of the officer temporarily assigned to watch them until my new assistant, a Jewish chaplain, was hired next month. Mr. Smith and three other inmates were reading *Decision* magazine, the monthly magazine that the Billy Graham Evangelistic Association faithfully sent us free of charge. Mr. Smith and one of the other inmates were wearing headphones—listening to gospel music no doubt. On my way to meet with Mr. Stone and Tom Daniels, I decided to stop by the chapel to check in and pick up something to take notes on, sure our meeting would prove to be noteworthy.

When Mr. Smith saw me, he jumped up and walked out into the hallway where I was unlocking my office door. "They's two who want to see you, Brother Chaplain," he said.

"Okay," I said, "but it will have to be when I get back. I've got a meeting with the superintendent in about ten minutes."

"Yesuh. I tell them to wait. It so hot out there, they won't mind waitin' in here where it nice 'n cool. 'Sides they got nothin' else to do."

"Thank you," I said and walked into my office. As I closed the door, the phone began to ring.

"Chaplain Jordan," I said into the receiver.

"Is this the chaplain?" a distressed female voice asked.

"Yes, it is," I said. "How can I help you?"

"This is Veronica Simpson. My husband Charles Simpson is an inmate there."

"Uh huh," I said encouragingly.

"I need to talk to him," she said, her voice breaking slightly. "I haven't heard from him in four months, and I need to talk to him right now. I'm not playing with you, and I'm not crazy, but I've got a gun to my head, and I'm going to kill myself and his two-year-old son if I can't talk to him right now."

My heart started racing. I couldn't believe what I was hearing. Whatever it took, I was not going to let another person die. So help me God, I was not. I had no way of knowing whether or not she would do it, but that really wasn't the point.

"Okay," I said, "now listen to me. I will let you talk to your husband, so just put the gun down and relax."

"I'm not crazy. I swear," she added quickly, her voice seeming to gain strength. "If I can just talk to him, I will not kill myself."

"The thing is, he is not here right now," I said talking very slowly. "It will take a few minutes, but I will have him called up right away. So, why don't we talk until he gets here. Would that be okay?"

"That would be okay," she said softly. She was beginning to sound calmer.

"I have to ask you to hold on just a minute while I call down to his dorm and have him sent up here, okay?"

"Okay. I'm not going anywhere. I'm all right, Preacher. I just want to talk to my husband. I won't do anything foolish," she said as if we had switched roles and now she was trying to reassure me.

As quickly as I could, I pressed the hold button, then the second-line button, and punched in the number to the control room. Without going into much detail, I told the sergeant in the control room to find Simpson and get him to my office ASAP.

I then punched line one again, praying that she was still there. She was. We talked for about five minutes, waiting for her husband to come to my office. Our conversation dealt primarily with all the pressures she faced being a single mom whose husband was incarcerated. I actually felt as if I did her some good, but chances were I'd never know.

When Simpson finally did arrive, after what seemed like days, I quickly put him on the phone and went into the other office, where I called the Tampa Police and reported her threat of suicide. While talking to her, I had discovered where she lived, and I told them. I then jotted down a few notes about what had transpired and called the OIC and filled him in. He advised me to fill out an incident report, which I did. I then walked back into my office and sat down at my desk.

Noticing that Simpson was crying, I busied myself with opening the rest of my mail. My mail consisted of roughly fifteen requests from inmates for everything from Bibles and greeting cards to phone calls. There were also two letters from citizen volunteers who ministered at the prison saying what a blessing they themselves were, a memo from the chaplaincy administrator about upcoming religious holidays that were to be observed by the Jewish, Muslim, and Christian inmates, and a single piece of typing paper trifolded and taped together on the end with the word "Chaplain" typed on the outside.

I unfolded the typing paper, tearing it slightly while removing the tape. It read simply: "I've seen you talking to her. I watch over her. If you don't stay away from her, I will kill you like I did that punk. She's an angel and I'm her guardian angel. She's mine. Stay away from her."

I reached into my desk and pulled out the request from Ike Johnson. I laid them both on the desk in front of me and began to compare them. Within seconds, I could tell they were typed on the same machine.

I thought of Anna as I reread the note a final time—when I realized that Simpson was talking to me. "I'm sorry, what'd you say?"

"Thank you, Chaplain. I thinks she going to be all right. I should have called her or written or something. It's my fault, but this place is getting to me. I don't know what to do."

"Why don't you start coming to see me every week for a while, and you might want to think about seeing our psychologist as well."

"Okay," he said. "I will."

"And, stay in touch with your wife. It's tough in here, but it's tough for her out there, too."

"I know. I will. Thank you."

"You're welcome," I said. I should have said more. I should have talked to him right then and there, but I couldn't. All I could do was think about Anna. Was she in danger? I talked to her more than anyone. Johnson had been assigned to her. Was he killed because of her? It was probably because I had just been with her, but I thought of Sandra Strickland, too. I could think of no other female staff members I had talked to recently.

Those questions would have to wait for now. I glanced at my watch and realized that I was already fifteen minutes late for my meeting with the inspector and the superintendent.

*T*EN

*T*HE SUPERINTENDENT'S OFFICE was neat, orderly, and as conservative as he was, with one exception. In the center of his wall of fame, amidst the diplomas, merit certificates, and department commendations, was a hand-drawn picture of a family: husband, wife, and child. The artist used crayons and showed great potential—potential he never got to live up to because of his untimely death at eight years old. Stone and his wife never tried to have children again after that, or so I'm told; I had been waiting for an opportunity to present itself for discussing it with him. However, since Edward Stone was involved, I realized it might not come in this lifetime.

When I arrived, Tom Daniels was already there. The two men grew silent when I walked into the room. Daniels looked as if a day's work felt like a week's. His shirt ballooned out just over his belt, the way you would expect it to if it had been worn all day without a retuck. His face was red. And large conspicuous drops of sweat trickled down the sides of his cheeks.

Stone looked as if he had just finished getting dressed—morning-fresh and military-crisp. His shoes, which were just visible underneath the desk, gleamed as the sunlight from the window, the only window in his office, spilled onto them.

"Good afternoon, Chaplain. You're late," the superintendent said as I was taking my seat beside Daniels, who neither looked at nor spoke to me.

"Good afternoon, Mr. Stone. I'm sorry I'm late. How are you doing?" I replied.

"Better now that something is being done about this situation we have on our hands," he said, nodding his head toward Daniels.

"Let's have a full report," Mr. Stone continued. "But first, shut the door."

He said this to no one in particular, but I quickly responded. Daniels never even flinched in that direction.

"Inspector, what do we have so far?" Stone asked.

"In some ways, a great deal of information," he said sitting up and leaning forward slightly. "But in other ways, not very much at all. I am finding your people very uncooperative."

"Surely the chaplain has been helpful with this," Stone said.

Daniels began to speak, but I beat him to the draw. "Mr. Stone, as soon as you left us this morning the inspector expressed his desire to work alone." I could feel Daniels's anger; it was palpable, but he never looked in my direction.

"Inspector?" Stone asked, raising an eyebrow, which caused his glasses to rise slightly.

"I've made it clear from the very beginning that I do not wish to work with him," Daniels said, the sweat on his forehead increasing. "I am fully capable of conducting this investigation on my own. I certainly do not need someone who is not even an investigator helping me. He would only botch up the case."

"If, as you say, you are fully capable of conducting this investigation on your own, how is it that you are having difficulty doing any investigating?" Stone asked.

"I'm not having difficulty investigating. I am having difficulty with these mother-loving rednecks around here. I have gathered a lot of information about the inmate who was killed, though."

"But that is only one investigation or one part of a larger investigation," Stone said.

Daniels withdrew a wrinkled, soiled handkerchief from his back left pants pocket and wiped his forehead. It merely smeared the sweat around. It also left some lint on his eyebrow.

"That's true, but—"

"But, you will work together, or I will call the secretary. Understood?"

Daniels did not respond.

"Understood?" Mr. Stone asked again.

Daniels made a slight nod with his head.

"Understood?" Mr. Stone looked at me.

"Yes, sir," I said. "I understood it the first time."

"Now, tell me what you have, Inspector," Stone said.

"I can tell you that Johnson was murdered," Daniels said with a swell of pride that changed his posture.

"Murdered? Being killed while trying to escape is justifiable homicide not murder," Mr. Stone said.

"Yes, but," Daniels said with obvious pleasure at the prospect of enlightening us, "it *is* murder when the inmate was unconscious before he was ever placed in the bag."

"And he was?" Stone asked with great surprise.

"That's what the ME says." Daniels looked at me to gloat. His face registered surprise at my obvious lack of it. He turned away abruptly. "Says he was full of enough chloral hydrate to be dead soon anyway."

"What is chloral hydrate?" Stone asked. It was obvious he was interested, but he was not excited. He didn't get excited.

"Sleeping pills," Daniels said with a small snort as if everyone should know it.

"Could he have taken them himself?" Stone asked. "Maybe to relax during his escape?"

"No, I don't think so. It would seem that someone drugged him. Someone who knew that putting him in the trash bag would get him stabbed to death."

"Did the ME say how the drug was administered?" I asked.

The superintendent said, "Why on earth would that matter?"

"Because," I said, "medical personnel would probably use a syringe, an officer might put it in food, and an inmate might give it to him in pill form as if it were some other kind of drug."

"I see," Mr. Stone said. "Interesting. Well, Inspector, how was it administered?"

Daniels's face registered his obvious embarrassment. "He was unable to say conclusively. We should know shortly." After this, Daniels, acting nonchalantly, made a few notes to himself on his legal pad. I was able to see that one of them read, "Ask ME dickhead's question." I assumed he was referring to me.

"What else do you have?" the superintendent asked.

"He had an abnormal amount of lacerations, even for an inmate. A few abrasions that were not related to his death."

Outside, a rather large female officer passed by the window. It looked like walking was difficult for her. She moved like she was on another planet with three times the gravity of Earth. I wondered how she would fair during a riot.

"Where did the fatal blow strike him?" Stone asked.

"Bottom part of his heart. The rod got stuck in his rib cage. Shutt broke several of them trying to get it free." Daniels hesitated a minute for effect and then added, "But that's not what killed him."

"What?" Stone asked.

"ME says that the rod scraped the bottom of the heart, but really didn't pierce it. The loss of blood would have killed him eventually. He lost a shitload of it in a hurry, but it still takes a while."

"What are you saying?" I asked, sick of the suspense.

"I'm saying that he didn't die immediately," Daniels said.

I thought about those lifeless black eyes and wondered if they were really lifeless or just drugged.

"He died as the result of a blow to the throat that dislocated his windpipe," Daniels said.

I thought about falling on top of Johnson and wondered if I had landed on his neck. I tried to remember, but I couldn't. Had I killed him? Did Shutt use me as a weapon like the rod?

"Could the officer have done that or even known what he was doing?" Stone asked.

"Maybe. I don't know. Your prime witness is sitting right across from you. Why don't you ask him?" Daniels said, tilting his head in my direction.

"I'll get to him in a minute," Stone said with a quick glance in my direction. "What else can you tell us?"

"He was a drug user. There were traces of crack and alcohol in his blood."

"Crack?" Stone said in shock. "I know we have the occasional marijuana smuggled in here, but crack—that is not possible."

Dust was visible in the sunlight shining in through the window. Specks danced around in the single shaft of light like performers in a spotlight. Amazingly enough, the dust seemed to avoid Edward Stone's shoes.

"Could his death be drug-related?" I asked, thinking that I should say something just to let them know I still could.

"That's an obvious possibility that we must consider," Daniels said to Stone, as if he were the one who had asked the question. "As you say, it's difficult to get drugs on the compound, crack especially."

"Aren't drug screenings done periodically?" I asked.

"Yes, they are. And to answer your next question, he was tested as recently as a week ago, and it was negative. Besides, he was in confinement most of the time, which makes it virtually impossible to get drugs—or anything else, for that matter."

As Daniels wiped his forehead again, the small piece of lint that was on his left eyebrow fell down and landed on the end of an eyelash, bobbing up and down as he blinked. It was very distracting. I found myself looking at it more than anything else in the room.

"That's not what I've heard," I said.

"Oh really, and just what have you heard?" Mr. Stone asked.

"I've heard that some very strange things go on during the first shift around here," I said, then added, "especially in confinement."

Daniels started to speak, but Stone lifted his hand and when he does that, as easily as a cop stops traffic, people stop talking. "I'll get to you in a minute," Mr. Stone said to me. Then looking back at Daniels, "Okay, drugs, what else?"

"He was a faggot. He had AIDS. Of course you already knew that. There were traces of dried semen around the anal region. It is being processed at FDLE. Maybe we'll get lucky and get something from it. Who knows?"

"Pardon my ignorance, but who has unprotected sex with an inmate who has AIDS?" I said.

"There are other inmates who have AIDS so they have nothing to lose, inmates who do not know because the other inmate has kept it secret, and then there are plenty of inmates who do not have unprotected sex."

"There are *condoms* on the compound?" I asked.

"No, of course not," Daniels sighed with impatience. "But many of the inmates use the latex gloves they wear when working in medical, food services, or caustic cleaning—and that's with no lubrication."

"Ouch," I said, giving Daniels the response he was looking for. He smiled.

"Sounds like your FDLE crime lab is working overtime," Stone said.

"They're good. Very good. Probably the best state lab in the country," Daniels said proudly, not realizing that Stone seemed to be saying that the lab was working hard but Daniels was not.

"How about you, Chaplain?" Stone asked. "Have you discovered anything useful?"

"I have more," Daniels said, playing it for all it was worth.

"Let's have it."

"The lab also found some unusual trace evidence—a PRIDE chemical, on his blues. It may very well give us an idea of where he was before he wound up in the trash heap. Which in turn may give us insight into who was responsible for him winding up in the trash heap."

"Thank you, Inspector. Now what did you learn around here today? All of this information seems to have come from the lab."

Daniels stopped smiling. "As I said earlier, your staff was not cooperative. Perhaps if you spoke to them."

"Perhaps I will. Chaplain, did you make any inquiries today?"

"A few rather discrete ones."

"Discrete?" he asked in shock. "That little fiasco in confinement wasn't very discrete."

"No, sir, it didn't turn out that way, but it was intended to be discrete."

"The road that leads to the opposite of where your boss lives is paved with good intentions. Well, no matter. But, did you meet with resistance from the staff?"

"No, sir, I can't say that I did, but I only interviewed a few of them. I just tried not to do it like an interview."

"What about you being our prime witness? Can you tell us anything else about the actual stabbing yesterday?"

"I really don't think that I can add anything to what I've already said. In fact, the further I get away from it, the more difficulty I'm having remembering it."

"Should Shutt be looked into?" he asked.

"Yes, sir. To eliminate him as a suspect if nothing else."

"Okay," he said, and then he looked at Daniels again. "Have you ever heard the old saying, 'You can catch more flies with honey than vinegar'?"

"Sure, I've heard it," he said.

"Well, the chaplain here is your honey. He is well liked and respected, and he knows at least half of the staff pretty well. So, you are to work with him and not without him, or you are not to work in this institution at all. Understand?"

"Yeah, I understand," Daniels said in a tone that said, *I'm not an idiot.*

"Understand, Chaplain?" Stone said to me.

"Yes, sir."

"Good. Now both of you get out of here. And go find out what's going on in my institution."

ELEVEN

NIGHTS WERE THE WORST. The tin man alone in his tin house. Loneliness, fear, isolation, and guilt tormented me mercilessly. I couldn't sleep. When I first got married, I found it rather difficult to sleep with another person in the bed. Every time she tossed, I turned. Every time she turned, I tossed. And the sounds that she made—the breathing, the little grunts and moans—I would lie awake in the dark listening to them. And then I got used to it—needed it, in fact.

After the divorce, I had many nights in which I would lie awake in the dark listening to the silence, trying to readjust to sleeping alone. I tossed and turned in the huge bed. Susan and I shared a king size, which dwarfed the double bed I did not sleep in now. Every move I made rumbled like a voice in a deep well; my movements were exaggerated and echoed in the absence of someone to absorb them.

At night, too, the demons came. I faced my greatest fears: those of meaninglessness—no hope, no future, no God, no purpose. Self-doubt and accusation rumbled in my head like thunder in a canyon. Also, the desire to drink was overwhelming. Alcohol offered a baptism into its depths that would cause the fears, demons, and, most of all, the loneliness to drown. I wanted to drown beneath the golden ripples of its surface and never come up for air. I didn't, but I don't know how I didn't. This, more than anything else in recent memory, convinced me of the existence of God. Alone, I could not stay clean and sober. And I was completely, utterly alone.

Earlier that night, I had gone to an AA meeting. I drove into the next county to attend it to ensure my anonymity. It helped, but not enough. I returned home and, in the absence of the prospect of sex with anyone other than myself, went jogging. Actually, much of the time I ran. I ran away from the case, the bottle, the loneliness that eventually chased me down and overtook me, no matter how fast or how far I ran. As I did, I thought about Bambi. She wasn't the answer—I knew that—but it doesn't mean that she couldn't be part of the answer. I came home, showered, changed, ate, and watched *It's a Wonderful Life* on cable—none of which occupied enough time. I then scratched out some notes on a legal pad, which I had recently heard was no longer used by the legal profession. I thought of everything I knew about the case and then wrote it down. It didn't take long.

After doing all of these things, it was only ten after ten. So I read, prayed, and ironed my clothes for the following day. At midnight, I turned the lights off. That's when the ugly neon lights inside my head came on. I looked at the clock: it was twenty after twelve. I rolled over and tried to direct my thoughts in a single, more productive direction. The phone rang.

Saved by the bell.

"Hello," I said, my voice sounding much sleepier than it was, probably because I hadn't used it for several hours.

"This the chaplain what work at the Potter Prison?" an elderly black woman's voice asked. I could hear a loud television and a dog barking in the background.

"Yes, ma'am, it is. John Jordan."

"This is Miss Jenkins. I'm Ike Johnson's aunt. I'm sorry to call you so late, but I just come from making the arrangements for Ike."

"Yes ma'am. That's okay. I'm so sorry about Ike."

"Thank you. The thing is, we realized at the funeral home we didn't know no one to do his funeral and wondered if you'd do it for us."

I was stunned. I didn't know what to say. I just continued to listen to the background noises. I picked out another one. It sounded like wind blowing into the phone, but it was intermittent. She must have had an oscillating fan.

"We not really church peoples," she continued. "And Ike's grandma, Miss Winger, said you was the nicest white man she'd ever spoken to."

I had spoken to Grandma Winger earlier that morning to tell her that her grandson, the one she had raised like a son, had been killed. At the time, I thought he was killed while trying to escape. She refused to believe it. She said that they were coming to visit him this Saturday, and he knew it. According to her, he liked prison and had no desire to leave. He told her that it was the best he had ever lived. I believed that, and it made me mourn even more.

"When are you planning on having the funeral?" I asked. I couldn't think of anything else to say.

"Saturday, if you was able to make it."

I was silent. The light from my clock cast a green glow at a fifteen-degree angle on part of the bed, the back wall, and the ceiling.

"Listen, Preacher, we know Ike was no good. We not asking you to say stuff that ain't true."

"Good, because I couldn't. And about Ike being no good, I've never met anybody that had no good in them."

"Well, he was close," she said.

"God loved him," I said.

She was silent. And then she said, "You really believe that? You just saying it?"

"I really do. Sometimes it's all that I do believe, but I never seem to be able to shake it. Probably because I need to believe it."

She didn't know what to say to that. I had said too much again. I often found myself telling strangers what I needed to say, though what I needed to say was often very personal and painful and often made them feel uncomfortable. I went to confession wherever I could—wherever it was safe and anonymous.

"Can you do it Saturday?" she asked, her voice sounding slightly desperate.

"Yes, I can. I will."

"Thank you, Preacher."

"You're welcome. Good night," I said after she gave me the time and place of the funeral on Saturday in Tallahassee.

I rolled over after hanging the phone on its cradle and stared up at the ceiling. It hadn't changed. The wind outside caused the aluminum of the trailer to bend in and out, sounding like a whip cracking. I looked at the clock to watch the minute change. It seemed to take far longer than sixty seconds.

I sat up and looked at myself in the mirror on my dresser against the wall across from the foot of my bed. It was dark, but enough light came in the window from the streetlight and in the door from the bathroom down the hall so that I could see myself in shadow. It looked artistic, like a low-lit black-and-white photograph. I lay back down and looked at the clock again. Everything I had just done took less than a minute. I decided to get up and work on my funeral sermon for Saturday. My thinking was that the challenge might exhaust me so I could fall asleep.

Preparing the funeral sermon of a stranger killed under suspicious circumstances was challenging. I grew weary, but I still couldn't sleep. At one point it got so bad, in fact, that I went into the den and watched nearly an hour of infomercials. I had to do something about this.

On my way back to bed, I stopped by the bathroom—mainly for something to do. Looking in the mirror, I discovered that I looked as tired as I felt, which wasn't good. As I turned to head back to bed, I noticed a small pile of clothes near the shower. It was about two day's worth. I smiled as I thought of how Susan hated that. Having that thought gave me a strong urge to leave them there, which I only overcame because if I left them in reaction to her, she would still be controlling my life. I bent down, scooped them up, slinging one sock between my legs as I did. When I reached for it, I saw something that froze me in sheer terror.

On the back of my left leg, there was a cut about two inches long.

I dropped the clothes and bent down even farther to take a closer look. It wasn't very deep, but it was deep enough—deep enough for AIDS-infected blood splattered on it to get into my bloodstream.

My heart, racing up until this point, seemed to stop altogether. I grew faint and nearly fell over, but was able to catch myself on the towel rack. Suddenly, I had the urge to jump into the shower and scrub the cut.

I did. In the shower, I inspected my body for other cuts and scratches. There were none. At one point, I stared at the violent scars on my upper body. It would be tragically ironic to survive a gunshot wound to the chest, a knife wound to the abdomen, and then die of a narrow two-inch long cut to the leg.

For the rest of the night I asked myself one question over and over, *When did I get the cut?*

Please, God, let it have been today.

At two thirty I was lying on my side in bed with my eyes closed counting deer, each looking like a female version of Bambi. I could feel my exhausted body giving in to the approaching sandman. My breathing became heavier and slower, and I was actually on my way to the land of dreams, or so I thought. As it turns out, I was headed to the land of nightmares—the waking kind.

The nightmare began when I found the cut and continued when, for the second time that night, my phone rang.

"Hello," I said after fumbling around with the receiver
for a few seconds. I sounded sleepy again. This time I was.

"John John," the voice said.

My heart started racing and I could feel the first of what
I knew would be many waves of nausea coming over me. I
wanted desperately to hang up the phone, but it was too late
for that now. A new rule: From this point forward, I would
not answer the phone after midnight.

"John John," the voice said again. That voice was slightly slurred, slightly desperate, and very scared.

It's amazing what can trigger a memory: a single smell, a
song, or a voice. And this voice, above all others, triggered
memories that I would pay to have surgically removed. It
was the voice that haunted me at night.

The voice was the voice I heard within the sound of my
own when I had been drinking. It was the voice of my mother, and she only called me John John when she was drunk. I
hated her. I hated her for who she was, but I hated her even
more for who I was. The fact that she had called at nearly
three in the morning meant that she was in a detox center
and wanted me to come and get her out. I didn't know which
detox center because I didn't know which city she was in
these days, but she had been in them all. When she and Dad
had divorced, I had actually believed that she was out of my
life, but like a recurring nightmare, she always forced herself
back in and always at night.

"John John, answer me. Are you there?" she asked like a
little girl lost in the woods at night.

"I'm here," I said, and that was the truth. I was here, and
she was there, and that was the way it was going to stay.

"John John," she slurred again, "they got me locked up

again. I'm dying. You got to come and see me."

"Mom, you're not dying; it just feels like that. You're just having withdrawals. Remember? How could you forget? You've done this many, many times. They'll pass eventually."

"No, you don't understand, Son, I'm dying. I haven't been drinking. Come see me at the hospital, Son, before it's too late. I love you. I love you, John. You've always been my favorite."

"That's what you tell everybody when you're drunk. And you are dying. I was wrong before. Alcohol is killing you."

"I know, Son," she said and then began to cough. It sounded as if she dropped the phone. Her act was definitely improving.

It took maybe two minutes, which seemed like thirty, for her to pick up the phone again. When she did, she said, "I've got to see you, Son . . . before I die."

"What you've got to do is get sober. I won't come near you until you're sober again. Got it?"

"I swear I'm sober, Son. You've got to believe me."

"I stopped believing you a long time ago. Get cleaned up and dried out, and then call me, okay?"

"You don't understand, Son—"

"Mom," I interrupted, "I'm hanging up now. You call me when you've been sober for at least a week." I hung up the phone.

I probably wouldn't hear from her for quite a while. She hadn't been sober a full week for as long as I could remember.

Please, God, help her get sober and to get her life back together. And, please, please, don't let me have AIDS.

*T*WELVE

*T*HE NEXT MORNING, INMATES STOOD outside the chapel underneath the brilliant sun that had long since burned off the fog and dew from the night before. The sun was so intense, in fact, that it seemed to explain why all the blues and grays in prison were so muted: it had faded them. After I was situated in my office, Mr. Smith began bringing the inmates in one at a time. The first one was a kid who had recently had some spiritual experiences that he didn't understand.

The second was a middle-aged white man who had been inside less than thirty days of a thirty-year sentence. Needless to say, he was devastated, not only because he missed his children and his wife, but also because he had killed two teenage girls while driving under the influence. He was remorseful and offered no excuses. I was moved by both his words and his actions. He spoke slowly, was silent a lot, and occasionally a single tear would roll down his cheek leaving a jagged streak on his sunburned skin.

We talked for a long time. I don't know if it helped him; though he said it did, I had my doubts. Before he left we scheduled a weekly appointment together for an indefinite amount of time, and he signed up to attend AA.

After he left, and before Mr. Smith could bring in the next inmate, the phone rang.

"I've got an emergency message for Tommy Hines," the shrill voice said over the noise of the bad connection. "I need him to call home."

"Okay, ma'am, if you'll hold on just a moment, there is an emergency notification form I have to fill out."

I retrieved the form. "Okay, the inmate's name is Tommy Hines?"

"Yes."

"What's the nature of the emergency?" I asked, flipping through the morning's mail that sat on the left edge of my desk.

"Whatcha mean?" she asked.

"What is the message?" I asked as I separated the inmate requests from the outside mail.

"His son was killed," she said quickly.

"I'm so sorry to hear that. Your relationship to the inmate?"

"I'm his wife."

"I am so sorry for your loss," I said.

"When can he call me?"

"I have to get some more information first. What is your phone number?" I asked. Then I saw it: another single piece of typing paper, trifolded, taped, with one typewritten word on the outside: "Chaplain."

"Nine, zero, four, eight, seven, one, four, five, six, one. But they's a block on the phone so he can't call collect."

When she said that, a little red flag went up inside my head. "Okay, I need the name and telephone number of the hospital or funeral home where he is."

"Whatcha mean?" she asked in surprise.

"Before we are allowed to give an inmate any information from the outside, especially a death message because of the security risk that it imposes, we must first verify it with an outside official: either a hospital or a funeral home," I said, but I was thinking: *Open the letter, see what it says. Is Anna in danger?*

"That's bullshit. His son is dead. Just let him call home, dammit."

"Ma'am, if his son is dead, then he will be at a hospital or a funeral home and all I need is the number to one of them."

"You son of a bitch. I hate you prison pricks." And with that, she hung up the phone.

I receive approximately six emergency calls a week for inmates. Of those calls, at least two are people who are trying to get in touch with inmates who stopped calling or writing. The inmate probably didn't have a son.

Daily, I am confronted by inmates who are running scams. They try to manipulate every situation—they know of no other way to operate. Many of their families do the same thing. However, there are those who truly desire help both spiritually and psychologically. The key is not to grow cold and cynical because of the abusers and to be able to discern the difference between the genuine and the con.

After I hung up the phone, I carefully peeled the tape back and opened the letter. I could tell almost immediately that it was produced by the same typewriter as the other one. It said: "Chaplain, if you don't back off, I'm going to kill you. Just back off, or you're dead. I will kill you and that girl you love. Killing's better than fucking. I love it. I will probably fuck her and then kill her. But I might kill her then fuck her. Back off!"

The institutional mail was delivered every day but Sunday. The note had probably been sent the previous night. Who was it about? I loved Anna, but was it that obvious? The other note had spoken of protection, now this one of threat. Were they about two different women? Anna and who? Sandy Strickland? Who else had I been seen with recently?

My office door opened while I was still rereading the letter. When Mr. Smith didn't say anything, I looked up. Tom Daniels was standing there. I nodded my head toward one of the chairs across from my desk as I carefully folded the letter and stuck it in my desk drawer. He sat down. He looked better than he had yesterday, like maybe this case had breathed some life into him. His face wasn't as red, and his eyes were not bloodshot. If the case continued to be eventful, he would probably replace his addiction with it for a while. I used to have the same experience from time to time.

He looked down at the clipboard that he was carrying, flipped through a couple of pages, looked back up at me.

"Look, the superintendent said we got to work together. Neither of us is happy about it, but whatcha gonna do, right?" He said it as if we were suddenly pals.

I knew that the superintendent's words alone were not enough to bring about this change in him, but I said, "Right."

"So, I say the investigation is more important than our dislike of one another. Wouldn't you agree?"

"I agree, but I don't dislike you. And before all of this is over, I wish you would give me the opportunity to talk with you about things."

"I've heard your excuses before."

"I don't intend to offer you any excuses, but then again I never have. You've only heard things from Susan's perspective."

"Listen, I don't want to discuss the past now or ever. Let's just concentrate on our jobs and do the work. I don't care for you, never have much, but we can work together. I can work with anyone."

"We *can* work together, and I apologize for any pain I've caused you and your family, especially Susan. I really loved her. Still do."

He was unable to hide his obvious awkwardness and discomfort at my apology. He'd never been good at dealing with personal things.

"Okay," I said. "What's our next move?"

"We need to follow up some of the leads that our physical evidence has produced—some of which you could do without anyone noticing. If the inspector of the prison system walks in and asks to look at things or asks questions, people get nervous."

So that was it. No wonder he was being almost civil toward me. He needed my help. It had nothing to do with what Stone said, although that made it so much easier for him.

"Like what?" I asked.

"The lab said there were traces of a chemical on his pants that's used in floor cleaner and wax in medical and dental facilities. We've traced the exact chemical to two types of cleaners manufactured by PRIDE."

PRIDE is the manufacturer of various products for prisons. It is operated by the Department of Corrections and staffed with inmates. Just one of the many ways taxpayers save money.

"The cleaners," he continued, "are used in the medical offices, the infirmary, and the dental offices."

"From what I understand," I said, "Johnson spent a lot of time in the infirmary."

"Yes, I think he did, but you couldn't get it on you from just being in medical or dental, even if you fell on a recently mopped floor. Besides, the chemical on his pants had not been diluted. He would have had to have been around the actual bottle of cleaner to get it on him, and it had to have been within a few hours prior to his death, according to the lab."

"Did he ever work with the cleaner?" I asked.

"Not that I know of. He was supposed to have worked on outside grounds. We need to check with his work supervisor," Daniels said.

"Perhaps I should. We went to school together," I said. "You know inmates' uniforms often get switched in the laundry. It may have come in contact with the cleanser when another inmate was wearing it."

He shook his head. "Maybe, but I doubt it. The chemical had not been through the washer and dryer, and the uniform had his name tag on it. It actually stuck to the spear. Okay. How about medical and dental?" he asked.

"I'll check them both over the weekend. I can't today because I have to continue my regular work as well. Also, I've been asked to do Ike Johnson's funeral tomorrow morning."

"Find out all you can about him from his family," he said. "They may know something useful and not know they know it."

"If the opportunity presents itself I will, but they've just lost a family member in a horrible way. I'm not going as a detective, but as a minister."

"You better go as both or some other family is going to lose their son."

"Like I said, I'll do what I can."

"I think it's best if we're not seen together. You do those things. I'll talk with Fortner, make him feel a part of the investigation, and continue to check with the lab. Why don't we meet again on Monday?"

"Sounds good. Where?"

"If I stop by here, no one really sees. Besides, I could be asking you questions like anybody else. You are a witness."

"Okay, but don't believe that nobody sees you. Somebody sees everything that is done in this place. Everything."

THIRTEEN

WHEN MERRILL MONROE AND I were in elementary school, the history books and the teachers that taught from them painted a benign picture of slaves singing soulfully as they worked on the plantations. It wasn't that they said slavery was right; they didn't tell us just how wrong it really was. The slaves were not happy, of course, but only because they didn't own the land on which they were working. Seeing the inmates, most of whom were black, harvesting the crops outside the institution brought this memory to mind, and I wondered if slavery really ever ended in this country. The two obvious differences between now and then were that they were harvesting watermelons and potatoes, not cotton and tobacco; and they were doing it under the watchful eye of a black man, who, as he put it, was the Head Nigga In Charge.

Being a black man in a small Southern town is not easy. Being an intelligent and ambitious black man in a small Southern town is nearly impossible. I first noticed Merrill's strength and intelligence in elementary school when I was learning about slavery. Merrill didn't learn anything during that unit; he already knew it all too well. Our friendship began then, and since that time I'd not had a better friend.

Merrill was a correctional officer sergeant in charge of the outside grounds of the prison. Inmates assigned to him were not considered to be an escape risk and, therefore, allowed to work outside the gate.

I found him in a garden to the left of the institution down on his hands and knees showing an inmate just how to plant the potatoes. The light brown sleeves of his short sleeve CO uniform were stretched tightly over the dark brown skin of his arms. Every time he moved, his muscles flexed, straining his shirt to the point of ripping.

As he instructed the inmate on exactly how to do his job, he spoke in slow, even tones. I had seen him stare down a gang of inmates, two with shanks, the same way. I had also seen him wipe out an entire gang by himself, never raising his voice and never acting as if it required much effort either.

"Sarge, you got a minute?" I asked as I came up behind him.

He stood, nodding at me and pointing at the row of potatoes to the inmate.

We walked away from the garden and the inmates who hear all and see all.

"I was thinking of planting some potatoes and needed some help."

"Sure, I can help you. Us colored mens knows how to toil under de sun. It what make us so brown and earthy," he said.

"I am really about to put some sod around my trailer. Want to help?"

"I'll help with some advice," he said.

"What's that?" I asked.

"Put the green side up," he said, and then a broad smile crept across his face revealing startling white teeth.

"Thanks for the tip."

"Us coloreds live to serve y'all, sir," he said. "It's what we here for."

We were both silent a minute. He glanced back in the direction of the garden. I could tell he was not happy with how the inmate was planting the potatoes.

"It's hard to get good help these days," I said.

"Yeah. Speaking of which, I heard about what you did in the sally port the other day. Very impressive for a skinny white boy."

"I'm not skinny," I protested. "I'm fit."

"You's fit before the Atlanta thing," he said, "Now you skinny."

He stood directly in front of me, positioning himself between me and the sun. The shadow he cast kept me from needing the shades I did not have. He was always doing things like that and never mentioning it. Any other white person in America, except maybe for Anna, he would have left squinting in the sun.

I could see my reflection in his glasses. I looked distorted, like my face was too big for my head and body. Merrill towered over my six feet by about four inches, totally eclipsing the sun.

"Anyway," he continued, "you did good. Showed some of these rednecks that a man can be civilized, even holy, and have balls, too."

"That's what I came out here to talk to you about. I need to know if Johnson worked for you and what kind of worker he was?"

"He worked for me on paper, but that's all. He was assigned to me, but he never came to work. Every month I get a note from Captain Skipper that he was using Johnson other places. Said I should go ahead and give him credit for working out here."

"And you did it?" I asked, a little surprised.

"Captain say do it, I do it. I not smart enough to think for myself. I a machine. They program me, I work. I don't ask no questions," he said, falling back into his favorite dialect for expressing his frustration.

Merrill thought for himself all right. However, his life would have been easier if he were a machine. He was as smart as any man I had ever met, but was unable to go to college until recently because of family and money problems. He had, however, spent much of his time at the public library and already had a much better education than most college graduates.

"Did he ever come out here for work?" I asked.

"When he was first assigned here, he came about three times. Didn't do a damn thing. Worried about his fingernails and hair too much. He should have been a woman. . . . From what I hear, sometimes he was."

"What have you heard?" I asked.

"Some of the inmates called him 'Godown—' " he said with a broad smile that showed off every one of his snow-white teeth again.

"Godown?" I asked.

"Yeah, because he would go down on anybody."

"Do you think that had something to do with his death?" I asked, trying not to smile too big.

"It sure as hell a possibility, now ain't it, Sherlock? Since your man David offed Uriah to have Bathsheba, people been getting dead over the nasty."

"What can you tell me about Officer Hardy, who works midnights in the infirmary?"

"Ex-military, still in the reserves, I think," he said. "One hell of a good officer. Smart. Tough. Fair. He's righteous."

"How did you know I was playing Sherlock?" I asked.

"I know things." He smiled. ·

"Do a lot of people know?" I asked.

"I don't think so," he said, "but it's just a matter of time. They's very few secrets when everybody lives this close together."

"Yeah, I guess so."

"So," he said, "you better watch your back, Jack. Sooner or later, the wrong person's going to know. And . . ."

"And?"

"Just watch your back," he said, tilting his head forward so that I saw his eyes above his shades. They were serious.

"How about you watching my back?" I asked.

"I'll do what I can," he said.

"Which is more than most."

"Which is more than most."

"You're pretty confident for a black man named after a dead white woman."

He ran his hand across his short hair and then started patting it. "I'm named after a beautiful white woman. And she was almost as pretty as me. You know Mama swears that we were kin to her somehow."

"You probably are," I said. "For her sake, I hope so. Can you tell me anything else about Johnson?"

"No, I really didn't know him that well. I'll tell you who can. There is an inmate named Willie Baker. He's probably the oldest homosexual alive on the compound, maybe even in the world."

"The one they call Grandma?" I asked.

"Yeah, that's right," he said with surprise and amusement. "You chaplains know the four-one-one, don't you?"

"That's me, Mr. Information. It's not the four-one-one, but the nine-one-one that has me concerned."

"Well, if it come to that," he said smiling, "I be happy to make the call."

"Thanks," I said, "that's very reassuring—speaking of which, I've received some notes that I think may be threatening Anna. Will you—"

"I will," he said, nodding his head definitively. And I knew he would.

I turned to leave and then turned back and said, "Oh,

yeah, could you recognize a request that Johnson typed if you saw it?"

"No, and neither would you," he said.

"How do you know that?" I asked.

"Because Johnson couldn't read or write. Just another dumb nigga'," he said smiling, "like all us darkies."

"You sure he couldn't write?" I asked.

"As sure as I am that desegregation didn't end racism in the South."

That was as positive as Merrill could get. Walking back toward the institution, I wondered who wrote the request for Ike Johnson and if they knew anything about the trouble that Ike was in or maybe who killed him. Maybe he'll come and see me before the day is over. And, maybe I'll wake up in the morning and racism will be over, too.

*F*OURTEEN

*T*HE COMPOUND WAS ALIVE with the noise of a crowd, distinct voices only heard occasionally— laughter, yelling, religious talk, and profanity, all whirling around together like a brackish whirlpool of sound. Blue movement was everywhere. The activity was astounding; the inmates were in perpetual motion. They buzzed around like bees going from one flower to the next, many of them spreading poison rather than pollen. In the distance I could hear shots being fired on the range, and I wondered if it registered with the inmates that the officers were preparing for the eventuality that they might have to shoot them.

The sun beat down with a vengeance. The only shade was provided by four pavilions that were constructed for just that purpose. Like everything else in the institution, they were uniformly gray. Perhaps they blocked the sun, but they were impotent against the heat. The heat was stifling. Breathing the hot, thick air in and out took extra effort. The breeze that was present at the end of spring had finally given up and left town about a week before. The air didn't move, which is why the constant movement of the inmates looked all the more out of place.

As I walked through the open population, I was again reminded that I was a stranger in a strange land. This was their world, not mine. Many of the inmates treated me as guests at a dinner party would a servant. Some of them didn't seem to notice me at all. Others spoke, many of them doing so very respectfully.

As I passed through their midst, I heard contrasting discussions, from talk about God on a seminary level—"The concept of the trinity is not the fixed state of God, but an expression of different ways in which God can be experienced"—to the proliferation of scatological language—"That motherfucker even think about fuckin' with my shit I'a fuckin' kick his motherfuckin' ass two times"—quite often from the same mouth. I heard deals being made, political and sports discussions, and what I never failed to hear anywhere in the prison: discussions of all that was wrong with the Department of Corrections.

I walked down to the recreation field where inmates were very seriously playing. Above the field, in the clear, blue sky, a small flock of birds chirped and sang as they flew—surely a sign to anyone looking: beauty was here, God was here. I usually visited the rec field once a week to be available to the inmates who would never consider coming to the chapel. However, I had already done that this week. This visit was to see Willie Baker, who hadn't shown up after I had him called to the chapel. I could've had security pick him up and bring him to me, but I thought that might make him less than cooperative.

I found Willie at the far end of the rec field sitting on the ground leaning up against the back of the softball fence. He looked about a hundred and fifty. His gray hair, what little there was, made a nearly complete circle around the crown of his head. His eyes were hollow, and his eyeballs seemed as if they would have been too small for their sockets if not for the yellow matter in the corners of them. His stubbly gray beard sporadically covered his gaunt face, dipping down in the recesses of his cheeks because he had no teeth. If he were in any way effeminate you couldn't tell it by looking at him. However, if he were alive, you couldn't tell it by looking at him either. Men and women look a lot more alike at his age anyway.

He sat with two other men, both in their twenties. I said men because that's all this institution incarcerates, not because they looked like men. They were as feminine as any girl I had ever dated, and more so than some. They worked their femininity for all it was worth, too. They were gay and proud; they also seemed to be advertising.

"I'd like to ask you a few questions," I said to Willie when I had squatted down in front of him.

Willie's expression didn't change. He continued to stare up, which made his pupils almost completely disappear, causing him to look like the blind dude in *Kung Fu*.

"Grandma," the inmate to his left said in a high falsetto voice, "the chaplain want to talk whichya."

Willie didn't respond.

In the center of the field stood a gray officer's station. Part of it was open, housing free weights and Ping Pong tables. Scattered all around it were card tables where small groups of inmates played checkers, chess, and dominoes. There was no gambling going on—just ask the inmates.

"Grandma," he said again, this time patting his cheek as he did, "wake up, old girl. They's a man what wants to talk whichya."

Willie's eyes drifted slowly back down to earth, landing somewhere in my vicinity. Then he said in a soft, airy voice, "Who . . ."—he breathed out and paused as if this would require the last bit of life that was left in him—" . . . is . . . it?"

"It's the reverend. The new one," he said.

"The fine one," the other one said. I smiled.

Willie leaned down and whispered something in the ear

of the inmate to his left. He was obviously the spokesperson for the group. His name tag read Jefferson.

"Grandma wants to know," Jefferson said, "if you think homosexuals have no hope of salvation."

"I don't think there's anybody with no hope of salvation. I say this because I am being saved or redeemed or whatever, and if I can, anybody can."

Willie leaned down again and whispered something else in Jefferson's ear. Behind us the other inmates on the rec field were loud and active, sounding like children on a playground. And, in many ways, that's what they were—children who refused to grow up, men who could find no benefit in becoming responsible adults.

"Grandma say what do you think about priests who molest children?"

"I think they need help. I think they do not need to be priests."

"Do you think that they do that because they fags?" Jefferson asked.

"Pedophilia and homosexuality are two different things, and rarely is a person both," I said.

Behind me on the track that circled the entire field, two inmates passed by and snickered. They said something I couldn't make out. Then they laughed some more. Again, Willie whispered something into Jefferson's ear. Their actions brought to mind Moses and Aaron.

"Grandma say you all right. What you want to know?" Jefferson said.

"I want to know everything there is to know about Ike Johnson."

"Grandma say he dead. What else is there to know?" Jefferson said after receiving instructions from Grandma to do so.

"I want to know all about him while he was alive so I can find out why he was killed," I said.

Beyond the blacktop court where young black men

played full-court basketball like they did in Miami, the elderly inmates played horseshoes like they did in retirement homes in Sarasota. Past them, the young white inmates played volleyball the way they did on Panama City Beach. Yet, beyond all of this, the wall of chain-link fence and razor wire served as an ominous reminder of exactly which part of Florida this was.

"Grandma say he a real faggot. A bastard of a faggot. Do anything. Worse than a ho. Say, him getting killed just a matter of time. Sooner or later his kind always get stuck."

"Did he belong to someone?" I asked.

"You mean was he someone's ho?" Jefferson asked.

"Yes," I said.

"Grandma say everybody think he belonged to Jacobson, but he didn't. Grandma say he belonged to another inmate, and they both belong to a cop."

"A correctional officer here at the prison?" I asked, though I didn't believe it.

"Yeah. But the point is," Jefferson continued, "he wasn't loyal to his old man. He would do anything anytime. He also had a big mouth."

"What else can you tell me?" I asked.

"Grandma say that all he can say, 'cause he ain't got a big mouth."

I thought about all the names that I had come across so far in this investigation. I wanted to ask him about at least one of them.

"Can you tell me who Johnson's real old man was?" I asked.

"Can't say," Jefferson said, and Willie nodded his head in agreement.

"What can you tell me about Captain Skipper?" I asked.

Willie said nothing, but for just a split second the seemingly knocking-on-death's-door old man was as alert as any twenty-year-old I had ever seen. He leaned over and whispered in Jefferson's ear again.

"Grandma say, he won't say nothin' about that redneck son of a bitch," Jefferson said.

"Okay, what about Jones, the inmate who works in the infirmary?"

Again the whisper, again Jefferson with the response: "Say all he know is he well looked out for. He in love with them nurses, especially Strickland. Jones say they do things for each other, but Grandma think it a one-way street. Grandma understand what Jones mean. Say if she was straight, she'd love Nurse Strickland, too." All three inmates smiled widely.

"How about a young officer named Shutt?" I continued.

"Must be new, 'cause Grandma don't know him," Jefferson said.

"I don't really know what else to ask you. I'm trying to find out who killed Johnson and why. Is there anything else you can tell me that would help me do that?"

He shook his head. And then he, and not Jefferson, said, "Look into sex and drugs. It gots to do with sex or drugs or both. Everything out here got to do with sex or drugs." The depth of his voice took me by surprise. It came out as a tired and painful exhale from vocal cords that sounded as if they had been rubbed with sandpaper.

"Only thing missing is rock 'n' roll," I said.

"We got a little of that, too," he said.

*F*IFTEEN

"**W**HO CAN I GET DRUGS FROM?" I asked a very surprised Anna Rodden.

"Excuse me," she said, moving her head from side to side in mock confusion. "Have things gotten that bad?" She was wearing a colorful jumper with blooming spring flowers all over it. It fit nicely, though not too nicely, which would have violated her oath. Her long brown hair was worn down in long rolling waves. She was lovely.

"If an inmate wants to buy drugs on the compound," I said, "how does he do it?"

I was seated across from her desk in a blue plastic chair that sloped down to the left. Behind her, through the window, I could see inmates mowing dead grass. The sun had taken a toll on everything this year, but the grass most of all. The waves of heat made the inmates look as if they were many miles away rather than a few hundred feet. An overweight officer with mirrored sunshades stood nearby to inspect their work.

"Well, let's see," she said, narrowing her eyes and tapping her pencil on her forehead. "First he would have to have something to buy them with. This could be cash from an outside account; personal property to trade—say, a watch, rings, or canteen items; or he could be willing to do something—sex, a hit, a favor."

"Do many of them have what it takes to buy drugs?" I asked.

The officer inspecting the crew outside behind Anna turned slightly to the side. He looked pregnant in profile.

"Not many have money, but almost all can do some service or something. We're talking about an economy like our own, the trading of goods and services."

"Just how available are drugs on the compound?" I asked.

"Not as much as you might think after working here and seeing all the crime, but a whole hell of a lot more than a person on the street would think."

Her phone rang. She picked up the receiver, tossing her head back and slinging her hair out of the way. It swung out to the right of her head and then settled back down to the center. It looked like silk and moved with the bounce of hair on a Breck commercial. If I had seen a more graceful or beautiful sight, I couldn't remember when.

"Classification, Rodden," she said into the receiver. "Yes, I'm in a meeting right now. I'll come over when I finish. Okay. Good-bye."

She hung up the phone and said, "Sorry. Where were we?"

"I was about to ask how the drugs get in? I mean how can an inmate get drugs past all of the security measures taken to prevent them from getting in?"

She smiled. "Some of the drugs on the compound are homemade. We have chemicals here and a pharmacy. Sometimes inmates get their grubby little hands on that stuff. Usually though, the homemade stuff is liquor. Real drugs come in because someone brings them in."

"Who brings drugs into a state prison?" I asked, though I knew the answer.

"Well, if you're asking for names, I can't help you, but generally it comes down to two types of people. First, there are family members who smuggle dope in mail packages, although that is extremely difficult. Most of the time, family and friends bring drugs into inmates when they come for visitation."

"But security shakes them down. I see them do it every weekend," I said.

"That's true, but you know that it would still be possible to hide the stuff, especially in certain body cavities or in certain parts of the female anatomy. And which officer is going to pull out an inmate's wife's tampon to see if she has drugs hidden in it?"

"I see what you mean," I said, unable to hide my disgust at the picture she had just painted on the canvas of my mind.

"Remember these are the families that produced criminals. Now, not all of them are bad, but some are criminals themselves."

I nodded my head in agreement. Then, I shook it in disbelief, thinking of the implications of all that she had said.

"Another way," she continued, "is for corrections officers to smuggle them in and sell them."

"I've heard of that, but does it really happen that much?"

"It's really hard to say, but drugs do get in, and it's too much to be coming in just through inmates who get visits. COs don't make a lot of money. Not often, but occasionally, there's a thin line between the captives and their captors."

"What is that thin line?" I asked.

"Time, place, luck—I don't really know, but I think it's always borrowed time."

"You believe in divine justice?" I asked.

"I've seen it too many times not to. It's just not like most people think. It doesn't come in the same way as the crime. It comes in guilt, paranoia, anxiety, fear, loneliness, and ultimately death—spiritual, emotional, moral death. And those who don't pay now will pay later."

"I wonder sometimes," I said and then fell silent, wondering. "What about drug screening?" I asked.

"Officially, they will tell you that we do random drug screening. Unofficially, most of them are conducted after we receive a tip from another inmate. And, of course, after an inmate tests positive once, he is watched very closely."

When she stopped talking and before I started, I found myself hoping the phone would ring just so I could witness an encore of her earlier Breck girl performance.

"If that is true, how could Johnson have been full of crack in confinement and then the infirmary, both of which did drug screenings that came back negative?"

"There are only three possibilities. The inmate somehow faked the test—traded urine with someone or something like that. Or, it was an honest mistake by the officer doing the test. Or, someone, I mean an officer or a staff member, was looking out for him."

"Who could tell me names of inmates and/or officers supplying drugs?" I asked.

"A lot of people, but they wouldn't do it. They wouldn't tell any of us—that would be crazy."

"Well, I just happen to know a crazy inmate."

"Who?" she asked.

"Jacobson."

"I said crazy, not psychotic."

"Speaking of which— This is off the subject, but have you received any threats lately?"

She smiled. "You mean in addition to the normal stuff?"

"Yeah."

"No. Why?"

"Just curious," I said.

"You're never *just* anything," she said. "Especially *just* curious."

"Well, just be careful."

"I always am," she said.

"Be extra careful for a while, okay?"

She nodded slowly. "Okay." Her expression said she trusted me and that she didn't have to ask why.

Like the answer to a prayer, Anna's phone rang again, and I got to watch a repeat performance of a woman who could force all the other Breck girls into early retirement.

"It's for you," Anna said, after touching the hold button. "She says it's urgent, but she'll only talk to you in your office."

"Who is it?"

"Molly Thomas."

"Okay," I said. "I'll take it down there. Will you transfer it, please?"

"Yes," she said. "But should I be jealous?"

"No," I said. "You never should, but you should be careful. And let's talk some more about that this afternoon."

"Okay, if you say so."

"I do."

"Just call."

"I will, " I said. "If for no other reason than to get you to do that thing with your hair again."

Sixteen

W HEN I GOT BACK TO THE CHAPEL, the transferred call was ringing through. Fumbling with
the keys, I rushed in and picked up the call. "Chaplain
Jordan," I said as I pulled the receiver to my mouth.

"Chaplain, this is Molly Thomas," she said in a soft voice.

Molly Thomas was the devoted wife of an inmate here at
PCI named Anthony Thomas. She was devoted enough to
her husband and their relationship to move up here from
south Florida when he was transferred here. She rented a
small trailer in a trailer park not very far from mine. She
moved all the way up here so that she could be with her husband for six hours every Saturday and Sunday each week.
She was either very devoted or very controlled. The romantic inside me said that it was the former. The cynic in me said
the latter. Both sides of me longed for someone to love me
like that.

"Hello, Molly. How are you?" I asked.

"Not very good right now. I was wondering if I might
talk with you?" she asked hesitantly.

"Of course, you know that," I said.

"I can't do it over the phone," she said abruptly.

"Why don't you come to the institution this afternoon? We can meet in the administration building."

The administration building is the only building that is not behind the fence.

"I can't meet you there either. I'm in a real bind, and I feel as if I need to be very careful. I'm scared. Can we meet somewhere in town?"

"I don't see why not," I said, though I really saw a lot of why-nots. "There's a conference room I use sometimes at the sheriff's station. We can meet there if you like."

She hesitated. "I can't really meet you there either."

"How about the Methodist Church on Main Street at one o'clock?"

"That would be great. Thank you, Chaplain."

"You're welcome. I'll see you at one."

After we hung up, Mr. Smith swaggered in with some inmate requests and passes for me. I took them from him and looked through them. Nothing urgent.

"Have a seat," I said. "I've got a few more questions for you, if you don't mind?"

"Nosuh, I don't mind," which is what he would have said even if he did.

"I need to know who supplies the most drugs on the compound."

"Probably the biggest supplier that is a inmate is Jasper Evans."

I sat there stunned, unable to speak or move. Mr. Smith sat quietly with no expression on his face.

"But he is our choir director and the most faithful member of the church," I said at long last, unable to conceal my shock.

"Yesuh, he is. He a good singer, but he a dope pusher, too."

SEVENTEEN

WEEKLY CHURCH ATTENDANCE across America was higher than it had been since 1962. This was not true of Pottersville. In most small towns, church attendance, like the population, rarely varies. People go to church in small towns for different reasons than they do in large cities. Attending church in a small town is as much social as it is spiritual—and often more so. It is also about family tradition and social acceptability. And, to be honest, there is less to do in a small town. Another reason for going to church—the reason in fact, that brought Molly and me to church today, and one that occurs more often in larger cities than in small towns—is having a genuine need or personal crisis. Molly had both.

When I reached the First United Methodist Church of Pottersville, Molly Thomas was waiting on me. The church was red brick with white trim and, like most Protestant churches, looked like an old schoolhouse. Recently, however, like many Protestant churches, it had undergone cosmetic surgery to make it look more churchy: stained glass, a statue of Jesus holding a lamb in the front yard, and a bell tower on the roof. These changes created a confusing look: part school, part church, and part brick home.

Molly sat in her car, an older dark brown Ford Taurus, with her window rolled down. Her auburn hair was moist, and sweat trickled down the sides of her cheeks. Her green eyes, aided by colored contact lenses, looked like the Gulf after a summer rain. She glanced around nervously and then got out of the car.

I got out, too, but without the nervous glances. Later, I realized I should have been glancing.

"Molly, how are you?" I asked when we were both out.

"I'm scared out of my mind. I don't know what to do. I need your help," she said frantically.

Her eyes moved rapidly around in their sockets like flies too hyped up on speed to light. She blinked often and jerked her head occasionally. I wondered if she were high or just needed to be.

"Come in. We can use the pastor's office. He's at lunch right now," I said, walking toward the office at the rear of the church.

She followed. Actually, she walked at such a brisk pace that she passed me, which I guess means I followed her.

Pastor Clydesdale's office was way too small, or his library was way too big. He had three rather large bookshelves that held approximately twice the amount of books that they were made to. The books standing vertically on the shelf held books lying horizontally, and the top shelf had four large stacks that reached the ceiling. The floor, or what could be seen of it, was covered with a dark green shag carpet from deep in the 1970s. A small window air conditioner, which was not in a window at all, but rather an oversized hole in the wall, pushed the sweet smell of pipe smoke around the room.

I sat in the pastor's seat, an old swivel desk chair with wheels on its legs, and as I did I could feel two small springs—one under each cheek.

Molly sat on an old couch that occupied the wall to the

right of his desk. The couch, which was beside his desk so the desk wouldn't serve as a barrier between the shepherd and his sheep, was covered with a thin rust-colored bedspread and sloped down at the rear. This made Molly look at least six inches shorter than she really was. It seemed to me to defeat the purpose of having the couch beside the desk, something I was sure that the sensitive Dick Clydesdale had worried about before.

"Why don't you tell me what's going on, Molly."

"I'm taking an awful risk in talking to you. I think I can trust you, but I'm not sure," she said.

"If you have any reservations, I would encourage you to speak with someone you know better and can trust more."

"I don't know anyone. I am all alone down here. I'm out of options," she said. Her auburn hair and green eyes were striking, and she looked as if she should have been beautiful, but she was not. It was as if individually her features were attractive, but taken together they were not. The total was not equal to the sum of the parts.

"Down here? I thought you were from south Florida," I asked, surprised.

"No, I'm from Michigan. We were in Miami about to leave for a two-week cruise when Tony was arrested," she said and smiled a sad, ironic smile.

"So you moved down here from Michigan just to be with him?" I asked, envious of him for having such devotion from his wife.

"No, I never went back. I had my sister send my things and sublet our apartment. I haven't left his side."

"Are you sure you want to talk with me?" I asked.

"I have no one else."

"Don't try flattery. I'm immune to it," I said. "But it is nice that you are confident in my abilities."

She did not smile. We were silent a moment.

"If you want to talk with me, there are some things you

should know first. I will keep confidential anything you say unless to do so would cause harm to you, someone else, or the security of the institution. Also, we are not alone here."

She startled. Sitting up in her chair, she asked, "What do you mean?"

"No one is listening in on us. We have privacy. I just have this rule. I do not meet with young women in a pastoral role alone. It's nothing personal; it's just the best way to do things."

"Who's here?" she asked, looking around the room.

"The pastor of this church, the Reverend Dick Clydesdale, is having his lunch in the other office."

"I understand. I guess that lets me know that I picked a trustworthy man."

I shrugged. "I try. Now, why don't you tell me what is going on."

"Okay," she said and took a deep breath. "Tony's been doing real good. This is his first time down, you know. I was worried about him at first. He's not tough like those other men. But he's doing good. A lot better than I ever thought he would."

"Is that why you stayed around, to look out for him?" I asked, still wondering what her real motivation was. I wanted to believe that it was pure love, but I found it difficult to believe.

"I thought if I was here, he wouldn't feel so alone, and that might help him make it."

"And it has."

"It has helped. But about a month ago, Tony started acting real sure of himself, like he didn't need me anymore. He said that the most powerful man at the institution was looking out for him and that his last year would be cake. He was so cocky I couldn't stand it. I hate it when he gets like that," she said shaking her head.

"Did he say who the man was?" I asked.

"No, he never did. I would go on the weekends, and he would have all kinds of money to spend on me at the canteen. He would also give me little presents: a nice watch, earrings, a bracelet. He also began to deposit money in my account at the bank. Large deposits, especially considering I was his only source of funds and I hadn't been able to give him any in a long time."

"Did he ever say where it came from?" I asked.

"No, he didn't. He used to say that the skipper took care of his mates. And," she started to cry, "that everything he was doing he was doing for me. That he knew the sacrifices I had made to be near him and he appreciated it."

She continued to cry. The right side of her face twitched along her jawline and her bottom lip quivered. I looked around for what I knew Dick would have close by. I found it on a small table at the left side of his desk. I held out a Kleenex box. She withdrew two of them and neatly folded each one. With the first, she dabbed the corners of it in the corners of her eyes. With the second one, she blew her nose. She seemed so frail. I wanted to hug her and tell her that it was going to be all right. I knew better.

"He appreciated it," she said with disgust, "like I worked for him or something. Anyway, I was so thrilled that he was doing okay on the inside that I didn't really think about what he was really saying. Then, last Saturday when I was visiting him, he said that he had something very special planned for us this week and that he would call me and not to be scared. It would be all right."

"What did you think he meant?" I asked.

"I had no idea, but, to be honest, I was excited. Anyway, I got a call from him on Tuesday night saying for me to come to the institution. He said he worked it out for us to be alone. I was horrified, but I went. I was kind of excited too, you know? When I got there, the officer at the control room said that Captain Skipper was expecting me and to come right in.

They didn't even have me sign in or take my driver's license or anything."

I sat in silent shock, not knowing what to say.

"When I got into the sally port, a big man in a white shirt met me and escorted me to the chapel. He wasn't wearing a name tag. I looked."

"The chapel?" I asked with surprise.

"Yes. No one was there. It was very dark. The officer told me to go into the sanctuary and wait for Tony. When I got in there, Tony was waiting for me."

She began to tremble, and her twitch grew worse as she continued her story through her tears.

"He took me from behind, like he was attacking me. He grabbed me and slung me to the ground. At first I didn't know who it was, but then he started talking, and I knew it was him. He was like an animal pawing at me. I tried to turn around, but he wouldn't let me. He had my jeans off before I knew it." She began to cry so hard that she was gasping for breath. "Chaplain, he was whispering the most horrible things in my ear. Words he never used before and saying things he would do to me that he had never done before."

In every counseling session that I had ever conducted I tried to sit quietly and nod my head as I listened intently. This one had been no different until now. I felt as if I were sitting there with my chin on the floor.

"Why don't you rest for a minute before going on," I said as I gave her the entire tissue box this time.

"I," she sobbed, "must," she sniffled deeply, "go on. It felt like he put his fist . . . Oh God, this is so hard," she said.

"Don't rush it. It's okay," I said.

"It felt like he put his whole fist inside me. He was completely out of control. He grunted and cursed and called me the most awful names. It wasn't like Tony at all. Then, he . . ." she started crying even harder, " . . . sodomized me," she yelled at last and continued to cry uncontrollably.

"I am so sorry," I said. And then we sat in silence for a long time. About five minutes after she stopped crying she spoke again.

"Chaplain, I'm no saint. Tony and I have had sex in every way conceivable, but . . ."

"But, with your consent," I said.

"He raped me," she said matter-of-factly, all her earlier emotion gone.

"There are doubtless many saints who have had sexual intercourse in every conceivable way, so don't exclude yourself quite so quickly. However, no one should have anything forced on them. I am very sorry."

"He hurt me, not too bad physically, but real bad emotionally. But the worst thing of all was before he was through, the big officer in the white shirt and two other officers in brown shirts came in. They pulled him off of me and cuffed him. I have never been so scared or humiliated in all my life. It was all like a horrible nightmare. One of the officers jerked me up, told me to get dressed, and then led me to the gate. I heard the other officers saying that Tony would get time in the box for this and that he should be taken for a preconfinement physical.

"I was so disoriented I don't remember anything else except being in my car about a mile from my house when I saw the bright lights of a truck in my rearview mirror. I sped up, and the truck behind me did, too. When I reached the trailer park, I pulled in quickly, and so did the truck. I parked in front of my trailer, jumped out, and ran toward the door. The truck pulled in behind me, and I heard the truck door open. When I turned around, I saw the big officer in the white shirt running towards me. I dropped my keys, but thankfully I had left the door unlocked. People do that in Pottersville.

"I ran in and locked the door just before he reached it. He tried it. It was locked. Then it hit me—my keys—they were out there on the ground. I put the dead bolt on and the chain. He came back and unlocked the knob, but couldn't open the door because of the dead bolt. He kicked the door. I could hear him cursing. I ran into the kitchen and called nine-one-one. When I went back, he was gone. When the deputy arrived, I told him that it was a false alarm, but he could tell that I'd been beaten up a little. I think I looked worse than I felt. Anyway, I convinced him that I was okay, and he left. I've lived in fear ever since. This is the first time I've come out of the house since then."

"Do you know the name of the officer, the big one in the white shirt?" I asked.

"No. I assumed it was Skipper, but I don't know. God, he's a psychopath. You should have heard him laughing at me just before they pulled Tony off me. I wonder how long they were there in the dark watching us."

"Have you ever seen him before?" I asked.

"No, never. I take it that he is either a captain or a lieutenant because of the color of his shirt, but I couldn't see his collar."

"What time did all this take place?" I asked.

"I'm not sure," she said.

"It's very important. Was it before or after eleven?"

"Oh, after. It was way after eleven. Why?"

"The shift changes at eleven. So does the shift OIC."

"While you were at the institution, how many different officers did you see?" I asked.

"There was only one in the control room and then the three in the chapel."

"Are you sure?" I asked.

"Yes. It was eerily quiet that night."

"I wonder how many officers saw you." I said, mainly to myself.

"Four," she said confidently as if I had asked what two plus two equaled.

"More than four. Certainly the officer in Tower One saw you, even though you didn't see him or her."

"Oh, I see what you mean. Is it real important?"

"It would give me an idea of how many are involved and how high this goes."

"What are you going to do?" she asked.

"I'm going to look into it," I said.

"What should I do?" she asked like a lost little girl.

"You should stay home as much as possible. I'll ask the sheriff to assign someone to watch you for a while. As soon as I know something, I'll be in touch."

"Can you get the sheriff to assign a deputy to me?" she asked, sounding impressed.

"I think so," I said confidently.

"You are something else, Chaplain," she said with a puzzled expression on her face.

"No, I'm not," I said. "I'm just related to him."

"Oh, I see. Chaplain," she said, turning deathly serious, "will you please check on Tony for me? I need to know he's all right."

"I will."

"Thank you."

"I haven't done anything yet," I said.

"But you will," she said. "I know it."

*E*IGHTEEN

"*W*HAT EXACTLY ARE WE DOING HERE?" Anna asked.

We were sitting at the large conference table in the medical break room designed more for meetings than breaks. In fact, it was a conference room with a Coke machine in the back of the medical building. The corridor leading to it led past the steel doors of the suicide cells on one side and the glass walls of the infirmary on the other. I was drinking a can of "pure Florida orange juice," she a Diet Pepsi, both produced by the vending machine.

"We're taking a break," I said. She looked confused. "You know, a break. We're state employees; we takes lots of them."

"Oh, we do?" she asked, raising her left eyebrow to a sharp point.

I had called her shortly after returning from my meeting with Molly Thomas. Just prior to calling Anna, I called Tom Daniels and asked him to quietly get the FDLE technicians to examine the chapel floor for trace evidence that might verify Molly's story. I had no reason to doubt her, but in dealing with inmates and their families I had learned to verify everything. Besides it was an incredible story. I also called Dad and told him about the case and asked him to look out for Molly.

"Okay, so we never do," I said, "but today we are turning over a new leaf."

She sipped some more of her Diet Pepsi. Where she'd found a straw, I had no idea.

"You know," I continued, "I never once saw Susan drink out of a straw. She said it causes wrinkles around the mouth."

"What?" she asked, rolling her eyes and shaking her head. Anna had never liked Susan, which was difficult while we were married, but wonderful now.

I shrugged. "She was always obsessing about something."

Anna sucked on the straw even harder; her cheeks drew, and gulping noises surfaced from the bottom of the can. Like everything she did, this, too, had the unique blend of sensuality and innocence. I'm not saying she didn't know she was sexy—she was far too confident in it. But just as those raised in wealth are unaware of their privilege, Anna never seemed conscious of her beauty.

"What we're *really* doing here," I whispered, "is looking around for clues."

Her eyes widened. "Clues? Like real detectives? Am I playing Watson to your Holmes?"

"Being my partner would make you either Curly or Moe, not Watson."

"I think I'll be Moe and let Merrill be Curly."

"Fine by me," I said. I then grabbed her nose between my first two fingers and brought my other hand down pretending to hit it and said, "Hey, Moe."

She smiled that smile. For just a moment, time paused. And the Stooges were the furthermost thing from my mind.

"Actually," she said, "I should be Nancy Drew or your Girl Friday, you sexist pig," she said with a different smile.

"You know, you're right. I almost forgot that you are a woman. I'll be James Bond, and you can be— "

"I will not be a Bond bitch," she said cutting me off.

"I think the term is Bond babe," I said through a laugh.

"Whatever."

I sat there preparing to talk to her about the letters. It was more difficult than I would have thought, primarily because of what I thought her reaction was going to be.

"I need to talk with you," I said finally.

"We are talking."

"We need to have a serious talk. I want you to really listen to what I'm going to say. I'm not joking."

"Okay, what is it?" she said, tired of the buildup.

"I've received a couple of letters threatening someone that I love. I think they're about you."

"What did they say?"

I told her.

"It's not necessarily about me."

"No, not necessarily, but I think it's probably about you. I love you more than anyone within miles of this place, and the letters are coming from within the institution."

"You're probably right," she said soberly. "What do you want me to do?"

"I want you to listen to me. If anything ever happened to you . . ." The thought just lingered in the air. I regretted saying it.

"Well, then, you'll just have to stop anything from happening to me."

"I don't trust me to do that."

"I do," she said, her voice full of certainty. "This is not Atlanta. I'm not convinced that was your fault anyway, but even if it was, it's time to move on. You're very good at what you do—at all the different things that you do. I trust you to take care of me, to solve this case, and to continue to do the work of God, too."

"And on the weekends, I could bring about world peace," I said.

"It *is* a lot, but you can do it. I'm serious."

I could tell that she was. "Thank you," I said. "I want to talk to you more about the whole Stone Cold Killer thing. Not now, but soon. I know you need to. For now, I want you to be very careful. Play it safe, okay? Don't go anywhere or do anything alone inside here, okay?"

"Okay. It's going to be all right. I'm going to be fine. You're going to figure all of this out. Once again, save the day."

We drank a little more. I knew that we needed to get on with our search, but I was content just to be in her company. She was refreshing. If being happy is being unable to think of another place you'd rather be than where you are, then I was happy.

"I need to look in some of the rooms down here, and I need someone to cause a distraction, and, honey, you are distracting," I said.

"You asked me down here just to be a distraction? I'm insulted. I am more than just another pretty face."

"Without question. You're a versatile woman who can do anything. And the anything that this situation calls for is distraction. Another time and in another place, you can use your other assets."

"As long as you don't forget that I am woman, phenomenally," she said, alluding to Maya Angelou's poem, which I wouldn't have known had it not been for her.

"Phenomenal woman, that's you," I said completing the line of the poem. "Now, what I need is for you to talk to the officer in the infirmary. And be as distracting as you can."

She was.

I decided to look in the caustic storage closets first since this was where the cleaning chemicals were stored. They were both locked. I reached in my back pocket and whipped out my Visa card, slid it down the side of the doorjamb, and the door opened—too easily. Someone had done this before—many times.

I glanced at my Visa before I put it back. It had a tear in

it that broke the magnetic strip. I smiled. It was maxed out anyway.

The first closet had a single metal shelf that looked like it should have been in someone's garage. It was filled with boxes of garbage bags, paper towels, toilet paper, and rubber gloves. The very bottom shelf was filled with white plastic bottles of PRIDE chemicals: wax, stripper, floor cleaner, and glass cleaner. There were also two cans of the cleaning spray that kills HIV and hepatitis that may live in body fluids found on contact surfaces like toilet seats.

I got down on my hands and knees to take a closer look. I resisted the urge to touch them, which made it tough to see well. I moved to the side of the shelf, and then I saw it. On the back side there was a bottle of cleaner leaking, the liquid standing around the base of the bottle, the shelf, and the floor. I had not done a lot of detecting lately, so I wasn't sure, but I thought this looked a lot like a clue.

Amazingly enough, I was right. It was another reason I had faith—anything's possible. I was so thrilled about being right and finding an actual physical clue that I decided not to check the other closet. Daniels would do it with crime scene investigators who were equipped to process it.

I walked back up towards the front. In the long corridor that led up to the infirmary, the elderly inmate orderly named Jones was mopping the floor. He was so quiet and his moves so understated that I probably wouldn't have noticed him except that he was whistling. It was a very soft, airy whistle. I wasn't sure, but the tune sounded like "As Time Goes By." When I arrived at the infirmary control room, Anna was still beguiling the young officer, Ron Straub. He never had a chance.

"How you doing?" I asked him when I walked in.

"Fine. How are you, Chaplain?" he said, not bothering to mask his irritation at the intrusion—the second one in as many days.

"Do you have an inmate in the infirmary named Anthony Thomas?"

He looked away from me very quickly, but it was in the direction of the infirmary, so I couldn't tell if he was just looking to see if Thomas was in the infirmary or if he was startled by the question.

"Jones," he yelled to the orderly, "wasn't Thomas put in confinement Tuesday morning?"

Through the windows of the control room, I could see the inmate slowly walking up the hallway toward us.

"Yes, sir," he said when he reached the door. And then he walked back.

"He's in confinement," Straub said.

"Thank you. I'll see him there. Have a good day," I said and began to walk away. When I began to leave, he smiled. When Anna joined me, he stopped.

"What did you find?" Anna asked when we were seated in her office again.

"I just may have found where the body was stored until the trash was taken out."

"Where?"

"In one of the caustic storage rooms at the end of the hallway past the infirmary. It would make the perfect place. That hallway is almost always empty, and next to no one goes into that closet."

"What made you look in there in the first place?"

I told her.

"Why did you ask about Anthony Thomas? I mean, does it have something to do with this case?"

"I honestly don't know. Why?"

She smiled that smile from ear to ear and shrugged as if to say, *What canary?* "Well," she began, "some men, most men, will brag when given the opportunity to do so to an attentive female."

"I quite agree."

"So, I gave Ron my full attention and just a hint of thigh and he sang like a Pointer sister."

"A Pointer sister?"

"They're making a comeback."

"I wondered where they had gone. I figured they found a man with a slow hand and just couldn't quite get back on the road anymore."

"I think he left them. Anyway, Ron told some tales, and one of them was about an inmate who was having an affair with one of the nurses."

"Thomas?" I asked

"Thomas," she said. "So I wondered how he figured into all this."

"I don't know how or if he does really. Did he say which nurse it was?"

"No. I don't think he knows. He was just showing off and probably feeling me out as to whether or not I would go with an inmate."

"I see. Well, what now?" I asked. "You're going to be extra careful. Lock your doors; don't go anywhere alone. Play it safe."

"And you," she said, "are going to continue your search—that is, if you are handling it as well as you seem to be."

I stood to leave. "It is no illusion. So far, I'm okay. But you go right on asking because it makes me feel looked after."

"I try," she said.

"No," I said. "You succeed."

NINETEEN

*B*ACK IN MY OFFICE, I sat entering all of the information I had about the murder into my computer when Merrill Monroe walked in.

He didn't knock, which meant he had asked Mr. Smith if anyone was with me. He would have knocked otherwise. He walked in and took a seat in the same way he did everything, with natural rhythm—like he was made to do it. I knew it to be over a hundred degrees outside, but not because Merrill showed any signs of it. He moved and looked as if he had just come in from an invigorating walk in the cool, crisp air of a fall morning.

"Wha's up?" he said when he was seated in front of me.

"Got me," I said. "You're looking at the man who knows the very least about the way things work around here."

"It *is* a different world, but you's a quick study, boss."

"Yeah, I've certainly proven to be lightning quick so far."

"You doin' okay. Got a lot of people talkin'. Something or somebody goin' to snap. Just keep pourin' on the heat, puttin' on the pressure, and eventually the cooker gonna explode."

"The very fact that people know I am investigating lets you know how poorly I'm doing."

"Well, it can work to your advantage," he said, instantly losing his dialect. "Have you rounded up the usual suspects yet?"

"Yes, and the butler did it."

"He's black, too, isn't he?"

"Of course. Come to think of it, there is really only one suspect of African descent."

"Everybody's of African descent. We were the first people on Earth."

"I should have said that there is only one black suspect so far."

"The nigga' got a name?"

"Name and a number," I said. "Allen Jones. Inmate who works in the infirmary. He's not really a serious suspect. He has no motive that I can see, but he was there and in charge of handling the garbage. He also has access to a typewriter. Most inmates don't. But Anderson says he didn't take the trash out on Tuesday. Speaking of which, what can you tell me about Shutt?"

"Not much," he said. "He's pretty new. Seems okay. For a white boy, I mean. He a suspect?"

"Yeah. He picked up the trash, and he's the one who actually did the deed."

"Shook him up like hell, too, though, didn't it?" he asked.

"Maybe. Did you ever see *Fatal Attraction*?" I asked.

"Did Spike Lee make it, or was Denzel in it?" he asked.

"No," I said.

"Then, no," he said as if stating the obvious.

"Well, anyway, it's about this lady who goes crazy for this married man she had an affair with. Threatens his family—tries to kill them, even boils their pet rabbit. Anyway, for the longest time, I thought Glenn Close, the actress that played the crazy woman, was really crazy—scary, you know. But a few years later, I saw her in another role, and I was convinced that she was a saint. There are some good actors in this world, and they aren't all in Hollywood."

"Who else?" he said, shaking his head at my Glenn Close analogy.

"Jacobson, of course."

"Of course. But do you really think he's the one?" he asked.

"Don't know. Not ready to rule him out yet. He's very smart. And, then there's Skipper."

"He's probably involved somehow. He's a mean bastard. Bad to the bone, and not in the good way either. Anybody else?" he asked.

"Anybody who was in medical that night—Anderson, Strickland, even Skipper was there. Or anybody else, for all I know."

"You've really narrowed it down, haven't you?" he said, shaking his head sadly. "Got a motive?"

"Seems to be either sex, drugs, or rock 'n' roll. Or something else maybe."

"You really good at this shit, Sherlock," he said with a wide grin.

"Aren't I, though."

"What about racial? Victim *was* black and most of your suspects *are* white. Besides, Jacobson is a full-fledged Nazi."

"That's true. See, I really am clueless."

"Have you talked to Anna about the notes yet?" he asked.

"Yeah," I said. "But I could tell that she didn't take it very seriously."

We were silent for a few minutes. Through the thin chapel walls I could hear a group of inmates having an argument. And, although I couldn't hear what the argument was about, I could guess. Most of their arguments were about either religion or football. Then I told him about Molly Thomas and her experience with Captain Skipper.

"What do you think of correctional officers?" Merrill asked when I finished my story.

"I think most of them are good people doing a very difficult job with little resources for little pay."

"You don't think they're all like Patterson or Skipper?"

"No, of course not. But, I don't think they're all like you either. I know there are very few Skippers or Pattersons in the department—maybe just the two. What concerns me even more is that there are very few Merrill Monroes in the department. The department's in such a hurry to fill positions that they're compromising standards."

"True enough. What's the solution?" he asked.

"Don't know. That's why I'm not very critical of the department in general. Crime and punishment is a complex problem that requires a complex solution that's beyond me."

"No, it's not."

"It's not? What is it?"

"A complex solution that *includes* you."

"Be nice to think so, wouldn't it," I said.

Shortly after Merrill left, Mr. Smith brought inmate Jesus Garcia in to see me.

"Chaplain," he began, "I been serving the Lord now for about six months. I don't miss church. I really been gettin' in the Word, you know. Jesus has changed my life. I'm a new creature in Christ. Since I been serving the Lord, I have been so blessed. I stopped having nightmares, and I been treating my wife a lot better. When we talk or write each other, we really get along. We stopped fighting and everything. I will never hit her again."

"That's really great," I said encouragingly.

"Yeah, but, she ain't saved. I told her that she had to get saved or I could not be with her when I get out."

I knew where this was going. "How old are you, Garcia?"

"Twenty-seven."

"Is this your first spiritual experience?"

"Yes. I played some religious games before, but I've never been, you know, saved before."

"I see. So, it took twenty-seven years for you to begin your spiritual journey?"

"Yes, I guess so."

"And, who made you begin it?"

"Nobody. I mean, I guess God did."

"That's right. Nobody and God. And that's who has to do it for your wife."

"But, Chaplain, she's Catholic."

He whispered the word "Catholic" the way people do "cancer" or "death."

It never ceases to amaze me how many inmates get a good dose of jailhouse religion and expect their families to get it just like they do. They become obsessive over the minutest details of their chosen faith, and they engage in endless debates and exclude other inmates from their circles if they disagree. It's probably because they have so much time on their hands, and many of them have severe mental and emotional problems to begin with, but in the words of Jesus, "They strain out a gnat and swallow a camel."

"There is nothing wrong with being Catholic," I said. "It is the oldest Christian church on the planet."

"They're not Christian. I told you they're Catholic."

"Catholicism is one branch of the Christian tree—still the largest, in fact."

"It's the harlot spoken of in the Revelation," he said with a straight face—something I could not return.

"Let me give you a little advice," I said. "Don't expect everyone to have the same spiritual experiences that you do or to experience spiritual things in the same way that you have. They will not. God is vast and limitless. There is room in God for all of us, and with our different cultures, backgrounds, families, and individuality, we will all experience God differently. So allow God to move in your wife's life, and don't try to force her to experience God in the exact same way you have."

"There's only one way," he said, rising to leave. "You're not even saved, are you? You need to repent. You are worldly. 'Come out from among them and be ye separate, saith the

Lord,'" he said, and then he slammed my door.

Religion has numerous dark sides, many of which rear their ugly heads in prison. Not all inmates have shallow, self-righteous jailhouse religion. Some of them are truly becoming men of God. However, many of them have a mean-spirited, separatist, militant religion based on hate and prejudice. This was true for all the religions on the compound and not limited to Christianity. I was confronted with this dark face of faith nearly every day.

In another few minutes, Mr. Smith brought in Sandra Strickland to see me. I was pleasantly surprised.

"How are you?" she said. Her voice was full of concern.

"I'm okay. How are you?"

"Pretty good. I just wanted to stop by and check on you. You seemed very upset yesterday. I was worried about you. Are you really okay?"

"Well, I am anxious to know the results of the test," I said, and because she was so warm and compassionate I added, "I found a cut on my leg last night. It shook me up pretty badly. I just don't know when I got it. It may have happened after the incident Tuesday morning. I just don't know."

"You poor man. I know the waiting's the worst part, but I really don't think you have anything to worry about. Even if you did have a cut on your leg, his blood would have had to seep all the way through your pants."

"I know, but it's just so scary."

"We are at such high risk here. It's not fair. Some of these inmates are the sorriest excuses for human beings I've ever seen. They're breaking our state, our nation, and they're not just killing each other, they're killing us, too. They are leeches."

I didn't know what to say. She had moved from friendly to furious too fast for me.

"Anyway," she said as she stood up and walked over to

join me behind my desk, her face softening again, "I just wanted to let you know that if there's anything I can do for you, don't hesitate to ask." She then patted my arm with one hand and rubbed my back with the other—merely friendly expressions of concern as best I could tell. Until she kissed me.

The kiss started out friendly enough, but then she lingered. I became uncomfortable and pulled away.

"Thank you, so much," I said. "I really appreciate it. You are an exceptional nurse."

"That's not all I'm good at," she said. She was silent a moment, then added, "How about dinner, tonight? My meals will make you want to kiss the cook."

"I can't tonight," I said.

"Perhaps later in the week?"

"Perhaps."

"And, you really are going to be all right," she said moving toward the door. When she had opened it and stepped through it, she said, "Anything at all, now, just call."

"Okay," I said. And, as she shut the door and walked away, I mused at all the female attention I was receiving lately—Anna, Bambi, Sandy. They were all like streams in the desert.

Thank you, Father. And please, please, don't let me have AIDS. You've given me some new reasons to want to live.

*T*WENTY

M Y HEAD WAS SWIMMING. Swirls of consciousness created a whirlpool of thoughts that included
Anthony and Molly Thomas, Bambi, Sandy, AIDS, blood,
murder, and Anna. There was a powerful undertow in the
center of this mental whirlpool, and I was being pulled
toward it. In fact, what was happening inside my head was
preventing me from hearing what was happening outside.

"Chaplain. Chaplain," Stone said. Tom Daniels and I
were seated in his office for another round of who-knows-
what and what's-going-on-around-here, but I didn't feel like
playing.

"Yes, sir. I'm sorry. I was just thinking."

"About what the inspector said?" Stone tilted his head
toward Tom Daniels.

"What did he say?" I asked.

Stone frowned deeply.

"I said," Daniels said, "I found out that our very own
Officer Shutt has been written up several times on accusations of brutality towards inmates—every one of them
black."

"What has been done? Did you know about this?" I
asked, looking at Edward Stone.

He frowned at me again. Again deeply.

"Not much has been done, as you would expect, because the grievances have been written by inmates. It seems that on a couple of occasions, he was reprimanded by his supervisor," Daniels continued.

"That'll teach him," I said.

Stone frowned at me again. The man was nothing if not consistent.

"You both know what it's like. We get grievances on staff members all the time from inmates. All some inmates do is write grievances. So, they are very often not believed or, at best, taken with a grain of salt. And remember, this may still be a case of a good officer being abused by some lowlife inmates. Good officers and staff get written up all the time. It's almost impossible to know. There's nobody in the entire department who has not been written up by some inmate at some time or another for something."

Both Daniels and Stone could tell that I didn't like what was being said. Stone frowned at me.

Daniels said, "What?"

"Nothing."

"What is it? You thinking, 'Poor, pitiful inmates. Another example of how they're abused by the man'?"

"I was thinking how high a price we all pay for the abuse," I said.

"There's no evidence that he abused them," Daniels said.

"No. I mean the abuse by inmates of the grievance procedure. Because of the abuse of some, all suffer. Because so many of them lie and misuse the system, none of them are believed. So, those who are abused are not believed because of all those who cry wolf."

"Yeah." He sounded surprised to find himself agreeing with me.

"However, Inspector, continued and consistent reports of abuse by an officer should be treated quite differently from the rare or even the occasional one. How many charges of abuse has he received?" Edward Stone said.

"Twelve," Daniels said.

"How many years has he been with the department?" I asked.

"Not quite two."

"That seems like a lot of smoke for there not to be a fire somewhere under there," I said.

"I agree." Stone also sounded surprised to be agreeing with me. "Watch him very closely, Inspector. If he's guilty, I want his ass," Stone said without emotion. He turned slightly towards me. "Please excuse my language, Chaplain."

I merely nodded.

Daniels started to say something, but I broke in. "Were any of the grievances filed by Johnson?" I asked.

He nodded.

Edward Stone's eyebrows peeked several inches above his glasses.

"Maybe you could call the chaplain at his old institution and ask him about Shutt, Chaplain," Stone added.

"Sure," I said. I then stood to leave.

"I've got more," Daniels said after he let me get almost to the door.

I sat back down.

"About the sleeping pills," he said, "the doc said they were not given by syringe or with food. It seems as if Johnson just took the pills himself. Some of the capsules were not even fully dissolved yet."

"Suicide?" Stone asked, his voice sounding hopeful.

"Who knows?" Daniels said. "But at least a possibility."

"But that rules out the medical staff and the officer, though, right?" Stone said.

"No," I said. "It's just another piece of the puzzle that may or may not lead to a possible solution."

Daniels frowned at me. Then to Stone he said, "It probably does remove the suspicion from the employees, yes, sir. Then again," he continued, "who better to give a patient pills than a member of the medical staff or the officer who helps them."

"But you're the one who said—" Stone said.

"I know, and it may still hold up, but none of this is cut-and-dried. It never is. What'd you expect?"

"I don't know, " Stone said. "But this isn't it."

"It never is," I said.

*T*WENTY-ONE

*T*HE AIR IN CONFINEMENT was ten degrees hotter than the air outside and lacked the breeze. The body odor hung in the air like a fog. It was so thick as to be almost visible. There was very little volume to the noise, only the occasional yell or scream, with a small but steady hum of voices sounding like bees at my ear. It was too hot to be loud—the heat had zapped the inmates' energy, drawing out their poison.

The officer at the desk, a thirty-something-looking guy with wavy black hair and a slight Latino accent, said that Thomas was in cell 155. When I reached his cell, he was kneeling at the tray hole as if he had expected me, which he probably did. The inmates' ability to communicate with each other, even in lock-down, was amazing.

"Anthony, how you doing?" I asked.

He shook his head slightly and stared up at me, trying to focus on me. His movements were slow and unsteady. When his eyes finally came within the vicinity of mine, he grinned with way too much familiarity.

"Hello, John," he said. It was the first time an inmate had ever called me John.

"How are you feeling?" I asked.

"Top of the world. Top of the fuckin' world."

"It appears you may have even left this world," I said.

He didn't respond.

"How is Molly?" I asked.

"Molly. Molly. Molly," he said and zoned out again. Actually he was zoned out when he said it. "Molly is my wife, but you, you are my true love."

"Me?"

"Sure you are. I really love you, man."

"Do you have a girlfriend here at the institution?"

"I have lots of friends."

"Like who?"

"Ike was my friend, but he's not my friend anymore. He's dead. He's like way out there, man."

"What can you tell me about Ike?" I asked.

"He was," he said and then paused, "my friend."

"I think we've established that. Anything you can add to the fact that he was your friend?"

"He was a good friend. He was a real sweetheart. I wish they didn't kill him."

"Who killed him?" I asked.

"That pigfucker Skipper. If he didn't do it, he had it done. He's . . ." he seemed to drift further out again.

"He's what?" I asked.

"He's . . ." he said in a near-whisper. "He runs this place. He's the skipper of this ship."

"What makes you say that?" I asked.

"He does what he wants to, man. He uses . . . abuses . . . nooobody can stop him. Stone's scared of him, too . . . unless he's working for him," he said and then looked off into space as if to contemplate a deep thought. "My name should be Stoned, too."

"How about Molly? Does Skipper use or abuse her?"

He began to cry. At first just small tears and then, gradually, bigger and bigger ones. "That fat bastard pigfucker son of a bitch," he said and sobbed even louder. "I'm gonna kill him, the prick sucker."

He leaned his head against the steel door and cried some more. In a few minutes, he was snoring.

I walked back down the hallway toward the desk to speak to the officer seated there. On my way by Jacobson's cell, I looked in. He was completely naked, standing in the center of the cell with a full erection.

When he saw me, he ran to the door and began to shout, "I'M THE DEVIL'S SON. I'M THE DEVIL'S SON."

"No argument here," I said and continued to walk.

"Got a question for you," I said to the officer when I had reached his desk.

"Shoot," he said.

"Is that inmate on any medication?"

"Jacobson, yeah. He takes sleeping pills. But, between you and me, he doesn't take nearly enough of them. I wish he would sleep all the time. Maybe even sleep the big sleep. You seen that movie? Bogart's in it."

"Yeah, I've seen it. Good flick," I said. "But, I was talking about Anthony Thomas in one-fifty-five."

"Thomas?" he shrugged, "beats the hell outa me, Padre. I don't know about Thomas. Better ask the nurse."

"Which one?" I said, finding it odd that he knew that Jacobson was on sleeping pills and didn't know what was making Anthony Thomas float around his cell.

"Any of them can tell you, I'm sure, but he sees Nurse Strickland the most."

"Thank you," I said and walked out.

I was walking back toward the chapel when I saw her. Actually, I didn't see her. What I saw was a one-ton white FedEx truck. She was headed toward the warehouse on the west side of the institution outside of the fence.

When I reached the warehouse the truck was still there. It was backed up to the loading dock with its flashers blinking. I walked up the ramp and entered the cargo bay. When I stepped inside, I could see her and the warehouse supervisor in his office. I walked over as nonchalantly as I could, which probably resembled running.

"Hello, Chaplain, what brings you out here?" Rick Spawn said when I stepped into the doorway of his office.

Before I could answer, I glanced in her direction.

"Hello, Chaplain JJ," she said with a big smile.

"Hello," I said, because it was all I could say at the moment.

"It's good to see you again," she said enthusiastically.

"You two know each other?" Rick asked.

"Yes," Laura said, "I bought the chaplain a pizza the other night. It wasn't a date or anything, but I think he's smitten. He's probably here to ask me out. Do you think I should go?" she asked Rick.

"No, you should go out with me," he said.

"I don't date married men," she said.

"He's married," he said, nodding his head toward me. "To his God. Besides, you're married too," he said to her.

My heart sank to the depths of my stomach. "You're married?" I asked, unable to conceal the disappointment in my voice.

"It's just a joke, Preacher," she said. "Don't lose your religion or anything. You almost made him cry, Rick," she said. "Be ashamed."

"Listen, you two, I have almost a thousand inmates inside the fence who will harass me anytime. I don't need two amateurs doing it," I said.

"Sorry," she said but didn't mean it.

"Kind of touchy, isn't he?" Rick asked.

"Yeah, but he's cute," Laura said, "in a discarded mutt sort of way."

"Okay, that's it. I'm out of here. I'm going to find some professional harassers."

"Aren't you forgetting something?" Rick asked.

"Like what?" I asked.

"Didn't you come out here for something?"

"I just stopped by to speak to you, you know, making the rounds."

"He came out here to see me," Laura said. "When he saw my truck, he nearly ran across the compound. It was embarrassing."

"Well, let me just say," I said as I turned to leave, "that if what you say is true, then it was worth it. For the abuse if nothing else."

As I was walking away, I heard her say to Rick, "I better go and check on him. He seems pretty fragile. Probably doesn't have a good woman looking out for him."

"Wait up," she said as she caught me on the exit ramp. "You're not going to break your neck running over here and then not even ask me out, are you?"

"Yes, that's exactly what I'm going to do."

"Well then, my mom would die if she heard this, but, I guess I'll just have to ask you out."

I didn't respond.

"Well?" she asked impatiently. "Are you going to allow your wounded inner child to keep you from possibly finding your soul mate?"

"Okay."

"Okay what, Caveman? Try to form a complete sentence."

"Okay, we can go out. Saturday morning I have to go to Tallahassee. You can come along, and we'll make a day of it."

"Doing what?" she asked.

"Whatever. I'll surprise you. It'll be fun, I assure you."

"Okay."

"What was that, Cavewoman?"

"Okay, I'll go. I mean how bad could it be. It's just one day, right?"

"Where do I pick you up?"

"Are you going to the jamboree tonight? You were the jamboree king back in the olden days when you were in school, weren't you?"

"Yes, I'm going. Yes, I was king. No, it was not the olden days."

"Then find me at the game, and I'll tell you where to pick me up. Besides, if you'll wear something besides that little priest's outfit, I might let you help me chaperone my little sister's jamboree jam dance. And if you are really right with God, you might even get to dance with me. Does he allow you to dance?"

"God?" I asked.

She nodded her head.

"Since he, or she, as a friend of mine would say, is the Lord of the dance, I do not see how he or she could object to me doing it."

"*She*, huh? I've got to meet this friend of yours. And, here's to a dancing God," she said and held her hand up in a mock toast.

And then she got into her one-ton truck and drove away. And I stood there and tried to catch my breath.

TWENTY-TWO

IT IS THE CHIEF PARADOX OF FLORIDA that the south part of the state resembles the north part of the country and the north part of the state resembles the south part of the country.

There are two Floridas actually—both of them like LA. The first one, the one that most people are familiar with, is the *Miami Vice* Florida, filled with bikinis, billionaires, and bars. It's like Los Angeles because of its beautiful beaches and beautiful people, all of whom live the jet-set lifestyle. It is a glamorous place where the women look like models and the men like movie stars.

The second Florida, the one most people drive through on their way to the first, is quite different. It is a Florida much like LA also, just a different LA—Lower Alabama. It is a Florida of pickup trucks with gun racks, house trailers with cars on blocks in the yard, and night spots named Bubba's. It is a rural Florida where segregation still exists and the black people are relegated to live in a part of town called the Quarters. It is a Florida virtually unknown to tourists.

Pottersville was a part of Gloria Jahoda's *Other Florida*, a rural town much like those of South Georgia and Alabama. Wealthy and well-educated people resided in Pottersville, just not very many. Many of its citizens were interested in having just enough money so they could buy beer and bait. They hunted, fished, and got drunk simply because it was Friday. In this town many people preferred not to wear shoes, and usually didn't. Some called black people niggers, and many survived on government checks, and, lest you forget, all of this took place on the verge of the twenty-first century.

Pottersville had other sorts as well; they were just not as colorful. They were hardworking people who were the salt of the earth. They looked out for each other's homes, farms, and kids. They went camping and to church and to family reunions—all on a regular basis. They ate fried chicken, homemade biscuits, and fresh vegetables—the latter from their own gardens or a neighbor's. They called the women, including their own wives "Miss," as in "Miss Julie." They obeyed the laws of the land—the important ones anyway, and they believed in God and his son, Jesus Christ, both of whom were assumed to be Southern gentlemen.

In a place like Pottersville, where there was not a lot to do, a Friday night high school football game was a social event, and if it were the July jamboree game, it was the social event of the year. Why football in the summer? It was Pottersville. Every other game was played in the fall, but the July Jamboree was reserved for midsummer, when the days were hot and long and the nights were filled with bored kids and reruns of shows that the people of Pottersville didn't watch the first time.

People poured into the gate of the football field with excitement and enthusiasm. Pottersville was a town with a lot of energy. It was by no means a retirement community like the ones taking over south Florida. Who would come to Pottersville to retire? Not even the heat could take the energy out of the air. Walking up to the gate, I could hear the band playing a popular song. I recognized the tune but couldn't think of the name.

When I walked inside the gate, Merrill was standing there waiting for me. His clothes matched his skin tone—midnight. He wore black tailored slacks with a thin white pinstripe, black-and-white wing tip shoes, and a black collarless long-sleeve shirt.

"Wha's up?" he said when I reached him.

"Jam, Bro," I said, looking around at all the people buzzing around like fireflies in the night sky.

People swarmed around everywhere. They lined the fence around the field; they stood in line at the concession stand and sat in the bleachers. Cheerleaders roamed around selling programs and blue-and-white shakers. The two teams were on opposite ends of the field warming up.

"I think the entire town is here tonight," he said.

In stark contrast to Merrill's cat-burglar ensemble, I wore Levi's 550 stone-washed-straight-leg jeans, leather deck shoes with no socks, and a white collarless long-sleeve shirt. We looked like day and night.

As we approached the home bleachers, Merrill extracted a quarter from his pocket. "Heads or tails?" he asked.

"Tails," I said.

Merrill flipped the coin into the air, caught it with his right palm, and slapped it on down on his left.

"Tails," he said, "you win. What will it be, eighty or twenty?"

For as long as I could remember, the bleachers had been divided up into eighty-twenty. The first eighty percent was the unofficial white section, and the last twenty was the unofficial black section. Merrill and I, when we came to the games at all, always sat together, which meant that one of us would be in the minority. I won, so tonight I got to call it.

"Twenty," I said. "Let's sit with the colored folk."

"We be honored to have you, missa' Jordan. You a important man, suh."

We walked along the narrow sidewalk at the front of the bleachers past the white section, where a few people spoke to us, down to the black section, where a few more people spoke to us.

We sat by a heavy black woman whom everybody called Miss Tanya. She said, "Boys, how y'all doin' tonight?"

"Just fine, Miss Tanya. How are you?" I said.

"Honey," she said in about five syllables, "I am so blessed. God is so good. 'Course you know that. You still preachin'?"

She asked me that every time she saw me, like she expected me to quit at any minute. "Yes, ma'am," I said.

"Oh, honey, I'm so proud of you."

"Thank you."

"Mer Mer," she said to Merrill, "how is school coming along?"

"Slow. I figure to be finished about the time Jesus comes back."

"Well, you hang in there shuga'. You makin' us all so proud. When I win the lottery, I gonna finish payin' for you schoolin'."

"Yes, ma'am," he said patronizingly.

When the game started, Miss Tanya yelled, "Come on, Tigers. Kick some butt!" Her whole body, all three hundred pounds, bounced up and down as she yelled.

Miss Tanya continued to talk to us and to the players throughout the first quarter. Mer Mer and I were quiet—he watching the game, I looking for Laura.

Near the end of the second quarter I spotted her. She was on the other side of the field helping the jamboree court prepare for its halftime program.

I could see that all of the young ladies on the jamboree court and most of the women helping them had on corsages, but Laura did not.

"Idiot!" I exclaimed.

"That *was* stupid," Merrill said. "The whole left side of the field was open."

"No, not that. I forgot something. Miss Tanya," I said

looking over at her, "where did you get that corsage?"

"From the school this afternoon. Shaniqua bought it for me."

"Are they still selling them?"

"I don't think so, baby. What is it?"

"I'm meeting a girl tonight and I forgot to get her one."

"Here," she said and began to pull the pin out of hers, "you take this one, baby."

"I couldn't," I said.

"Don't you argue with Miss Tanya. Now go on—take it, boy. Go on now. Take it to her."

"Thank you," I said and gave her a hug. "I'll see you in a little while," I said to Merrill.

"If things don't go well, you'll see me in a little while. If things go well . . ."

"I'll see you Monday."

As I walked over to the visitor side of the field, I thought about how generous Miss Tanya had been. Every time I wondered why I was living in a place like Pottersville, something like this happened to remind me.

Laura was straightening the corsage on her sister when I reached her. She wore a peach sundress with shoulder straps and light brown sandals. Her tan skin set the peach color off beautifully. I quickly glanced at her feet. I've always thought that feet say a lot about a person. They were beautiful—not too small, and her toenails were painted to match her dress. Her light brown hair, roughly the color of her sandals, was held in a ponytail by a peach bow. She was lovely—the first serious competition for Anna I had ever seen around here, maybe anywhere.

"Certainly the prettiest woman in the county needs a corsage, wouldn't you agree?" I whispered when I was right behind her.

She spun around, her brilliant, deep brown eyes twinkling flirtatiously. She was breathtaking.

"The county?" she said. "The county? It's a pretty damn small county."

"I meant the state," I said. "May I?" I asked as I held up the corsage.

She hesitated, then looked around. "You seem to be my only suitor. Go ahead," she said in mock exasperation.

As I pinned it on her dress, I said, "I seriously doubt I am your only suitor."

"Well, maybe not my only one. Watch your hands there, Priest. I wouldn't want to be an occasion of sin for you."

"More like an occasion of grace," I said almost to myself.

She let that one go. Then she said, "Speaking of priests, you don't look half-bad without that silly collar on. I might just dance with you tonight."

"Now that you mention it, you look lovely, not that you don't in your FedEx shorts, mind you, but even lovelier tonight."

"Thank you," she said softly. Then, "How long is this going to take?"

"I'm almost finished."

"Poor priest. Is this your first time?"

I looked up with surprise.

"Pinning a corsage on a woman," she said. "Is this your first time pinning a corsage on a woman?"

"Of course not, but it has been a while."

"I'm sorry I'm giving you such a hard time," she said.

"No, you're not. You're loving every minute of it."

"Are you finished playing with my breasts yet, Preacher?" she said rather loudly.

Before I could respond, Laura's sister walked back from where she had been giggling with some of her friends.

"This is Father John," Laura said. "He's the priest who wants to have an illicit affair with me."

I smiled—I could do nothing else. "Hello, I'm John Jordan, and I'm not a priest. As to the affair, well let's just say that your sister is the one who keeps mentioning it."

She laughed. "I'm Kim," she said. "And she likes you."

"She has a funny way of showing it."

"Well," she said and then hesitated, "she just needs someone to settle her down a bit."

"Have you tried Ritalin?"

Kim laughed.

Laura punched me in the arm.

"Hey, JJ," Ernie yelled from where he stood with the rest of the kids waiting to enter the field.

"Well, I've got to go," Kim said as the last seconds of the first half were ticking down.

"Good luck. You look great," I said.

Later that night we danced slowly to Boz Scaggs's "Look What You've Done To Me" and to other songs, most of them unfamiliar to me. It reminded me of high school—distant dances and young love. She danced close to me, but not too close. Actually, not nearly close enough.

"I think your dress is overpowering me," I said as we danced to a ballad Richard Marx had written for his wife.

"Why do you say that?" she whispered, seemingly in some sort of trance herself.

"Because I would swear that your hair smells like peaches."

She smiled.

Still later that night, I took her home and kissed her good night—a perfect first kiss: gentle, slightly lingering, and hinting of more, much more. It was a perfect night.

Even later that night, I went to bed with a smile on my face and dreamt of picking peaches in what must have been paradise, maybe even the Garden of Eden, but I assure you they were not forbidden fruit.

They were fruit from the Tree of Life.

TWENTY-THREE

THE GREAT FIERY EYE IN THE SKY was covered in a thick asbestos blanket of rain-threatening clouds. Relief. It was the coolest morning in weeks—still, it never dipped lower than ninety. Many of the Native Americans in our area had been doing a ceremonial rain dance for weeks. Had we known how to do it, many of us Other Americans would have joined them. Perhaps today our prayers and dances would be answered.

Laura and I were driving east on Highway 20 toward Tallahassee in my dad's new Ford Explorer. It was white with tan leather interior that still smelled new. My old Chevy S-10 was not an appropriate chariot for the Lady Laura. The Lady, who was less talkative than the previous night, looked regal in her long, fitted black dress, her hair down, small gold loop earrings, and a single gold chain around her neck. Her look was as understated as it was devastating.

For the first part of our trip she said very little. She looked and sounded sleepy. I couldn't help but wonder what waking up beside her would be like. I couldn't imagine ever wanting to get out of bed if I did.

"When are you going to tell me why we're dressed like this?" she asked.

I was wearing a black Mark Alexander suit with a gray pinstripe, a black shirt with an Episcopal collar, and black wing tip shoes.

"Did you bring a change of clothes?" I asked.

"Yes, but that doesn't answer my question," she said, her eyes twinkling though they still looked half-asleep. I guess I should have said half-awake.

"You don't like surprises?" I asked.

"As a matter of fact, I don't," she said. Her face, besides looking slightly sleepy, looked pure and childlike, due in part to its sleepiness and in part to its natural look. If she had any makeup on at all, it was not visible—with the exception of a small amount around her eyes.

"That figures," I said.

"Oh, really," she said, leaning forward preparing to engage. The new leather creaked as she moved. "And exactly what does that mean?"

"You're just too guarded, too addicted to control to like surprises," I said.

"Listen," she said, her irritation showing, "I'm pretty close to getting my master's degree in psychology, so I don't need some prison priest who's taken a few psychology classes spouting off psycho babble to me."

"I see," I said.

We were silent for a while. I couldn't help smiling.

"Why are you smiling so big?" she asked behind a smile of her own.

"I enjoy your company," I said. "I also enjoy giving you a dose or two of your own medicine."

"I am working on my OC tendencies," she said. "How about you?"

"What about me?" I asked. I felt the muscles in my stomach tighten.

"Are you actively working on your recovery? I've heard a few things about you, you know."

"Been checking up on me, have you?"

"A girl has to be careful these days."

"You're not a girl, and I have no doubt that you can handle yourself quite well. As to your question, I do not miss my two AA meetings each week, I have a sponsor, and I read a lot of recovery books."

"I know. I just wanted to see how honest you were about it. You think I would go off with a recovering alcoholic without being sure that he was, in fact, recovering."

"It seems you know a good deal about me. Tell me about you."

"I will. Just as soon as you tell me where we're going."

"Okay," I said trying to think of how to tell her. "Here goes. We are going out for lunch and to a jazz concert in the park and to spend a leisurely afternoon in our state's beautiful capital."

"Don't you mean lovely?" she asked. "And, I am talking about this morning. What are we doing this morning?"

"Well, on the way to an exciting afternoon, we're going to a funeral."

"You are taking me to a funeral on our first date?" she asked and then opened her mouth to speak again and could not.

"I can't believe I was here to see it," I said. "You're speechless. You are actually speechless."

"Wouldn't you be?" she said. Her smile had completely vanished now, replaced with the look of disgust ordinarily reserved for perverts. "I can't believe this. I hate funerals."

"I don't know anybody who loves them, but it's certainly an important time of ministry for me. People experiencing loss need help. However, I did arrange for you to stay with a friend of mine during the funeral if you want to."

"Whose funeral is it?" she asked.

The sides of the highway, like every highway in northwest Florida, were lined with rows of pine trees. The occasionally visible sun behind the rows of trees caused them to cast shadows like prison bars across the highway.

"One of the inmates from Potter," I said.

"Do you go to all of the inmates' funerals?" she asked. She seemed to really be trying to understand. Gone was her look of shock, replaced now with a look of curiosity.

"No. Actually, this is my first one," I said.

"Why this one?" she asked.

"His family asked me to do it."

"You're *doing* the funeral?" she asked, her eyes widening. I nodded.

"Did you know the family from before?" she asked.

"I've never met them, and if I met the inmate, I don't remember it."

She was silent, her eye taking on the abandoned look of someone in deep thought.

"Listen," I said, "I'm very sorry about this. You were giving me such a hard time yesterday I thought I'd pull this little surprise on you, but I shouldn't have. It was inappropriate, and I'm sorry. But I did think it would be nice to get out of Pottersville together, and since I had to make this trip anyway . . . And well, I probably didn't think it's such a bizarre thing to go to a funeral because they are so much a part of what I do."

"I've never thought of it that way," she said, her expression changing from contemplation to compassion. "You must stay depressed."

"I have my fair share of depression, but probably not too much more than most people."

"I would think that someone in your position, whether it be a chaplain, minister, or priest, would either have to totally disassociate or vicariously feel depressed most of the time."

"You're right that many people in helping professions maintain a professional aloofness in order to protect themselves, but as someone whose primary job it is to follow Jesus and enter into the sufferings of others, I can't do that. The foundation of ministry is compassion—to feel with others."

"No, I guess you can't disassociate," she said, "not like us cold clinical shrinks anyway."

"To be honest, I think the best caregivers, whether counselors, doctors, nurses, or ministers, are those who risk truly caring."

"Maybe. But who can do that without eventually burning out, or worse?"

"It is a tightrope. And I fall off it quite often. But I've been through some pretty dark times in my life, and those who tried to help me from a safe distance out in the light were unable to."

"So, what do you do?" she asked.

"I care. I get my heart broken. I get manipulated. I get depressed, but only occasionally. And that's because I care for people, but I don't adopt them. I do all I can, and if they need more, then God will send them someone else who can give them more, and if she doesn't, well then she must not want them to be helped anymore. I try to be responsive to needs, and I try not to take responsibility for people."

"And that works?" she asked with genuine interest.

"Not very often. No. But in theory . . . in theory, it's great."

She laughed. It was a nice laugh and the first time I heard her laugh genuinely. Every other time I had heard her laugh it was at me and it had come out forced and a little mean.

"I bet it does work for you," she said, becoming instantly serious, "and I have a lot to learn before I begin my practice."

"Anyone who says they have a lot to learn is someone I trust. I'm willing to be your first client and send you my referrals. And, if you ever get to the place where you feel like you don't have a lot to learn, let me know, because I'll need to terminate our sessions and find someone who does."

"It's a deal," she said, but then seemed to reconsider. "However, if we have a relationship, won't that be unethical, you know, dual relationships and all?"

"So you think we might have a relationship then, huh?"

"We have a relationship now, but I would say that if I don't drive you off and if your God decides that he—I mean *she's*—not overly jealous, then we might have even more of a relationship by then."

"She is very jealous, but she will share me with one other lover, so long as she's good for me and she knows who's the wife and who's the mistress."

We were silent again. The sun peeked out from behind the clouds and reflected off the car in front of us. I put on my shades. They improved the situation only slightly. I pulled over to the left to pass, and when I did, I noticed that Laura eased her right hand over to the door and held onto the handle. Her knuckles turned red and then white.

After we had safely passed the car and she had time to recuperate, she said, "I would like to go to the funeral with you, and I'm sorry for before."

The clouds covered the sun again. I pulled my shades off.

"Now, will you tell me about yourself?" I asked.

"I don't know. You seem to see way too much as it is."

I looked at her with an expression that said, *I don't buy it.*

"Well, the short version is that I'm working at FedEx while I finish up my master's at FSU. I should finish this fall or at least by the spring. I would like to have a practice in Tallahassee, but the field is so flooded now that it's doubtful that I will."

"What about family?" I asked.

"My dad lives in Tallahassee. He was a deputy with your dad at one point. He and my mother divorced when I was thirteen. My mom and my sister live in Pottersville."

"You too, right?"

"No. I just visit on the weekends. You think I would let a strange man come to the place where I live?"

"Strange?" I asked.

"You're taking me to a funeral on a date."

I gave her a small shrug, conceding the point.

"My mom teaches school, and Kim is going to attend TCC in the fall. My mom's brother is the president of the bank in Pottersville."

"Have you ever been married?" I asked.

"I'm not ready to discuss that yet."

"Okay. I understand."

"Have you?" she asked.

"Yes."

"Kids?"

"No."

"Me neither."

"Anything else I should know?" I asked.

"Yes. I've always been a sucker for compassionate men who look like Catholic priests and take me to funerals for our first date."

"That's good to know," I said.

THE FUNERAL HOME WAS ACTUALLY a small double-wide trailer. It was only slightly larger than my trailer, but it was way too big for the number of people who showed up for Ike Johnson's funeral. In addition to Laura and myself, there were four other people there—two elderly black ladies, his grandma and aunt, and two young people, his sister and his friend. The funeral home was named Jack's. It didn't even say Jack's Funeral Home on the sign—just Jack's. There were an uneven number of wooden pews on the right and left sides of the chapel. They needed another couple of coats of paint. The thin red carpet had stains and smelled like old socks.

I had wrestled with what to say all week. I felt it must be something about God's love and his ability to redeem the worst of situations and people.

I said, "God's mercies, the Bible says, are new every morning. That means that every single morning, God's infinite mercies are fresh and unused and waiting for us. They were waiting for Ike this morning no less than for you and me. You may say that Ike didn't live the way he should have and so surely God's mercies were not available for him. But I say that it is when we don't do what we should that we need mercy most, and it is also when mercy is most available to us.

"Grace is not what we deserve, but what we need. Justice gives us what we deserve, but grace gives us what we need. If God doesn't love Ike as much as he does you and me, then God's love is conditional and the Bible is wrong. But if the Bible is true, if Jesus was right, then God is love, filled with compassion even for those who make themselves his enemies. God is love.

"All I ask of you today is to believe and trust in the absolute love of God. A God, who like the father in Jesus' story of the prodigal son, welcomes us home even after we rejected him and ran away to a foreign land to get as far away from him as we could. This past Tuesday, Ike closed his eyes in this world and opened them in the next. He opened them on the familiar and loving eyes of God, who, as a father, loves Ike and loves you and me, his children. Johnathan Edwards, the famous Puritan preacher, was wrong. We're not sinners in the hands of an angry God. We're sinners in the hands of a merciful God. Dare to believe in love, in God. For God is love."

Throughout the entire message no one made eye contact with me except for Laura. That's not a complaint—even from ten feet away her eyes were incredible. She looked at me the way some people do when they hear you speak for God. It was a very dangerous thing, and I could tell that she was seeing far more than was there. Or perhaps more likely, she wasn't putting what she saw into the full context of my broken-down life. I closed with the hope for atonement that extends past the borders of this world and the few nice things that some of the inmates had said about Ike. The latter I stretched so far they almost broke.

After the funeral, the family thanked me and tried to pay me. As Laura and I were preparing to leave, the young man they had said was a friend of Ike's asked if he could talk to me, which was funny because until that moment he hadn't acknowledged my presence at all.

"Preacher, I loved Ike," he said, still looking down at the floor. "I even went to see him a couple of times in prison. But then something happened to him. Drugs, I think, but something else too. He got in over his head. I think they killed him. I wanted you to know."

"Who do you think killed him?" I asked.

"Whoever he was involved with," he said.

"What's your name?" I asked.

"Don Hall."

"Is there a number I can reach you at if I find something out or need to ask you some questions?"

He shook his head and walked away. After taking about five steps, he stopped, nearly turned around, but then continued walking. Laura was waiting for me in the back near the door.

"Do you believe all that?" Laura asked when we were back in the car.

"Believe all what?" I asked.

"All those things that you said in your sermon, which, by the way, was excellent."

"Yes, I do."

"How can you believe such hopeful things when the world is such a hopeless place?"

"How can I not? Besides, the world is filled with hope as

well. Grace shows up all the time; we just usually miss it when it does."

"What grace?"

"Dancing with you last night, that was a grace. And your peach perfume, that was a grace, too. A good night's rest is a grace, a rainy night, the weekend, the love of a parent, the loyalty of a friend. God speaks through all of these things and more. In fact, she speaks through the bad things as well—it's just usually things we don't want to hear."

"But how can you know all of this has meaning?" she asked. Her voice said she wanted to believe.

"I admit that it's wishful thinking," I said. "But certainly it is not blind faith—there is evidence. However, the fact that I find meaning in them says something, doesn't it?"

"I guess it does," she said. She shook her head slowly. "I've never met anyone quite like you." She reached over to the armrest where my right arm was and took my hand. "You did a good thing back there. You're a good man."

I didn't respond. I didn't have the heart to tell her how badly she was mistaken.

Lunch consisted of Chinese takeout from the Ming Tree, which we ate beneath the shade of a live oak tree in the park around Lake Ella. The park was brimming with signs of life—from both creatures and creation, the lively jazz issuing forth from the gazebo at its center adding to the effect.

For the rest of the afternoon, we clung to each other, savoring every moment. I could tell that the crisis dynamic of the funeral had had a profound effect on us. We were grasping for life, hoping to find something within each other. We were moving too fast, and I knew it, but I lacked the will to do anything about it.

TWENTY-FOUR

UNDER COVER OF A SMALL OAK GROVE, I parked on an old twin-path logging road in my dad's Explorer. Dan Fogelberg sounded rich and full on compact disc played on the vehicle's expensive stereo system. One of the few things I was left with after the divorce was a rather nice collection of CDs. Susan was never into music much, which was a downer while we were married but turned out to be most beneficial when we divorced. The only other thing that I escaped life with Susan with was my stereo system, which, combined with my CD collection, was worth more than the trailer in which I kept them.

I had taken Laura home after our day in Tallahassee, and now I was parked on the old logging road because it gave me a good view of the prison without being observed by Tower One. If I had been observed, the roving patrol would have driven out to investigate. If an officer had driven out, I would have been in trouble in more ways than one. There was, I discovered, a firearm in the vehicle, a fact I had just uncovered after searching underneath the seat for a flashlight. Firearms on state prison property were against the law. In addition to the Smith .38, Dad also had an expensive pair of binoculars. For the latter I was grateful. Without them, I would have seen nothing. As it turned out, because of them, I saw everything.

I sat there in the dark listening to Dan and thinking. My window was open slightly, and the woods all around me were alive. The bitter sweet smells of oak, pine, gopher apple, and honeysuckle wafted into the vehicle. I could hear a cricket symphony, the occasional bark of a dog, and the hum of mosquitoes. The last made me roll the window back up. I had done very few stakeouts in my time, but on each of them, amidst all the waiting and watching, I found myself doing a lot of thinking. I thought about my life up until this point—all the wasted time and money and all the pain, felt and inflicted. Of all the evil in all the world, addiction topped any list I would make.

The mood that my thoughts led me into was in sync with the music that was playing. Dan's album of lost love and deep wounds, *Exiles*, played softly in the background. I was usually thoroughly depressed when I finished listening to it, but it was a comfortable, soothing depression that never lasted too long—or long enough. I couldn't listen to it without thinking of Susan.

I thought of Laura, too. At times she tired me out, making me feel as if I were swimming upstream. At times she refreshed me like floating down that same stream on a soft inner tube. My thoughts turned to Anna, the woman by whom all women in my life were judged. It was not fair to compare other women to Anna, but, then, who said life was fair? Besides, Laura didn't do too badly against her.

Dan was depressing the hell out of me when I saw Captain Skipper near the front of the institution.

I could see Skipper walking an inmate into the sally port and getting into a van. Totally contrary to DOC policy, the inmate was not cuffed or shackled, and there was no armed officer accompanying them. The van pulled out of the institution heading down the two-mile county road to the main highway into town.

I followed.

Following someone was always very tricky for me, even if they didn't expect it. If they expected it, it was impossible. This was true anywhere, but especially in Pottersville, where there was very little traffic most of the time, and virtually no traffic at one in the morning. However, I had the advantage of being in my dad's vehicle, which would be unknown to the captain.

Nevertheless, I kept a safe distance.

The night, several degrees cooler than the day, was pleasant. The moon was nearly full, the sky clear, and the stars out. Dan continued to sing to me as I followed a full mile behind the van with my lights off. When the van reached the main highway, it turned toward town. About a quarter mile before I reached it, I turned my headlights on. As I came to a stop at the intersection, a car passed me. I followed closely behind the car that had fallen in right behind the van.

At the next intersection, which was two miles from Pottersville, the van turned left and the car between us continued straight.

When the van had a sufficient lead again, I turned and followed. The highway was desolate, with only the occasional house or trailer, most of which sat a good distance off the road under the cover of pine trees.

Unlike most places, there were no zoning laws in Pottersville, which meant that houses and trailers and even businesses were often side by side. On some streets, you would pass a hundred-and-fifty-thousand-dollar brick home with a fifteen-thousand-dollar single-wide house trailer next door. This road was such a place.

I gave the van as much of a lead as I possibly could, which forced me to use the binoculars. Maybe a mile and a half up on the right, the van signaled and then turned. It was a residence, and from the road only the mailbox and the first thirty feet of the driveway could be seen. However, this was Pottersville, and I knew who lived there, and it didn't make me happy.

The mailbox had small, neat letters reflecting in my headlights the name R. Maddox. The home belonged to Russ Maddox, the president of Potter State Bank and the wealthiest man in Potter County. He was also Laura's uncle.

Russ Maddox, as far as I knew, was a finicky, middle-aged bachelor. He had lived alone for as long as I had lived in Pottersville. He had more dollars than sense and a slightly feminine way about him, which certainly gave rise to more than one small-town rumor. He was rich, though, and from what I remembered, a pretty fair banker, as bankers go.

By the time I reached the driveway, the van had disappeared into the woods that served as Russ's front yard. I pulled the Explorer off the road about a half mile down from the driveway and moved through the woods towards the Maddox mansion, as it was known.

The light from the moon and the stars shown down so brightly that the pines almost cast shadows. There was no breeze, no visible movement of any kind. Moss hung still from the few tall cypress trees standing in the midst of the pines. The wire grass and weed undergrowth was thick and green in its summer prime. It came to just below my knees and made a swooshing sound as I trudged through it.

The undergrowth was so thick, in fact, that it camouflaged a fallen scrub oak tree. My right shin struck the tree full on, and I fell over it, suppressing a yelp of pain as I did. The ground was damp and the grass moist and much cooler than I had expected it to be.

When I reached the edge of the yard and the end of the woods, I could plainly see the front of the house. The interior of the house was dark, and the only illumination of the exterior was provided by a security light near the garage. The garage doors were closed. In front of them, I recognized Maddox's dusty-rose Lincoln. Parked beside it was a car I didn't recognize: a gray Toyota Tercel.

From where the yard began to the porch where Captain

Skipper and the inmate stood was a hundred feet. Skipper looked frustrated and angry as he continued banging on the imposing solid oak door with no response. From the distance that separated us, it took the sound of the knock about a second to travel to my ears. The inmate, who was in his prison uniform, looked from the back like nearly every other average-height, average-weight white inmate. Something, possibly the Holy Spirit—who speaks to me on the odd occasion—told me it was Anthony Thomas.

After about five minutes of banging on the door of the dark house, Skipper and the inmate turned to leave. When they did, I saw that it was indeed Anthony Thomas, which meant that it must have indeed been the Holy Spirit. Thomas walked like a drunk man.

Skipper helped him into the van and then jumped in himself. In another few seconds, the ignition started, the lights came on, and the van began to turn around in the massive driveway. I glanced at my watch. It was one forty-six.

I ran toward the Explorer, though not as quickly as I could have, remembering the tree my shin had kissed on the way to the house. I was running for two reasons: one, I wanted to follow the van; and two, if the captain turned left out of the driveway, he would pass the Explorer, which might make him suspicious.

And, if he was doing all of the things I thought he was doing, then he had good reason to be suspicious. It took me three minutes to reach the Explorer—far longer than Skipper needed to reach the end of the driveway. I paused at the edge of the woods to allow Skipper time to pass. When he didn't, I stepped out of the woods and looked both ways. Nothing. Then I jumped into the Explorer and continued past Maddox's place for about two miles. Nothing. I then turned around and drove back the way we had come.

He was gone.

TWENTY-FIVE

R ARELY IS WITNESSING AN EVENT, even an event that was supposed to be secret, as revelatory as it seems at the time it is witnessed. People who have witnessed plane crashes, automobile accidents, even assassinations, often know little more than those who were not there at all. I had seen Skipper take Thomas to Maddox's house last night and I had no idea what it meant. I had seen one isolated incident out of context. Of the several things it could mean, I had no way of knowing what it actually meant.

Under the clear blue skies that had appeared again when the sun rose Sunday morning, I was returning Dad's Explorer. He lived about fifteen minutes from me on a secluded five-acre farm. I tried to enjoy and appreciate the beautiful creations all around me as well as interact with the creator, but I could think of little else besides the events of the preceding night. I thought maybe I should tell Dad what was going on, but then again, I thought I probably should find out what was going on first. It seemed reasonable.

As I rounded the last curve and put my left blinker on, preparing to turn into Dad's driveway, the phone rang. At first I didn't know what it was. I thought maybe a bird had somehow gotten in the vehicle, because of the chirping sound. After the third ring, I deduced that it was a car phone—I'm nothing if not quick. I answered it as I came to a stop in front of my Dad's little red farmhouse.

"Hello," I said into the small phone.

"John," Dad said, "we need to talk. How long will it take you to get over here?"

"Not long," I said.

"Well, that's too long. Come as quick as you can."

"Sure, Dad, I'll be right there," I said.

I hung up the phone, got out of the car, and walked over and knocked on the front door.

He looked puzzled when he opened the door. He was wearing a red flannel shirt and a pair of blue jeans that were no longer very blue. His white tube socks matched his jeans—his laundry skills had never been his strong suit. His salt-and-pepper hair, which was receding only slightly, looked to have not seen a brush this morning. His brown eyes, which almost always looked sad, looked especially sad today.

"How the hell did you get here so fast?" he asked.

"I was in your driveway when you called. I'm returning your truck. It made the trip to Tallahassee seem like a vacation. Thanks."

"You're welcome. Come in. We need to talk," he said as he turned and walked down the short hallway that led to his den.

His den was actually a great room with very little furniture, the first clue that this was a bachelor's pad. There was a large stacked-stone fireplace on the back wall, which we faced as we entered the room. It had an unvarnished wood hearth that was filled with pictures and marksman trophies. Above the fireplace on the dark paneling wall the head of a large elk was mounted. On the other wall to the left, where the TV sat on a built-in shelf, hung other animal heads—deer, bear, boar, and moose. Dad was a real man's man. I was a real disappointment to him in this regard.

He took a seat in an old gray recliner that was positioned in front of the TV. It creaked when he plopped down in it. The only other place to sit was a dark gray couch in front of the wall opposite the fireplace, but to sit there was to sit behind him, so I stood.

The house smelled as it always smelled—dusty, slightly mildewed, and like a pack of wild dogs lived there. The pack-of-wild-dogs smell came from Wallace, an Irish setter who was currently occupying the couch—another reason I stood.

I glanced over my shoulder toward the kitchen, where I could see food on the small yellow table and dishes piled in the sink, a look not unfamiliar to me. I looked back at Dad. He was staring at the TV, which showed two boxers—a white one and a black one. The black one was being cruel and unusually punishing to the white one. Dad leaned forward slightly as if to hear what the announcers were saying, but the sound was muted.

"Dad, you okay?" I asked. He was always quiet, but now he seemed depressed, preoccupied. As always, his expressions and gestures were small and understated. He was the kind of man who would walk not run out of a burning building.

"Yes, I'm fine, but your mother's not," he said without his usual disgust when she was the topic of conversation.

They were divorced when I was fourteen, when her drinking had progressed to the point that it was no longer safe to leave my brother and me with her. He divorced her after almost eighteen years and about a million second chances. The patience of Job comes to mind. It was at this time that my sister Nancy divorced herself from our entire family and moved to Chicago. My brother Jake and I lived with Dad until, at seventeen, I started drinking, at which time I lived with Mom for a short time. It was during that time that I discovered that I didn't like her any better when I was drunk.

"I know that," I said. "I've never seen her when she was fine. Why are you telling me what I know so well?"

"She needs someone, and it needs to be you," he said, only looking away from the boxing and up at me momentarily.

"Dad, we've been over this. I'm a recovering alcoholic. That comes first. I have a difficult enough time staying sober myself. I cannot keep her sober as well. I'm sorry, but I'm not responsible for her sobriety, and I do not hold her responsible for mine."

"I'm not asking you to keep her sober," he said, his voice cracking a little. "I'm asking you to comfort her. She's dying, John."

"She's not dying," I said. "She's manipulating you, Dad."

"No," he said. "It's not like before. She really is dying. I talked to her doctor. She has cirrhosis of the liver and kidney failure. She won't last long."

"What?" I asked in shock, waves of guilt beginning to roll over me.

"She's dying," he whispered. "She doesn't have too much longer, though the doctor doesn't know for sure how long."

God forgive me, I'm a heartless son. She was reaching out for me on the phone the other night, and I was so hateful to her.

"Are you sure?" I asked again. "She called me the other night, but she sounded drunk, not sick."

"It's her medication. She's in the hospital. It makes her sound drunk, but she's really not."

"I can't believe it," I said. "I was so mean to her. She's dying."

Suddenly my dad stood up. He was still an imposing man, with a large frame that was agile for his age.

"Listen to me, Son," he said forcefully. "You are not to feel guilty for the other night. She told me what happened, but I told her that it was her fault. She's cried wolf too many times for any of us to believe her. Hell, I wouldn't have believed her if I hadn't talked to the doctor. It's not your fault, understand?"

That was a classic Jack Jordan statement. He said I was not to feel guilty, so that was that—I was not to feel guilty, as if I could just turn it off. However, it was classic also because he did his best to make sure that Jake and I were not manipulated by her when we were kids. He said not to feel guilty, and I didn't, and that's what bothered me the most. I felt guilty in my head. I knew I had been too harsh on the phone the other night. But in my heart I felt no guilt. I felt nothing.

"She needs someone right now," Dad said, "and that can't be me. Jake's not cut out for it, and the only thing Nancy's going to do is dance when she's dead. It can only be you. You're a minister, for God's sake."

"Yeah, I'm a minister. And, I would find it easier to minister to anyone in this world other than her."

"You can't do it?" he asked.

"I am going to do it," I said. "I just question how effective it will be."

"You'll do great, Son. You've got a gift. Now, sit down here, and let's watch some boxing." I knew he would say no more about Mom.

"I've got to go, Dad. I've got a service to do at the prison. Sorry."

"That's okay. By the way, how's the investigation going?"

"Barely going at all, I think, but it's hard to tell. You can go along and think you've got nothing, and then you've got everything. Who knows?"

"Well, you keep me posted. This is still my county."

"I will, Dad," I said. "And, about Mom, too."

"Yeah, thanks," he said but his mind was back on boxing.

*T*WENTY-SIX

"*I* KNOW OF NO OTHER WAY TO PUT THIS," I said, "so I am just going to come out and say it."

"Okay," Jasper said as he nodded his head up and down. He was as big an inmate as we had on the compound—well over six and a half feet tall and well over two hundred eighty pounds. He had skin the color of Tupelo honey and teeth to match. His hair was always unruly, and his two front teeth were separated by nearly a quarter of an inch, causing him to look like a black David Letterman.

"I hear that you're one of the main suppliers of drugs on the compound."

We were seated in my office in the chapel on Sunday morning around ten. My eyes stung, and I spoke, as best I could, between yawns. I needed some rest. I needed some sleep. I also needed to know if I had the AIDS virus floating around in my blood.

It was less than an hour until the service, and the sounds of the choir rehearsing could be heard from within the chapel sanctuary. The song they were rehearsing for today's service was "Power in the Blood." If Jasper Evans were dealing drugs, then I wanted him to deal himself out of that choir.

Would you be free from the burden of sin? There's power in the blood, power in the blood; Would you o'er evil a victory win? There's wonderful power in the blood.

I was anxious to get the conversation over because when I had arrived at my office, I had discovered in my mail another letter from the killer. I was dying to read the letter, but I had to wait until I was alone.

Since he didn't answer, I asked him again, "Are you?"

There is power, power, wonder-working power in the blood of the lamb. There is power, power, wonder-working power in the precious blood of the lamb.

He continued to look as if I had asked him to explain to me the theory of relativity. Finally, he shrugged, tilted his head to the left, and made an expression that said, *What can I say?*

He didn't seem overly concerned that I knew.

"How long has this been going on?" I asked.

"A while," he said.

"And you saw no conflict between what you're doing and being our minister of music?"

"Two different things. I know that doing dope is a sin, but I don't do it. And I only sell the small stuff. I don't sell no crack or shit like that. But, Brother Chaplain, I love to sing in the choir."

Would you be free from your passion and pride? There's power in the blood, power in the blood. Come for a cleansing to Calvary's tide? There's wonderful power in the blood.

"I know you do, and you are very good. In fact, I don't know what I am going to do without you, but you must realize that I can no longer allow you to lead the choir."

"I got to sing," he said emphatically as if he were saying, *I've got to breathe.*

"Certainly you can sing, but not in the choir and especially not as the choir leader."

"Why not?" he asked.

"As a leader you take on more responsibility and accountability to the group, not to mention God. You have to attempt to live in such a way as not to bring reproach on the Body of Christ."

"That what you do?" he asked.

"I certainly do the attempting part, but I do not succeed."

"How you can be the chaplain then?"

"The requirements do not involve being perfect."

Through my window I could see the inmates fortunate enough to receive a visit from their loved ones in the fenced-in visiting park. I felt guilty for not dropping everything and visiting my mother in the hospital right then, but I wasn't ready yet. I would have to prepare. Couples walked around the yard holding hands, families sat at tables eating ice cream, children ran and played—remove the chain-link fence and razor wire, and you'd have an average Sunday afternoon in any park in America.

"But you say you don't do it," he said, trying to understand.

Would you do service to Jesus your King? There's power in the blood, power in the blood. Would you live daily his praises to sing? There's wonderful power in the blood.

"Yeah, but I'm not out doing illegal things either. I mean, I am not as mature or integrated in most areas of my life as I want to be, but I'm not doing anything illegal or even immoral. That's the difference."

We were silent for a moment. "You say you don't sell the hard stuff?" I asked.

"That's right," he said with pride.

"Who does?"

"Don't nobody on the 'pound. It's too hard to get, too much trouble. Not many inmates can afford it anyway."

"Are you saying that there is no crack on the compound?"

"None that I know of. And I'd know. When it come to

drugs, I the man," he said defiantly. Then he realized whom he was talking to.

"Did you know Ike Johnson?"

"Knew of him."

"What can you tell me about him?"

"He was taken care of."

"What do you mean?"

Jasper rolled his eyes in exasperation over having to explain so much to this naive chaplain.

"Somebody took care of him. But it wasn't no inmate. It had to be an officer. He do whatever the hell he want. He get high every day, and he stopped getting it from me a long time ago."

"Is there another inmate he could have gotten it from?"

"No."

"How do you get the drugs that you sell?"

"Can't say, sir. Get lotsa people in trouble. People that can give me a world of trouble if they want to."

"So you're saying that it comes from the staff?"

"I ain't saying."

"Okay. If you think of anything else you can tell me about the drug trade inside here, I would sure like to know. You coming to church this morning?"

"Am I going to be singing?"

"No," I said.

"No," he said.

There is power, power, wonder-working power in the blood of the lamb. There is power, power, wonder-working power in the precious blood of the lamb.

As soon as he left, I tore open the letter. "Chaplain, I not going to tell you again. This is your last warning. I will kill the bitch if you don't back off. I'll kill you too. It's going to hurt. Now's a good time to take some time off."

I read and reread it several times. Maybe the letter wasn't from the murderer. It could be from a witness or about something that was totally unrelated. I wondered if

Anna was in any real danger. I thought about taking more precautions, and, as it turned out, I should have.

"TODAY WE ARE HERE TO RECEIVE the holy Eucharist," I said, beginning my Sunday morning chapel communion service. All week I had been thinking, even obsessing, on the power of blood. I was interested in seeing how it would affect what I was going to say.

"We are here to eat the body and to drink the blood of Christ. On the night of the feast of the Passover, Jesus revealed to his disciples that he was about to become their Passover. His blood would be shed for an entirely new Passover. This was, of course, very familiar to them. Their minds raced back to the time when the people of their great nation were little more than a band of slaves in Egypt. Daily they cried out to God for deliverance. God answered them after four hundred years—for God is never in a hurry. God's answer came in the form of a deliverer.

"God's unlikely deliverer was a Hebrew shepherd who had been wandering in the wilderness for forty years. His name was Moses, and his mission was to go and tell the pharaoh that God said, "Let my people go." He did. Pharaoh, however, was resistant to this idea, so God sent plagues, each one an affront to the gods of the Egyptians. Pharaoh, however, continued to resist.

"So it was that on the Hebrews' final night as Egyptian slaves, God sent a death angel to kill the firstborn of every family. This would be the final straw that would break the back of the pharaoh, and he would then indeed let God's people go. God's instructions to the Hebrews were for each family to sacrifice a lamb and smear his shed blood over their doors. Thus, seeing the blood, the death angel would pass over and allow their firstborn to live. Because of the blood, the death angel passed over—only because of the blood.

"So when Jesus said that his shed blood would be the

beginning of a brand new Passover, the disciples understood him to say that they would be spared from eternal death because of what he was about to do. Christ, our Passover, shed his blood for us. As we prepare to receive the body and blood of our Lord Jesus Christ, I want to remind each of you that there is power in the blood. There is power in his blood. We are about to receive Jesus' own blood, and as we do, we will receive forgiveness for our sins, restoration of our inheritance, and eternal life. The death angel will pass over and not come near us. There is power in the blood.

"The shedding of blood represents covenant. A covenant is a sacred and binding agreement that demands the death of the one who breaks it. When a man and a woman enter into the covenant of marriage, the consummation of that covenant involves the shedding of the woman's blood.

"God's grace is not cheap. It is costly. When we partake of the cup of Christ, we are accepting the costly gift of forgiveness. Realizing that we could not pay the price ourselves, we accept Christ's free, but costly, gift. We acknowledge that it is only through the painful shedding of blood that our sins are blotted out. There is power in the blood. Life is in the blood. Death is in the blood, too. Christ exchanges the life in his blood for the death in ours.

"So come to the altar and receive the body of our Lord and the cup of Christ, and as you do, receive healing, recovery, and redemption. And also, too, remember what it cost Jesus."

Serving communion to my congregation, the inmates of Potter Correctional Institution, I dipped the wafer, which was his body, into the cup of juice, which was his blood, saying, "The body that was broken for you. The blood that was shed for you"—all the while wishing, praying that it were true.

After serving everybody else, I partook of the body and

blood of Christ, praying: *Let your blood become mine. Life for death. Give me life, for I receive and accept your death. Please don't let me have HIV, but if I do, please cleanse it now from my blood with yours.*

ᴀFTER CHURCH, I DECIDED to look around the medical building again. I knew the body had been hidden in the closet there. I knew that Johnson, Jacobson, and Thomas all spent a great deal of time there and were all involved in this thing. Whatever this thing was.

"Hey, Chaplain," Nurse Anderson greeted me loudly as I approached the medical building. She was standing outside smoking. She was a large attractive woman with bleached blond hair, green eyes the color of lime Jell-O, and bright red lips.

"Good afternoon," I said. "How are you today?"

"Just fine, thank you. How are you?" she said. Smoke came out of her mouth as she talked. The moment the last word came out of her mouth, she brought the cigarette back to her mouth. In contrast to the dainty Capris that Sandy Strickland smoked, Anderson smoked full-sized Winstons. She held the pack, along with a lighter and a cup of coffee in a paper cup with large red lipstick stains on it, in her left hand.

"Fine, thanks. Is there anyone in the infirmary today?"

"Yes, we have two convicts today," she said. She waved the Winston with her hand as she talked. Her gray uniform matched the buildings around her, and its wrinkles matched those around her mouth as she sucked on the cigarette.

Behind us a steady stream of inmates, returning from the chapel, library, or dining hall, made their way back to the dorms. A couple of them remarked on my message as they went by. Many of them spoke or waved to Nurse Anderson.

She was warm and friendly, brightening up their day with her sweet smile.

"Don't you mean inmates?" I said with a smile.

"No, these are definitely convicts," she said. She spoke more loudly than was necessary, and regardless of where I stood, she moved toward me and invaded my space.

"Good for them," I said.

"Good for us," she said and laughed. When she laughed, her large breasts bounced up and down with the buoyancy of a cork in the Apalachicola River.

"This is a pretty popular place, isn't it?" I asked.

"You have no idea," she said with a wink. "A lot of these men just need some feminine TLC, if you know what I mean."

I hoped I didn't. "So, you all are consistently busy?"

"It's always busy," she said after a long drag, "but at night, for some reason, things really get crazy."

"ATTENTION ON THE COMPOUND," a loud voice said over the PA system. The words echoed off the buildings. "RECALL. INMATES RETURN TO YOUR DORM. RECALL. INMATES RETURN TO YOUR DORM." The stream of inmates behind us became a river of blue. Many of the inmates carried paperback books in one hand, a few had their Bibles, nearly all were talking and laughing.

"Aren't you usually on the night shift?" I asked.

"Yes, but we're all working overtime to prepare for the ACA inspection," she said. "I work midnights, but Sandy, she runs the show. She's one of the most competent nurses I've ever seen, both medically and administratively. She's the best. She really does care."

"I saw her in action when the inmate was killed in the sally port. She was very impressive. Cool as a cucumber under extreme pressure."

"I've heard the same about you," she said with a small nod in my direction and a quick wink.

"Thank you. That was an awful thing that happened, wasn't it?"

She took a big gulp of her coffee. "Wasn't it though? I just can't believe it happened. He was here the night before it happened. I talked with him for a pretty good while. We weren't that busy. I just can't believe it. It's really freaked me out," she said.

"I can imagine," I said. "Death is always difficult, but when it's so brutal and so bizarre, it's even worse."

She took her last puff, a long, slow drag that caused her cheeks to grow hollow—well, hollower. Her face said that it was as satisfying as she thought it would be. She ground the butt down into the sand of the ashtray.

I always thought that smoking, unlike alcohol, involved much more than just an addiction to a drug. It was oral, busy, and nervous. Smokers enjoyed the lighting, the extinguishing, and especially the fondling of the cigarette.

"Who was in the infirmary that night?" I asked.

She thought for a minute. "Let me see," she said, "seems like it was only Thomas, Jacobson, and Johnson. I think that's right. We usually have more than that, so it sort of stands out, you know? Especially after what happened."

"Anthony Thomas?" I asked.

"Yes, I believe so. I mean, I know he was in there. He's always down here." She leaned in and whispered, "He's in love with Sandy." She leaned back and continued in her normal tone, which for her was loud. "I don't think there was anyone else that night. Come on, let's go back there and take a look at the log, then I can tell you for sure."

"Sure," I said.

She set her coffee cup down on the counter of the nurses' station and began flipping through the pages of the log book. Her movements were awkward and overstated like her speech. "Just Johnson and Jacobson according to this," she said, looking at the log, "but I know Thomas was here. I remember. Oh well, somebody forgot to write it down."

"Somebody forgot to write it down?" I asked, my voice revealing my skepticism.

"I know. That shouldn't have happened, and it usually doesn't," she said, then thought about what she had said and added, "At least I don't think it does. But, I know he was here. I saw him with my own two baby blues."

"Blues?" I asked.

"Oh," she said loudly, "I have colored contacts on." She rolled her eyes.

"So Johnson, Jacobson, and Thomas were the only ones here last Monday night, right?"

"Right. I'm sure of it."

"Who took the trash out that morning?" I asked.

She gave me a large shrug. "That's the sixty-four-thousand-dollar question, isn't it?" She leaned in closer to me and whispered, "I can tell you who it wasn't. It wasn't Jones. He was cleaning up a urine sample for me. I saw the bags when I went and got him, and when we went back, they were gone. Oh, and it wasn't me. I was with Jones the whole time."

"Did you see him go into the caustic storage room at anytime that morning?" I asked.

"When we saw that the trash had disappeared, he tried to look into the caustic closet, but it was locked. He said it was unlocked just an hour before, but I tried it, too, and it *was* locked."

I went by the infirmary and prayed with the two inmates, who were really not inmates at all, but convicts, before I left medical. When I walked back out into the late afternoon sun, I saw spots. I considered going to confinement, but a voice inside my head said for me to go home instead. As it turns out, it was the voice of God. Another voice said I should go and visit my mom, and I tried to pretend that it was the devil's voice, though I knew it wasn't.

*T*WENTY-SEVEN

*L*ONELINESS EATS AWAY AT YOU from within and without simultaneously. Within, it's the dull ache of emptiness and the sharp pains of hunger—hunger for another. Without, it's the dull hum of silence when noise stops and the sharp pains of a body needing to hold and to be held. The only thing wrong with going home was that I would be alone. Actually, there were other things wrong with going to my current home: like the fact that it was not a home at all, but a trailer. And the fact that it was not just a trailer, but a butt-ugly trailer with several inches of crud on it, alone, like me, in the middle of a prairie of poverty around a lonely, dried-up palm tree. However, the worst thing about going home was being alone.

When I got home, there was a powder-blue '66 Ford Mustang parked in my driveway. I was wrong; it was not parked. It was backing out. I pulled up behind and blocked it in. I wanted to know who was at my home when I wasn't. I honked my horn to keep the car from hitting me. The driver slammed on the brakes, pulled back into the driveway, and got out of the car. It was Laura. Like a person out of uniform, I hadn't recognized her out of her truck.

I backed up and pulled in beside her. The gravel crunched under my tires.

"You scared I was going to leave without saying hello?" she asked when I opened the door of my truck. The sound of her voice was barely audible over the creak of my door.

"Something like that."

"Where have you been? I called earlier, and since I was out driving anyway, I decided to stop by."

"Unlike most people, my primary workday is Sunday."

"Oh, that's right. I forgot."

"Can you stay for a while, or do I have to block you in again to prevent you from leaving?"

"I *am* leaving, and that's why I stopped by, but I can stay for a little while."

"You're leaving. That's sort of sudden. Usually women I'm seeing don't leave me until at least the second or third date."

"Relax, you're not getting rid of me that easily. I'm just going home now."

"Words cannot describe my embarrassment at having you see this place," I said when we were seated in my living room, each of us with a tall glass of iced tea.

"Don't be; it's your place. It's a part of who you are, or at least who you are becoming,"' she said.

"That is truly a scary thought," I said.

"Not at all. It says that you're a survivor. You've gone through the most difficult thing that you are likely ever to go through, and you are surviving. Granted, it's not in good shape, but it's neat and as clean as you could make it and, in some unique way, homey. It says that you are independent, strong, and resourceful. You could live with other people in better homes, but you do not. You need space—autonomy."

"This trailer says all that to you?"

"And more."

"I agree. It is a part of who I am becoming or have become.

I got into the ministry to serve God and to help people. I lost sight of that as my church in Atlanta got bigger and bigger. I had to have increasingly nicer clothes, cars, houses, and stuff to keep up with the Joneses—my congregation. I was never about that. And, now that my world has fallen apart, I am a prison chaplain, which, like you said, is for those who can't make it on the outside. A tin man living in a tin box. But, I'm happier. And, I'm doing what God created me to do."

"You are anything but a tin man."

"I'm nobody. Who are you? Are you nobody, too?"

"As a matter of fact, I am. I'm a thirty-two-year-old virgin who drives a FedEx truck for a living and who has only recently decided what she wants to do when she grows up."

"You're a *virgin*?" I asked, shocked beyond description.

"I have intimacy problems, in case you haven't noticed."

"No, I hadn't noticed," I said, and we both laughed, which is what we needed to do at the moment. "I *would* like to know more," I said.

"Yes, I know you would, and that scares the hell out of me. But I want to tell you more. I want to move forward, but there couldn't be a more unnatural thing for me to do."

"I understand," I said.

"I think you really do. I think I can trust you, but I want to know."

"You want to know you can trust me?"

"Yes."

"You realize that you can't."

She stood. "I can't trust you?" she asked, her voice quivering.

"No. Sit down. That's not what I meant. What I meant was that you can't know that you can trust me. You can never know that you can trust someone until they have repeatedly kept your trust, which they cannot do until you first give them your trust."

"So I'm damned if I do and damned if I don't."

"You're damned if you don't trust somebody, not necessarily me, but someone."

"I usually trust the wrong people," she said with an ironic laugh.

"Maybe, but I figure you've never completely given your trust to anyone, so in that respect, you've never truly trusted the right or the wrong people. But to live is to learn to trust—God, others, yourself."

"You trust yourself?" she asked with the awe of a child. Gone was her adversarial demeanor and quick-witted verbal cuts.

"I trust me with everything but liquor, but I trust myself not to trust myself where liquor is concerned."

"I am getting to the place where I can truly trust me, but it will be a while for God and people, men especially. With the possible exception of you."

"It makes sense to make exceptions for exceptional people," I said and laughed.

She smiled, but not much. It was not the time for jokes.

"I'm sorry. You're trying to be intimate, and I'm trying to make it easier for you, and that can't be done," I said.

"I appreciate it, but you're right. It's hard, and it has to be. It's no small thing that I'm contemplating. I've known you such a short time, but I really do feel like I can trust you. It's just that my judgment has been so bad before."

"I know."

"I want to share who I am with you, and I think I can, but. . ."

But, what?" I asked.

"I need to know if you feel like we might have something here. I think I can trust you, but if this isn't going anywhere, then I don't want to do it."

We were silent. I tried to take in everything, to be fully present in the moment.

Finally, she said, "Well, what do you think?"

"I think," I began very slowly—I was walking on eggshells with land mines beneath them, "that you would be a lot of work. You are, to use the words of Jesus, 'a treasure hidden in a field.' You are going to . . . *We* are going to take a lot of work."

She looked down. I placed my hand under her chin and lifted her head up. I gazed into her eyes and caught a glimpse of her soul.

"You would be a lot of work, but, in my estimation, very worth it. You should be encouraged that I don't have unrealistic expectations going in. It means I will be less likely to become disillusioned later."

She smiled a wide, full smile. The skin under her chin tightened. I wanted to kiss her, but it was not the time. She had much more that she needed to say. Kissing, while very nice, would hinder true intimacy. I knew that. I had used it for just such a thing many times before.

"I'm trusting you," she said as she pulled my hand from underneath her chin and held it in her lap, "with my secrets. Which means I am choosing to trust you."

I nodded my head slowly.

"I'm the child of an alcoholic. My dad is a recovering alcoholic. For as long as I can remember, Dad was an alcoholic. I have not one memory of my dad ever really being with me, like you are right now. I feel your total attention."

"You have it," I said.

"I never once felt like my dad was around, even when he was. Most of the time he would get drunk and pass out on the couch, but not always. Sometimes he would get violent, slap Mom around a little, but that didn't happen very often."

"I am so sorry," I said.

She stared off into something I could not see.

"How are you feeling now?" I asked.

"So far so good, but there's more."

"There always is," I said.

"On a few occasions when he was really drunk," she began, her lower lip quivering as she did, ". . . I'm just not ready. Is that okay?"

"Of course," I said.

She looked deep into my eyes, searching for reassurance. I looked back. When she found what she was looking for, she leaned forward to kiss me. When she was within an inch of kissing me, she stopped, allowing me to kiss her.

I did.

The kiss was everything it should have been at that moment. It was gentle and powerful, a touch that offered each of us the reassurance we needed. I felt at home in her arms, and I could tell that she felt the same.

After we embraced and kissed and cuddled for a while longer, we cooked dinner together. We also ate together, cleaned up the dishes together, and went for a walk together. Eventually, the evening reached its inevitable conclusion.

She was preparing to leave when I said, "Would you sleep with me tonight?"

She hesitated, considering me intently.

"Before you answer or slap me, let me explain. I was married for nearly ten years, during which time I got used to sleeping with someone. Since that time, for a little over a year now, I've not had a good night's sleep. What I'm asking is for you to sleep in the same bed with me. I am not asking you to make love with me. I just need someone to hold me while I sleep—someone to watch over me. Maybe we can keep each other's demons at bay tonight."

"I will" was all she said.

We were lying together in my bed—she propped up on two pillows, I with my head in her lap. She held my head tenderly, as if it were precious to her, and ran her fingers along my cheeks and through my hair. At one point I thought she was going to sing to me.

Instead, she said, "Tonight when you asked me to sleep with you, before I knew what you meant, although I guess I suspected, I seriously considered it, something I've never done before. You're unlike any man I've ever met."

I fell asleep hearing such things and slept like a baby full of mother's milk, safe in its mother's arms. I slept better than I had in a long time—until three, when she woke me up to tell me the sheriff was on the phone for me.

*T*WENTY-EIGHT

"*I* THOUGHT PRIESTS HAD TO SLEEP ALONE," Jake said when I arrived at Russ Maddox's house. Jake and I were brothers. So were Cain and Abel. He was waiting for me in the driveway, standing with his chest out and his arms hanging wide of his body to make room for his muscles and his gun. He had obviously watched one too many Western movies.

Jake Jordan, two years my junior, also had brown eyes and light-brown hair. Although we were both roughly six feet tall, he outweighed me by almost fifty pounds. His dark green deputy sheriff's uniform shirt was at least two sizes too small, and his pants puckered and pulled at the pleats.

"We're not having this discussion, Jake. But I will say that I let my conscience be my guide."

"You should know better than to listen to *your* conscience by now," he said with a sneer. I noticed part of a toothpick hanging from the corner of his mouth.

"Where's Dad?" I asked, too tired for another verbal sparring match.

"He's inside doing what the sheriff is supposed to do when there's been a crime committed." Jake rubbed the wooden handle of his pistol with his index finger. The small, tender caresses were those of a lover.

When Jake and I were growing up, we both competed for the approval of our childhood hero, our dad. We both received Dad's approval; however, I received more and was more like a friend than a son. Jake hated me for it. When I moved away, Jake moved in, and when I left law enforcement to enter the ministry, it seemed as though I was no longer a factor in the dysfunctional equation. However, ever since I had moved back to Pottersville, Jake's insecurities had kicked into overdrive. He perceived me as a threat and was even more obnoxious than usual. Had he possessed the slightest insight, he would've known that I was an outsider and would forever remain outside, the prodigal that could never fully return home.

"Why are you out here?" I asked.

"Waiting for you," he said as if it were obvious. "I needed to talk to you." He removed the toothpick from his mouth and twirled it between his thumb and forefinger.

"How thoughtful, Jake," I said. "I'm touched."

"Yeah, in the *head*," he said and then began laughing as if the joke were the funniest thing he'd ever heard. "Anyway," he pointed the toothpick at me, "I wanted to warn you to be careful. You seem to be doing okay now, and I wouldn't want you to lose it again. Besides, you've embarrassed Dad enough. Think of him. Back off, and play it safe."

I started walking toward the house.

"Wait," he said. He put the toothpick back in his mouth and dropped his hand down again where it hung wide of his body. "I'm serious. You've been gone a long time. Dad's getting older now. You don't realize how much he depends on me. He knows he can count on me." He began to finger the butt of his gun again. "Anyway, he thinks that you're a pretty good investigator since you worked on those two big cases in Atlanta. The thing is he doesn't realize that a lot of people worked on those and that you actually screwed one of them up pretty bad. I want what's best for Dad. And I don't want to see you on the sauce again."

"Thanks for your sincere concern, Bro," I said. "Now, tell me what's going on here?"

"Russ is dead," he said emotionlessly.

"Dead?" I asked. "When?"

"Probably sometime last night," he said.

"How?"

"Not sure," he said. "But it looks like he was murdered. It's neat, but it still feels like murder. Pretty exciting, isn't it? Two years without a homicide in Potter County, and now we have two in a week."

I nodded.

"When are you going to see Mom?" he asked.

"Soon," I said. "I'm not exactly sure when. How about you?"

He shook his head. "I just can't deal with that kind of shit. I mean, I know she's . . . I think Dad and I are going to ride over together. Maybe next weekend. I don't know."

"Does Nancy know?" I asked.

"Dad said he was going to call her tomorrow, but I told him he shouldn't. Hell, she ain't even a part of this family anymore."

I waited, but he had nothing else to say. "Well, let's go in," I said.

"You think you can handle it?" he asked in disdain. "Don't forget Atlanta. What was the name of that girl you got killed?"

"I realize," I said, "that I'm not a professional deputy of a big-time sheriff's department like you, but I'll try my best to handle it. Besides, if I can't, you're a trained professional. You'll know what to do."

Inside, Jack Jordan, looking tired and older than he

should have, spoke with the county coroner in hushed tones that reminded me of church. His wrinkled clothes and uncombed hair said that he, too, had been in bed and he, too, lived alone.

The body of Russ Maddox was slumped over in an uncomfortable-looking wingback chair covered in plastic and positioned in front of the television. Like the chair, the entire house looked uncomfortable. If the house were lived in, I couldn't tell it.

"John," my dad said when he saw me.

"Dad." I nodded my head. Neither one of us was what you might call a gabber.

I walked over to the chair where Russ's obese body sat crumpled. His head hung down, the fat gathering beneath his third chin and in large rolls of white blubber around his midsection. He was wearing a white silk robe, which gaped open revealing white silk boxer shorts and a tight white silk T-shirt. He looked like the Stay-Puff Marshmallow Man. Beside his chair stood an ornately carved wooden TV tray with an open bottle of wine, a wineglass, and a small china plate with caviar and crackers on it.

My eyes widened when I noticed the two long, sharp kitchen knives lying near the plate. The knives seemed to be spaced too far apart from the plate, and they were positioned funny. It was just an impression, but it looked as if they had been added later. I looked back at Maddox. There was no sign of violence or trauma anywhere on his body. In stark contrast to the last death I had witnessed, there was not a single drop of blood.

"That *is* caviar, isn't it?" I asked.

"Yes, it is," the medical examiner said.

"Is it generally eaten with large carving knives?"

"Curious, isn't it?" he asked.

"You ever been accused of exaggeration, Roger?" I asked.

He smiled, but did not comment. I looked over at Dad. He just shrugged.

"Any prints?" I asked.

"On the bottle, the glass, the plate, the tray—everything but the knives. They're clean," Dad said.

"I did find small traces of the light powder residue that is usually associated with surgical latex gloves," Roger stated as if he had said that he had found wine in the wine bottle.

"Well, now," I said.

"Yeah," said Dad. I could tell we were thinking the same thing.

"Is it okay to look around?" I asked no one in particular.

"Everything has been dusted, if that's what you mean," Jake responded. He took his toothpick out of his mouth again and tucked it into the left breast pocket of his deputy's shirt.

"You can take a look," Dad said and then gave Jake a look that said *back off*.

I walked across the sculpted Berber carpet, which covered the entire house save the mahogany floors in the kitchen, dining, and foyer areas. In the kitchen, brass pots, colanders, and ladles hung over the butcher-block island. Like the counters, there was nothing on it, and it had been cleaned to the point of shining. Expensive wineglasses were suspended under the glassed cabinet housing his fine, and I do mean fine, china.

I walked out of the spotless kitchen into the formal living room, continuing my journey through the showpiece of the Potter County Tour of Homes. Every single piece of upholstered furniture sported carefully placed afghans, as if being preserved for an event yet to come, and every piece of wooden furniture was fitted with a sheet of custom-cut glass to cover the top. In fact, with the exception of the dead body in the living room, the entire house could have been a fine furniture store showroom.

Evidently the crime-scene investigation was nearly concluded when I had been called. The house was virtually empty. I did, however, pass by a young female deputy as I was walking up the stairs, but she didn't seem to be investigating. I smiled politely at her. She didn't smile back. She obviously felt the need to establish that she was a serious crime-scene investigator. She convinced me.

The second story of the house was as immaculate as the first—nothing out of place and no sign that human beings lived there. Every hallway had a long plastic runner covering it, which caused my shoes to make a noise similar to that of a small Skilsaw as I shuffled along them.

There were three bedrooms. If someone had ever spent a single night in any of them, I couldn't tell it. The one I assumed was Russ's, because of its size and attached bathroom, was nearly two times the size of my trailer. The bed, a king-size monstrosity, was at least four feet off the floor with massive spiral posts at each corner and looked to be mahogany. The other furniture in the room seemed to be an eclectic gathering of priceless antiques gleaned from different parts of the world: an armoire, tallboy, full-length freestanding mirror, vanity, and dresser. I was certain their value could have purchased any modest home.

The walk-in closet was neatly organized. The back wall was covered with shoe bins from floor to ceiling: each containing a pair of polished shoes. Each side of the closet had a rack with clothes hanging on it, suits and dress shirts mainly. I looked around the closet and the bedroom and found nothing unusual. In the bathroom, however, I did.

Under the expensive porcelain sink with gold and brass fittings, there were three very large jars of Vaseline, four tubes of K-Y personal lubrication jelly, and two rather large boxes of condoms. This was very unusual since Russ was thought to be about as sexual as the lint that gathered in the large black hole of his navel. It was also an inordinate amount. Unless these were tributes to wishful thinking, there should have been more Russ Maddox grist in the Pottersville rumor mill.

The other two bedrooms were a lot like the larger one, only smaller. They were showroom-clean and decorated like the ones seen in magazines. I made what I thought was a pretty thorough search of the rooms and then went back into the master suite. Looking through Russ's drawers was like shopping at Macy's. Everything looked new, and there were several packages of underwear and socks that had never been opened. I thought how embarrassed I would be if some-one were searching through my drawer of holey underwear and dirty socks. I walked over and looked under the bed. It was spotless. I was beginning to think that Russ Maddox was a little on the obsessive-compulsive side, but it was just an impression, and I knew the dangers of formulating rash opinions.

After finding nothing on the back side of the headboard and the mirror, I opened the two doors of the armoire, expos-ing a 32-inch television, VCR, and camcorder. On a shelf under the TV and VCR, there were several videotapes. The movies ranged from *The Sound of Music* to *Rocky*. I pulled a few of the tapes out of the boxes. Their labels matched the boxes. I popped a few of them into the VCR. They were what they appeared to be. As I started to replace them, I noticed that behind them, lying on their sides, were four of the oversized Disney movie boxes. I pulled them out. There was *Bambi, Dumbo, Beauty and the Beast,* and *The Lion King.* I stood them up vertically alongside the other tapes and closed the armoire doors.

I started to leave the room, and then it hit me. Why would somebody as obsessive-compulsive as Maddox lay the Disney tapes horizontally behind the others? When I saw them, I had figured it was just because they were too tall to fit, but putting them back like the others disproved that. It also proved that there was room for them. I also wondered why a man like Russ Maddox would have Disney movies anyway. I went back and opened the doors again and then the Disney boxes. The labels on the tapes corresponded with the boxes, but they were typed homemade labels and not the printed labels that usually were affixed to tapes in the dubbing houses. Homemade labels would have made sense if the tapes were copied, but if they were copies, they wouldn't be in the Disney boxes.

I placed one in the VCR. The TV screen blinked from royal blue to a shot of two men having sex on the bed in the very room in which I stood. The camera seemed to be shooting the video footage from where it still sat on the shelf beside the VCR. The room was well lit, and the camera was obviously an expensive one because the picture was crystal clear. It showed a fat white man from the side hunched over a thin black man. The fat white man was Russ Maddox. He was moaning and occasionally blurting out obscenities. The other man, whose face I could not see, was making noises, too, but his seemed to be pain rather than pleasure. However, the two are hard to distinguish sometimes, and I could have been projecting.

In another minute or so, Russ had climaxed and collapsed, the black man disappearing beneath his blubber. I hit the fast forward button on the machine, and in a few seconds the black man beneath Russ began moving slightly and Russ finally rolled off him. The black man jumped up. When he did, he came face-to-face with the eye of the camera. I paused it on the familiar face. It was Ike Johnson.

As I stopped the tape, I heard a voice from the hall.

"JJ, your dad would like to see you downstairs," the serious young female officer said when she reached the door to the bedroom.

"Thank you. I'll be right down," I said. Quickly replacing

the tapes in their original place behind the others, I closed the armoire and walked down the stairs.

Downstairs I found my dad and brother in the living room talking. The body, along with everyone else, was gone.

"JJ, the reason I called you is probably obvious. We haven't had a homicide investigation in this county in several years. And this week we have two mysterious murders. Do you think they could be related?" Dad said.

"I think it's possible," I said and felt guilty for not telling him everything. I wasn't even sure why I didn't. It was probably the mode I was in—I wouldn't say anything to anyone until I knew more. I hated to be less than honest with him, but it wasn't the first time. "Like you say, it seems a little much to just be a coincidence. Was Russ murdered?"

"It looks like it. Like maybe he was poisoned. We'll know for sure in a day or so. What have you found out about the other murder so far?"

"It's still just bits and pieces now, but I hope to put it all together soon."

"Why the hell do they have you looking into it?" Jake asked. "Aren't you just the convict preacher?"

"Yes, I am. And I'm not conducting the investigation I'm just assisting in it."

"With your father-in-law?" Dad asked.

"Yes, Tom Daniels," I said.

"I'm just glad to hear you're using your God-given abilities again. It's been too long. You are a damn fine investigator. I'd like to have you in our department."

When I got out of law enforcement and went into the ministry, it broke my dad's heart. Since that time, he and Jake had been extremely close, and I had been the odd man out.

"Thank you," I said, "but I really am just assisting. I love my work as a chaplain."

Jake snickered softly. I didn't look his way.

Dad ignored him, too, and said, "If there is a connection,

I wonder what in the hell it could be. I mean, what do a black convict and a white fat-cat banker have in common?"

"If their deaths are connected, we will find out what they had in common. And, thanks for calling me, Dad. It really means a lot."

"Let's get out of here," he said. He looked at his watch. "Rudy's opens in another ten minutes. Let's go get some breakfast together."

"You two go ahead. If you don't mind, I'm going to look around some more first and then I better get back home."

Jake laughed again. Dad smiled and said, "That's right, you weren't alone." The pride in his voice was obvious.

"Well, it's not what you think or what Jake thinks anyway. But this man was her uncle, and I need to go and tell her."

"Okay, Son. We'll let you know something whenever we do. You do the same, okay?"

"Yes, sir," I said.

They left.

I went and took another look upstairs, got the tapes, and went home.

TWENTY-NINE

"I THINK CAPTAIN SKIPPER has been supplying inmate prostitutes to Russ Maddox. And Ike Johnson was one of them," I said. I was sitting with Merrill and Anna in her office on the morning of the longest Monday of my life, a day which I began in the company of my friends and ended in the hands of my enemies.

Anna looked pretty this morning, though a little sleepy. And Merrill looked as he always looked, like he didn't have a clue as to what was going on around him and didn't care. But it was just a look. I had seen him look the same way just prior to nearly killing a classmate of ours who had attempted to rape his little sister when we were in high school. Anna did not look as devastatingly beautiful as she usually did. I wondered if it were just that my eyes were still full of Laura. I looked at her again and determined that's exactly what it was.

"You want to run that by me one more time?" Anna said.

"You heard me. The two people who have died recently both have ties to Skipper and each other."

"What do you mean?" Anna asked.

I told them. When I finished, they were both silent. I could see the wheels turning in Anna's head. I knew that wheels were also turning in Merrill's head, but I couldn't see them.

"It's just not possible," Anna said at last. "There's no way Skipper could pull it off. It would take . . ."

"Help from higher up," Merrill said.

I shrugged. "It's a possibility."

"At least," Anna added. "But he couldn't do it without getting caught."

"He could do it without help from Patterson or Stone. They're never here during the late shift. Besides, he is getting caught," I said. "We're catching him."

"No *we* are not. I am just a weak little woman," Anna said.

Merrill and I both laughed as hard as we ever had at anything.

"I'm serious," she said. "We need to call FDLE and let them handle it."

"I plan on telling FDLE, and the inspector, as far as that is concerned, but I need to know a little more first."

"Like what?" Anna asked.

"Like what else is on the tape," I said. "I need something that implicates Skipper—money swapping hands or him on video. So far there's nothing that directly connects him to any of it. I need more evidence."

"How are you going to get that?" Anna asked.

"I was hoping you would have an idea."

"You're joking, right?"

I shrugged. "I would be happy to entertain any suggestions either of you might have."

"Why don't you get his niece's help? You've slept with her recently, haven't you?" Merrill asked.

"As recently as last night," I said, "but enlisting her help would be tricky. And you weren't supposed to mention it."

Anna sat up and leaned forward, her eyes growing wide and slightly wild. "What did you say?" she said to Merrill.

Before he could answer, she said to me, "What did he say?"

"As it turns out, I started seeing Laura Matthers this past week, and she is Russ Maddox's niece."

"Whoa, wait just a damn minute. Why wasn't I aware of this?" she asked.

"I was going to tell you today. It just happened this weekend."

"You all are joking, because I know the next time you sleep with a woman, it will be in a marriage bed."

"Thank you," I said. "I've been having a hard time convincing these jaded men of that."

"Why would they think that you did?" she asked suspiciously.

"When Dad called, Laura answered the phone, and technically we were sleeping, and technically we were together, but we were not sleeping together, if you know what I mean."

"Your dad called in the middle of the night, and she answered the phone?" she asked in disbelief.

"She tried to wake me, but couldn't."

"I don't believe you."

"It's true. It was the first good night's sleep I've gotten in over a year. That was until I was awakened to go to the scene of a murder."

"If you slept like that, then this is serious, and I should have known about it."

"It was just one of those things that happened. It almost all took place this weekend."

"Your weekend was a hell of a lot better than mine," Merrill said.

I shrugged. "It was a grace."

"She really loves you," Anna said.

"You don't even know her," I said.

"I wasn't referring to Laura, but to God," she said with a warm smile. Her eyes twinkled.

"I really love her."

"And Laura knows that?" she asked.

"Of course."

"You said that you saw Johnson on the tape. Was there anybody else on it?" Merrill said, changing the subject.

"Actually that is the only one I saw, and it was very short. Russ is what you might call a minute man. I thought maybe you would be willing to come over tonight and watch the others."

"If it's all men, I couldn't do it. You know that," Merrill said with an exaggerated shiver.

"I have no idea what's on the other tapes."

"Just the same, you better count me out," he said, still shaking his head as if to rid it of the mental pictures his mind was developing.

"Sounds like you may have some repressed or latent homosexual desires," Anna said to him.

Merrill did not respond. He looked as if he had heard nothing.

"Are you saying this is a cultural thing, Merrill?" Anna continued. "Like, for example, heterosexual black men can't tolerate even the thought of homosexuality, black men are more well-endowed, and they won't perform oral sex on a woman."

"Generally, I'd have to say those things are true," he said.

"Well, I'll help you review the tapes if you want me to, John," she said.

"I hate to ask you to watch those things, but I'd really enjoy your company."

"Okay, it's a date. I'm a married woman going to a minister's house to watch homemade porno tapes. Sounds like fun."

"People gonna start calling you Jimmy Swaggart," Merrill said to me.

I let that one go. "Let's not call it a date," I said to Anna.

"And I definitely think that Merrill should have to join us."

"Yeah, Merrill, you can't break up the three musketeers," Anna said to him.

"The three stooges," he mumbled.

"Hey, Moe, so you'll join us?" I said.

"I'll come, but I'm not watching."

Anna started to say something, and from her expression I knew what it was going to be. I held my hand up to stop her and said, "We better break up this little meeting before it degenerates any further. I'll see you both tonight at six o'clock at my house."

"Let's make it seven. I need to eat first," Merrill said, and with that we were walking out the door.

I went back to my office and ordered flowers for Laura. I had them write on the card, "The scent of peaches still lingers." I also ordered flowers for her uncle's funeral and my mom's hospital room.

Next, I called her to see how she and the family were doing. Last night, or rather early this morning, she took the news exceptionally well. I first considered that she might be in shock, but later determined that she was genuinely okay.

"Hello," she said.

"Laura?" I asked.

"No, this is Kim. Who's this?"

"This is John Jordan. How are you doing?"

"I'm fine. How are you?" she said.

"I'm good," I said.

"Listen, let me grab Laura," she said. "I know she's dying to talk to you."

"Why do you say that?"

"I can just tell. She's like spazzing out over you."

"Thank you, Kim. That's good to know."

In a moment, Laura picked up another extension and, after Kim noisily hung up her extension, said, "Hey, you."

"Good morning. How are you doing?"

"I'm okay," she said. "Actually, I'm having contradictory feelings. Coming off the high of a wonderful weekend with you and then the shock of Uncle Russ's death.

"How's your mom handling the loss of her brother?"

"She's okay. They weren't real close. He was so weird. He was not really close to anyone that I know of. Still it's a shock."

Scenes from the video flashed on the screen of my mind. *He was very close with some people*, I thought, but had the good sense not to say it. Instead, I said, "Is there anything I can do?"

"Yes. Could you come by after work?"

"I certainly will," I said, and, though I never made it, I meant it when I said it.

I said good-bye and hung up just as there was a knock at my door, followed by Mr. Smith bringing an inmate pass in and laying it on the desk before me.

"Brother Chaplain, I think you better talk with this inmate. You need to hear what he need to say."

"Okay, send him in."

"Chaplain, I need to talk with you right away," Jefferson Hunter said when he entered my office. Mr. Smith closed the door, and I motioned for Hunter to have a seat.

"What's on your mind?" I asked.

"Chaplain, you know I ain't down with the religion thing, and I really don't like white people none much, but I got the four-one-one you need."

"No matter what the information is, I cannot pay you for it in any way."

"No, I know you wouldn't. That's why I'm here. You okay. They's lots of mean sons a bitches around here, but you different. When my mother passed, you really helped me a lot, and I remember that."

"Thank you," I said, not knowing what else to say.

"Chaplain, you in trouble, in danger, you know."

"What do you mean?"

"See, they's this dude what handles things for people on the 'pound. Now I ain't gonna say his name, but I want you to know he come up to a small group of inmates. Some real badasses, you know. He say he got lotsa money for a hit. He say it's protection on the 'pound and about three hundred in canteen. I never heard anyone offer that much for anything. Then he say who he want hit. It you."

I was silent. I couldn't believe it.

"It really surprise me, you know, because you the most popular chaplain we ever had. Everybody on the 'pound say you really care and shit. So when he say he want a hit on you, I just really couldn't believe it. I thought you should know. But I mean, I ain't no squealer or nothin'. I just doin' you a solid like you done me when my moms was dying. So we straight, and you didn't hear it from me."

"We're straight. And thank you. I know you didn't have to do it. I appreciate it."

"Just stay off the 'pound awhile, and watch your back," he said, rising from his seat. And then he left.

No sooner had he gone than Mr. Smith knocked on the door.

"Come in."

"Brother Chaplain, are you okay?"

"Yes, thank you. How much weight should I give to what he says?"

"About most things, an ounce to nothin'. But about this thing, a ton. He know what he talkin' 'bout. He a bad dude. I still can't believe he come up here and told you. You really liked on the 'pound. That's why I can't believe this is happenin'."

THIRTY

I HAD MADE A DEAL WITH THE DEVIL, and I knew it
would come back to haunt me. I knew better than to deal
with the devil, of course, but I didn't feel as though I had a
choice. I also didn't realize that it would come back to haunt
me quite so soon. But even as we sat down, I could hear the
slithering serpent hissing my name.

"What have we got so far?" Edward Stone asked.

We were back in his office on Monday afternoon discussing the investigation.

"We've got a lot for such a short time into the investigation," Tom Daniels replied. "Let me go over what we know,
and then we can discuss what we think. We know that
Johnson was murdered. He was put to sleep in the early
morning hours last Tuesday. We know that his body was kept
in the caustic storage closet."

"We do *know* that now?" I asked.

"Yes. The lab tested the cleaner that we found and some
fibers that were found on the floor in there and made a
match. We think he was drugged between six and seven."

"Which means the medical shift would have just been
changing," I said.

"Right," Daniels said, "but security wouldn't have changed yet."

"You both act as if staff members are the only ones being considered here," Stone said.

"That's the way it looks. It would be nearly impossible for an inmate to orchestrate all this," Daniels said.

"Don't forget that this murder took place in a prison where there are over twelve hundred criminals, four hundred of them killers," Stone said.

I wanted to say that there were far more than twelve hundred criminals here, but I decided to keep that one to myself.

"I'm not ruling out inmates or inmate involvement, but we'd probably know a lot more than we do now if an inmate had done it. They almost always tell on each other."

"Just don't rule out the possibility that an inmate did all this," Stone said. "In fact, an inmate named Jacobson is in confinement, and he was there with Johnson the night he was killed. I had Captain Skipper search his cell this weekend, and an entire bottle of sleeping pills was found. Apparently, he's been saving them up. Keep that in mind. Now, what else do you have?"

"We haven't ruled him out," Daniels said. "I think he's involved somehow. We also know that Johnson was an active homosexual and that he was on drugs, not small stuff either. Where he got it, we do not know. We know he spent a lot of time in medical and confinement. And, I want you to know that much of this information was gathered through us working together and sharing information," he said and nodded in my direction.

I felt bad for keeping so much from him, but I still didn't know what it meant and who I could trust.

"I'm pleased to hear that," Stone said. "What about motive? Have you found any real motives yet?"

Daniels looked at me and said, "That's his department. I've been working primarily on the physical evidence while he's been asking the questions."

They both looked at me. "I've looked into Johnson's life somewhat, and I believe that his death was connected to either his prostitution or his drug use, but how or who did it, I do not know yet. I also don't believe that it is purely coincidental that much of this case and other problems originate in confinement and medical."

"That may be due to the fact that the worst inmates are the ones in confinement and many times medical, too. They go to the box for discipline. Many times they go to medical for fighting, sex, and drugs."

I didn't say anything. I just sat there and nodded my head. It seemed to me as if Stone was unwilling to hear anything negative about his institution. I wondered, so I tried something out on him. "I've gotten a lot of reports about what goes on here at night. I've heard that there are both institution and statute violations taking place."

"What?" Stone asked in shock. "Listen, Chaplain, you've got to learn that an inmate will say anything. They lie. They can't help but lie. Of course they're going to tell you that illegal things take place. They don't like it here. But guess what? They're not supposed to like it here."

That answered that question. I was glad that I didn't share with them everything I knew. My only other hope was that Daniels would remember not to discuss the chapel situation in front of the superintendent. I had asked him to examine a sample from the chapel floor where Molly had alleged her husband had raped her. If that were mentioned in front of the superintendent, it would open another whole can of worms. With everything that was going on, I couldn't figure out if Stone was in on it or not. I also wondered if they had heard about the death of Russ Maddox.

"What's this I hear about another death in town last night?" Stone asked.

It was Pottersville; I should have known that everybody knew it by now.

Tom Daniels looked blankly.

"It was Russ Maddox, the president of the bank in town," I said.

"Was it a natural death or murder?" Daniels asked.

"I don't believe they know yet," I said.

"It figures," Daniels said, "hicktown sheriff's department. They couldn't find their own assholes with two hands and a flashlight."

I let that one slide. This was not the time nor the place.

"Well, we need to monitor that pretty closely. It would be an unlikely coincidence that the only two murders to occur in Potter County in years were this close together and unrelated."

"Yes sir, I agree," Daniels said. "I think Jordan should be our liaison with his dad's department."

"That's a very good idea," Stone said. "We sure don't know much yet, do we? Is there anything else?"

"I called the chaplain at Calhoun Correctional, where Shutt worked before transferring here," I said. "He said that he got nothing but complaints about Shutt,"

"Yes, but—" Stone interrupted.

"From staff as well as inmates," I continued.

"Okay," Stone said. "We'll watch him very closely. Anything else?"

"The chaplain had us do an analysis of some of the carpet in the back of the chapel," Daniels said.

And thus the serpent raised his ugly head.

Stone lifted his eyebrows and tilted his head severely to the left. I was seeing his puzzled look and perhaps an annoyed look, as well. "What's this?" he asked.

"I was told that inmates were having sex in the chapel," I said, telling only a half-lie.

"What bearing does that have on this case?" Stone asked.

"I'm not sure. At the time I heard it, I was in the very early stages of the investigation and I wanted to consider every possible lead."

"We did find small traces of blood and semen. Which means someone has been having sex on the floor in there."

"Well, whether or not it has anything to do with this investigation, it must be looked into. We cannot have inmates having sex in the chapel," Stone said, his anger showing slightly, which is more than I had ever seen it show before.

"Just wait; there's more," Daniels said, enjoying every minute of this. "The lab also found traces of vaginal fluid and female pubic hair."

Stone kicked his desk, pushing his chair backwards, and stood up. "What? That can't be right. There must be some kind of mistake."

"It's no mistake," he said.

"Chaplain, what the fuck has been going on in your chapel?" Stone yelled.

"It sounds like you answered your own question, but that's exactly what I am trying to find out. That's why I asked the inspector to take the samples. I assure you it is not happening when I am here. I was told that things like this are going on at night."

"I just can't believe this," Stone said again. He was shaking his head, which he had turned to look out the window behind his desk. His back was to us. "Inspector, I want you to look into this personally. This kind of shit does not happen in Edward Stone's institution. I want daily reports from you. I want to be informed every step of the way. Now, you two get out of here and go find out what's going on in my institution."

Daniels and I both rose to leave. I walked quickly, trying to avoid any interaction with him. I was far too upset to even talk to him. In fact, it would have been better for me to go to the chapel and pray awhile before I talked to anyone. In the corridor of the administration building about fifteen feet from the superintendent's office, he caught up with me.

"Jordan, I need to ask you some more questions about the

chapel evidence," he said. I was amazed at his audacity.

"I think it best if you don't attempt to do it now," I said. I reached the door and proceeded out of it without slowing. When I stepped outside, the heat overtook me like an attacker. It was brutal, making my walking labored and my vision nearly nonexistent.

"Listen, you little prick, consider yourself under investigation. That building is your responsibility. If you refuse to cooperate, I can have you suspended or worse, so don't fuck with me."

"I have no intention of doing so," I said, continuing to walk.

"What's your problem? We are supposed to be working together."

"That's right. We are, and you deliberately brought up the chapel incident without talking with me first."

"No, I didn't. But this is not a game, boy. If you're holding back, you better come clean before you take the fall for someone else. And, if you're guilty, I will find out about it eventually, so you better tell me now. I'll go easy on you," he said with a wicked smile.

"Guilty?" I asked incredulously. "Of what? You're just using this as an opportunity to harass me."

He smiled. "Perks of the job."

"I've done nothing wrong. I uncovered this in an investigation that *you* are supposed to be conducting. So from this point forward, I'm going to allow you to conduct it. I'm going to get out of your way. I wouldn't want to hold you back. I'm sure you're about to crack this thing wide open."

"I'll crack your head wide open if you're not careful. I'll stop by to interview you later. If you want to, you can call your lawyer. But, I wouldn't get that clown you had during the divorce. Susan's kicked his ass," he said. He then laughed obnoxiously and turned back toward the administration building.

The truth was I told my lawyer to let Susan have everything she wanted. I hadn't counted on her wanting everything, but no matter. I was free.

After closing the chapel's sanctuary doors behind me, I paced some more, but this time I prayed, too. I walked and prayed until I found peace. Then I walked back out again to finish this thing I had begun.

I was walking out of the chapel on my way to medical when I heard my phone ringing. It was the quick double rings of an outside call, so I unlocked my office door and answered it.

"Dad wanted you to know that it *was* murder," Jake said when I answered.

"What?"

"*Hello,* is anybody there? Stay with me, okay? Russ Maddox's preliminary autopsy results are back. He was poisoned."

"With what?"

"I don't know why Dad wants you to know all this. He must want you to work the faggot connection."

"Jake, what was used?"

"Chloral hydrate," he said, not knowing what he was saying or how to say it.

"Do you have the time of death?" I asked.

"Doc says it was between twelve thirty and one thirty A.M.," he said.

"That's pretty accurate," I said. "How can he be so sure?"

"Russ ate at Rudy's that night. Doc could tell by the stomach contents."

"And it wasn't Rudy's food that killed him?" I asked.

"That's a good one," he said, laughing a little too much "I'm going to tell Dad that one." When he had stopped laughing, he said, "Oh yeah, guess what? Maddox's mansion was broken into late last night or early this morning. You were the last one to leave. Did you lock it?"

"Yes," I said defensively. "Of course I did."

"I know," he said. "If you hadn't, they wouldn't have had to break in, now would they? See, you ain't all that smart, are you? Just lucky sometimes is my guess."

My guess was that Skipper was looking for Maddox's little home movies.

"Do you know anything else?" I asked.

"No, but Dad wants to know if you think the deaths are related?"

"Yes, I do. Tell him I'll call him tonight when I know more."

"Listen, you better remember that you ain't no cop, okay? Don't screw around with this thing. Leave it up to us. Best thing you can do is to forget about all of this and concentrate on not missing your meetings," he said patronizingly.

He always used that against me. I was the first and only Jordan to admit I was an alcoholic, which is not to say that I was the only alcoholic. It is ironic how the one that breaks out of the unhealthy cycle is viewed not only as the sick one, but the traitor as well.

"You got your bags packed for Atlanta yet?" he asked. "Think you'll say good-bye this time?"

"Jake," I said. "I'm not going anywhere. But I'm also not going to interfere with your relationship with Dad. I know you all are close, and I'm very glad . . . for both of you. You have no reason to feel threatened by me."

"Threatened? By you?" He started laughing. "Drunk ass faggots who tuck their tails and run anytime there's trouble don't threaten me." His breathing was heavy and his voice tight. "Oh, there's one more thing." He paused, taking in a breath and letting it out slowly. "Something that you and Maddox had in common."

"Yeah? What's that?"

"He had AIDS," Jake said and started laughing again. "He's a queer, too."

I was stunned. I couldn't speak. I was overcome with anger, fear, and embarrassment.

How could he know? Did she tell? Who else knows? Oh, God, please help me.

"Hey, Dickhead, are you there? Didn't you think that was funny? Come on now, you know all you boys wearing your collars backwards are either fags or child molesters. Which are you? Y'all all going to die of AIDS sooner or later."

I hung up the phone. Actually, I slammed it down and began to cry.

I walked back into the chapel, fell on my knees at the altar, and began to pray again.

THIRTY-ONE

A S I APPROACHED THE MEDICAL BUILDING, I could see Julie Anderson out front smoking again. She perked up when she saw me coming.

"Hey, Chaplain, come here," she said. Her voice changed, and she began to whisper, which was roughly the volume most people use in ordinary conversation. "I really felt bad yesterday because of our log book not having Thomas and all. Anyway, I called the sarge at the center gate to see if he could remember who went through on their way to medical that night, and guess what, he did. He said that Thomas didn't come through the gate but that he did go to medical that night—just from the other side of the compound."

"Did he remember anyone else going in or out?"

"Yeah, he did. I didn't ask him or anything, but he said that later, after my shift was over, he let another inmate through the gate to go to medical, but that he came back in just a few minutes and said he couldn't find anybody in medical, and, anyway, he didn't want to be charged the three dollars."

Because of all of the abuse of the medical facilities by inmates who just want to get out of the sun or see a pretty nurse, the department had instituted a policy that made inmates pay three dollars to the department if they declared a medical emergency and they really didn't have one.

"Did he say who it was?" I asked.

"He couldn't remember," she said.

"Thank you. I sure appreciate it."

"You're welcome. I'm just sorry somebody was so careless. You going to say anything to anybody about it?"

"No, don't worry. I'd like to talk with Nurse Strickland though. What time does she come in tonight?"

"You're in luck. We're both pulling a double. So, she's here today."

"You've both been doing a lot of that lately," I said and began to walk into the medical building. "Thanks again for all your help."

"You're welcome, and thank you for not making a big deal about the mistake," she said and turned to take one last draw from her cigarette.

I walked through the waiting room, where twenty-five inmates were staring at the wall in front of them in silence. A few of them whispered greetings to me. A couple asked to see me later in the day. I entered the door on the left, which led to the exam rooms and the infirmary.

Strickland was not in any of the exam rooms, nor the nurses' station, nor the infirmary, but standing outside of the infirmary, I heard her. She was seated in the break room at the end of the hall talking with someone I couldn't see. As I approached, she glanced my way and then quietly said something to the person she was with. I couldn't hear what she said, but then that was the point. When I reached the door, inmate Jones walked through it. He didn't speak, but his body language was loud enough.

"Hello, Chaplain," she said. "How's it going?"

"Fine. How are you doing?"

"Right as rain, thanks," she said and started to get up.

"Before you go, I wonder if I might ask you a few more questions?"

She looked at her watch, "I can give you a couple of minutes. I'm sorry. We're just very busy today."

"Then I'll talk fast. I'm still trying to find out what happened the night and morning before Johnson was killed. Can you tell me anything else about that night in the infirmary?"

"I heard that you were conducting the investigation, but I didn't believe it. You're the chaplain, not the inspector."

"That's true. The inspectors are in charge of this case. I'm primarily a gopher for them," I said, wondering how many people knew what I was doing and how they knew.

"Well, anyway, there's not a lot more to tell. It was an unusually quiet night in the infirmary. I forget why Johnson was there. Something related to his AIDS case, but it was in no way critical. Like I said, it was just quiet."

"Too bad they can't all be like that," I said.

"That's true," she said.

"I'm still not clear on when Thomas came to the infirmary that night," I said, "and how long he stayed."

She sighed impatiently. "I told you Thomas wasn't there," she said. "Not on my shift. On my shift Johnson and Jacobson were the only inmates down here, and it's a good thing because, like I said, I was alone."

"Where was Nurse Anderson?" I asked.

"Where she always is," she said angrily. "Waddling around, flirting with inmates and avoiding work."

"Is there anything else you can think of?" I asked.

"No. It was quiet," she said, sliding her chair back and standing up. "Well, I've got to run. You have a good day, Chaplain, and when you finish playing Sherlock Holmes, we have some inmates down here that need you to talk and pray with them."

"Thank you. I'll see them today. You have a good day,

too," I said to her back as she walked down the hallway. She was not nearly as helpful as she once had been. She seemed scared, though. I had an urge to rush to her and offer to protect her. I do not, however, give in to all of my urges.

"Oh, one more thing," I said to her as she reached the door. "Is there a typewriter down here that you all use?"

"We have a typewriter, but we all use the computer."

"Does your inmate orderly use it?"

"Jones? I don't think he knows how to type very well, but I've seen him pecking away on it before."

"Does he have access to it at all times?" I asked.

"Yes, I guess so," she said.

"Where is it?" I asked.

"It's in the first office on the left when you enter the medical department. Just before the nurses' station."

"Is it locked?"

"Oh, no. We just keep some extra furniture and a few office supplies in there. It stays unlocked all the time."

"I see. Thanks again. Sorry to have taken up so much of your time."

"No, it's not that. I'm just so far behind in preparing for our ACA inspection, but you're no bother at all. In fact, I enjoy seeing you. You are like a breath of fresh air around this place."

"Thank you. I think the same of you."

Now is the time for all good men to come to the aid of their country. What does it profit a man if he gains the whole world and yet loses his soul? After typing these sentences on the typewriter I found in the empty medical office, I pulled out one of the letters I had received and compared them. They looked identical—the t's were missing the right side of the crossbar. The o's were missing a small place in the bottom center. And, the a's, as in angel or Anna, were darker than all of the other print.

The letters I had been receiving were typed on this

machine, but that didn't tell me who'd been typing them. I suspected it was an inmate, however. Any other medical staff member would have typed the letters on some other machine—or at home maybe. But, an inmate wouldn't have access to any other machine.

I walked out of the office and down the hallway to the nurses' station. There I found an elderly white nurse who seemed to be dozing.

"Hi," I said.

She jumped slightly. "Hello," she responded after recovering.

"How are you today?" I asked.

"Just fine, thanks. How are you, Chaplain?"

"I'm okay. I was wondering if I might ask you a question."

"Sure, sweetie. What is it?"

"Have you ever seen anybody use that old typewriter in the front office up there?"

"No, I sure haven't. I don't think it works."

"Nobody? Not even an inmate?"

"No, I don't think so. Sorry," she said, sensing my disappointment.

"Oh, that's okay. It's no problem. I appreciate your time."

"Anytime, sweetie. Anytime."

THIRTY-TWO

WHETHER IT WAS THE PRESENCE of a spiritual entity or the collective soul of its inhabitants, confinement felt oppressed by the dark forces of slothfulness and depression. The thick, pungent air seemed to me to be a natural manifestation of the spiritual condition. I signed in at the sergeant's desk, told the officer that I had received a note from the first-shift sergeant asking me to check on an inmate named Larkins, and began walking down the long hallway toward Larkins's cell. Halfway down the corridor, about a hundred feet from where I was, I saw a small group of inmates. Something was wrong. If these were confinement inmates, they should have been in their cells. If they weren't, they shouldn't have been here at all. As I looked at the inmates, I thought about what Hunter had said about the hit out on me. Ordinarily, I walked among the biggest, baddest inmates in this place without giving it a single thought; now I was getting paranoid.

I didn't like what I was thinking. I wasn't going to give in to fear; I continued to walk. I was also not going to be stupid; I glanced back at the sergeant's desk. He was gone. When I looked forward, the group of inmates was walking towards me, seven of them—all black, all big.

A loud, familiar voice in my head screamed for me to run, but I couldn't, and I don't know exactly why. I began to pray. The line "Though I walk through the valley of the shadow of death" crossed my mind. So did "To be absent from the body is to be present with the Lord." I was not particularly comforted by either of them.

They were closing in on me, which means they must have picked up their pace, because I hadn't sped up. As they walked toward me, I could see the white shirt of an officer just behind them. As they got closer, I could see that it was Matthew Skipper.

At first, I was relieved to see him, but almost immediately thought better of it. For all I knew, he was the one who put out the hit on me. For all I knew, he was about to do it himself and save the money. In another five seconds, we came face to face. The inmates surrounded the two of us, putting Skipper and me in a circle of black and blue—most likely the color I was about to be.

Some of the inmates, none of whom I recognized, were panting with excitement. They smelled blood. They also smelled.

"Chaplain, I hear you're confused about exactly what your job is around here," Skipper said. His breath had the overpowering smell of tobacco and coffee.

He stood probably six-four, but he slumped, as if the weight of his belly pulled him down and forward. We would have been eye to eye, but he wore mirrored sunshades, which were at least a decade out of date, not to mention totally unnecessary in the dark hallway. So rather than staring into his eyes, I was staring into my own. In them I saw fear.

"My job is to do the work of God, which involves both justice and mercy," I said, my voice sounding much stronger than I thought it would. A pleasant surprise.

"Your job is to give this bunch of inmates some religion. Not to be sticking your nose where it don't belong."

I was silent. It seemed a wise move at the time.

"Well, boy," he yelled, "whatcha need, some job counseling?"

"Is that what these men do, job counseling?" I asked.

"When it's needed."

"And I thought I was doing such a good job here. I really thought that I had found my vocation, a reason to live."

"Funny," he said, "how your purpose for living is gonna get you dead."

"That is funny," I said sarcastically. "Come to think of it, though, the same thing happened to Jesus."

"You boys do crucifixions?" he asked.

They laughed. It was a mean, humorless laugh.

"Perhaps we should go speak with the superintendent about my job description," I said and started to move away from him. The inmates closed in tighter around us. There were less than six inches between us.

"Everybody knows I run this place, not Stone. He just thinks he's the head nigger in charge. I'm the man around here. I'm the man. Stone's scared of me. He'll do what I say. You or nobody gonna change that. Nobody."

"You're the man, huh? You the man that did Johnson and Maddox?"

"I'm the man, period. All you need to know is that I'm the man that's gonna put you in a fucking box. Okay, boys, do your thing."

"I won't fuck with no preacher," one of the inmates said.

"Sounds fun to me," another one said and then hit me hard in the kidney. My knees buckled, and I started to go down.

On the way down, one of them caught me, lifted me back up, and then punched me hard under the chin. My head began to ring, and the room began to spin all around me. I fell to the floor. This time no one caught me. I hit the bare, rough concrete floor at full force. It was a welcome relief compared to the two other blows I had just received. My vision was blurred. I tried to lift my head. I not only tried, but succeeded—only a few inches, however. Those few inches were just enough for me to see the blood on the floor beneath me. Not a lot of blood, but any blood of mine that is outside my body is too much blood.

"Inmates," I heard someone yell. "Inmates, face the wall with your hands behind your head. Captain, I'll have you and the chaplain secure in just a moment," the officer said.

I looked up. All the inmates were still, each looking at Skipper. Just then, he reared back and swung his fist at one of the inmates, hitting him square on the nose.

"Get against the fucking wall," Skipper yelled. "Officer, call the control room. Tell them to get the riot squad down here immediately. DO IT! NOW!" he screamed. The inmates quickly lined up against the wall. The officer did what his captain told him to do using the radio clipped to his belt. "Call medical for the chaplain, too," Skipper yelled again. "NOW!" He then knelt beside me and asked if I were okay. I was unable to answer. I just prayed that the CO at the end of the hall wouldn't turn his back on us. Thank God, he didn't.

Thanks.

Within a few minutes, I was being treated in the infirmary by Sandy Strickland under Anna's watchful eye. I felt like I had just been fifteen rounds with Foreman. In actuality, I only had a cut under my chin and a small abrasion on my right cheek. I had no idea where the captain was, but I found myself periodically looking over my shoulder.

"It's funny that the captain didn't sustain any wounds at all," Anna said to no one in particular.

"He never sustains any wounds," Strickland said. "He makes sure of that. Chaplain, you better watch your back. You have no idea who you're dealing with."

"Yeah, but you do. Why don't you help me? You have to be aware of what's going on here at night. Why won't you help us put a stop to it?"

"He scares the hell out of me. He's a psycho."

"Is that your medical opinion?" Anna asked.

Strickland smiled. "You don't need an M.D. or a Ph.D. to diagnose that one."

"I guess not. How are you feeling?" Anna asked me.

"Yo, I don't want no rematch," I said in my best Rocky Balboa voice.

She smiled, but I could tell it was only a courtesy.

"I feel okay. How do I look?"

"Still the best-looking man in the institution," Anna said.

"I concur," Strickland said.

"Are you going to help me?" I asked her.

"Haven't you had enough? This is only a taste of what he will do. I can't help you. I've got a little girl. She doesn't have a daddy, and I'm not going to make her an orphan."

"If you change your mind, you know where to find me," I said and eased off the bed.

"The institutional inspector is going to want to talk with you. He's in confinement locking up those inmates, but he's got to fill out the incident report within twenty-four hours."

"Tell him that the chaplain will be in my office," Anna said. And we slowly walked out of the infirmary. Slowly.

*T*HIRTY-THREE

"*A*RE YOU OKAY?" Anna asked as she handed me a can of orange juice and a bottle of aspirin. We were seated in her office. She was seated. I was more like a blob in the chair. My head ached, throbbing with the rhythm of my heart and the ringing in my ears. My mouth felt like I'd just received a root canal. When I tried to speak, I sounded drunk and drool rolled down my bottom lip.

"I'm okay. Really," I said as best I could.

"You're sure?"

"Yes."

"Then tell me just what the hell is going on," Anna said. "What happened in confinement?"

"Skipper."

"He did this to you?" she asked in shock.

"No. He had it done. When I walked in there, they were waiting for me. The confinement sergeant left his desk, and it was just me, Skipper, and the seven inmates. He said that I wasn't doing my job or I was doing more than my job. He knows I'm on to him."

"This is still all so unbelievable. You're sure he's been taking inmates out of the institution for Maddox? I mean, come on, it wouldn't be an easy thing to do."

"No, but a lot easier on the first shift than any other. We

228

don't really know what goes on out here at night. This is probably just the surface of what Skipper's been doing. He has to be supplying the drugs, too. Evans said it was too difficult and there wasn't enough demand for the expensive drugs like Johnson was on."

"What's next?"

"I don't know. I think it's a little premature to go for Skipper. He's dangerous, but he's not stupid. The evidence is mounting, but it's not enough yet."

"Yeah, but you have to tell the inspector or the superintendent what happened today down in confinement. If you cover it up . . ." Before Anna could finish what she was saying, there was a knock at her door. Pete Fortner, the institutional inspector, entered the office. He was followed by Matt Skipper.

"Pretty exciting day, huh, Chaplain?" Fortner said. I couldn't tell for sure, but he seemed to be oblivious to who or what Skipper was.

"Pretty exciting," I said as I stood and walked behind the desk where Anna was seated and leaned against the wall. There were only two seats in front of her desk, so Fortner assumed that I was giving the seats to them. I was actually trying to put some distance and a rather large desk between myself and Skipper.

"You need to sit down more than I do, Chaplain," Fortner said. Skipper remained silent. He still had his shades on, his eyes hidden.

"I'd rather stand right now. I still have large amounts of adrenaline pumping through my veins."

"I know what you mean, son," Skipper said and smiled broadly. His teeth were white with only the slightest tobacco stains.

I did not return the smile.

"Miss Anna, how are you today?" Fortner asked.

"I've been better," she said curtly.

"Her boyfriend just got beat up and nearly killed, Pete. How else would she be doing today?" Skipper said and smiled again.

I could only see Anna's profile, but I could tell that she was giving the severest of looks to Skipper. Fortner grew awkward and uncomfortable.

"I've already taken Captain Skipper's statement. Why don't I read it to you and see if there's anything you have to add, okay?" Fortner asked.

"Sure," I said.

"Okay, let's see." He opened a file folder on his lap and flipped through a few pages.

As he continued his search, Skipper began tapping his ring on the wooden arm of his chair. It was a big class ring, high school no doubt.

"Here it is," Fortner exclaimed. "Do you want to read it or do you want me to?"

"You can," I said.

"Okay. At approximately twelve thirty P.M. Captain Matthew Skipper walked into the west end of confinement corridor B and saw seven inmates surrounding Chaplain Jordan. He then reached for his radio to call the control room and found that it was dead. He ran towards the group, jumping in the center with Chaplain Jordan. Together, they kept the inmates at bay for as long as possible. The inmates then attacked. The captain used defensive tactics to defend himself, and the chaplain used his head. The captain landed a couple of good blows against one of the inmates, but it seemed as if the inmates were going to overtake them, until the other officer showed up. He radioed control, and the inmates dispersed. The riot team responded within five minutes, and the situation was squashed quickly. The inmates were locked up, and the chaplain was taken to medical." Fortner looked up. "Do you have anything to add, Chaplain?"

"No," I said and then went back to biting my tongue.

"Do you know any reason why these inmates would want to hurt you?"

"I tell you, Pete, I really can't think of anything right now. I'm still sort of out of it. Why don't I stop by your office tomorrow," I said.

"Yeah, Pete, the boy's been through enough today. Give him a break. Come on, let's go," Skipper said.

"That arrogant son of a bitch," Anna said when they had gone. "Did you see how cocky he was? He sat in here knowing you wouldn't turn him in. Why?"

"He probably thinks I'm scared."

"I know better than that."

"He doesn't. He's been dealing with inmates and inmate families too long. In those dealings, he's had all the power. They are powerless in most situations. He's operated not just above the law, but as the law. It's made him like that, but it will be his downfall. Pride comes before a fall. Believe me, I know."

"Why didn't you say anything to the inspector?" she asked.

"It's just not time. He's coming down, God will see to that, but I don't have enough evidence yet. And you know how easily evidence can cut both ways. If I've learned anything in my few years on the planet, it's not to jump the gun."

"Still, not to say anything could work against you too, couldn't it? I mean, if you agree with Skipper at first and then change your mind later, won't that look suspect?"

"I didn't agree with him. I just didn't add anything. I told him I would talk to him tomorrow. I want the night to figure out what to do. But, you're right. All of this is like playing with fire, and that's true of most investigations. The trick is to get as few burns as possible, because rarely do you not get burned at all."

"Just be careful. You're not the man you used to be.

You've become a lamb, and you are definitely among wolves now."

"Well, I'm trying to become a lamb. But this wolf's apparent strength is actually weakness."

"And your apparent weakness actually strength?" she asked.

"If the Gospel is to be believed."

"And it is," she said.

"You think so?' I asked.

"You think so," she said, "and that, more than most things, makes me think so."

I was caught off guard. For a moment, I was speechless. I felt tears stinging the corners of my eyes. "Thank you. That means more to me than anything. I want to do that for people, you know, point them in that direction, but I fear I fail most of the time."

"Believe me," she said, sounding slightly irate, "those fears are unfounded. You make a big difference around this place."

I didn't respond.

"It's true," she said.

At that moment there was a faint knock on the door. I walked over and opened it, and Sandy Strickland walked in. She looked as if she were having a hard day. Her pale-blue nurse's uniform resembled surgical scrubs. Her hair was done up in a topknot, and her face was hard and wrinkled. Small lines cut through her makeup like tunnels in an ant farm. She was still beautiful, if no longer very attractive.

"I didn't test Thomas," Strickland said when I was seated.

"Why not?" I asked in surprise. I had asked her to test Anthony Thomas for drug use.

"I didn't have to. I know that Captain Skipper has him on all kinds of drugs," she said. Her voice quivered slightly.

"You two don't look very surprised," she said.

"We're not," Anna said.

"He's been doing all kinds of shit at night when no one's around to see. He uses inmates to do his dirty business. He's a sick prick, and I want him stopped."

"Why are you just now coming forward?" I asked.

"And why to us?" Anna added.

"I've been scared, okay. He's got a lot of people working for him and some inmates who will do whatever he says. They'd kill for him."

"Believe me, I know," I said.

"That was just a taste of his brutality. You've never met anyone like him. He'd kill me if he knew I was here. I need some help."

"And why me?" I asked.

"Listen, a lot of people know you're looking into that murder, and when you found out about Tony, I knew you were on to something. I want to help you so you can put him out of commission. I can't do it. I'm not strong enough, but you are. And you have the inspector's help. What are you going to do?"

"I was just asking myself the same question," I said. "Why don't you tell us what Skipper's been doing, and we can go from there."

"What he's been doing is whatever in the hell he wants. He's got free reign over this place at night. He treats people like animals and inmates worse. He uses drugs and favors to get them to do whatever he wants. But he doesn't have to use too much because they're so powerless and defenseless anyway. They're human," she said with conviction.

"I agree," I said.

"I agree that *some* of them are human," Anna said and smiled.

"I stand corrected. Some of them are animals." She practically hissed. She looked at Anna. "You know what it's like to be a woman. . . ."

Anna smiled and said, "Ah, yes. I guess I do."

"We're vulnerable in a place like this. We need men who can protect us from some of these less-than-human men around here—not just inmates either. Men like Skipper. They're more dangerous than the inmates. They make me scared. He even makes the inmates worse than they have to be by all the shit he pumps them full of. Besides, this whole place is one big boys' club. If you don't have a dick around here, you don't get dick done around here. Don't you agree?" she asked Anna.

"That this is essentially a boys' club? Yes, I do agree with that," Anna said.

"I mean, my God, what are all these damn towers around here except huge phallic symbols?" Strickland said with a mean laugh.

"I have to agree with that, as well," Anna said to my surprise and then added, "And what about the batons the response teams use?" There was the slightest hint of sarcasm in her voice.

"Exactly," Sandy said.

"What else does Skipper do?" I asked, trying to get her back on track.

"He supplies drugs, fixes disciplinary reports, changes job assignments, gives canteen, and arranges special visits at night, too."

"What do you mean?" Anna asked.

"I mean, if one of Skipper's drones misses his missus, Skipper will have her come in and have a conjugal visit with him. What they don't know is that he has a few conjugal visits of his own with their wives after they are locked back up. He never lets any ugly ones in."

"If inmates are having conjugal visits, it's only through Skipper, because we haven't had legitimate ones in years," Anna said.

"And half the people who come into the infirmary," she

continued, "do so because of Skipper. Many of them give up their manhood and even humanity for him because it beats having him harass or kill them, and he still treats them like shit."

"What does he get out of it?" I asked, playing dumb.

Actually I wasn't playing.

She gave an elaborate shrug. "They don't have any goods, so it must be services—and there's one service that's older than all others."

"Do you know who his customers are?" I asked.

"Only rumors, but there can't be too many of them out there in Mayberry RFD."

"Is there anybody else involved in this?" I asked.

"What do you mean?"

"Are any of the administrators involved?"

"How could they not be? I mean, I don't know. But, how can he do all of this without them knowing?"

"That brings up a good point," I said. "How long has this been going on?"

"He's been crooked from his mother's womb," she sneered.

"He's been doing all these things the entire time he's been here?" I asked.

"Well, maybe not all these things, but he's always broken the rules and gotten away with it. And, no woman could ever have done that. I'll bet you that."

"How do you know all of this?" Anna asked.

"Because I've been around. I keep my mouth shut and my eyes open."

We were all silent.

Finally she asked, "What are you going to do?"

"I'm going to look into it. Gather some more information and maybe even a little evidence, and then turn it over to the inspector."

"Well, I'm going on vacation. I don't want to be here

when all of this hits the fan. I told you, he scares the hell out of me. The reason I wanted you to know all this is that I've been watching out for some of the inmates that Skipper has been using and I won't be here to do it for a while. I'm especially worried about Anthony Thomas in DC 101. If Skipper was willing to kill Johnson, I'm sure he would kill Thomas."

"You think Skipper killed Johnson?" I asked.

"Yes, of course. Have you been listening?"

"Do you know Russ Maddox?" I asked.

"The banker? Yes, I know of him. He died recently, didn't he?"

"Yes. Do you know of any connection he may have had with Skipper?"

"No, none. Do you think Skipper murdered him, too?" she asked, her voice full of excitement and interest.

"I don't know. I'm just looking for a connection. You knew so much about everything else I thought you might know if there's a connection."

"Well, I don't," she said rising from her seat, "but I wouldn't be surprised. Anyway, please hurry and take care of this. There's a lot of people at risk, yourself and this pretty lady included," she said, motioning towards Anna. "And, watch out for Tony and all the men in confinement, okay?"

"I'll do what I can," I said. "But, up until now, that hasn't been a whole lot."

When she left, Anna said, "She's right, you know. Something has to be done about Skipper. It's not safe around here. Not that it ever was, but you know what I mean. What do you think?"

"I'm not sure. You're the better judge of women, but something wasn't right. Why, after all of this time, would she come forward?"

"Maybe she sees the net being drawn in around Skipper and feels confident that she's going to be safe. Who knows?" Anna said.

"I don't," I said, "but I plan to find out."

My head was hurting, and the cut under my chin felt like it was gaping into something the size of the Grand Canyon. I was about to say things couldn't get any worse when the phone rang. When Anna said that it was for me, I knew instantly the foolishness of the thought I had just had. I just didn't realize how extremely foolish it was.

"You have three minutes," Tom Daniels yelled into the phone, "to have your ass in the superintendent's office. I told you if you stepped out of line, I would bury you. Guess what? You dug your own grave. Now, I'm gonna dump a load of dirt on your ass!"

THIRTY-FOUR

WHEN I ARRIVED at the superintendent's office, Edward Stone sat behind his desk, Tom Daniels and Pete Fortner in front of it. The three men looked as if they were sitting in a surgical waiting room, preparing to receive bad news. The only thing inaccurate about that analogy was that, unfortunately, the bad news was for me.

"Have a seat," the superintendent said, his voice low and flat.

I sat down between Daniels and Fortner.

Edward Stone looked over at Tom Daniels once I was seated.

Daniels said, "Chaplain Jordan, we've received some very serious allegations concerning your conduct while an employee of the Department of Corrections. We've made the decision to suspend you without pay until a thorough investigation can be conducted. However, we wanted to give you the opportunity to respond to the allegations before you are made to leave."

I was in shock. I couldn't speak. In fact, I found it difficult to swallow. Maybe it was because of all the cotton in my mouth. My mind raced down dark streets and alleyways searching for an incident or the source of the allegations. I could find none. Every street was empty. Every alley deserted. My mind said, *It's fabricated.* And, then it said, *Of course, it's fabricated, but who fabricated it and why?*

A moment of silence passed while Daniels flipped through a few papers in an open file folder on his lap. The silence was maddening. My mind continued to race chaotically. Images flew at me like rain at a windshield; I couldn't focus, each object a rapidly moving, overexposed blur.

"We received a call," Daniels began again, "charging you with forcibly having sex with the wife of an inmate in the chapel and then having her husband locked up and threatened in order to keep her silent."

"That's ridiculous," I said.

As if I had said nothing, Daniels continued, "She is demanding the immediate release of her husband from lockup and an investigation. She's putting a lot of pressure on Tallahassee."

"I don't believe this. There's not one shred of truth in any of this, and you know it. You've already made the decision to suspend me and to investigate without even asking me or looking into it further."

"Tallahassee knows that if it's true," Stone said, "there will be hell to pay in the press, so they want to say they acted quickly."

"The press?" I asked.

"She's threatened to call the press," Daniels said. "We don't know if she has or not."

"I still don't get it. Why are you treating me as if I'm a criminal? I've done nothing wrong. It's just so absurd. Does the department always respond this way to idle allegations? I mean, anybody could say anything. How can you suspend someone with no corroborating witnesses or evidence?"

"If you'll recall," Daniels said with a knowing smile, "we

found female pubic hair and vaginal fluid on the floor of the chapel. I know you. I know how you are. This time, you've been caught."

Stone said, "Inspector Daniels, we are not going to make this personal."

"But that's exactly what it is. This wouldn't be happening if he didn't have a personal vendetta against me. Mr. Stone, I am the one who asked for the tests to be conducted. I haven't done anything wrong," I said.

Fortner spoke up, "This is not just personal. I would do the same thing based on the woman's testimony and the evidence we have. It looks real bad for you, pal."

"So far, all we have is an allegation and evidence that requires an investigation," Stone said. "So, if you're innocent, we will clear the whole thing up. Guilty or innocent, though, you had better retain a lawyer."

It was happening again. My mind raced back to Atlanta and the painful experiences of losing my marriage and my church. My whole body tingled, as if it had been asleep and I was just getting the feeling back. I was floating in a black hole, suspended above the abyss. There was no gravity, nothing to hold on to. I was powerless. I was lost.

"So, that's it?" I said. "You don't want to hear my side of what's going on here? Evidence I might have to contradict all of this?"

"Now is not the time, Chaplain. Let these men do their jobs. If you are innocent, it will all work out and we will owe you an apology. But, as they say, it does not look good for you right now. You have done an excellent job here, and I hope, even pray, that this is some kind of horrible mistake, but if it's not, we are going to move forward with prosecution to the fullest extent of the law."

"When was this alleged to have happened?" I asked.

"I can't say," Daniels said.

"How can I offer a defense if I don't even know with whom or when I'm to have done this?"

"Chaplain, now is not the time for defense," Stone said. "I will have an officer escort you over to your office to gather your personal things."

"FDLE will send an investigator to talk with you. If you're innocent, it's in your interest to cooperate," Fortner said.

"Remember," Daniels said, "do not leave town. Do not attempt to contact anyone involved."

"I don't know anyone involved, because I'm not involved." I stood up and walked out.

THIRTY-FIVE

THE RADIO WAS ON, but I didn't hear it. The heat was stifling, but I didn't feel it. The scenery was pretty, but I didn't see it.

My mind was frantically searching for something, anything, that could make sense of what was happening. I didn't understand how or why or even who was behind all this. I wondered if the allegations were related to my investigation or if they would have happened anyway. I was clueless. And yet I couldn't help but feel as if the answer were in my mind, somehow encoded in all the data I had collected.

I was driving my rusty old S-10 in the direction, of town—a direction, not a destination. I needed some time to air out, to think for a while. I had canceled my date with Anna and Merrill to watch the videos. I really didn't feel like it, and besides, I was no longer on the case. I was a chaplain without a church and an investigator without a case. I was lost, and I didn't know who to turn to for direction. Laura had enough going on without this, and we were too newly together. Anna and Merrill were still at the prison, a place I was not allowed in. My dad was involved in a prisoner transfer. So, I drove.

I considered calling Susan to ask her to get her dad to back off. I hadn't talked to her in over a year and had no desire to do so now, but I was desperate.

I pulled into the Jr. Mart parking lot and used the pay phone. She was not home. Thank God for small favors. Her answering machine said, "We are not at home right now." I wondered who the "we" was, but only for a minute. Whoever the "we" was, they were entangled and endangered. Even in the midst of my present crisis, my heart found the grace to rejoice to be free of Susan and the sickness that was our marriage. I then called the prison and asked for Anna, but the switchboard operator recognized my voice and said she had been told not to patch through any calls from me. She then apologized profusely.

I got back in my truck and continued to ride. I thought about going to my dad's place or the state park, but in the end I just drove.

I drove for an hour or more, most of the time not aware of where I was. I needed a destination. I didn't have one. My truck, which was approaching ten years old, didn't have a low-fuel light. However, I knew from experience how far I could let the needle approach empty. When I looked at it, for the first time since I had been driving, it was at that point. I figured I had just enough gas to get back to town. Then I realized that I didn't know how far town was because I didn't know where I was.

I slowed and pulled off on the shoulder to get my bearings. I was at Potter's Landing, which was about ten miles south of town.

I began to make a U-turn, waiting long enough for a white Ford Bronco to pass by, but it didn't. It slowed and pulled off the road at an angle blocking me from the front. It was Matt Skipper, and he was not alone. Three other men were in the Bronco with him—all white, all COs, although not in uniform. One of them was Shutt. I could tell by their expressions that this was not a social call.

I jammed the gear shifter in reverse—it ground in protest—and punched the gas pedal. I began to move backwards, although not very fast because my truck had some carburetor problems. I did move away from them, though, and that was the point. When I looked over my shoulder, something I usually do *before* I start to back up, I saw a car approaching in my lane. The car, a green Buick, was maybe twenty yards away. I jerked my steering wheel hard to the right, and in a few seconds I was off the highway again. I slammed on my brakes just before plowing into a rather large pine tree.

I thought about flagging down the Buick, but as it got closer, I could see that it was an elderly couple. There was nothing they could do, except let me use their car phone, if they had one. I had a fleeting thought of the luxurious car and car phone I had in Atlanta. I missed them both, but mostly the car phone at the moment.

Once the Buick passed, I gunned it back onto the highway and headed toward town. Skipper was close behind. In a matter of seconds, he had caught up with me, my old Chevy no match for his new Ford. He pulled up beside me in the left lane, not a problem on the desolate road. He swerved away from me going to the edge of his lane and then swerved back and slammed into me.

I tried to steady the wheel, but it was no use, both of my right-side tires went off the road. The truck bumped and bounced hard on the uneven ground of the shoulder. I resisted the urge to jerk my steering wheel back toward the road. Instead, I slowed and eased back on. Skipper was maybe ten feet in front of me now, still in the left lane.

I wanted to stop. I wanted to go in the other direction. But to get any help at all and not run out of gas, I had to continue toward town. Glancing at the gas gauge, I knew I wouldn't make it. I looked up again to see Skipper slowing to match my pace.

As he did, I sped up and passed him. I downshifted, which was the only way to get any power out of my little truck, and floored it. I gained speed, but I lost precious fuel.

In less than fifteen seconds, Skipper caught me again. This time he came up from behind. When he caught up with me, he didn't slow down. He hit me hard from the back. I was thrown forward in a classic whiplash motion and realized that in my disorientation at the afternoon's events, I had failed to put on my seat belt. Needless to say, I remedied the situation.

After buckling up and praying to arrive alive, I checked my rearview mirror. Skipper was no longer right behind me. Now there were maybe fifty yards in between us. I checked my gauge again, not good, and looked at the road in front of me again. It was empty. When I looked back for Skipper again the distance between us had increased to a hundred yards.

And then he began to increase his speed, decreasing the gap between us. He was coming up fast. It was decision time. I knew I couldn't outrun him. I knew I couldn't outmaneuver him. I was in trouble. I had the gas pedal to the floor, and I was doing just over sixty-five. Before I could think of what to do, he was right on me again. I braced myself.

He plowed into me hard. I pitched forward, but the seat belt snapped me back. My bumper dropped off, causing Skipper's Bronco to bounce up in the air as he ran over it.

That was it. He had bumped me hard, yet I had managed to keep it on the road. I felt encouraged. Pottersville was less than seven miles away now. I just might make it.

And then my engine died. I was out of gas—literally and figuratively. How, I do not know, but I had the presence of mind to pray.

When my truck finally rolled to a stop on the right shoulder of the road, Skipper and company were right behind me.

They jumped out quickly. I knew it was only delaying the inevitable, but I locked my doors. Within seconds a tire iron crashed through my window. Glass shattered everywhere. My eyes fixed on a single shard of glass as it slid the length of my dashboard.

When you get hit on the nose, it has a feeling all its own, and, besides being hit in your credentials, nothing hurts worse. This is especially true if you are hit very hard in the nose with a tire iron.

Blood spurted out; cartilage shifted, and bone crunched; my eyes filled with those painful, I-got-hit-in-the-nose-with-a-tire-iron tears; and the pain made me nauseous. I fell over to the side, but not very far—the seat belt held me up. Somebody grabbed me by the shirt, which ripped open as buttons shot like bullets across the cab.

Someone snatched me hard from the seat, but the seat belt held. He yanked even harder, jarring me unmercifully. My brain felt as if it were rattling around inside my skull. Finally he figured out that the seat belt would not give me up, so he unbuckled it. He yanked at me again, and this time I went flying out.

I had probably seen him at the prison, but everything was blurry, and I didn't recognize him. He reared back and hit me hard in the gut. I fell down as my lunch came up.

I knelt there vomiting as they stood around laughing. On my last heave, I fell forward. With everything in me, I tried to get up, but I couldn't.

"Search the truck," Skipper called to Shutt. I lay there with tears, blood, vomit, and dirt smeared all over my face while they searched the truck.

"It's not here, boss," Shutt said.

"Get him up," Skipper yelled. He got out right in front of me after two of his men were holding me vertically again. "You like movies?" he asked.

I tried to respond, but couldn't.

"You know," he said, "videos. Do you have any Disney tapes? Maybe some that don't belong to you?"

I thought I answered, "I don't know what you're talking about," but evidently nothing came out.

"Answer me," he yelled again, and this time his spit joined the other disgusting things on my face. Of everything, it disgusted me most.

He turned, and with his back to me he said, "Okay."

That was just what the two men holding me were waiting for. One got behind me to hold my hands back as the other one moved into position in front of me. They were placing me in the classic working-over pose. However, rather than keeping me from defending myself, the man behind me was actually keeping me from falling to the ground.

The guy in front of me began working on my midsection as if he were doing a heavy-bag workout. My knees buckled, but the officer behind me held me up. I began to heave again, but everything in my stomach had been purged. I coughed in between heaves. The heaving and the coughing only produced blood. It wasn't a lot of blood, but it was my blood, which made it way too much blood.

"My turn," the officer behind me said with an evil sneer.

He was enjoying this way too much. Come to think of it, they all were, with the possible exception of Shutt, who seemed not to have the stomach for violence.

The officer released me, and I crumpled to the ground as they switched positions. I could see the boots of Skipper and the other officer on the other side of the truck, and it looked as if they were still searching through it. When the two officers had switched positions, the one behind me kicked me hard with his pointed-toe boot and said, "Get up, you big pussy."

I tried.

Finally, he yanked me up, primarily by my hair.

The officer in front of me said, "Hold him still now. I

don't want no moving target. I held him still for you." The officer holding me began to push me from side to side as if I were a boxer bobbing and weaving. "Cut it out," the one in front said.

"We got to give him a fair chance now, Jeff, don't we?"

He continued to jerk me from side to side, but I could tell his arms were getting tired. As his grip loosened, I thought of trying to break free to run. When he finally did get so tired that he released me slightly, I fell to the ground again.

When he pulled me back up to my feet, he said, "Now be still, boy. Can't you see we got work to do? The one in front drew back like he was about to pitch a baseball and swung his fist fast and furiously toward the left side of my head. The blow landed between my ear and eye.

And then the strangest thing happened. Somebody turned off the lights.

T HIRTY-SIX

I AWOKE TO THE MUTED SOUNDS of soft, constant beeps, whispering voices, and the low hum of an air conditioner. Everything sounded as if I were in outer space or under water.

When my eyes finally opened, they closed again from the assault of the bright light.

Someone said, "Close the blinds. He's waking up."

Someone else said, "Okay." Both voices sounded excited.

My eyes opened again. I saw white light, less bright now, but still very present. A TV mounted on the wall in front of me played CNN. I lifted my right hand. Something was attached to my forefinger. I tried to remove it, but a hand descended out of the sky and prevented me.

My eyes followed the hand up the arm to the body to which it was attached. It was a beautiful goddess with large brown eyes and long brown hair. Beside her was another one. The second one looked like Bambi with a broken nose. Bambi? Laura. And Anna.

Thank you for letting me live. I love you.

"I must be in heaven," I said. There was laughter, so my words must have come out, but I hadn't heard them.

The loudest laughter came from the left of the bed. I

249

looked over to see Merrill standing there with a wide grin on his face.

"Oh, no. It must be hell," I said. And this time it was the ladies who laughed.

"How are you feeling?" one of the ladies asked.

I turned in that direction again, which didn't take more than five minutes, and said, "Who said that?"

"I did," Laura said with a warm, adoring smile as she rubbed my leg. Anna had dibs on my hand and arm.

They would just have to share.

"I feel like I just went fifteen with Foreman," I said.

"You look it, too," Merrill said. This time I didn't attempt to look at him.

I looked up at Laura and said, "Anna, Merrill, this is Laura Matthers. Laura, this is Anna and Merrill."

They all laughed. "We know each other pretty well by now," Anna said.

"We've been in here looking over and praying for your white ass for the past three days," Merrill said.

"I don't remember."

"You've been resting," Laura said.

I was puzzled, which must have registered on my face.

"You been out cold, man," Merrill said.

"What? For three days?"

They all nodded.

Then I remembered what Skipper had been looking for. "There're some Disney tapes in my trailer," I said. "I need them."

Their faces registered concern.

"There ain't no VCR in here," Merrill said. "'Sides, I'd be too embarrassed to come visit your sick ass if you up in here watching the wonderful world of Walt Disney."

"No, I don't want to watch them," I said. I just need them out of my trailer. They're—"

"I'll take care of it," Anna said. Don't worry about it."

"You'd better be worried about how you look," Merrill said.

"How do I look?" I asked.

Laura started to speak, but Merrill beat her to it. "You look like you went fifteen with Foreman and him fighting with a tire iron."

"You look ruggedly sexy," Laura said. Anna nodded in agreement.

"That's two against one for ruggedly sexy. Sure you don't want to reconsider your assessment?"

"I calls 'em likes I sees 'em, boss. We never lie to a white man, boss. Nosuh."

"You got a mirror? I'd like to judge for myself."

"Doctor say no mirror for at least a month. He scared you off yourself if you see what you look like," Merrill said.

By the time Merrill had finished saying that, both Anna and Laura were offering me mirrors. I tried to take one. It didn't work.

"Here, let me," Laura said as she held the mirror in front of my face. Anna backed away gracefully.

My nose was taped up with some sort of plastic device to support it. Both eyes were black. There were a few cuts and scrapes on my face, many already well on their way to healing. The underside of my chin was split open pretty badly, but there didn't seem to be any stitches, just butterfly Band-Aids.

"A ruggedly sexy raccoon. Why am I not dead?" I asked.

"You look pretty bad, but it's not worth ending it all just because you ugly," Merrill said. "You's ugly before."

"I guess you're right. Why didn't they kill me? What happened?"

"Some loud Negro in a big-ass pimpmobile-looking car scared them off."

"What were you doing driving your uncle Tyrone's car?" I asked.

"He needed my truck to haul his old lady's dresser. She leavin' again. Twice every year he has to borrow my truck. Once to move her big black ass out and again to move it right back in. Come to think of it, it's four times a year. Her ass is so big it take two trips each way."

"How many years have they been doing this?" I asked.

"As long as I can remember. Anyway, Anna told me to look out for you. She say you could probably use a big, strong, handsome, black bodyguard 'bout now."

"She was right. What took you so long to snatch me from the jaws of death?"

"You's drivin' everywhere. Never stopping. I didn't know how long you's gonna ride. I finally had to stop for gas."

"That's what I should've done," I said.

"You can say that again."

"That's what I should have done. What happened when you pulled up in the pimpmobile? Did they come over and ask you for some ladies?"

"I made a lot of noise coming in—horn honking, firing a gun. They took off."

"White flight," I said. "It happens when you black pimp-mobile-driving hoodlums move into the neighborhoods."

"I suppose so."

"Did you see who it was?"

"Sure did. Now they in your daddy's jail. I've heard complaints of police brutality, but I said that police don't be brutal to no white men, especially fellow law-enforcement officers."

"Especially them," I said.

"Skipper's going to pay for what he's done," Anna said. "Merrill and I went forward with everything you had told us. He's already been arraigned. Now he's just waiting for a probable-cause hearing."

"For what?" I asked.

"Murdering Johnson and Maddox, of course," she said.

She could tell by the look on my face that something was wrong. "Are you all right? What is it?"

"What other charges were filed against Skipper?"

"Just attempted murder, for what he did to you. The DA said that was enough. Don't you think that's enough?"

"No. It's not nearly enough," I said.

"Why?" Anna asked.

"Because he didn't do it."

"He tried to kill you twice," she said emphatically.

"Yes, but he didn't kill Maddox or Johnson."

"Of course he did. Who else would have killed them?"

"I've got some ideas, but it doesn't matter. I'm no longer involved. I'm suspended, and I feel like I'm lucky to be alive. They won. I quit."

"I think he's guilty," Anna said. "Skipper's the worst kind of cop. He's rotten to the core."

"He is rotten, and he's guilty as sin, but he didn't kill those men, and they'll figure that out."

"Who?"

"The inspector, FDLE, the sheriff's department. Somebody."

"And, if they don't?" Anna asked.

"He get what he deserve anyway," Merrill said.

"Right," I said.

"No, it's not right, and you know it. If you really believe Skipper didn't kill them, you have to do something. You can't just allow this to happen. You're not even sounding like yourself."

"Anna's right," Laura said. "You're not a quitter. You have to see this thing through."

"Sorry to disappoint you," I said, "but quitting is what I do best. I've been practically fired and practically killed, and I've had enough. If you all are so concerned about Skipper, go and do something about it. I'm not. I don't have nine lives."

"He's just upset," Anna said. "He's been through so much."

"That's not it. You were right," I said. "I had no business getting involved in the first place. I was meant to be a chaplain, and now I've screwed that up, too."

"There are other jobs," Laura said. "I'm just grateful you're alive."

"So you not going to do anything about Skipper?" Merrill asked.

"No. My religion forbids retaliation. I've turned both cheeks, and he's pulverized them both. You going to do anything about him?"

"I haven't decided yet. Are you going to do anything about your job?"

"Clearing my name, all that stuff? I don't know. We'll have to see what happens."

"What about this?" Merrill asked and slung a newspaper on my chest.

"Merrill, no," Anna said, "now's not the time."

I attempted to pick up the paper. When I had struggled with it for maybe five seconds, Laura picked it up and held it in front of me. It was the *Tallahassee Times*. The headline just above the fold and to the right read: "Former Atlanta Pastor Charged with Sexual Misconduct Again."

A wave of sickness crashed over me, and I began to heave—a deep, painful, dry heave. It was happening again. My world was closing in on me. I felt as if I were suffocating.

"I told you he didn't need to see that now," Anna said. "My God, he's been in a coma for three days."

"He need to see it now more than ever. He need to finish what he started."

"Merrill's right. I needed to see it. I can't hide from it."

I looked up at Laura. Her eyes were warm and reassuring. "Lucy," I said in my best Cuban accent, "I got some splainin' to do. I'm just not up to it right now."

She smiled at my lame joke and said, "You have nothing to explain to me. I've spent the night with you, remember? I know you. Besides, Anna told me everything."

"She doesn't know everything," I said and laughed.

"She knows a lot," Laura said and smiled.

Anna smiled, too.

It was overwhelming.

After they left, I went back to sleep. I slept the rest of the night and most of Friday, only waking long enough to eat and move around the room a bit at the doctor's insistence. Late Friday night I eased into my wheelchair and slowly, dreadfully rolled to Mom's room. I felt so guilty, a feeling not uncommon to our relationship over the years. I couldn't believe it had taken me being put in the hospital myself to make me visit her. I had told Laura how important it was for me to reach out to people when they were in crises—death, terminal illness, loss—and that was all true. But, I found that going into the room where my own mother lay dying I had nothing to say—no words of hope, inspiration, comfort. Such is the hypocrite I am.

"Mom," I whispered when I had rolled up beside her bed.

She didn't respond. Her back was to me. I sat there and stared at her for a while before I attempted to rouse her again. She was emaciated. Her hospital gown, which she should not have had to wear because I should have brought her one from home, was only tied at the top, revealing a backbone and ribs that protruded so far out as to make her look like a sack of bones. She reeked of urine, sweat, drool, and a few other chemicals that were foreign to me.

"Mom," I said a little louder this time.

She slowly raised her head and then let it fall back down again. I wheeled around to the other side of the bed. What I wanted to do was to wheel back out of the room and say, "Well, I tried."

"Mom," I said even louder and this time directly towards her wrinkled, seemingly lifeless face.

Her eyes opened, and in them I saw fear—fear of death, fear of life, pure fear. In that moment, all of my rage toward this wounded old woman seemed to melt like the numerous candles I had lit for her. Now, in liquid state, it ran out of me, across the floor, and out the door.

She closed her eyes again. I think the closeness of my eyes to hers made her uncomfortable. She probably needed a drink. I sure did. I rolled the chair back slightly, and this time, when she opened her eyes again, that is how they stayed.

"John, John?" she asked, her voice warm and refreshingly sober. "Is that you? What happened to you?"

"I was in a little car accident, but I'm okay. Looks worse than it really is," I lied. "Mom, how are you?"

"I'm dying," she said flatly.

Her honesty was so refreshingly simple that I decided to return it. "That's what I hear. I'm very sorry. I love you."

"John." She seemed unable to say more, but then she said, "I'm so sorry."

"Mom, it's nothing really."

"No. I mean for what I've put you through. You were always so sensitive. It's no wonder you turned to the bottle with a mother like me. I just wanted you to know, if I could have stopped, I would have, for you. Hurting you is what hurt the most. God, forgive me."

"He has," I said, with as much conviction as I had ever said anything.

"Can you?"

"I have," I said.

And though that was not the end of the pain or resentment, it was the beginning of the end.

THIRTY-SEVEN

I WAS LYING ON MY COUCH, my head propped on
several pillows. It was Saturday afternoon. Anna and
Laura had driven me back to Pottersville from the hospital
and tripped over each other trying to wait on me once we
had arrived. They had already cooked and cleaned in prepa-
ration for my homecoming, and my tin house sported a dull
shine and the smell of pine. Finally, after nearly three hours,
I had convinced them to leave so I could take a nap. They
agreed to do so only with the understanding that they would
be back and soon.

I attempted to lean forward slightly and sit up some so
that I could read the newspaper accounts of what was happening in my life. My entire body was stiff and sore. The
pain, like small needles, shot through me in sharp staccato
punctures. It took awhile, but when I was finally up, I pulled
the papers up towards me, letting them rest in a neat stack on
my upper abdomen.

The first story was in Tuesday's *Times*. It said I had been
suspended pending an investigation into sexual assault allegations. It detailed how the accusations concerned things
done in the chapel of Potter Correctional Institution. The
report went on to say that although there were no charges

filed yet, they were believed to be forthcoming. The article quoted not one source and failed to mention that I had been hospitalized after being beaten by correctional officers.

There were three papers that carried the story on Thursday—the *Panama City Tribune*, the *Potter County Examiner*, and the *Tallahassee Times*. The *Tribune* repeated what the *Times* reported the day before, adding only a few minor details, including a quote from some local ministers who said that the Christian community did not need any more scandals and that I was in the hospital in connection with an automobile accident.

The *Potter County Examiner*, where my uncle was the editor, said that a man is not guilty just because some inmates or their families accused him and that everything the *Tribune* copies from the *Times* is not necessarily true. Thank you, Uncle Mike.

The most damaging report of all, however, came out of Thursday's *Tallahassee Times*. It detailed the current charges in three paragraphs and then went on to report that the *Stone Mountain Home Journal* had carried a story nearly two years ago accusing me of sexual misconduct. It highlighted the best parts of the *Journal*'s articles, including my alcoholism, divorce, and being asked to leave my church. I felt all of the old embarrassment and depression rolling over me like a fog, but the worst was still to come.

Friday's *Times* carried an additional article complete with quotes from some of the members of my church in Atlanta and my ex-wife, Susan. The members said how they never would have believed it and still couldn't. I was, in their opinion, a wonderful pastor and a good man, but they somehow conveyed the impression that theirs was the minority opinion.

Susan said that she knew me better than anyone and that none of this surprised her. She said that, although it was never proven, I was suspected of stealing funds and having an affair with a depressed woman I had been counseling at the time. I was pond scum, she was convinced of it, and soon everyone would know it.

No one mentioned the Stone Cold Killer case or anything else about my work at the Stone Mountain Police Department.

I sat there in shock. My head was light, and the room was spinning. Thoughts shot through my mind at warp speed, and all of them were as black, cold, and empty as I was. I wanted to run away. I wanted to move to a foreign country where nobody knew any of this stuff and where nobody cared.

Of all of the depressing thoughts that plagued my mind, one turned over and over like clothes tumbling in a dryer. The inmate library at Potter Correctional Institution received daily copies of the *Tribune*, the *Times*, and the *Potter County Examiner*. All of the work I had done to establish trust and confidence with the inmates was being leveled with a wrecking ball known as the free press. I was thinking seriously about having my first drink in two and a half years when I heard a knock on the door.

Like an idiot, I said, "Come in. It's open."

A young woman with light-blond hair, pale white skin, and light-blue eyes came in. She was wearing a blue business suit roughly the color of her eyes, and I thought I detected a shoulder holster underneath her jacket.

"Reverend Jordan," she said as she walked in, "I'm Rachel Mills. How are you doing today?"

"How do I look?" I asked.

She laughed. "You do look like somebody got ahold of you." She seemed nervous and awkward. "Do you mind if I sit down?"

"That depends on why you're here."

"I'm with FDLE. I need to ask you some questions."

"Have a seat. I thought you might be here to ask me out,

in which case you couldn't be seated because I'm seeing someone."

She looked at me as if I had just exposed myself.

"It's a joke."

"When one is charged with sexual assault, one should not joke about such matters," she said in an old maid school mistress tone.

"When one is innocent," I said, "one should feel free to joke about whatever one wishes. Besides, I thought you were here to ask me about the charges against Matt Skipper. He has been charged, not I. You made the same mistake as the paper by saying that I was charged with sexual assault, when really I've only been accused of sexual assault."

"It's practically the same thing," she said.

"If one were more professional," I said, "one would realize the day-and-night difference between an accusation by a private citizen and a charge by a state or federal agency."

"I did not come to be insulted by you. I came in search of the truth," she said defensively.

"Truth is the last thing you're here for, if you believe that an inmate's wife's accusations are practically the same thing as charges from your office."

"Well," she huffed, "I happen to be passionate about the rights of inmates and prisoners, and I'm sick of the people who exploit them because they are powerless to defend themselves."

"It sounds like a good crusade, but if it blinds you to the truth, then it's evil. Like all inquisitions, crusades, and witch hunts, passion must be tempered with wisdom and an open mind. If you are convinced of something before you investigate it, you will only prove what you already believed."

"Fair enough. I am in search of the truth, and you are innocent until proven guilty."

"Or in this case, just plain innocent," I said.

"I sincerely hope so, of course. The church sure doesn't

need another scandal these days—crooked televangelists, pedophile priests." She paused for a minute and shook her head slowly. "Well, I really do need to ask you some questions."

I nodded.

"Where were you last Tuesday night? By the way, do you mind if I tape this?" she asked, pulling out a microcassette recorder.

"No, I don't mind. And I was in the hospital, I am told. I was unconscious."

"Oh no, I meant the Tuesday night before that. If you will lead me through all the events of that night."

"I was at an AA meeting in a Sunday School room of the First Methodist Church of Panama City, Florida, from six until eight. I then went to Applebee's on Twenty-third Street with two of the members of that group. I then drove home, arriving about twelve forty-five. I read a little and then went to bed . . . alone."

"Can someone corroborate your story?" she asked.

"AA is anonymous. It would be their choice, but I'll ask."

"It's not that important. The crime was said to have occurred later anyway, but if they're willing, it wouldn't hurt. Did you speak to anyone after you got home that night who could confirm your whereabouts?"

"No."

"Do you know Molly Thomas?"

"Yes."

"How well do you know her?"

"I've probably spent a sum total of three or four hours with her. Most of that time has been in the visiting park of the institution. I've counseled her and her husband during some of their visits together, at their request, of course. They, like most inmate couples, were having some marital problems and wanted my help."

"Were you able to help them?"

"Apparently not. I thought so at first, but then lately something has happened to Anthony, her husband. He is on a serious downward spiral."

"Have you ever met with Molly Thomas by herself at or away from the institution?"

"Yes, I have. Last Friday. I mean a week ago last Friday—she called and asked to see me, saying it was an emergency and she was scared to come to the institution. So we met in the pastor's office of the Methodist church in Pottersville."

"What was the nature of that meeting?"

"She described what took place the Tuesday night before when she was raped at the institution and asked for my help."

"Who did she say raped her?"

"Her husband."

"He's an inmate. How could he have even seen her?"

"Captain Skipper arranged it, according to her, but interrupted them in the middle and then stalked her that night and tried to break into her home."

"Why didn't you come forward with this information?"

"I've been in a coma, but it was premature anyway. It was part of an ongoing investigation that I was still conducting, and I was looking for other evidence to corroborate it."

"Was there anyone present at your meeting with Molly Thomas that Friday?"

"Yes, one of my few rules is that I will not counsel a woman alone. The pastor of that church, the Reverend Dick Clydesdale, was in the next office monitoring the session, and I told Molly that he was."

"Would you be willing to submit blood and semen samples? If you're telling the truth, it will clear this up quickly."

"From what I've seen so far, telling the truth does no good and nothing can clear this up quickly. I'm being drawn and quartered in the press. Can you clear that up?"

"If you will submit those samples and they test negative, I will guarantee you front-page coverage of that fact and a chance to tell your story. What do you say?"

"I say, pardon me if I've become cynical, but I don't believe you. However, I will submit the samples, because I *am* telling the truth," I said. I thought, *Great, another blood test. And I still don't know the results of the most important one.*

THIRTY-EIGHT

AFTER READING ALL THE ACCOUNTS of my alleged misconduct in the papers and talking with Rachel Mills, I was exhausted. I took a nap, but not before praying for my total recovery and for me not to have AIDS.

Please, God, anything but that. I couldn't handle it; you know that. I'm not nearly strong enough for that.

It was at that moment that a voice inside my head said that God would never put more on us than we can bear.

That's not what I want to hear right now. I want to hear that there is power in the blood. Power to cleanse me. Power to heal me. Power to kill HIV if it's in my blood. I want to hear, by his stripes we are healed.

And then I fell asleep and had more bloody nightmares.

I awoke to the sound of the phone ringing. Since it was probably a reporter, I decided to let the machine catch it. I nearly broke my neck and reopened all of my wounds trying to get to the phone when I heard Sandy Strickland's voice.

"Wait, I'm here," I said, snatching up the receiver.

"I don't blame you for monitoring your calls today. You're really in a bad way, aren't you?"

"Pretty bad."

"I've heard some very disturbing reports about some

things you've been doing—crimes, I mean, and against women. I was shocked. I was also confused. I thought you were different."

"Me, too. They're not true," I said, but it didn't sound very convincing.

"Well, where there's smoke, there's fire. And there's a lot of damn smoke around here."

"I'm sorry you feel that way. All I ask is that you withhold judgment until all this is cleared up. It won't be long. Are you back at the prison?" I asked.

"Not officially, and I'm glad. It's a zoo out here. You've made it difficult for all of us."

Her words and anger stung like slaps.

"Sandy, please listen to me. I didn't do those things—any of them."

"You're lying, you son of a bitch. I hate men like you. I'm glad you have HIV."

"What?" I whispered as the breath suddenly rushed out of me.

"That's right," she said and began to laugh. "What does the Bible say? You reap what you sow."

"I can't. I—"

"You do. And it's called poetic justice," she said.

And then there was a click. And in a few seconds, a dial tone.

I sat there with the phone still at my ear. I couldn't move. I was seized by fear. It wasn't shock. I wasn't in shock, because she gave me the news I had expected. I knew that I had HIV the moment I had discovered the cut on my leg.

"Well, that's that," I said as I hung up the phone.

I now knew that I was going to die—sooner rather than later. Death had come into the room with me and said, "You're mine."

That was it. That killer had done this to me. I was another of his victims. He had killed me, too, probably didn't even know it. I made a vow, then and there, to find him and make sure he knew that I was one of his victims—find him, so we could die together. I was dying, but before I did, I was going to find the man responsible and woe be to that man.

I was climbing on a pale horse to go and track him down, and the name of that horse was death, and hell followed after him. In that moment, I pushed the knowledge of the disease so far down inside me that it became nearly unconscious. I was going to die, but there was no reason to let that rob me of the little life I had left.

And then I broke. I cried for hours. I also searched my house for liquor, but found none. I buried my face into my pillow, baptized by my tears, and fell asleep and dreamed of death. I did, however, wake up. I woke up a new man—a man on a mission.

THIRTY-NINE

THERE ARE A FEW PLACES IN FLORIDA that have within them all that Florida has to offer—fields, forests, rivers, lakes, and beaches. Potter County is just such a place. You can stand in the middle of the huge trees of the Apalachicola National Forest and feel as landlocked as if you were in Montana, but a twenty-minute drive brings you to the Gulf of Mexico. Pottersville is home to farmers and fishermen, and I love its duality. Of all of Pottersville's natural resources, one of the most beautiful and most powerful is the Apalachicola River.

On Sunday afternoon, in record-setting heat, I was lying under a tall bald cypress tree near the bank of the river, my head on Laura's lap. Her lap was not as comfortable as the soft stack of pillows in the hospital and in my trailer; there were, however, other consolations.

The base of the bald cypress swelled to four times the circumference of the rest of the trunk, and there were cypress knees shooting up all around it. The grayish brown, spiraling base of the tree was normally covered in water, but the summer was dry and the river low.

Dammit, why do I have to die now? Why? How cruel to do this to me now.

She sat there gazing down at me, as if I were the man of her dreams, rubbing her fingers through my hair—the only part of my body that didn't hurt. Occasionally, she would run her fingers delicately along the edge of my cheek, tracing the beard line. Although she barely touched it, it still hurt. It was, however, worth it.

"I was so scared in the hospital," she said, her voice barely above a whisper. "I thought I might lose you, and I had just found you. I prayed like I never have before. I remembered some of the things you said at that funeral. . . . Anyway, I want you to hang around a while and teach me more, okay?"

"I plan to."

"You know how you said that stuff about grace, about things being a grace, like dancing with me that night or a good night's sleep?"

I nodded. *Where the hell is my grace?*

"You're a grace for me." Tears formed in her eyes. She smiled.

"There's nothing I want more."

A small breeze rippled the top of the muddy, coffee-colored water, and the moss hanging from the cypress limbs above us swayed slightly. Upstream, a fish jumped and made a loud splash.

We were silent, both fully in the moment. A single small tear fell from her left eye into my right.

"Tears form in my heart, but they fall from Laura's eyes," I said.

"That's beautiful," she said, and then more tears came.

"It's from one of Dan Fogelberg's songs—'Anastasia's Eyes'."

It was a very romantic moment, considering that I looked like a raccoon that had barely survived being hit by a car . . . and was going to die anyway.

The branches of the bald cypress were too high and too

small to provide any real shade, but a large live oak about ten feet away shaded the entire area of the bank and part of the muddy river. The water looked like just-stirred coffee as it swirled around the cypress trunks and the edge of the bank. The lapping of the water on the trunk of the trees reminded me of the bow of a boat breaking waves in the Gulf.

"I was a pretty successful pastor in Atlanta," I said. "When I finished seminary, I served for a short time as an associate of one of the larger churches in the area, and then two years later I was the senior pastor of the second largest Methodist church in Atlanta. I drank like a fish when I was in high school, college, and shortly after that when I was working with the Stone Mountain Police Department, but I stopped when I received my calling. I didn't seek help or look at why I drank so much. I just stopped."

"And, stopping like that is always temporary," she said.

"Yes, it is, especially because I had an extremely horrific case with a very traumatic ending just before I quit the department. I didn't drink while I was the associate and for two years after I became a senior pastor. I threw myself into my vocation."

"You exchanged one addiction for another," she said.

"Yep, I was a classic workaholic. Now, this whole time I'd been living as a dry drunk, and that was okay with Susan, because that's what she was used to. We had a nice, comfortable, unhealthy relationship. We didn't see each other that much, and we lived in a glass house, so when we did, we were usually doing our best to win an Oscar."

"All the world's a stage," she said.

"Uh huh," I said. "Finally, with all the pressure of being a pastor of a large church, never having gotten over my last case, and no personal life whatsoever, I began to drink again. Small amounts at first, but then I tried to swim in the bottle, and that's when I drowned."

"How did Susan respond?"

"Like an old pro at enabling. She was the best. The silence, the secrets, the excuses, and the justification."

"Sounds like a perfect setup. What happened?"

"Remember that grace we spoke of earlier—she stepped in. I saw that I needed help, and I went looking for it. I started AA, I read the books, I got a sponsor, and I made one fatal mistake—I became honest about my addiction. Susan couldn't handle it. It's funny, but it wasn't my addiction that split us up, but my recovery. And the church, the last thing they wanted was an honest recovering alcoholic for a pastor. I was too real, too much of a reminder of their own needs."

She nodded encouragingly.

"Things got worse from there. I was faithful during all of this time. To be rigid enough to be a dry drunk meant that it was not a problem to be rigid enough to not be human. However, Susan and I had never been all that human with each other either, if you know what I mean. We were probably down to once a week, sometimes less. So, when the charges came that I was having an affair with one of the wives of a board member, she believed it. She was always so insecure anyway; that was all she needed."

In the distance, the hollow tapping of a woodpecker started. It echoed off the trees and surface of the water, sounding like a family of woodpeckers at work.

"Why do you think the woman accused you of adultery?" Laura's eyes were filled with compassion and understanding. Her mouth stayed slightly parted when she wasn't talking—desirous, it seemed, to drink in my pain.

"She didn't. Her husband did. She had come to see me because they were both alcoholics. She wanted help. He didn't. He fixed her. Not too long after that, she committed suicide, and the papers had a field day. It all hurt like hell, but the worst thing was the way the church turned me out to the wolves."

"Probably a lot of wolves within your fold."

"Yes, there were. And every one of them had on sheep's clothing. I didn't see it coming, and I didn't know what hit me."

"So, you moved to this luxurious home," she said, looking back at my trailer, "in sunny Pottersville, Florida."

"Right here," I said. "All of this came on the heels of a disastrous case I worked on with the SMPD. I quit. I ran away. I wanted to die. But, I didn't drink, and, somehow, I didn't lose my faith, in myself or in God. So, I've been demoted to a convict preacher."

"You don't see it as a demotion," she said. "I can tell."

"Well, maybe not. But, it was certainly a demotion as far as everyone else was concerned."

"I think it's a grace. The inmates at Potter CI have a priest who knows what it's like to fall from grace."

"You're beginning to see grace everywhere, aren't you?"

"Obi-wan trained me well," she said and started to laugh.

"There's just one thing. Grace was the only thing that I didn't fall from. I actually fell into grace's gentle embrace."

"You're right. But I was using it as an expression, not literally." I knew I had to tell her about the AIDS soon, but she'd had enough of my confessions for one day.

We strolled back to the trailer in no particular hurry. We laced our fingers together and held hands, weary of traveling alone. When we walked into the trailer, the phone was ringing, and I knew it was bad news.

It was.

It was Merrill. Anthony Thomas had been murdered in the infirmary the night before—stabbed and raped with a surgical scalpel, which the murderer had left in the body.

FORTY

"**Y**OU LOOK AWFUL," Molly Thomas said when she was seated in the only chair in my living room. She was wearing a pair of dark blue jeans, a white oxford button-down shirt, and white leather Keds. The large shirt, probably one of Tony's, was not tucked in, and the tails were wrinkled. Clasped in her right had was a small wad of tissues that were wrinkled, too.

When she'd knocked on the door, Laura had greeted her like any Southern lady would, not realizing that she was the woman who had accused me of raping her in the chapel of PCI. I agreed with her, I did look awful, but she looked worse. She looked like the grieving widow she was. Her eyes were deep and hollow with big black bags underneath. Her auburn hair was thin and wispy, part of it standing up, but she didn't care. She had aged ten years in the ten days since I had last seen her.

"Molly, I don't think it's a good idea for you to be here," I said, sounding too harsh even under the circumstances. "I'm very sorry about Anthony, but I'm not the one to help you right now."

"I've got to talk to you," she said. Her voice was flat and

as expressiveless as her face was expressionless. "I know what I've put you through, but I'm going to make it right. I'm so sorry." She began to cry. Women seemed to be doing a lot of that around me lately. "I just didn't know what else to do."

Laura stood over near the door, giving Molly room but keeping watch over me. I hoped for Molly's sake that she didn't try anything crazy or make any sudden movements. I could picture Laura pouncing on her and, quite frankly, kicking her ass.

"What are you talking about, Molly?" I asked.

She tried to speak, but nothing came. She cleared her throat. "I'm talking about calling the superintendent and telling him that you were involved in the thing in the chapel." Her voice was weak and sounded hoarse. "I didn't tell him you did it or anything. I just told him that you were involved. I'm so sorry. I was just trying to protect Tony. I was so scared they were going to kill him."

When she said "kill him," she looked as if she had just revealed the most horrible secret. The shocked expression on her face turned to rage and then pain in seconds. She cried for two minutes, her red eyes unable to produce enough tears for more, and then talked the rest of the time through sobs and gasps for breath.

I looked over at Laura. She looked relieved. Her small smile said that her trust in me had been validated. She seemed as proud of herself for trusting in the right man as she was happy for me actually being innocent.

"Skipper said if I accused you," Molly continued, "he would let Tony out of confinement and take care of him. I just didn't know what else to do. I was so scared and so alone." She lifted the wad of tissues to her eyes, her hands trembling like those of an elderly woman. "You were the only one who had ever helped me or even treated me with any decency, and I stabbed you in the back."

I wondered if she knew how Tony was killed. Judging by her composure when she said "stabbed you in the back," she didn't know. I was glad. I wished I didn't.

"I killed him," she continued. "If I had not done what I did, he might still be alive."

I thought the same thing—he was a lot safer in a confinement cell than in the open bay infirmary, but I said, "You did not kill your husband. It was probably just a matter of time. He had fallen in with some very bad people."

"He wasn't bad when he went to prison. I mean, he had broken the law. He was no angel, but he was no devil either—but that's what he was the last time I saw him."

"When you called the superintendent, did you accuse anyone else of being involved?"

"No, not to him, but he had me speak with some sort of inspector. I told him that Captain Skipper was involved, too. But, he only wanted to know about you. He acted as if you were the only one involved. I was making it up, but I didn't know what else to say, so some of the things that Skipper did, I told him you did."

"Did you tell him that Anthony was there?" I asked.

"Yes, but that he was made to be. I thought that might make them sympathetic to him. Oh, God, I'm so sorry, but I was just trying to help Tony. He was so powerless, you know. They could do anything they wanted to him, and there was nothing he could do."

"I understand," I said. What I didn't say was that he was still responsible for the wrong he did and that he probably got hooked up with Skipper to begin with because he was looking for a way to beat the system.

"I'm going to make it right," she said, nodding her head rapidly. "I'm going to the press and to the superintendent tomorrow and tell the truth. I will clear your name. I've wronged you like no other person in my entire life, and I'm sorry. Just please believe that it was all for Tony."

"I do, Molly," I said, waiting for her to look into my eyes. "He was very lucky to have someone who loved him so much."

Suddenly and unbidden, a jolt of enlightenment surged through my mind like lightning running down a tree.

When Molly left, Laura said, "That's good news, isn't it? Won't she clear your name?"

"Maybe, but I doubt it," I said, not realizing how right I was. "It's already so public, and most people probably will not see her real story, and of those who do, most will not believe it."

"Come on now," she said. Her eyes were wide, searching for strength in mine. "Don't give up. . . . I'm not going to."

"I just think that the damage has already been done. Words are something that can never be taken back. Never. I just wonder what my inmates are thinking. How can they ever trust me again?"

"From what I've heard, they know what's going on. They probably all know about Skipper, and it sounds like most of them are discovering what a wonderful man you are. They're probably a lot more forgiving and believing than someone on the street."

"The vast majority of them are guilty and have no difficulty believing that everybody is guilty. They probably aren't surprised by what they've heard about me, but they probably do believe it."

"So what are you going to do?" she asked.

"I am going to testify tomorrow in Skipper's probable-cause hearing and see what happens, but I can't imagine ever going back to Potter Correctional Institution."

"Well, you obviously don't have much of an imagination," she said and then smiled warmly enough to melt some of the ice of my isolation.

FORTY-ONE

THERE WERE REALLY ONLY TWO QUESTIONS that Skipper's lawyer had for me. They had already established an alibi for Skipper during the time in which Johnson was killed. Skipper's lawyer, Gilbert Hamilton, was a short, round man from Alabama with a Southern gentleman's exterior and a predator's interior.

He was overweight by at least a hundred pounds, and he carried it all at the center of his body. His hair, what little of it there was, he wore closely shaven in a partial crew cut. He was wearing a light blue pinstriped suit with a white shirt roughly the size of a two-man tent, a burgundy tie with navy blue stripes, and matching suspenders. He reminded me of Boss Hog.

"Now, Mr. Jordan, I have only two questions for you, which if answered honestly will prove that the state does not have a case against my client, Captain Matthew Skipper."

He pronounced it "Skippa."

"First, in the matter of attempted murder, did Captain Skipper, at any time . . . Let me rephrase the question. Has Captain Skipper at any time ever laid a hand on you?"

I started to answer, but he continued to talk.

"Has he," he continued, enjoying listening to the sound of his voice reverberate off the wooden walls of the small courtroom, "ever so much as laid a finger on you?" He pronounced it "finga."

I looked at him to see if he was through.

"You may answer the question, son," he said.

"No, sir. He has never laid so much as one finger on me," I said, being careful to enunciate properly. I did not wish to sound anything like the man questioning me.

"Thank you, sir, for your candor and honesty. I have always found it to be the best policy, haven't you?"

I started to respond, but he continued talking.

"Now," he said, "think long and hard about this next question before you answer, and I remind you that you, sir, are still under oath. On Saturday night a week ago, were you following Captain Skipper between the hours of twelve thirty and one thirty A.M.?"

I started to answer, but he continued. "All I am looking for here is a yes or no answer. Were you following him during the time that the county medical examiner says Russ Maddox was murdered?"

"Yes, sir, I was," I said, followed by an audible gasp from the courtroom.

"So you are saying that you are his alibi then, sir?"

"Yes, sir, I guess that's exactly what I'm saying."

"Nothing further, Your Honor," Hamilton said, and it sounded like "Nuthin' futha, ya hona."

I was Skipper's alibi. That was the kicker. I looked over at Skipper, seated with Hamilton at the defendant's table. When he caught my eye, he winked and smiled widely, showing me all of his yellow tobacco stains. He looked happier than I had ever seen him look. He was now more convinced than ever of the myth of his invulnerability. But I knew better.

My entire appearance in court had taken less than fifteen minutes. I was exhausted. I went home to rest—but not for long. I had to figure out whodunit, so I went in search of clues. The only problem was I couldn't find them because of the vigor with which Laura and Anna had cleaned my trailer.

I looked high and low. I searched every room, every cabinet, every closet, and every nook and cranny. Still I couldn't find them. I called Anna at the institution.

"How did your day in court go?" she asked immediately. I told her, but she knew already. After all, this was Pottersville.

"Are you okay?"

"I'm okay," I said, "but I'm feeling felinely and trying not to get killed."

She thought for a minute. "So, what are you so curious about?"

"Very good. I didn't think you were going to get that."

"Scary, isn't it? So, how can I help with your feline pursuits?"

"You can tell me where you put the videos that were on top of my TV."

"The Disney tapes?" she asked immediately.

"Yes."

"I took them to watch. I've heard how good *Aladdin* and *The Lion King* are. I wanted to watch them. You don't mind, do you?"

I laughed. "Those are the tapes from Maddox's private collection."

"What? He hid them in Disney cases? That's sacrilege! You don't think there could be children on them do you?"

"I hadn't considered that, but considering what he hid them in, it is a possibility. I need to watch them."

"I'll bring them over this afternoon. I want to watch them too. Does that make me a pervert?" she asked sincerely.

"No, a voyeur or very curious."

"Either one of those sins?"

"Not that I'm aware of. But like most things, they can be. It all has to do with the circumstances and what's going on in your heart."

"So what you're saying is that as long as I don't lust after Russ Maddox's fat, hairy ass, I'm probably safe."

"In which case, you're very safe," I said.

"Very," she said and then hung up the phone.

WHEN ANNA ARRIVED, she found me asleep on the couch.

When I opened my eyes, she was standing over me saying, "Ricky. Ricky. Wake up."

"Ricky?" I asked. "Who's Ricky?"

"Ricky Raccoon," she said and started laughing.

"Cute," I said. "Very cute. Did you bring the tapes?"

"You mean the wonderful world of Maddox's Magic Kingdom?"

"The very same."

I put the tapes in a stack on top of the television, which was an old, thirteen-inch number on an old-fashioned TV stand with a VCR on the uneven shelf below it.

The first tape was the one I had already seen. It showed Maddox and Johnson together again. We didn't watch very much of it—I had seen it, and Anna wanted to see as little as possible of it. I couldn't blame her. We watched roughly two minutes of it. They were the last two minutes though, and when I ejected the tape, I noticed that there was at least three quarters of the tape unused.

I put the tape back in and began to fast forward it. The snow on the screen looked no different in the fast forward mode than it did in the normal play mode, with the exception of the lines at the top and bottom of the screen that looked like wrinkles. After about five minutes or so, I ejected the tape, concluding that there was nothing else on it.

The second tape was of Maddox alone. When the first image flickered on the screen, it was of Maddox's bare chest. It was roughly the color of cotton and covered with white hair, which added to that comparison. He was obviously leaning over the camera to turn it on. He then backed up, bent down, and looked right into the lens. His fat, out-of-focus face filled the screen. I could see the reflection of the red recording light flashing on his left cheek. He turned and headed toward the bed, and the light could then be seen flashing on his other left cheek.

Waiting on the bed for him were a remote control and a jar of Vaseline. He pointed the remote in the direction of the camera, and the TV began to play. The sounds of sex began to fill the speakers. They sounded as if they were coming from his TV, and because the video camera was so close to the TV the sound was distorted, but it was still unmistakable. It sounded like the tape we had just watched. Russ was watching himself with Johnson.

He removed the lid from the Vaseline jar, scooped out a heaping amount, and began to masturbate. He thrust hard up and down and moaned with pleasure. It was a sick, contrived moan, like he needed to hear himself make it. It made me feel sick.

I suddenly became very uncomfortable. I looked over at Anna. She seemed fine, but if we were watching a tape of her funeral, she would probably look the same way.

"Are you uncomfortable?" she asked.

"Slightly," I said.

"Why?"

"I don't know. This just seems so personal, even more personal than watching two people have sex."

"There's more to it than that," she said. "What is it?"

"I don't know," I said.

"Do you?" she asked.

"Do I what?"

"Do you, you know . . ." she said and nodded toward the TV.

"We are not having this conversation," I said. I then added with a smile, "It really is the safest form of sex, you know."

"Just one question," she said.

"What?"

"Do you ever think about me when you do it?"

I choked and stuttered as I tried to speak, which was admission enough for her. She smiled.

I smiled.

"I think that's enough of that one," I said and stopped the tape. I pushed the fast forward button. This time it fast forwarded the tape without previewing what was on the screen. I pushed play again. There was nothing, just snow.

"You know, you are a very attractive guy: single, smart, sensitive, and to top it all off, you are very spiritual. I know you find me attractive, and we are alone in your trailer. Why don't you seize the opportunity?"

"Besides the fact that you're married and I look like Ricky Raccoon?"

"Yeah, besides that," she said.

"I would never . . ."

"That's precisely my point. You're different from Maddox. In fact, you're different from any man I know. I would never do this with any other man. I would never talk this way with any other man, but you, I can trust."

"Don't trust me too much. It might get you in trouble."

"I'm not saying you don't have a healthy libido. It's just that you are to be trusted."

"Don't believe that," I said.

"I do. I'm not saying you don't have your struggles like everyone else, but I can tell things about people, especially men. I know you. I trust you."

"Do you trust Merrill like that?"

"I trust Merrill, but for different reasons."

We turned our attention back to the tapes. The third tape was Maddox and Johnson again. It was shot in black and white, which, because of the contrast between the two men, took on an artistic look.

The last tape, or what I thought was the last tape, was the kicker. It was Maddox in the starring role again, but this time his co-star was Anthony Thomas. Thomas was not as willing a participant as Johnson and seemed to be drugged.

When we finished watching the tapes, I felt like I needed a shower. The world looked like an ugly, dirty place, and I didn't like seeing it that way.

"What do you think?" Anna asked when I had stopped the last tape.

"I think what you think, that everybody on these tapes is now dead. I thought there were five cases?"

"There were, but one of them had a smaller tape. Audio-tape, I guess."

"Where is it?"

"It's in my purse. Let me get it," she said.

"Anna," I said chastisingly, "it could be very important."

"I know. I brought it with me. I just forgot to get it out of my purse. But it might just be music or at best just sounds. How is that going to help?"

"I need to hear it to know."

She retrieved the tape and brought it over to me. It was not an audiotape, but an eight-millimeter videotape.

"Anna, this is a videotape."

"But, it's so small."

"It's eight millimeter."

"What does that mean?"

"It means it's from a different camera than the one in Maddox's bedroom. It's not standard VHS, like these other tapes. It means that it was shot by somebody else."

"Let's watch it and see," she said.

"You girls are so untechnical. We can't watch it. I don't have an eight-millimeter VCR."

"Well, who does?"

"Susan still has ours."

"Great, let's drive up to Atlanta and see if she'll loan it to us."

Just then the phone rang, and I knew it was bad news again. I was almost to the point of not answering my phone anymore.

It was Dad.

Molly Thomas was dead.

FORTY-TWO

*U*NDER SHADE OF MASSIVE LIVE OAK TREES dispersed among the bald cypresses that lined the banks, a small hill—the highest point in Pottersville—sloped down into the muddy waters of the Apalachicola River. The crooked cypresses, both in and out of the water, were silhouettes against the neon orange and pink of the setting sun. The natural slope down to where the swirling water patted the red clay of the bank was most often used as a boat launch. It was in this picturesque spot, where I had learned to water-ski and later had been baptized, that the car of Molly Thomas was being pulled from the river.

Apparently, Molly Thomas's car had raced down the hill at high speed and crashed into the river below. When I arrived, two deputy sheriff's cars, one city police car, one highway patrol car, one game warden's Bronco, an ambulance, a tow truck, and Dad's Explorer, which had the windows rolled down because Wallace was inside of it, were parked at odd angles around the scene.

The yellow crime-scene tape, stretched between two cypress trees near the water, rippled in the small breeze coming off the water, making a small and lonely whipping sound.

Molly's car could just be seen breaking the surface of the

water. A cable attached to her back bumper was spinning around the winch of the tow truck, pulling the two vehicles ever closer to one another. At certain points along the way, the steady hum of the winch was interrupted by the grinding of metal on metal as the river begrudgingly released the car.

"Is this the girl you were dickin'?" my charming brother asked when I walked up to where he, Dad, and two other officers stood. Jake and the two officers laughed. I was amazed we were from the same family. I suspected we were not. There had to have been some sort of terrible mix-up at the hospital. Jake felt the same way.

"Does it look like suicide?" I asked Dad, ignoring Jake completely.

"Yes, Son, it does. There are no signs that she tried to brake or that another vehicle was involved."

"You were such a bad lay that she offed herself," Jake said to even more laughter than the first time. He now had them primed. "She left a note addressed to 'Dear Pencil Dick.' We saved it for you."

More laughter.

"Is it okay to walk down there?" I asked Dad.

"Sure, Son. Go ahead," Dad said in a voice that told me he was sorry for what Jake was doing but that he wasn't able to stop him.

As I walked away, I heard Jake say something about having sex with a raccoon. There was more laughter, but this time it was forced, like men wanting something to be funnier than it was. As I walked down to the river's edge, I felt awkward and self-conscious.

I knelt down on one knee by the river and quietly began to cry. I was crying for Molly, a good woman who had loved her husband. I was crying for Anthony, who went to prison on a marijuana possession and came out a crack addict prostitute in a body bag. I also cried for me. I was a total stranger in a place I once called home. I had never fit in like Jake—my neck had never been that red—but now I was totally alienated.

The isolation was painful.

When I finished crying, I got up and walked over to where the car now sat on dry land. Molly's wet auburn hair was matted, and it hung forward with the rest of her slumping body that only the seat belt held vertical. The officers and ME had opened her door maybe ten minutes ago. Water was still draining onto the ground. The hair covered her face, and for that I was glad.

There was a strong odor coming from the car, but it wasn't Molly, not yet anyway. It was the mix of the river water, including the things that are in it, and the interior of the car. I smelled fish and mildew.

I walked around to the back of the car and studied the bumper. It was bent slightly, but there was no way to know when it had happened. There were a few dents and some white paint from another vehicle on the back right quarter panel. The paint could have been on the car for six months or six hours; there was absolutely no way to know. But I knew. This was the work of Matt Skipper. Molly had lost the love of her life. Having nothing else to lose, with the exception of her own life, she was very dangerous to Skipper. He no longer had power over her, because he no longer had total power over her husband.

I walked back up the hill, picturing in my mind how the deed was done. This time I didn't stop where the officers stood, but continued to where I thought Skipper would have tried to stop. I found tire marks on the road, not acceleration marks, but the skid marks of Molly's car as she tried to stop. I pictured Skipper hitting her one last time, knocking her unconscious, sending her car down the hill and into the river. A second tire track was visible on the edge of the road in the dirt.

The tire track could just be seen beneath the highway patrol car that was parked on top of it, whose front tires had already ridden over it. It came as no surprise to me that the highway patrolman was one of Skipper's biggest hunting buddies. I didn't see any point in mentioning what I had discovered. . . .

Or in any longer seeking justice in the manner I had been.

*F*ORTY-THREE

*T*HE QUARTERS, THE NAME given to the black section of town by a certain segment of the white population, was roughly two hundred acres on the south side of Pottersville, only part of which was inside the city limits. A single row of small, red-brick duplexes provided by the government for low-income housing was the only part of black Pottersville actually located within Pottersville.

The low-income housing, known as the black projects, was a mirror image of the government housing on the east side of town, known as the white projects. The only difference in the two projects was color. Thus, it was more of a negative than a mirror—the negative of a hateful and ugly picture of humanity.

I drove past the row of identical duplexes and found myself again surprised by how widely the yards varied. In front of most of the dwellings, the yards were barren, a mixture of dirt, weeds, and trash. Others, however, had neatly trimmed lawns and a shrub or two. Most of the houses did not have vehicles in front of them. Of those that did, many were tireless heaps up on blocks and covered with plastic tarps. Two of the units had late-model Cadillacs that gleamed even under the late evening sun.

Beyond the projects were the houses and trailers of African Americans who could afford to own their own homes. These dwellings were as eclectic as any in the world. White prosperity and poverty in the rural South were separated from each other—relegated to certain well-defined clumps and clusters. However, black prosperity was scattered like leaven within the lump of black poverty. To my left stood a nice brick home with a paved driveway, two-car garage with the door closed, and a large yard in which a flashy bass boat sat on its trailer. To my right an old, faded single-wide trailer with its insulation hanging loosely underneath sat unevenly on cinder blocks with at least six dogs lying on the bare dirt yard scratching and licking themselves.

On the corner, a small fire burned surrounded by three men and a woman—all holding tall beer cans in their hands. Across the road and down two yards, at least twenty children were playing various games under the watchful eye of an elderly, gray-haired lady rocking on the front porch. Occasionally, she leaned forward and spat her snuff-filled spittle onto the front yard.

A little farther down, I passed a small travel trailer that served as home for three adults and four children—a digital direct TV satellite dish mounted to its upper right-hand side. Next to it a twenty-three hundred square-foot home stood as it had for the nearly twenty years it had been occupied with no brick or wood on its exterior—only faded gray sheets of once-silver Thermo-Ply. The modest, freshly painted clapboard house with the manicured yard next to it was Uncle Tyrone's.

When I arrived at Uncle Tyrone's house, his numerous children sitting on his front porch told me that Merrill and Tyrone were already at his shop. Uncle Tyrone owned a shoe shop just over the tracks in Pottersville. This meant that although he lived on the wrong side of the tracks, Tyrone owned his own business on the right side of the tracks. His

was one of only four black-owned businesses in Pottersville
and the only one that was located in the white part of
Pottersville.

He wasn't very far across the tracks, but it was far
enough to suit him and close enough to the tracks to suit the
white establishment. I had heard some of that white establishment refer to him as a "white negra." No one had ever
said anything like that to me, because they knew what I
was—what I had been labeled since the eighth grade when I
had fallen in love with Merrill's little sister, Kyria—a nigger
lover.

"Cousin John," Tyrone said as I walked in, giving me his
usual greeting, "how are you?"

"I'm okay, Uncle Tyrone. How are you?"

"I'm hangin' tough, but you, you don't look okay. You
tryin' to become black the hard way," he said, laughing.
Merrill and I laughed, too. "You ought to just have the opposite of that treatment Michael Jackson's having. Be a lot less
painful."

"I'll keep that in mind," I said. "Thank you. You sure
know a lot about Michael Jackson to be an old man."

"I watch a lot of BET. And, what they forget to tell me I
read in *Jet*." We all laughed some more. "So, let me see your
tape, son." I reached into my pocket to retrieve the tape. "Is
it standard eight millimeter or high eight?"

"Standard," I said as I handed him the tape.

"Ah, yeah, I can handle this. Right back here," he said as
he began to walk through the faded curtain behind his
counter.

In the back of Tyrone's store was an office roughly the
size of my trailer. It was filled with shelves, which were filled
with shoe boxes. On a table that stood against the right wall,
there were all sorts of electronic equipment—VCRs, TVs, and
stereo components. The eight-millimeter VCR sat on top of a
small, square monitor in the center of the table.

"You the only white man who come in here," he said, smiling broadly. "Any other one see all this stuff think I stole it for sure." We all laughed, though it was more true than funny.

He popped the tape in.

"I have no idea what's on the tape. Would you mind if Merrill and I previewed it alone?"

"You scared if I see some white man screwing a black man, I might go off. Well, I wouldn't. I see that all the time," he said as he began to walk back toward the front of the store. "Just push play when you're ready," he said.

I did.

The first scene to fill the screen was of a floor whose carpet looked familiar to me. It was the chapel at PCI. There was very little light, making the picture on the screen grainy, like a special effect for a rock video. When the camera tilted up and panned left, it showed Molly Thomas walking hesitantly into the dark chapel. She was shivering.

Within seconds, Anthony had pounced on her like a leopard and begun to rape her. She didn't scream very loudly, but you could tell that she was in pain. In between the screams, she tried to reason with Anthony. They both seemed unaware of the camera's presence in the sanctuary. One time Anthony looked straight at it without looking into it. His eyes were wild, darting back and forth, as glazed over as a frozen pond and just as cold. In a few moments, before climax, Skipper came in and broke up the little party.

The small video did two things. It showed that I was not involved and that Skipper was. However, Skipper was only shown as breaking up the violation and not as instigating it.

Within another minute, the chapel was empty, and the camera stopped recording. The monitor went blue. I stopped the tape. The whole incident lasted less than five minutes.

"Looks like you've just been cleared," Merrill said.

"Maybe," I said.

"Ain't no maybe about it. You be just like Rodney King. Got the shit on tape."

"That's what I'm afraid of," I said. "Things didn't turn out too well for Brother Rodney."

"Now you know how we feel. Guilty until proven guilty."

"Yeah."

"What's your next move?"

"I think I'll show this tape to the superintendent and the inspector."

"Not the others?" he asked.

"They don't prove Skipper did anything. And the fact that I have them makes it look like maybe I was involved. My ex-father-in-law would love that," I said. "What do you think?"

"Couldn't hurt."

"Are you sure?" I asked.

"Not much in this world's for sure."

"That's for sure."

*F*ORTY-FOUR

*T*HE DEPARTMENT OF CORRECTIONS of the state of Florida incarcerated just under 65,000 inmates at a yearly cost of roughly 1.5 billion dollars. The number of people required to operate this department was 23,732. I was now one of those people again.

It was an overcast Tuesday morning, and I was sitting at my desk, again active as the chaplain of Potter Correctional Institution. I had been reinstated thanks to the videotape of the chapel incident, or I should say a VHS copy of that video that Uncle Tyrone had dubbed for me in about ten minutes. Being at work again was not only a result of the tape, but also of a feisty, blond FDLE investigator named Rachel Mills, whom I showed the tape to first and who was by my side as I showed it to Daniels and Stone.

It was nice to be back at work. It was even nicer to see Daniels so disappointed at my return.

As I had expected, Stone and Daniels, and even Rachel Mills, were not willing to say that Skipper did anything but break up an illegal activity. The superintendent did, however, demand a full investigation, especially since, as they said, Molly Thomas had committed suicide. They even allowed

293

Skipper to assist in the investigation since he had been acquitted by the grand jury. The man had nine lives.

A few members of the staff seemed genuinely glad to see me back, but most, like most of the inmates, were tentative and seemed reserved around me. Mr. Smith was excited. Well, as excited as he ever gets. He said he knew I was innocent and was hoping Skipper wouldn't kill me. I had hoped that myself, still did in fact. What I didn't say, because I was trying not to think about it, was that someone had already killed me.

I called Laura to tell her the good news of my reinstatement as chaplain. She was, at the same time, happy for me and scared, too. She asked if I had changed my mind about finishing the investigation. I realized that I had started investigating again without telling anyone, and then I remembered why. I could not tell them about my new mission, nor could I tell them about my deeply personal motivation. I determined that I had decided to do it for Molly. She deserved better than what she got. I intended on finding out who took her life from her—not that I could get it back and not that I could take theirs, but just because I needed to know, and so did the authorities. No doubt the killer would face a higher court and give an account to the Most High Judge one day, but I wasn't willing to wait that long. I guess I've not perfected my passivity yet, nor my patience. Nobody's perfect.

After talking with Laura and coming to the realization that I was indeed still trying to figure out whodunit, I was more determined than ever to find out what happened that Monday night, just two weeks ago, in the infirmary. Two weeks ago, there were four people alive who weren't alive now, and I wanted to know why. I think better around smart people, so I decided to go think with Anna in her office. When I opened my door, Officer Charles Hardy was standing there.

"I'm sorry it's taken me so long to see you, sir," he said. "Several people told me you wanted to talk to me about the morning Johnson was killed, but I've been out of town. I'm in the reserves, and they sent us to help with some hurricane damage in Charleston."

Charles Hardy was an excellent correctional officer. Like most of his fellow officers, he was a good, decent man doing a difficult job. His crisp uniform and patent-leather shoes betrayed his military training, so did his comfort with authority. He accepted the authority of those above him with honor, and even more noble was the fact that he never abused his authority over the inmates.

"That's okay," I said. "I appreciate you stopping by. I realize this is not your shift, and you don't have to talk with me. I'm looking into this very unofficially."

"I understand, sir," he said. "I'll answer any question you ask."

"Thank you," I said. "But please call me John. I was just about to walk down to classification. If you're headed that way we could talk while we walk."

"Yes, sir," he said. "That would be fine."

We walked down Main Street Institution, alone because it was still early and the inmates had not been released from the dorms yet. The cloud-covered compound was even more depressing than usual, and the humidity came at you like the small side spray from a slight breeze blowing through the stream of a water hose.

"In the early morning hours of Tuesday, two weeks ago from today, two inmates started fighting, according to Nurse Strickland," I said. "She said that you were not at your desk and that she and Captain Skipper broke them up."

He nodded.

"Where were you?" I asked.

"I'm surprised they didn't tell you," he said. "When Captain Skipper came into the infirmary, he sent me to confinement to pick up an incident report. When I got back, he was gone. Nurse Strickland told me that Captain Skipper had left word for me to take Jacobson to confinement. So I turned right around and went back to confinement, this time with Jacobson in tow."

"So you took Jacobson to confinement per Nurse Strickland's message that Captain Skipper said to do so, but you never heard it from the captain."

"Right," he said. "The strange thing was she made me fill out the DR. Said Captain said for me to do it. I didn't want to, but I did it. I know how to follow an order. Later, when everything went down in the sally port, I was glad that I was not in the infirmary just before it happened."

"What time did you get back to the infirmary that morning?" I asked.

"I didn't," he said. "I was in confinement until a few minutes before seven. When I walked back up to medical, Officer Straub was about to go in to begin his shift. I gave him a report of the night's events. He went in. I walked up front."

"Who else was in the medical building that night?" I asked.

"Nurse Anderson, and the orderly, Jones . . . and another inmate was there for a while." He tilted his head back and closed his eyes to concentrate on recalling the nearly forgotten name. "Thomas. Anthony Thomas was there for a while, and that's it."

"Thank you," I said. "I appreciate your help and the way in which you do your job."

"You're welcome, sir," he said. "And thank you, sir."

I felt as though I should salute. I did, however, suppress the urge.

WHEN I ENTERED ANNA'S OFFICE, I told her about all the things that were twirling around in the whirlpool, or perhaps cesspool, of my head—all the things related to the case. I didn't mention that I was dying.

"Even before you realized that Skipper didn't have the opportunity to commit the murders, you thought he was innocent," she said. "Why?"

"I never said he was innocent, just that he didn't commit those particular murders. The reason had to do with motive. I couldn't see how killing Johnson or Maddox could have benefited Skipper in any way. Maddox was his best customer, and Johnson was his best product. He was making his own kind of killing on the little arrangement, so there was no reason for him to do any killing. He would have been putting an end to a serious paycheck, so why do it?"

"Maybe they were going to tell."

"I don't think so. Maddox wouldn't because it was his secret, too. A secret that he more than anyone wanted to keep quiet. Not to mention that it was a crime and he would have lost everything. And Johnson's an inmate. Nobody would believe him, and he didn't seem to mind it too much. He was being treated like a king: drugs, alcohol, no work, and no trouble."

"There's always the possibility of a motive that we can't see."

"There's always that, but I don't think so. It feels wrong."

"What do you mean?"

"If it were just motive, that would be one thing, but it's means, as well. I mean, if someone like Skipper wanted to kill an inmate, he wouldn't do it in the garbage truck. He would do it by having him killed on the rec field or shot during an escape attempt or beaten to death in confinement."

"Like he tried with you."

"Exactly," I said. "But, there's more. All but one of the murders were particularly bloody, and the third would've been. I think Skipper interrupted that one. They were all stabbed and disfigured. It's personal, not business. A business kill is a dispassionate single gunshot wound to the back of the head, but personal is more like beatings, knives, and pain. This is a nice cold dish of revenge. It reminds me of love," I said. Anna looked puzzled. "What is the opposite of love?" I asked.

"Hate," she said.

"No. Disinterest is the opposite of love. Hate is closely related to love. Both are passionate; both burn white-hot. Those we hate most are often those we've loved most at some point."

"Like a parent that betrayed us or a spouse," she said.

"Right. Divorce, when amicable, is because there is no passion, but when it is heated, it means at least one still cares or is hurt so deeply precisely because he or she cared so deeply."

"Damn, you *are* good. I can see why your dad wants you to be a cop. You have the mind for it. And, yet, you're far too sensitive and caring to be a cop. Besides, you're such a good minister. Maybe you really are meant to be a modern-day Father Brown."

"Maybe. Or maybe I'll just be lucky to get out of this one alive and should go back to just ministering."

"There is a distinct contradiction in the two things," she said, "but you are both of them. You, like most of us, are not just one person. I think you must do both or you will be miserable."

"There's always that," I said.

"So who do you think did it?" she asked.

"Someone who has a very personal stake in all of this," I said. "This is about love and hate, not money or cover-up. Unless, of course, it was made to look like something it wasn't."

Anna's eyebrows shot up into twin peaks. "Do you think all the brutality could be a cover?"

That same bolt of enlightenment surged through my

head. That was it. "I don't think so," I said. "But it could be. I still think it's twisted love, passionate revenge. Because even when something is made to look like something it's not, it usually still feels like what it really is. I said something to Molly Thomas the other day that reminds me of this. When she was explaining why she had made the accusation against me, I told her that Anthony was lucky to have someone who loved him so much, and I had the same feeling I'm having now. Like that's the key."

"You don't think Molly had it done, do you?" she asked.

"No, but she wasn't the only one who loved him. I need to find out who else did."

"How are you going to do that?"

"This is prison. People know things and people can be persuaded to talk about things."

"In other words, you don't know," she said.

"In other words, I don't know," I said.

After leaving Anna's office, I walked out into the waiting room where a dozen inmates stared at the blank wall in front of them in silence. A couple of them nodded to me. I nodded back. A few of the inmates were engrossed in paperbacks. I recognized Zane Gray, Robert B. Parker, and Stephen King. I started to walk out when I heard the faint tappings of an electric typewriter coming from behind the door to medical. I pulled out my keys and opened the door.

Standing next to the storage room where the typewriter was, Nurse Anderson jumped when I opened the door. The door to the storage room was parted slightly, and she moved in front of it.

"Chaplain," she said as the typing stopped. "How are you—"

"Who's in there?" I asked.

She shook her head. "I know they're not supposed to use that machine, but—"

I pushed past her and opened the door. Inside, Allen

Jones was stuffing a sheet of typing paper into his pants pocket. I reached out and ripped it from his grip, tearing the corner of the paper as I did.

One glance let me know it was another letter warning and threatening me. I looked at Jones.

He was looking down at the floor, his weary shoulders slumped forward, his head downcast. "I's just trying to protect her," he mumbled.

Nurse Anderson appeared behind me. "What's this all about? What is that?"

"Another piece of the puzzle," I said and walked out of the room.

"Chaplain, wait," she called after me. "You don't understand. I was only—"

Her voice stopped abruptly when the door to medical closed behind me.

FORTY-FIVE

I NOW KNEW OR THOUGHT I KNEW who was responsible for the murders. I also thought I knew why. But why kill all of them, and why now? I pondered these and other questions that plagued my mind as I paced up and down the length of my trailer. I was just getting used to walking well again, and the more I walked, the more the muscles in my legs and even in my upper body began to loosen and relax. I knew that I needed to go jogging again soon, but I wasn't quite up to it yet.

There was something else bothering me, something my subconscious picked up on that hung onto the edge of my memory like a name once known, but now forgotten.

Before finally giving in to pacing and thinking I had tried to do many things when I had come home after work, among them, watching the local news, which had yet to clear my name; reading Crossan's book, *The Essential Jesus*; and cooking a real meal, which I later abandoned in favor of a peanut butter-and-jelly sandwich.

As I paced through the tight quarters that I called home, I occasionally bumped into the thin walls or the cheap furniture.

As I walked and thought and bumped my way along, I wondered how Molly's death figured into all of this. Skipper most likely killed her in order to keep her quiet. She was the only one who could link him to all of the crimes he was involved in, and she had nothing to lose by telling all. Nothing to lose, that was, except her life. I should've thought about that. I felt responsible for her death. Had I not been on such a pity-party binge, I probably would've thought of it. I was to blame. Just then it came to me. The thought at the edge of my consciousness slowly drifted in. I saw the stack of videotapes. Images of Maddox, Johnson, and Thomas flickered on the screen of my mind. What was it? What had I missed when I previewed the tapes?

I walked over and pulled the tapes out of the linen closet. I placed them on the floor in front of the TV stand and pulled a chair, my only chair, over in front of the TV. I turned on the TV and VCR and popped the first tape in. As it began to play, the images that had been floating around in my head the last few days came back to life, accompanied by the tape's dull moans of both pleasure and pain.

I tried to watch other parts of the frame this time, forcing myself to look away from that which most drew attention to itself in each frame. Nothing. I did this with all the tapes and still nothing.

I sat there staring at the TV screen, now playing the late news. The anchorperson was saying that Molly's car accident was believed to be suicide. She went on to say how distraught she had been over the death of her husband, an inmate in the local state prison.

I wasn't really listening to her, though. I was still trying to think of what I had missed. I was sure it was on one of the tapes. What had it been? And, then it hit me like a tire iron across the face. I jumped up and ran toward my bedroom, bumping into the walls of the narrow hallway as I went. I retrieved the other tape—the eight-millimeter one—from the drawer in my bedside table and ran back into the living room, where the light was better.

While pastoring in Atlanta, I had helped our church begin a television ministry. We had a very small budget to begin with, so we used high eight tapes and equipment and did most of the work ourselves. I learned a lot about video production during that time. One of the things I learned was that it is best to fast forward a new tape all the way to the end and then rewind it to the beginning before you begin to record with it. This caused all of the loose magnetic particles on the tape to drop off so there would be fewer fade-outs during recording and playback. Most amateurs, however, did not practice this technique.

Therefore, you could tell how much tape they had used in recording because once the tape had been rewound the part that had been used was not level with the part that hadn't been used on the spool. This was because the tape that had been used was looser and uneven, whereas the tape that was unused was still wound tight and smooth.

As I looked at the eight-millimeter tape from Maddox's collection, I could tell that an amateur had done the recording. Over half of the tape was loose and uneven, while the other half was smooth and tight. This meant that only half of the tape had been used before it was rewound. This also meant that an hour of footage was on the tape because it was a two-hour tape. However, we had only viewed a few minutes of it. There was more footage on the tape. I called Merrill, and in twenty minutes he was at my trailer with Uncle Tyrone's eight-millimeter VCR.

"This better be good, man. I's already asleep. I pulled a double today," Merrill said as he entered the front door carrying the VCR.

"No promises, but a lot of potential. A lot of potential."

"What is it?" he asked.

"I think there's footage on this tape we didn't see."

"What? You called me over here for this. It could be Russ Maddox's family reunion or something."

"No, it's not Maddox's tape. He doesn't have an eight-millimeter machine or camera."

"So whose is it?" he asked.

"I think it's Skipper's. He would be able to shoot footage in the prison, and most people wouldn't."

"Well, let's see, Sherlock," he said and plopped down on the couch, the couch squeaking in protest as he did.

I put the tape in and pushed the fast forward button. After passing through the chapel scene at rapid speed, the screen turned to white noise and then to blue. I continued to fast forward it. In a few minutes, I thought I saw something. I punched play and an image appeared on the screen again. It showed the infirmary at night. The camera was actually positioned in the hallway outside the infirmary and shooting through the glass windows. Inside the infirmary, Johnson and Thomas were the only patients. They were both on the far wall, and there were three beds in between them. The screen turned to snow again and then to blue, but before I could hit the fast forward button, an image flickered back on again.

It was a close-up of Johnson and Thomas having violent sex together on one of the beds in between them. They looked like animals, gnawing and pawing at each other. I saw no evidence of love or affection; they were both fully intoxicated. In about another minute, Strickland entered the room and caught them. She walked right up to where they were before they knew she was there. No sound could be heard from inside the infirmary, but there was a lot of sign language to hear. She addressed all her rage at Anthony. She obviously cared for him, but she looked as disgusted as any-one I had ever seen. She looked sick from her disgust and rage.

At first, Tony bowed his head and looked like a wounded little boy, but as she continued to blast him, something began to change. He glanced over at Johnson for his response to the whole scene, and that set him off. He punched Strickland hard in the stomach. She bent over and stepped back. Within seconds, Johnson was behind her forcing her down on the bed.

Like animals, they hit her some more, never on the face though. Experienced batterers. They ripped her clothes off and began to beat her and rape her. It seemed surreal to watch all of this violence and brutality in silence, and though there was no sound at all, the expressions on the faces of the men said it all. They smiled and laughed wickedly. They had become sadistic. I thought of Skipper—they had a good teacher. Within ten minutes, both Thomas and Johnson had raped, beaten, and sodomized Strickland.

First, Molly Thomas and then Sandra Strickland— Skipper was making his own little rape tape. I could tell that the second rape had actually occurred before the first one— Jacobson wasn't in the infirmary like on the night of the murder, and Sandra Strickland wore the old gray nurse's uniform that had since been abandoned by the department for something a little brighter. Why was it second on the tape? Skipper must have recorded a lot of footage during the first rape that he deemed unworthy, so he erased it and taped over it.

As I continued to watch, something caught my eye—two things actually.

"Did you see that?" I asked Merrill.

"Yeah, they beat hell outa that white woman," he said. "They both beat and raped her, but she killed the black one first."

"No, not that. Look," I said as I rewound the tape. I played it back. At some point near the end, a door opened into the hallway where the camera was positioned. "Did you see it?"

"What are you talking about?" he said.

"Watch," I said. I rewound the tape and played the same footage again. This time when the door opened and the light poured into the hallway, I pushed the still button. There he was. When the light came into the dark hallway, it made the glass the camera was shooting through reflect images like a mirror. It showed who the cameraman was. It was Matthew Skipper.

"Son of a bitch," Merrill said in disgust. "He sat there and watched the whole thing—like the fool who filmed Rodney King getting the shit kicked out of him by some Cracker cops—and didn't do a damn thing about it."

"There's more," I said. "Look just over his right shoulder."

"Son of a bitch," he said again. Standing just behind Skipper in the doorway to the caustic storage room was Allen Jones, the inmate orderly. "Jones."

"Uh huh."

"Why would Skipper record them doing that rather than cracking their skulls?"

"Because Maddox would pay mucho dinero for something like that," I said. "Plus, he can use it against them."

"He's one sick bastard."

"And then some," I said, "but he didn't kill those inmates and Maddox."

"No? Who did then?"

"Who had the motive to kill them? Strickland," I said.

"So what are you going to do?" he asked.

I looked at my watch. It was nearly midnight. "I'm going to have a little chat with Sandy Strickland," I said. "Her shift is just getting started."

"You want me to come along?" Merrill asked.

"There's no need. I think I can handle her," I said. "Remember, you're not the only badass around here who's had defensive tactics training."

FORTY-SIX

SEEING HER DIE HAUNTS ME STILL.

The veil of darkness covering the compound seemed spiritual as much as natural. I was alone in that darkness. And yet, I couldn't help but wonder if I was in the darkness or if the darkness was in me. I had entered the institution just a few minutes before to the amazement of the control room officer, who asked why everybody was working so late tonight. I told him that duty called and that I would be in the infirmary. He said, "Ten-four." And then I asked him who else was working late tonight.

He responded, "That tall, pretty classification officer. Medical called her in on an emergency transfer."

Immediately my heart started racing. I jerked my entire body around and quickly scanned the parking lot with my eyes. To my horror, they locked on her car.

Why had she come? Hadn't I warned her? God, please let her still be alive.

The noise and movement of inmates and officers during the day was replaced by an eerie silence and the lonely still-ness of night. I quickly walked to the medical building. The officer's desk was vacant. I walked past the nurses' station to find one elderly nurse dozing with her head on the counter.

I continued toward the infirmary to find that there was
no officer in the infirmary control room either. I walked
through the control room and discovered that there were no
sick inmates in the infirmary, which explained why there was
no need for an officer.

When I walked into the infirmary, I saw Sandy Strickland
sitting alone in the far corner of the room on an exam stool in
between the last two beds. Her upper body was draped over
the bed in front of her, her right hand extended, rubbing it
gently. She was crying and between sobs saying a single
word: "Tony." I recognized the bed as the one Tony was in on
Skipper's video.

As I approached, she must have heard my footsteps. She
jerked up, looked puzzled, and began wiping her eyes.

"What the hell are you doing here?" she asked.

"I just came from viewing a videotape of what Thomas
and Johnson did to you here in this very room."

"I don't know what you're talking about," she said nervously. "What video? What do you mean?"

"I mean Skipper recorded a video of Thomas and
Johnson's attack on you."

"What are you talking about?" she said, trying to sound
outraged, but her voice broke, and she began to cry.

"Skipper got it all on videotape, so there's no point in
denying it," I said.

"That son of a bitch," she said, expressing the same sen-
timent that Merrill had. And then it hit her. "Oh, my God, he
could have stopped it. That sick bastard." She was silent as
she contemplated what he had done to her. Her face
expressed the horror of what she was experiencing. After a
long time, she said, "Why?"

I couldn't answer that question.

She cried.

I was trying to be gentle and patient with her. I had to
keep reminding myself that she was a murderer. "I think I

know why you killed them, but I still don't understand why you just didn't turn them in. They would've been punished."

As I neared her, I could see that someone was in the bed behind her. She blocked my view of the head and upper body, but I could see the outline of legs and feet beneath the thin infirmary sheet.

"Who's on the bed behind you, Sandy?"

She shook her head and waved her hand as if a bee were buzzing around her.

"I didn't want Anthony to be punished. I loved him. I just wanted to free him from that nigger inmate and that fat bastard banker's grip. Before they filled him full of dope, he used to be so gentle and kind. They took that away from him. He never made love to me again," she said and began to cry even more. After she cried for a minute, her face turned hard and bitter. "After they sank their claws in him, it was just fucking. They gave him AIDS."

"What?" I asked in shock. As I continued to move toward her, I tried to get a look at who was on the bed.

"Yeah, me too. It's just a matter of time for me anyway. I'm dying. You're not. They gave it to me, not you."

"But you said . . ."

"I know, but I had just found out, and I was so angry, and I knew you were looking into what had happened. So . . ."

"So you lied to me."

"Yes, why not? You're just as guilty as everyone else in this fucking place."

I was within ten feet of her now. "Who's in the bed behind you, Sandy?"

She didn't answer. Instead, she seemed to begin a mental meltdown. Her right hand began to jitter, and her left eye began to twitch. She looked off into nothing and began to mumble beneath her breath.

I stopped walking.

"You didn't blame Skipper for what happened to Anthony?" I asked, trying to get her back on track, but thinking, *I don't have AIDS. I'm going to live—a little longer, anyway. Thank you. I'm sorry for being so angry with you. Please forgive me.*

"Yeah, I blame him the most. He's hard to get to though, but eventually I will."

"No, you won't," I said. "I've got to turn you in."

She looked at me with pure rage. "Of course you do—you're a man, aren't you? All you pricks stick together, when you're not sticking each other," she said as the bitterness and bile spewed out of her mouth. "Sick pricks, every one of you."

I didn't know what to say.

"I loved Tony. He was different. You should understand that, you're a preacher. I'd kill that nigger Johnson all over again for turning Tony into a monster. I loved him."

"Then why did you kill him?" I asked.

She looked confused. "I loved him," she yelled. "I didn't kill him. I killed those other buttfuckers to protect him. I didn't kill him."

"Well, the courts will have to decide that," I said. "Now tell me who's in the bed behind you."

"The courts," she said with a bitter laugh. "What're they going to do, sentence me to life? I wish to God they could. No, you won't turn me in. I've got that bitch from classification that you're in love with. I'll kill her. I'll slice her open, you prick," she yelled.

She spun around on her stool to face the bed behind her, pulling off the sheet in one fluid motion.

On the bed behind her, Anna was bound and gagged. Her eyes, filled with tears, expressed the terror she was experiencing. For one brief moment, when our eyes met, there was a quick flash of relief. But that soon changed when Sandra Strickland pulled out a scalpel from her pocket and placed it at Anna's throat.

Oh no. No, God. Please save her. Don't let her die.

"No, Sandy. Don't. Please don't," I pleaded. "Why are you doing this? Why now? Why her?"

"Because it's all over. Tony's dead. Nothing else matters. I knew you'd be getting around to me when you realized that it wasn't Skipper. Monday morning my supervisor will be notified that I have HIV. Everyone will know. I'm not going out that way—suffer and die while everyone watches. I've watched it too many times. I'm going to join Tony." She looked back at Anna. "And I'm not going alone."

"But Sandy—"

"This is for you, you bastard. You let them kill Tony. I told you they would. You didn't care. . . . He's just an inmate, right? I bet you care now. Pretty isn't she? You think she'll be as pretty in death?"

"No. Sandy, don't. I'll do whatever you want. I won't tell anybody. Just let her live. Take me. Cut me instead. I'm a man. I know you'd rather cut a man, wouldn't you?"

"Yeah," she said excitedly, and as she did she pressed the knife too hard against Anna's throat. As Anna began to scream, muffled by her gag, blood started pouring out of a small opening on the right side of her neck.

"Here I am, Sandra. Cut me. I have all the evidence. She knows nothing. If you kill me, then all of this will be over. Cut me, Sandy."

"I will," she said as she stood up. "I'll cut you bad. I'll cut you good. So good. But it won't bring Tony back, will it? WILL IT?" she screamed.

"Miss Sandy, you okay?" Allen Jones asked as he stepped into the infirmary.

"Yeah, I'm fine," she said as he walked over towards her and stood between us. Her knight in shining armor. He quickly glanced at Anna, but made neither expression or comment.

She looked back at me. "I was on vacation, out of town,

when my Tony was killed. I didn't do it. I loved him. I couldn't kill him. I want him back."

I glanced at Anna, the blood still oozing out of her precious neck.

God, help me save her. Don't let her die.

I decided to go in a different direction to see what would happen. "That's what killed him," I said. "Your love for him got him killed by someone who loves you."

"What? Who?" she asked, shocked that someone would kill her Tony because of her.

"Him," I said and gestured with my head toward Allen Jones.

The moment of truth was upon us. It hung in the air like a bad smell. I saw the look of revelation and realization on her face. I pressed on.

"He was watching that night," I said. "He can be seen just behind Skipper watching what they did to you on the video. So he decided to kill them, but you beat him to the punch on Johnson, so he waits for his chance to get Thomas. When you were away, his wife got him out of confinement by her accusations against me, and it got him killed. Her, too."

Jones looked away from me and back toward her. She looked at him with pure contempt.

She said, "I loved him, not you. I loved him, and you killed him. You stole him from me." She started toward him on the offensive. When she reached him, she slapped him hard across the face. He didn't flinch. "You dumb nigger, you took him from me. I loved him. I didn't love you. I *DON'T LOVE YOU*," she yelled even louder.

Strickland swiped at Jones's face with the scalpel, slicing his cheek open about three inches. As the blood began pouring out of his cut, it spilled onto the ground and mixed with Anna's blood—his blood defiling hers.

And then it happened. Jones brought both of his arms up

in one quick motion, wrapped his hands around Strickland's neck, and snapped it like a twig. Her body went limp, her head fell unnaturally to the side, and when he let go of her, she crumpled onto the floor as if all her bones had been removed. Jones spun around and ran straight for me.

Not so long ago, I had made a vow not to injure another person ever again as long as I lived. But, what I did, I did out of instinct and training, not pledges or promises. It was strictly action and reaction, nothing more. And it was more in hopes of saving Anna, who lay unconscious now, than defending me.

Just before he reached me, I snapped out a hard right jab square on his nose. It stunned him, and blood started to pour out of it, but he was not about to stop. He came again, this time ducking his head down and tackling me like a football player. I was still sore from my last beating and I felt it everywhere as I hit the floor. He sat back onto my chest now, brought his left hand down hard on my chin.

I brought my midsection up, rocked forward, then back, and brought my legs up and wrapped them around his neck. I jerked them back down again hard, and he went down with them.

I jumped to my feet and looked around. There was still no one in sight. Anna's entire bed, once white, was now crimson. She was dying. I ran over to the door. It was closed, which meant it was locked—it locks from the outside. Normally, just inmates were in here.

I turned around to see Jones getting to his feet and reaching into his back pocket. He produced a surgical knife similar to the one he had used to kill Thomas.

"You get my letters, fucker?" he hissed at me.

"Yeah, but you just *killed* the woman those letters were meant to protect," I said in a voice that said, *You're not only a psychopath; you're an idiot, too.*

"Well, think about this," he said. "When I finish with you, she's mine." He slung his head toward Anna.

"You won't touch her," I said, rage taking over. "I won't let you touch her. IT'S OVER!" I yelled.

He rushed me again, holding the scalpel at gut level. I braced myself for impact, crouched in a defensive stance. About halfway to me, his feet flew up into the air, and he came crashing down to the floor in a hard thud. He had slipped on Anna's blood. Her blood saved me.

He got to his feet again, though, his face registering the stunned feeling he was experiencing. He rushed me again, only slower this time. Just before he reached me, he stopped, his eyes focusing on something behind me.

I spun around to see Merrill Monroe, my friend.

Merrill pushed open the door and stood with an officer's baton ready to do battle against the forces of darkness.

"Come on, nigga," Merrill said in his don't-fuck-with-me voice as he stepped in front of me. "Let's get it on."

Jones's eyes widened, and just before he started his run towards Merrill, he looked like a rabid dog I had once seen. He ran towards Merrill with his knife in his right hand, extended up and pointing towards Merrill's heart, unaware that Merrill didn't have one when he was in these situations. Merrill seemed to wait until it was too late. Jones was right on him before he chopped the baton down on his head. Jones stopped, bent down, and dropped the knife. Blood continued to pour from his nose and cheek. He did not, however, fall to the ground. His mistake.

Merrill brought the baton back and down across the left side of Jones's face. His whole head jerked back to the right, and blood and teeth spewed out in that same direction.

"Don't fuck with my only white friend," he yelled. And that was that.

"She cut Anna," I said, gesturing toward Sandra Strickland as I ran over to Anna's bed. "We've got to get her to a hospital, now." Reaching down to apply pressure on her wound, I felt her long, elegant neck, her precious warm blood, which there was a lot of, and a faint pulse. I felt a pulse!

"We're *in* a hospital. Let's see if we can wake somebody up around here," Merrill said as he dashed off to get some medical personnel to come and help save our friend's life.

Which they did. Not, however, without laying me on a bed beside her and taking some of my blood and pumping it into her. My precious, powerful, virus-free, life-giving blood.

*F*ORTY-SEVEN

*P*ERCEPTION IS REALITY.

Like the family member who breaks out of the dysfunctional cycle, Merrill and I were viewed as troublemakers at best and traitors at worst. We had delved into the sewer, and we wreaked of it. Those investigating the matter felt that the smell of the sewer on us pointed to our guilt. Like rape victims, we were being blamed for what had happened.

The next three days were filled with interviews, inquiries, and reports with both the DOC and the FDLE. They grilled us for hours—they smelled smoke and were diligently searching for fire. Merrill and I were treated with suspicion and sarcasm. It was as if we were inmates who were suspected of committing a crime. When they finally finished with us, they said that although they couldn't prove that we had committed crimes, they did, however, hold us responsible for Sandra Strickland's death. We had let a staff member be killed by an inmate, and it didn't matter to them that she was in the process of killing another staff member or that she had already killed two people.

I held me responsible, too. I just didn't see it coming. Through it all, Tom Daniels avoided being in the same room with me, and when that failed, he avoided eye contact and interaction. He had begrudgingly accepted my evidence and testimony and closed the case, but told me privately that he would keep an eye on me.

I did not, however, lose any sleep over it.

It was late Friday afternoon, and I was seated on the edge of Anna's hospital bed. The sun, refusing to go quietly into the night, shone brightly through the open shades, striping the bed and warming the room with a natural heat that made me long for an afternoon nap in a hammock. The door was closed, and we were alone.

Anna was wearing an oversized cotton nightshirt with bouquets of violets against a soft yellow background. Her hair hung straight down to the smattering of dark freckles just above her breasts and had the fluffy look of having just been blown dry. The bandage on her neck was smaller than the one the day before, and when we had hugged, I had smelled the slightest hint of her perfume.

"Thank you," she said when I had pulled back from our embrace. Her voice was soft and had a sleepy quality that matched her relaxed mood and heavy, slightly hazy eyes. She was seductive without trying to be, a rare combination of purity and sensuality.

I reached out and ran the back of my fingers across her face and down over her wound. When I reached the wound, I let my hand linger on it lightly while I prayed for her. When I finished praying and opened my eyes, I saw the faint outline of her breasts pressing against the soft cotton of her nightshirt. My hand wanted to continue its journey. . . .

I pulled my hand back to safety, but before I had it on the bed beside me again, Anna grabbed it.

Pulling my hand up to her mouth and kissing it gently, she said, "You're blood's in my veins."

"Yeah, I know," I said. "I can't quit thinking about that."

"Me neither."

We were silent for a long time as we experienced a connection beyond words.

Later, after the moment had passed, an elderly man in a pale blue hospital outfit brought a food tray and set it on the table beside Anna's bed. When she smiled at him, he blushed, and I could tell he did not want to leave her room. When he left, she asked me about the events that led up to my confrontation with Strickland in the infirmary on Tuesday night.

After I had given her a brief account of what had happened, she said, "You suspected Strickland over the other nurses, even before you saw the tape. Why?"

"There were several reasons," I said. "She was the first one to appear on the scene that Tuesday morning in the sally port. At first I thought that the medical department had just responded quickly, but the more I thought about it, the more I knew there's no way they could have gotten there that quickly."

"Why was she there?"

"I think she was there to make sure that Johnson was dead. If he were just injured, she could finish the job. And that's exactly what she did. She smashed his windpipe. She was the only one who could have. She climbed on the back of that truck not as a healer, but as a killer."

Anna was silent as she pondered what I was saying. Then she said, "What else?"

"Julie Anderson could have only done it if she and Jones were connected somehow, and that didn't seem likely. I knew she was kind enough to let Jones con her into doing him favors—like using the typewriter, but she's no killer. She had no idea what he was typing."

"Exactly how did Strickland do it?"

"She had Hardy take Jacobson to confinement so she could drug and dispose of Johnson. She put him in the caustic storage room, then locked it so that Jones couldn't get in. Then she spilled a urine sample in the exam room and had Anderson supervise Jones cleaning it up. When Shutt pulled up and knocked on the door, she didn't answer it. When he walked over to laundry she carried the bags out and put them in his truck."

"How was she able to lift him into the truck?"

"Johnson was a small inmate to begin with," I said. "But he was also HIV positive and very thin. And can you imagine how much adrenaline was pumping through her at that point? She had just committed murder. Besides, she was a nurse. Lifting bodies was part of her job."

"My God," Anna said. "She was so cold-blooded."

"I kept remembering what Strickland said to Officer Shutt. She said, 'I am *so* sorry—' like it was her fault. And it was. She also came to us with her concerns about Skipper at a very convenient time. I just kept wondering why she did it when she did. She had so many other opportunities. And, she was genuinely concerned about Anthony Thomas. That's what she was doing: asking me to protect him."

As she nodded, she squinted slightly, and I could tell that she was picturing everything I was saying.

"And also, I really had a feeling," I said, "you know, an impression, that she was involved somehow."

"That's not fair. You cannot use divine intervention and expect the criminals to have a fighting chance."

"Of course, when I saw the video, I knew it had to be her and then I also knew why. And it doesn't mean as much as it once did, but poison is historically a woman's method of murder. Both of her victims were poisoned or drugged. The violence was never direct, except, of course, for Anthony Thomas."

"What about Thomas?"

"Well, I suspected Jones of being involved, too. I knew he had typed the letters to me and Johnson's request threatening suicide or escape—come to think of it, Strickland could've typed the request after she killed him. One of them did it to divert suspicion. Anyway, I knew Strickland hadn't killed Anthony Thomas. Again, it was direct and brutal violence, the kind she really wasn't capable of. That night when it all went down, I was just playing them against each other, which is what got Strickland killed."

"I'd have to disagree with you about Strickland being incapable of direct violence, and so would my neck," she said, rubbing her bandage gently.

I nodded. "I think she was degenerating fast. She certainly seemed to have had violence planned for Maddox, had the knives out and everything, but Skipper and Thomas banging on the front door scared her off."

"And John, sin got Strickland killed. The wages of sin are death. She was reaping what she had sown. You didn't kill her. She killed herself. Got it?"

"Got it," I said, though it would be a while before I did. "You know, you just preached a powerful little sermon with one incredible object lesson."

"I was just trying to talk in a language you'd listen to."

"I always listen to you," I said.

"Then listen to this," she said gravely. "Take it slow with this thing with Laura Matthers."

"I will," I said and mused at her reason for saying it.

"Now, what about Molly Thomas? Who killed her?"

"That's a good question," I said. It's Dad's case. I personally think Skipper did it, but I can't prove it."

"So Skipper had a prostitution ring, sold drugs, had you beaten up, and has maybe murdered someone, and he gets away with it? Why don't you show Stone and Daniels the tape?"

"I did," I said. "They're meeting with him on Monday morning—if he lasts that long. Word's gotten out about his systematic abuse of power. But, physician, heal thyself. Have you already forgotten the little sermonette you just preached? He's not getting away with anything. You reap what you sow. The wages of sin is death. There is a justice that is higher than any we can exact. Nobody gets away with anything. Some just get away with it for longer than others. Besides, think of the price he's paying for his sin right now. He's not enjoying anything he's doing. He's not living at this point; he's just surviving. And, he probably won't do that for long."

"You're right," she said. "Do you think Stone or Patterson were involved somehow?"

I shrugged. "No way to know," I said. "I certainly don't have any evidence that they were, but I'm going to keep an eye on them. Patterson was away at a pretty convenient time."

"But how can you wait patiently for Skipper and those other officers to fall after what they've done to you?"

"True justice is often too slow to suit me, but it is sure. I also know that injustice is temporary, but justice is for eternity. If I worried about all of the injustice in the world, I wouldn't be any good to anybody."

She looked at me like she wasn't convinced.

"You can't live the way Skipper's living for very long," I said. "Besides, his treatment of inmates has gotten out on the compound. All this will come back to haunt him."

When we finished talking, I hugged her then stood and walked to the door.

"John," she said just before I opened the door.

"Yeah," I said.

"I love you," she said.

"I love you," I said.

"Thanks for saving my life," she said. "It belongs to you now."

I smiled at her, opened the door, and walked out. I stumbled down the hallway feeling intoxicated, the irony of the situation not lost on me. What she had offered, what I most wanted, was neither hers to give nor mine to take.

*F*ORTY-EIGHT

"*S*O MY UNCLE WAS KILLED by that nurse because they loved the same man?" Laura asked.

We were driving east on I-10 into Tallahassee on Saturday afternoon. Mom's condition was stable, and she was being sent home to wait—wait for a kidney and undergo a transplant or wait to die. All she could do now was wait. And she wanted to be home to do that.

"I'm not sure I'm comfortable calling it love," I said. "But they were both, ah, involved with the same man."

"And he was married?"

"The inmate? Yes."

"So, he's in prison, and he's still having a whole hell of a lot more sex than I am," she said. "What's wrong with this world?"

"Indeed," I said.

"Maybe that will change soon." She smiled broadly.

"I know it will," I said. "He's dead."

She punched me in the arm. "Watch it."

We rode in silence for a while. The traffic on I-10 seemed slower than usual. Gone were the FSU flags flapping from antennas that would return with the rush of the fall. I was in the slow lane with the cruise control set on sixty. We were in no hurry. We were in Dad's Explorer—his contribution to Mom's recovery. It still had that new-car smell, but I detected the slightest whiff of Wallace, which would no doubt eventually take over.

"He was such a creep," Laura said.

"Who?"

"Uncle Russ. I used to hate going to his house. Of course, we didn't very much. Mom hated him, too. Now he's made her rich beyond belief."

"Family," I said and shook my head.

"Yeah." She leaned up and turned on the radio, sat back and listened for a moment, and then leaned up and turned it off.

"What about us?" she asked. "Where do we stand? Where do we go from here?"

I was silent. Contemplating. "Forward, I think."

"Could you be a little more specific?" she asked with a smile.

"Not and be honest," I said.

"And you couldn't lie?"

"Not and be a Boy Scout."

She shook her head. "You're not a Boy Scout," she said. "Saint, maybe, but no Boy Scout."

I shrugged.

"It's a tough world for an honest man," she said.

"I'm finding that out," I said and continued driving forward.

FORTY-NINE

THE FOLLOWING MONDAY MORNING, I was standing at the gate looking in his direction when he was killed. Thick clouds had rolled in during the early morning hours replacing the sunny skies of the weekend, the gray day matching the buildings of the institution. In the sally port, Merrill Monroe was busy stabbing trash bags with an iron rod on the back of a flatbed truck. His graceful, fluid motions made him look as if God had created him to stab trash bags. However, God had created him with such strength and beauty that everything he did seemed as if he had been created to do it.

Seeing me at the gate when he had nearly completed his search of the trash, he said, "Somebody say somethin' 'bout me bein' a spear-chucker . . ." He held up the spear. "I'a show him why we called that."

"Of that I have no doubt," I said—and was about to ask how he got this choice assignment, for I had never seen him doing it before—when, in the strongest sense of déjà vu, I froze in midsentence. In stunned silence, I watched as Merrill unsuccessfully attempted to withdraw the spear from the trash bag he had just punctured in the center of the truck. On his second attempt, Merrill snatched the spear free, sending it flying through the air. It struck the fence nearest me, splattering blood on steel and concrete.

Merrill looked at me, slowly shaking his head in disbelief, as the officer in the control room buzzed me through the two gates that separated us. I rushed into the vehicle sally port as in a recurring nightmare and, climbing onto the back of the truck, joined Merrill in a small pool of blood seeping outward from the bag.

"I being set up?" he asked, slightly out of breath, his coal-black face glistening like silk in the sun under a fine sheen of sweat.

I shook my head, for I knew what we were about to discover in the fated green bag.

"I off the wrong nigga before?" he asked.

"No. Jones was a killer. Strickland, too. They just weren't the only ones," I said as I bent over to finish ripping open the bag. Plastic slipped from my grip, and warm blood bathed my fingers as I split open the bag to reveal the lifeless, bloody body of Matthew Skipper. His vacant blue eyes were filled with far more peace in death than they ever had in life.

I looked back at Merrill. His facial expression was a complex mixture—weary of the violence and bloodshed in general yet deeply satisfied at this violence and bloodshed in particular.

"Inmates?" he asked.

"Probably," I said.

"Jacobson got out of confinement last Thursday."

I looked down toward the compound. Beyond the medical and security personnel running toward us, a small group of inmates had gathered in front of the medical building. There in the midst of them, straining to see like the others, was Jacobson, a wide grin seeping across his face like blood from an open wound.

"That look like poetic justice to me," Merrill whispered as officers and medical staff began flooding the sally port. "What's it look like to you?"

"Divine justice," I said and then bowed my head and said a silent prayer for Ike Johnson, Matthew Skipper, Sandy Strickland, Allen Jones, and Mr. and Mrs. Anthony Thomas— all of whom were now sinners in the hands of a merciful God.